Wands l

CW01639552

Wands up Witches

N.JOY

0

Wands Up Witches

Thank you Lain for the hours spent adding and removing commas!!! Your editing skills are the perfect compliment to my creativity.

Wands Up Witches

This novel is a bio-fictional work with elements based om actual written accounts from the time. The background, appearance and circumstances surrounding the actual events and characters are the work of the author's imagination. Any resemblance to actual events relating to any persons is entirely coincidental.

Printed and bound by Amazon

Find out more about the author and her work @ www.nljdesigns.co.uk

ISBN 978-1-9997358-3-8

To all those that are different – You be you my wonderfuls and don't let the world change you.

And it harm none, do as thou will.

Prologue

Olivia Blackwell carefully turned the crisp and ancient pages of the family grimoire. Her grandfather had uncovered the heirloom which had been hidden for centuries.

Under threat of a witch hunt, the Blackwell ancestor had concealed the book of magic, along with some crafting tools within an alcove at the family home. Sealed crudely with a false stone wall, the book would lay undisturbed for hundreds of years. The owner unable to retrieve the sacred text from its hiding place.

On the passing of his father, Olivia's grandfather had become guardian to the crumbling archaic cottage. Tracing the source of a mysterious leak resulted in the stone wall being pulled down and the discovery of the relics of the past. The Blackwell's Book of Shadows was one of many that belonged to a practitioner of witchcraft and had been buried, burnt or secreted away in an attempt to prevent their owners from being hung or burnt as witches. Concealing the evidence had not saved Olivia's descendant from the noose.

The mysteries of the book had not been shared with Olivia's father. A money-orientated devout Christian. In Olivia, her grandfather saw a kindred spirit. One who would honour the family's history, and not sell it on eBay for a few quid.

Mr Blackwell senior had entrusted the book to his beloved granddaughter before he had passed. She kept it in a box of Barbies under her bed, and then, when she had outgrown her desire to play with dolls, she has wrapped it inside an old jumper and hidden it at the back of her wardrobe, beneath discarded memories of her ever-dwindling childhood. He hoped that she would discover it's secrets. Secrets he had been too scared to discover for himself.

When she was younger Olivia had enjoyed looking at the illustrations. Pretty drawings of flowers and plants, of strange looking animals and beautiful geometric designs. The understanding that someone had died to guard the knowledge in the book was not lost on Olivia, even as a little girl. As she got older, she began to understand the symbols and decipher the words, to truly comprehend the power that her relative gave their life to protect.

She studied books on the occult in the library, watched shows about the supernatural and practiced simple illusion and card tricks, entertaining her family and friends. Her perfected sleight of hand made her an excellent thief, pilfering chocolate bars or the odd stick of lipstick or mascara but only from the big stores that would neither notice nor care. Never from independent traders. She had morals and only took from those that could afford to give, and only if she couldn't pay or entertain her way.

To the outside world, Olivia's tricks were just that, tricks, fakery, illusion. Olivia knew she had uncovered some of the books enchantment, cracked it's secrets. She had told her mum once that it was real magic, that she had found a spell that made objects move. Her mother humoured her, watched her perform with genuine enthusiasm but Olivia knew she didn't really believe what she was seeing, would assume it was only pretend, that she had rigged up invisible wires or magnets. Her father refused to even acknowledge what he called her 'childish fantasy and whims' and he openly chastised her mother for encouraging behaviour that went against the fundamental teachings of God.

The more she practiced the better she got. The better she got the more her confidence grew. With increased confidence, Olivia used the charms in the magical book to her advantage. A love spell here, a spell for abundance there. She made a meagre living performing on stage so was forced to subsidise her passion with a job stacking shelves at the local supermarket. A band of dedicated followers on her YouTube channel boosted her ego but not her bank balance. She was training for a spot in a televised talent show, practicing hard for her biggest stunt yet. She had passed the first round of auditions with a series of illusions where objects disappeared, floated or otherwise defied both physics and logic.

The second round she had secured with a yellow canary that metamorphosed into a bat which flew around the auditorium before bursting into an explosion of glitter that rained down on the judges.

The third round, and her ticket to the semi-finals, rested upon her ability to successfully teleport herself and a lightweight gleaming Honda motorcycle from the stage to the doors at the rear of the gigantic room.

For this performance she would be using illusion, sort of. The technique of teleportation had proved a difficult task to master and her results had been inconsistent, and sometimes terrifying. She had found the manipulation of time an easier lesson to learn. The instructions had been precise. Olivia learnt to focus all her energy into her solar plexus. Once she could sense the ball of energy building she exhaled at a specific rhythm, in harmony with the universe's pulse. She worked with the vibrations to influence the fabric of time with a resulting rippling slow motion effect.

The side effects of playing with time were unpleasant. Olivia experienced the sensation of a sensory overload, a rush of adrenaline, felt nauseous, had vertigo and struggled to catch her breath, all at the same moment. It lasted for the same period that time was delayed. A cosmic consequence. Afterwards she would be zapped of energy. Her legs seemed like they were made of jelly and her mind drifted on a euphoric cloud of endorphins. Experience had taught her that she needed lots of fuel to control time, so she ate gluttonous amounts of sweets and chocolate that she washed down with calorie laden cola before a performance.

"Olivia Blackwell". Her name was shouted through the building's speakers and the room erupted into a thunderous crescendo of applause and whoops. She revved the engine and rode the bike onto the stage. She talked to the judges, performed a little sideshow magic then prepared herself for her big finale.

Placing her rhinestone customised helmet over her head, she focused on her central chakra. The lights were blinding and an anticipating hush had fallen on the audience. Inhaling deeply through her nose, she closed her eyes and slowed time. Slamming the bike into gear she shot off the stage and raced up the walkway.

Olivia focused on the backs of hundreds of heads as time caught up and her senses were assaulted. She waved at the astonished crowd and judges who took a moment to locate her. The smell of petrol hung in the air. Olivia walked back towards the stage on legs that felt like they'd give way at any second. She relished in the smiles and looks of wonder that captivated the faces that watched her stroll to her destiny. Her body shook gently as she stood on the stage, facing judgement on her act.

The judges were impressed but not enough to put Olivia through to the penultimate round of the national competition. She went home feeling dejected but pleased with herself. Now that she had used the book to gain notoriety, maybe she would use it for the benefit of others. The grimoires not only contained magic for showmanship but were a key to the natural essence that underpins the universe. They held an insight into a superior world of abundance and love and were waiting for their true purpose to be revealed. Mankind however, twisted, perverted and used the knowledge for personal gain and not the greater good.

Olivia wasn't the only pawn of the ever-waging battle between good and evil to have discovered the power in the ancient pages and poetic verse. Others had uncovered the carefully hidden gems and used them for their own personal goals of power or vengeance. Some were more dynamic or blatant with the use of magic and gained great notoriety or wealth. They ignored the hallowed messages inscribed on the pages. The magic was bound to the four elements - earth, air, fire and water. Each book could be manipulated, the spells for protection used to corrupt and destroy. A small proportion of the Books of Shadows consisted of a handful of beautifully illustrated pages; the others were substantial volumes.

Few used them for the purpose of education or encouragement to return to the old ways and beliefs. The occasional maverick portrayed themselves as modern day witches or warlocks, masters of the unknown. Most took a lesson from history and pretended it was just an illusion, a party trick, to avoid ending up as a lab rat, experimented on or ridiculed.

The Past

1

Mud squelched under Temperance's feet as she snuck along the track that lead to Daddon farmland, a large estate comprising of cordoned off tenant farms. She had made this journey many times over the last few months. The secret trysts with William Herbert had started innocently and were still innocent of behalf of Mr Herbert. Temperance however was in very real danger of losing her unrequited heart, at least. On his way out of town Mr Herbert would toss the old crone a farthing in exchange for one of her rosy, red apples but only when his son was not in attendance. They had apples aplenty growing from the trees in their orchard. Mr Herbert was a generous man; his son was not.

With a frayed woollen shawl pulled tight over her head to form a bonnet, Temperance would position herself at the entrance to the top of town. A stone archway led to a bevy of drinking establishments and neglected houses.

The dirt track swept down towards the bustling harbour, past the prison and the kilns. Following the path upwards would lead you away from the town, through the luscious countryside to the large residences and established farms. A rickety wooden crate served as a table two hundred yards from the small cottage in which she had lived since she became a widow. A task that had taken longer than she had ever hoped for but accomplished without a hint of suspicion.

William had been charmed by the old woman's tenacity and crooked gappy smile. Williams wife had been dead going on a decade and though he was not looking for a replacement, he did enjoy the company. For an extra bundle of firewood or a pitcher of cow's milk, Temperance would entertain Mr Herbert in her tiny abode or walk with him through the woods. He had been unwillingly pursued by the local widowed population but had so far rejected all advances although he took pleasure in them trying to win his hand and heart. This was much to the delight of the younger Mr Herbert who was desperately concerned that his father would marry again and the fortune he would be due to inherit would be squandered.

Not that the younger William was in need of the funds, he had a successful blacksmith business that he operated from a workshop on the family's land. Billows of smoke were seen daily emanating from the forge and a range of horseshoes, pots and pans hung from nails he'd crafted himself along the west side of the barn. His cart was loaded with axes, cowbells, hoes and various other tools used by farmers and labourers, ready to trade at market. He worked with iron the way Shakespeare worked with words and was a master of his art.

The pottery trade had only recently been established in the town and the blacksmiths still held the advantage, though the emerging domestic farm earthenware was becoming increasingly popular, despite its risk of breaking. By the end of the century almost every home would have a harvest jug or butter pot crafted by local skilled hands and fired in the great kiln that dominated the southern riverbank.

William, the elder, was unaware that Temperance was on her way to surprise him. A faint orange glow could be seen from the steamed-up kitchen window. The closer Temperance crept, the brighter the reflection of the flame and she could make out the outline of two people.

A cold shiver gripped her heart as she realised that one shadow belonged to William and the other belonged to a woman. Dainty black gloves covered the long slender fingers of the hands that were draped around Williams shoulders.

Temperance recognised the malnourished frame of Lydia Burman.

Temperance pressed her face against the icy pane of glass. The cold February night suddenly chilling her to the bone but she couldn't turn her gaze from the sight of the man who she had hoped she would eventually coax into her arms, and bed. He danced slowly, his female companion smiling as they rotated around, in time to the crackle of the heat from the hearth.

Two empty plates and two half full glasses were left on the table with a candle that was burning down to the wick. From the top of a rectangle bottle of black glass the purple ear shaped petals of the aconitum hung from the velvety green stem.

The monkshood roots had been crushed into a fine powder and sprinkled over Williams meal.

A strangled cry made its way from Temperance's lips, but it was lost to the night, consumed with the owls hoots and the badgers low pitched growls.

In that moment, Temperance prayed to the Dark Lord.

She called upon Hecate to do her bidding.

"I call upon you now, great Goddess. With the gush of the wind and the flame of the fire, may his heart know no desire." She twisted a clump of greying hair that she had ripped from her own scalp around a nail she had stolen from the blacksmith's workshop.

"Pricked will he be until he has eyes only for me."

As she spoke the words Temperance could feel a foreboding energy all around her. The darkness became absolute, even the stars hide themselves from the might of her wrath. In her peripheral vision she thought she glimpsed the image of a hound.

She kissed the encased nail and having made a hole in the ground with the tip of her boot, placed it hastily inside and covered it with the dirt she had dug out.

"So mote it be."

With tears gushing from her eyes, Temperance took one last blurry look through the window and started to return the way she had come. Her spirits were low, and her heart crushed. She didn't see the younger William as he drunkenly stumbled home, but he saw her. The contentment he had felt from his recent clandestine hook-up with Anne Fellow turned to rage. He slurred a string of insults in her direction and wailed incoherently about not replacing his deceased mother.

Fortunately for Temperance William had little control over his limbs and they would not comply with his desire for vengeance, which he would become hell bent in delivering. Temperance, in a fog of grief, was sensible enough to scarper, her old bones moving slowly over the muddy ground, but steadier than William who fell several times, allowing Temperance to deepen the distance between them.

As William wobbled towards the farm house he heard an ear-piercing scream. He burst through the kitchen door, causing Lydia to jump in fright and a jug to fall from the dresser and smash into lots of jagged pieces on the stone floor. At her feet lay the crumpled body of his father, whose breathing was shallow, his eyes unable to focus.

Between them they managed to drag the semi-conscious older gentleman up the staircase, to his bedroom. William lay fully clothed on his bed, his stomach contracting with the urge to be sick, his pulse weakening. William put the back of his hand against his father's forehead, which was cold and clammy. The adrenaline that was coursing through the younger Herbert aided in sobering him up.

The old man reached out a shaking arm that tingled in pain and pulled his son close.

"Stop her." William senior whispered.

"Who did this to you father?"

"I have been bewitched to death!"

"Who has bewitched you father?"

"You and the others must look for prints or marks upon my body."

"Father, I must call for Dr Beare." William exchanged worried looks with Lydia who seemed incapable of moving. Frozen to the spot through fear of discovery or death, her face did not reveal which.

William slurred his speech as his tongue became numb, the poison taking hold.

"Who has bewitched you father?"

"T..T...Temperancccce Lloooyd..... she.."

Were the last words William Herbert spoke before he slipped into a coma, from which he would never regain consciousness.

Temperance woke early the next morning. The images of last night swam in her head. The wet dirt camouflaged against Temperance's worn leather boots, a stark reminder of her presence at the farm.

She was not ashamed of her actions; she was hurting and in the moment she had meant every word. The effects of her curse on William should wear off with time, but the harlot Burman needed to be taught a lesson.

She kept her head down for a few days, plotting her revenge and licking her emotional wounds. Susanna called in with a crust of bread, followed like a lap dog by Mary who had nothing to offer other than a friendly face.

"Susanna. I have run out of belladonna. Can you please gather me some more?" The bell- shaped flowers grew in abundance, spurting from pathways and in the woodland, but few others were aware of its deadly properties.

"Remember not to touch it. And some of the berries too." Temperance disappeared out the back door and returned moments later. "Here, take this leather." Temperance handed Mary a strip of leather, which she folded and placed inside a secret fold in her skirt.

"Just three stems should be enough."

Temperance pressed the pretty violet flowers and vibrant green leaves between two pebbles, smoothed over time by the waves rolling them over the sand. She had collected the stones herself; one had a dip in the top, forming a natural basin, the other, smaller and elongated, acted as a pestle.

Murky liquid seeped from the picked perennial. Temperance prised up a floorboard and retrieved a small glass vial, capped with a cork. There were only a few droplets remaining. The shiny single black berries were hung from a string and placed on a hook, hidden inside the chimney breast. She could just reach it with her fingertips.

Once dried, and resembling a raisin, she would use the berries in hex bags, alongside other ingredients such as hair or nail.

Temperance was too scared to venture to William's farm to ensure he had recovered, or to ask after his health. She choose to wait in her usual spot in the hope that he would come to town, and she would see him, a basket of scarlet and jade apples propped against the wall, ready to offer him.

He did not.

She feared that the force she'd used against him was greater than she had intended. She had meant to cause him pain, for him to suffer, but only temporarily.

Each night, under the cover of darkness, she would sneak out, the bottle of poison tucked inside her sleeve and pass the doorway of Ms Burman.

This was not the first occasion that the women had come into each other's orbit but it would be the last. Lydia had never been short on male company, though she could convince none to put a ring on her finger, a feat accomplished by her nemesis.

A woman having to fend for herself, Lydia would take employment whenever it was offered. She could often be found at the house of Humphry Ackland who brewed a delicious scrumpy that was fermented to perfection and an amber ale that glowed golden in candlelight working as a product tester.

The door to his home was often ajar to release the suffocating smell of the hops. A constant buzz of insects, attracted to the rotting smell of fruit, kept a tune to which Mr Ackland had become accustomed, though Lydia found the flying pests a dangerous menace and dented many a tankard in her attempts to swat them.

Paid in produce, after a session brewing Lydia would stagger home, her lips as loose as her knickers. Wages were cheap as Lydia could not hold her alcohol. A few mouthfuls worked like a truth serum, and she kept Humphry amused by spewing out insults and unfavourable remarks about those that had spurned or scorned her.

Cackling laughter drowned out the bugs drone. "She's a pig, a haggard old red pig." Giggled Lydia, gyrating around the room in a mocking dance. Mr Ackland, who humoured his worker, was grateful of the company. One wife was dead and buried, the other was infirm. Lydia may have had plans to become the third Mrs Ackland, but they were not shared by Humphry, who did not share her opinions either.

An opportunist, Temperance would wander leisurely past Humphry's neighbouring residence, in the hope he would purchase the apples she had procured but one day she overheard the name calling. Lydia's slight would not be forgotten or forgiven.

Carefully Temperance tipped the bottle of cultivated liquid, so a few drops fell onto the door handle.

Lydia lived alone. She had yet to find a suitor willing to take her as his wife. Prone to bouts of hysteria all her life, Lydia dismissed the hallucinations and ignored the encroaching delirium. She possessed no mirror to note her dilated pupils and put the deterioration of her eyesight down to her age. She swore to herself that she would call on the services of Dr Beare if she did not improve.

She would not recover.

2

At midday on Friday the fourteenth of March two men bashed loudly on the shabby wooden door. The old town area high above the harbour was a bustling hub of homes, stables, taverns and the drum field, in which many a man and boy had stood to attention, practiced drills and signed up to fight for king and country. The houses had been constructed from the salvaged timbers of shipwrecks, the walls insulated with cob and horse hair and plastered with a lime and aggregate mixture.

A basket of apples she had scrumped in the early morning light sat beside the doorframe. Susanna Edwards had moved into the adjoining property following the death of her husband. Their children had grown up, moved out and married leaving Susanna destitute and unable to pay the rent.

She was cheapened to the small hovel and asking for help from the state, thankfully provided in the form of legacies from those whose wealth far exceeded their life span. Temperance would make a claim for aid too, and receive a pittance, but enough to sustain her.

Temperance was stirring a pot of woodland stew; nettles, berries and fungi foraged from the fields and hedgerows that backed onto the two roomed cottage in which she dwelled. She had moved in shortly after the terrace had been constructed. Designed to house the poor, it was a welcome upgrade from the cramped conditions she had found herself in following the death of her husband. Wells had been dug so that they could earn their keep as washer women, their minute back yards turned into laundrettes.

Temperance and Susanna's friendship blossomed over a bucket of soaking slacks. With the passing of Mr Edwards, Susanna had clung to Temperance as a life line, finding herself at the mercy of the state, a woman destitute of finance and love. Her children were in service or earning a living to provide for their own families, having neither the inclination nor the funds to support their poor mother.

Grace Thomas also lived alone, in a petite cottage by the stream that ran through Westcombe Lane. Her friendship with Temperance was strained. Once close acquaintances the women had become mortal enemies. Both falling for the same man, Temperance's strong personality and pretty face had won over Grace's frumpy frame and dull persona.

Grace didn't attend the wedding.

It wasn't the first occasion they had fallen out over a boy but it was the final time. Usually they made up quickly, the object of affection having fallen short of their initial wanting. They had once stolen a bottle of moonshine, spending the evening in a deserted barn with a farmhand, who fortunately was as barren as the desert.

As teens, the girls would meet up and do their laundry in the stream, their toes dangling in the cool water as they laughed and made daisy chains. They shared a passion for nature and manipulating the elements.

They balanced each other out. One good, the other bad.

However, one would go on to worship the dark arts, the other would embrace the light.

The widowed Mrs Lloyd thought her theft had been reported but the crime for which she was being arrested was far greater than stolen fruit. The makeshift police overlooked the woven container of pilfered produce.

Temperance was roughly escorted to the town hall where she was informed that she had been accused of practicing witchcraft upon the body of William Herbert. William junior stood solemnly in the corner, he wanted justice for his father and would see it done, after all it was he who demanded she be arrested.

Jeers could be heard from the adjacent bridge hall. Two drunks had been apprehended the previous evening and were serving their punishment in the stocks. Bound over to keep the peace on their release, the reprobates had to endure a day of festering in the damp air and the humiliation of being targets for the seagulls droppings and peers jibes. Several of the boys kicked them as they left school, a reward for hours of boring lessons.

A chill, the likes of which she had never known in her long life, cooled every fibre of her being, from her toes to her nose. Temperance was in mortal danger, and she knew it, the second the charges were announced. She had to come up with a plan, and quickly, her life depended on it.

William stated his case and how his father had uttered Temperance's name on his death bed.

She pleaded not guilty.

She would deny any and all charges.

The justices discussed the case.

Unable to reach a satisfactory conclusion and under pressure from Mr Herbert's son, Temperance was transported to the castle at Exon to stand trial.

Frustrated, William stormed home in a foul temper. He could do no more. Since his father's death he had become the head of the household and boss of two businesses, he had little time to spare and would have to trust that the judges in the city would come to the same verdict as he.

He let off steam in his workshop. Stoking the fire, he heated an iron rod until it glowed. Placing the burning metal onto the anvil, William took his trusted hammer and repeatedly hit it, with no purpose other than to pulverise something.

The journey to the county's capital was bittersweet.

It was the first time that Temperance had strayed beyond the borough, but she couldn't appreciate the encapsulating beauty owing to the knot of dread that twisted in her stomach. Her thoughts were so full of ways to escape that the new sights were squandered in a jumble of alibis and excuses.

Temperance was scared.

The cart skidded to a halt outside the north gate; a dual layered square tower topped with a flag and home to a single archer, poised for action.

A mismatched row of cottages lined the street on both sides, creating a tunnel of taverns, brothels and family homes leading to the bustling metropolis. Streams of black smoke could be seen billowing from the chimneys of properties within the city walls. Temperance lost her balance and was thrown to the floor, onto the heap of straw and mess that she had carefully dodged on the bumpy ride. She could see nothing save the reinforced stone wall that boxed in the city as they waited for the portcullises to be raised.

From the confines of the city Temperance could hear the echo of various church bells chiming, residents flogging their wares but what astounded her was the smell, a combination of poor sanitation, foul-smelling trades and livestock. It was worse than the stench of the rubbish filled, swine infested streets she longed to return too.

The steed had made good time, thundering in the direction of the assizes. The streets were wide but the driver was forced to decrease his speed to negotiate the public and other hazards that spilled into the street.

The walls of the castle rose into the sky. Temperance was pulled from the cart and marched to the cells where she would be chained, abused and underfed until her trial.

3

The date was Friday the 14th of March in the year 1670.

The day of Temperance's arraignment had arrived.

Judge Sir Thomas Raymond walked into the room with the officiality his position afforded. In court dress comprising of a full-length black robe topped with a miniver made from the unspotted coat of a red squirrel. Temperance would not experience the striking red robe and contrasting pink taffeta, worn in Summer, for over a decade. A resistive cincture was tied tightly around his waist. He deliberately made the girdle too tight, so that he felt a measure of being as uncomfortable as those that stood before him. It helped him to keep his compassion and focus. A trait that infuriated his fellow magistrates. A ringleted cream wig hung limply over his shoulders.

The jury assembled on hard wooden benches before Temperance was removed from her cell and presented to the panel of men who would decide her fate. She leant against the wooden bar for support. The tiered public gallery was crammed with men and women eager to witness the witch at the trial of her life.

Above judge Raymond an intricately carved coat of arms was fastened to the wall. Two magnificent Pegasus reared either side of a shield featuring the castle in which temperance found herself, on which balanced a knight's helmet and on top of that perched the royal lion. Plaques inscribed with the names of previous officials decorated the room and thick embroidered pelmets hung over the windows.

Two armoured guards with menacing polearms were posted at the door and one stood adjacent to the suspect, just in case Temperance made a break for freedom.

Temperance knew full well, why and how, she found herself at the county's assizes. All she could do was hope for a merciful judge who would be swayed by the charming lies that were to roll from her tongue.

"Are you Temperance Lloyd? A widower of the borough of Biddiford?"

In a feigned feeble voice Temperance confirmed she was the accused. Her identity had been established so there was no point in an elaborate ruse to convince them they had the wrong woman. Although she considered it for the briefest of moments.

"You are indicted for practicing witchcraft upon the body of one William Herbert, late husbandman of Biddiford."

Temperance looked suitably confused at the accusation.

"How do you plead? Guilty or not guilty?"

"Not guilty. Your Honor." Temperance's face now depicted the impression of innocence.

Sir Raymond recounted the details of Williams death and his son's accusations following his father's death bed revelation.

"Did you not prick the said William Herbert unto death?"

"No sir." Temperance allowed her voice to crack, as if she were on the verge of tears. "He showed me a kindness his son does not possess. I ask you why I would harm the dear Mr Herbert" She went on to describe the generosity of the deceased, embellishing the facts and exonerating herself of any blame.

The judge read from the witness statement provided by the younger William, considering the circumstantial evidence and hearsay the document contained.

The panel of educated men had deliberated and Sir Thomas Raymond was ready to deliver the verdict.

"Temperance Lloyd, the jury find you not guilty of causing the death of Mr William Herbert through the means of witchcraft. You are free to go."

4

Temperance was relieved to be walking through her own door. She had feared that she may never see the town, or her friends again.

She was dirty, tired and starving.

Her feet were bloodied and blistered.

Her dress was ripped and her hair was matted with leaves and twigs. William Herbert would not learn of Temperance's acquittal for some time but when he did he would make it a personal mission to destroy her.

Abandoned outside the gates of the city, it had taken her five days to walk home. A farmer had taken pity on her, and she had the luxury of riding upon a bale of hay for a mile but was soon forced to resume her journey on foot.

She followed the path of the canal and waterways where she could but was forced to trek cross county, through fields and woodlands, seeking shelter from the burning sun and cold nights.

She was pleased that Lydia was at death's door, and that she was safe from suspicion. Susanna had continued with the campaign against Lydia whilst Temperance had fought for her life at court.

Ms Burman was suffering terribly and welcomed death. Every part of her body ached. Over the weeks the poison had been absorbed though her skin and had filtered into her organs, coursing like blood through her veins.

The news of Lydia's demise brought a smile to Temperance's wrinkled mouth. It was two days before the neighbour smelt the unpleasant odour and alerted the authorities who discovered the remains. Her death was not treated as suspicious.

Lydia's bloated corpse was placed on a stretcher, and she was buried, wrapped in a shroud of used linen, in an unmarked grave.

The three women understood the need for secrecy. They had missed their mentor in her absence. The potency of their spells lacked the venom of the experienced practitioner.

Temperance had been lucky.

Matthew Hopkins was a man who had made a career of travelling around the country, to the benefit of the kingdom, ridding towns and villages of the scourge of their society. He had been responsible for committing hundreds of women and men to the noose by the time his lungs were blackened by tar and disease, and he too was dragged to meet his maker.

Devon had largely escaped the attention of the infamous witchfinder and subsequent generals but the fear of prosecution hung in the air as others stepped into Hopkin's shoes. Witches and warlocks throughout the country hid their magical tools and sacred books. To the religious men, intent of discovering demons, there was nothing more dangerous than a scorned woman who could wield magic, believing they could decimate a whole area if they weren't stopped.

His contemporaries treated his writings about how to identify and slay a witch as a guide, negating their conscience and aligning their behaviour with God.

Taking measures to avoid being spotted with one another during the day, the women met under the cover of darkness.

Climbing over the gate that secured the throughfare to the next village, Temperance held the folds of her pleated skirt to prevent it snagging or dipping into the boggy undergrowth and betraying her night time activities. A secluded copse marked their meeting place.

Susanna was next to arrive, quickly followed by Mary.

The three women embraced.

Temperance rifled through a pile of leaves to retrieve a small iron pot and placed it upon a tree stump which acted as a natural altar. She added a feather to represent air, Susanna scattered ash from her hearth to represent fire and Mary sprinkled a vial of her tears into the mixture for water. The element of Earth was covered with a handful of dirt, a pinch added by each woman. They invited spirit to join them.

Holding hands, the ladies skipped in a circle, three times, like overgrown children. Somewhere a clock chimed on the stroke of midnight.

Temperance sang the first line solo. As she sung the second line, Susanna began singing the first, with Mary joining the chanting in a harmonious perpetual canon.

"Mount water to the skies!
Bid the sudden storm arise,
Bid the pitchy clouds advance,
Bid the forked lightnings glance,
Bid the angry thunder growl,
Bid the wild winds fiercely howl,
Bid the tempest come again,
Thunder, lightning, wind and rain."

5

The sorry demise of Lydia was soon forgotten. Her cottage rented out before the lingering scent of death had left.

Temperance's sights were set on another.

Her recent brush with the law had left her feeling vulnerable yet invincible. Her acquittal had given her a false sense of security and an inflated ego yet her poor position in society meant she was at the mercy of the generosity of the men folk of the town. Her husband had died with not a farthing to his name.

Born into a working-class family, Temperance had always strived for a life that would remain largely out of her reach. Even when her husband was alive and bringing in a paltry and sweaty living as a lime burner, she subsidised their income.

She stole scrap iron from the ornamentation and sundial added to the raised parapets during the restoration effects to prevent the ancient crossing from crumbling into the salty water. They survived on scraps and leaves when her husband spent his earnings in the pub.

Mr Lloyd lost several jobs as an agricultural hand and was not skilled enough to gain employment as a ship builder, who paid less for brawn than brain and favoured the manual labourer of youngsters, being stronger and inexperienced.

Stoking the flames in the kiln rendered Temperance's spouse physically exhausted. Depending on the commission he could work throughout the night. He enjoyed the importance his role brought him in the community and took pride in looking at structures the mortar he created helped to build.

He had no time for his wife.

Temperance was lonely.

No-one would live up to the romantic notion she had in her head from the tales her father had told her of a highway man named Tom Faggus. Originating from North Molton, Tom used the deep valleys and winding lanes of the North Devon landscape to steal from the rich and make his escape on his enchanted strawberry mare, Winnie, who would come at the sound of his whistle.

The amazing roan often won awards, taking prizes from the elite's pedigree stock. Once a talented and respected blacksmith, he was betrothed to his beloved fiancé Betsy Paramore. Winnie scooped the prize for best-shoed horse, donning shoes forged by her master, which angered the owners of the competition, the Bampfyldes.

In his victory he lost his livelihood and his love, forcing him to turn to a life of crime. He became a local hero, Devon's Robin Hood. Generous with his bounty, he developed a reputation for being a courteous thief whose victims were left poorer but uninjured and evaded capture by cunning and daring feats of horsemanship.

Tom's infamous reign was brough too an end by a devious constable disguised as a beggar, who apprehended him with the offer that no man would turn down, free alcohol. His escape plan had been dispatched with a knife to her equine throat.

Tom's fate was less certain than his trusted four-legged steed, but Temperance liked to think that he escaped the hangman's noose and roamed still in the countryside.

Women were jealous of Temperance's flirtatious behaviour, or wary of her confidence. They always had been, and despite the wrinkled face and stooped spine, Temperance had a timeless beauty that enchanted others.

Mr Lloyd was unaware that his chosen profession was exposing him to a toxic fume and an early grave. He had been complaining of a headache for weeks and appeared confused when Temperance tried to make sense of his baffling behaviour, but he refused any assistance from the town physician, even when gripped by a debilitating seizure.

Temperance brewed ginger tea to help with the nausea and milk infused with garlic to ease the pains in his chest. Temperance learnt the skill of milking as a young girl, hired out as a farmhand. She squatted at the udders of several heifers, moving stealthily to avoid being spotted by the farmer as she had no intention of offering payment.

Her herbal remedies soothed the symptoms but did not alleviate the cause.

With a little help from her botanic buddy, she hastened her husband's final journey.

The smells from the market were both mouth-watering and torturous. Temperance had no money to buy any produce but she put on a crooked smile and her stained shawl in the hope that pity would be bestowed upon her.

It wasn't.

"Lamb pies. Chicken thighs." The alluring voice of Jane Dallyn rang out amongst the traders. Temperance shuffled past, casting her eyes at the farmer's wife, who, aware of the beggars tactics, refused to make eye contact. Temperance continued down the line of stalls. Her basket was empty save a potato with more eyes than a nest of spiders and few slug eaten cabbage leaves. Mr Eastchurch was generous to a fault and could be relied upon to spare what he could. Today's offering was a crust of stale bread that crumbled to the touch. She would add it all into a pottage, along with what she could forage and share it with Susanna and Mary.

Temperance passed Jane several more times in the vain hope she would be sympathetic to a woman in need. Jane saw through Temperance's ploy and offered her nothing other than a scowl. She toiled from dawn to dusk on the farm, feeding, cleaning and cooking and saw no reason to give away food. She would rather feed leftovers to her husband's cattle than offer salvation to someone she saw as unworthy. Temperance would not forget her treatment.

The news of her arrest had circulated around the town. Local women noticeably moved their children away in case they were cursed by the evil eye. Temperance would never harm a child. She would happily see them orphaned at her hand, but she would not cause them physical injury.

Suspicion fell on her as a child was taken ill, a piece of unchewed apple lodged in their windpipe. The mother accused Temperance, but no one could testify where the child had got the fruit, having been permitted to roam without parental guidance. Temperance denied adamantly that she had any involvement in the subsequent death of the youngster. With no evidence to the contrary, Temperance was not prosecuted further than a demeaning slight on her faltering reputation.

Her preferred place to steal apples was from the orchards by the sea, the dock men to distracted by the precious cargo. The only nature that concerned them was the changing of the tides and storms that could beach or sink a vessel. She was eating more than she was selling and at risk of cyanide intoxication. She tried her hand at offering tobacco in exchange for romantic favours, but her skin sagged, and her clothes smelt of smoke, and there were younger, fitter options available in every port.

Biddiford had become the epicentre of southern trade and brought vessels from around the world. The waterways became congested with ships that were held in the bay whilst awaiting room to dock on the quay, which the town was forced to extend, under the direction of Inkerman Rogers.

Piracy was a threat that hung permanently in the salty air, though the men of the town were a force to be reckoned with and wouldn't be taken without a fight, which they were more than happy to start. She recalled the tale she had heard as a young girl about the pirate named Thomas Salkeld. A pompous, yet good looking, wealthy rogue, the entitled swashbuckler declared himself king of Lundy, a largely unpopulated and barren island that was visible from the mainland as a protrusion on the skyline. His reign was short lived as the slaves he had taken with him revolted and threw him overboard, where he perished in the unforgiving waters of the Bristol channel.

Temperance stood on the bridge looking down the estuary. The landscaped swept to the left and right with the open sea and flat horizon separating them. She wiped her grubby hands on her equally grimy apron and adjusted the bonnet that kept her wispy grey hair from fluttering in the cool breeze. She concentrated on the murky water that churned below her.

She closed her eyes and took a deep breath, inhaling through her nose and exhaling through her mouth, then focused her energy on the river and attempted to conjure the elements to rock the waiting ships. She mustered a violent surge that resulted in the boats bobbing unsteadily in the choppy waves, but none capsized. One sailor lost a tankard of ale overboard as he fiddled with the shroud at the bow of the ship.

Between the three friends they devised a plan to lure one of the unruly hogs to the drum field opposite their residences, where they planned its slaughter.

The plan was easier thought of than executed. No amount of pushing or pulling would coax the pig from its diet of rubbish. Susanna successfully secured a rope around the animal's wide neck but couldn't budge the boar. A slap to the pigs rear end was barely felt through its thick hide and they had nothing tantalising with which to encourage it. Somehow they accomplished enticing the beast as far as the custom house when it fled their capture, and they gave up on the idea of bacon for tea.

There would be only vegan food that night. Temperance feared using fish as it once brought her out in an unsightly rash.

Temperance hurried to the woods to gather what she could to bolster the ingredients. She headed towards the great oak, plucking nettles with a strip of leather as she went. Her pockets bulged with acorns as she trekked back over fallen branches, trying her best to avoid crushing young saplings.

Temperance wasn't the only one in the woods that evening. Grace Thomas was hunting for ingredients of her own, but they weren't for culinary use. Her basket contained sprigs of rosemary and lavender with a handful of hazelnuts rattling around. She was on her way to collect the oak tree's seeds when she came across her old acquaintance.

The women exchanged pleasantries, with Grace taking her leave before Temperance tried to coax her to the dark side.

Grace missed the danger and excitement but morally she knew that Temperance was a wicked soul and the devotion to her Goddess and the desire to do good kept them apart. Temperance looked longingly at the retreating form of her former confidant. Shaking her head sadly, the old lady trudged back home.

The other two had taken a sneaky trip to the cornfield. Mary acted as scout whilst Susanna crept stealthily down the row and broke of three ripe ears of corn.

Temperance stirred the bubbling pot and thought about Jane Dallyn. She thought about her as the three ladies consumed their supper. She thought about her as she fell asleep.

6

The annual horse show brought profit and merriment to the little town with big aspirations. Temperance could live for a month, if she found the right marks. Farmers came from miles away to sell and show off their livestock.

Beautiful garlands of pink and red peonies, lilac rhododendrons and cream-coloured thorny roses were woven between the iron bars of the archway. The labourers and breeders cared not for the floral decoration, but the women and girls marvelled at the pretty displays.

Grace Thomas and her band of do-gooders had been up before the sunrise to ensure that their efforts were fancy and fresh. Temperance's preferred spot had been taken up with sacks of spuds, boxes of carrots and bundles of leeks. Not that she minded, she would fare better within the grounds than grovelling outside it. From her back hung a bag full to the brim of apples and another hung awkwardly at her side, this one containing figures made from twigs, their features twisted into shape.

The nimble fingers of Agnes Whitefield and her associate seamstresses worked day and night to produce rosettes created from scraps of fabric saved from projects throughout the year.

The equine fair was held at the top of town, away from the town centre, which was noisome, dirty and stunk of waste. There was little appreciation from the townsfolk with litter thrown into the hedges and drunken brawls a regular aspect. The sound of hooves almost drowned out the church bells as those coming from Amberley made their way to the show.

To visitors arriving from foreign shores the quay appeared to be a thriving, bustling, cosmopolitan market town and port but if they scratched beneath the surface or looked beyond the shining facades of the homes of the wealthy, cultured and educated elite they would see the heart of the town - deprivation and filth.

Many riders stopped off at the Pynecroft drinking pond, allowing their beasts refreshment before parading them in the sweltering sun. Hip flasks of whiskey or corked clay bottles hung from their steed's saddles, offering them the nourishment needed for a day of haggling.

Susanna and Mary picked feminine pastel tones of sweet peas, tied together with reeds. Mary, with her unassuming temperament sold her assortment before the midday rush for the food stalls. Susanna was more aggressive in her sales tactics and scared her clientele into parting with their hard-earned cash.

Susanna's forthright attitude had seen her rise from the stigma of being an illegitimate child, her father being present no longer than the time it took to conceive her and to break away from the life of poverty, the only one her single mother could give her. Racheal Winslade loved her daughter beyond words but the life she gave her was hard and unforgiving. Susanna found salvation in her marriage to David and the birth of her children, but it didn't last. When she fell in love her hands were coarse and pitted with calluses, but by the time she was widowed they were smooth and elegant. That too wouldn't last.

She was working in the rope factory, and he was a dock man, directing vessels through Raleigh so they could deliver their cargo direct to the premises, and then back into the open seas, to the next port in their travels. The death of her husband cost Susanna her status and security.

With her children grown and with families of their own, Susanna became a burden of the state and was housed in a small damp cottage next to a woman who would become her best friend, and the cause of her demise. Hooks that she had borrowed, on a permanent basis, were suspended from the ceiling, from which hung lengths of yarn. Herbs were also innocently hung, to dry out for use in recipes, or spells.

"Where did you get those apples?" Demanded Joane Jones.

Temperance's spirits sank as she realised she had been spotted. "What business is it of yours?"

"Be gone or I shall inform the clerk of how you conduct yourself." Threatened Mrs Jones, who was utilised by the town to carry out tasks deemed inappropriate for the men.

Her services had first been used to search Grace Ellyott for the mark of the Devil. She had been unsuccessful, and Grace had escaped the accusation with little more than a short stay in the town's overcrowded, smelly jail and the loss of a few pounds around her midriff, which she could afford to lose, and felt the better for it.

Blessed with the gift of being a seer, Grace was protective of her ability and who she exposed it to, yet a careless remark had nearly cost her life. She had been taught the craft by her mother, who had learnt it from her mother, and so on through the generations.

She had heard the tales of witch finders and the sorry demise of the Pendle coven and was determined not to suffer the same fate. Her young apprentices were left without a tutor, leaving the fledglings vulnerable and their training incomplete.

Temperance Lloyd and Grace Thomas were among those students. The two young friends, close and trusting, would come to tread different paths, one of lightness and harmony, the other of darkness and pain, which would rip their friendship apart.

Temperance considered a confrontation but thought better of it. It pained her like the sting of a bee but she had no desire to fight for her life in the court for a second time. Victorious, Joane watched Temperance with narrowed eyes, as she slunk through the crowd in the pretence she was departing the fair. She discreetly handed some of the juicy rosy fruit to Mary who hawked it on her behalf.

Though Mary longed to have had the male companionship the others did, it was through her own making. She did not remember her mother, gone before she had taken her first steps. Her own daughter, born out of wedlock, had lived only a short time but the pain of the loss scared her indefinitely and she swore she would never be in that position again, choosing to be celibate for the remainder of her years.

It wasn't only Temperance who had to scratch a living from the dirt, just to survive. Before her breasts swelled with puberty, Mary posed as a lad and worked in the paint mines at Amberley, extracting culm. The black pigment was used in the ship building industry as a natural water proofer.

Temperance had three apples left. One was bruised, the fruit beneath the dented skin turning to mush. The other two nearly suffered the same fate as Temperance was knocked to the ground. A disgruntled farrier, who received no recognition for his craftsmanship, blamed his horse and drowned his sorrow. He recklessly whipped the losing beast as it bolted up the road and around the corner at Catshole turnpike. He was heading down to Ford farm and the fording place to cross at low tide and save himself a longer journey through the steep hill of Amberley. He didn't see Temperance until it was too late, not that he would have slowed if he had with the red mist of failure clouding his vision. All he had to show for his efforts would be a knackered nag and a sore head. Other grumpy farmers with unsold stock drove them back through the designated routes, the favoured being through Bowden and into the lush rolling fields of Littleham or via Moreton to the surrounding villages.

It took Temperance some time to recover from her ordeal. Susanna comforted her whilst Mary cooked the apples into a sweet lumpy pottage with sage and lavender.

Temperance could scarcely muster the enthusiasm to eat. She stewed on being run down and the injuries she could have sustained, but didn't, and was furious with herself that she was too shocked by the incident to retaliate. In her right mind, the rider would have been hexed for his insulting demeanor. Instead, her thoughts turned to Jane Dallyn.

Taking a piece of cured cow hide, Temperance worked the tanned leather between her fingers, visualising the downfall of the woman who had again refused her. Using an awl, she crudely etched a drawing of a person with basic features, her skill as contemporary as Picasso.

One thing she hated more than being rejected was being ignored, and Jane had acted as if she wasn't even there.

Holding the awl tightly in her right hand, Temperance stabbed the leather. She used such force that the sewing implement penetrated the thick material and pricked her own leg. A droplet of blood swelled to the surface and she swore at herself for her carelessness. Using the blood, she smeared it into the cloth as she worked the awl over the placement of the effigies eye.

"With this mark may you not see, this torment I cast on thee."

7

Jane Dallyn woke screaming.

It felt like her eye was on fire. The sclera was bloodshot, and her iris was cloudy.

Within the week Jane would be dead.

Temperance gloated internally that suspicion did not fall at her door. Her crime would go unpunished, for now.

The fight between the rich and the poor, between religious factions and political parties are all carried out on a public platform, but there was a quiet war being covertly waged on the banks of the estuary, one between good and bad.

Grace and Temperance's closeness had fizzled from existence, the admiration turned to resentment long ago. Relationships often faltered, some for petty reasons, others for outrageous betrayals, friends became enemies and enemies became lovers.

An unlikely pairing was that of Susanna Edwards and Elizabeth Eastchurch. They had come to be acquaintances working side by side in the rope factory. They had spent many hours dangling their feet into the cold water and drawing patterns in the wet sand with their bare feet, giggling about cute sailors and dreaming of imaginary futures in faraway lands with exotic princes.

They were comfortable in each other's company but that changed as their bodies did and they experienced feelings that conflicted with the accepted norms of society.

Standing on the footbridge, that arched over the inlet from the river, the adolescents watched the workers as they scurried around unloading crates of goods. For a brief moment, their pinkie fingers touched and a bolt of desire shot through Susanna. Neither woman moved, their gaze transfixed on the bobbing boats as they entwined their digits. They grew closer over the coming months, their hearts skipping a beat when their skin brushed. Their gaze held longer and deeper.

It was Susanna's heart that was the first to split. Torn, she embraced the surge of wanting that David stirred inside her, yet at the same time she grieved for the friendship that was slipping away, and a future that she knew was never obtainable, no matter how much she dreamt of it.

Elizabeth would go on to win the affection of Thomas Eastchurch, an educated young man from a successful family. Elizabeth's prospects were turned around after she accepted his proposal of marriage and for many years she didn't give her old life, or friends, a second thought or glance.

With her children grown and caring for families of their own, Elizabeth found herself at a loose end. They had two girls in their employ, one to cook, the other to clean, leaving Elizabeth to occupy her time with embroidery and other leisurely pursuits.

She was an accomplished artist and took a great deal of pleasure in her study of nature. She would sit for hours sketching, her fingers black from the charcoal, her book full of observational drawings.

Owing to her husband's business accruement, Elizabeth was privy to the finest powdered pigments exported from Europe but also made her own by extracting the colour from plants. Iron pots of berries and petals lined the shelves of the pantry. The purple heads of the gomphrena flower hung limply over the side. Mixed with honey or water, Elizabeth took pride in developing new shades.

Thomas was a thoughtful man, for their twentieth wedding anniversary Elizabeth was presented with a set of brushes, made from horse hair and cedar wood by a local carpenter. Her first set of brushes had been crudely constructed with locks of her own hair, but it served the purpose.

The Eastchurch household were early risers, Thomas hadn't amassed his wealth by lazing around in bed. Elizabeth, attentive in her wifely duties, exited the marital bed in time with her spouse. Usually, she would potter around her garden, listening to bird song, attending to her plants as the staff prepared breakfast.

Today she was restless, her mind unable to focus on any tasks. She loaded a basket with art equipment and headed to the woodland behind Parsonage Close.

She wasn't the only person in the woods that morning.

After an unsettled night, plagued with dreams of flames and damnation, Susanna decided to take a stroll. Her appetite was as melancholy as her mind, after a few bites of an apple she put it back in the bowl and headed out, her shawl pulled tight around her head and shoulders. Susanna was drawn to the woods. Lifting her dress over a fallen tree, she followed the path that descended down from the solitary oak tree.

Elizabeth had her back to the approaching figure, who had not noticed the crouching form of the amateur painter. A twig breaking under Susanna's foot gave away her location. Elizabeth's head spun round to see who was interrupting her tranquillity. Her eyes were narrowed to slits and her mouth tightened. Susanna's eyes widened and she bit her bottom lip. For several moments, the aged women held each other's gaze, neither moving a muscle.

Elizabeth's features softened and Susanna relaxed, the tension ebbing from her body. She was about to turn and retrace her steps when Elizabeth, against her better judgment, tapped the moss-covered bank on which she was perched. Apprehensively, Susanna closed the gap, half expecting it to be a trap.

They sat in silence, barely inhaling, staring straight ahead. Elizabeth could no longer concentrate on the intricate details of the dandelion that she was midway through, an unfinished brush stroke marking her distraction.

"Susanna, I..." Elizabeth's voice was gentle but hesitant. They sat in silence; Elizabeth unable to say what was on her mind.

Elizabeth turned her head, just a little. Susanna's hands were bunched together on her lap, the top of her boot teased a long blade of grass before she pushed down firmly, crushing it.

"Um....Well... I... How have you been?" She knew it was a lame question, she knew that her former pal was destitute, and she knew she had done nothing to prevent or cure it.

"Well, it is what it is." Susanna was wary. She was torn between wanting to give in, embrace the time they were sharing, and being scared of falling foul of a deception, and she wasn't going to provide any ammunition.

"I'm sorry. I should have.....I mean I....." Elizabeth sighed. She'd grieved the loss of their friendship all those years ago but sitting in such close proximity she felt the spark of fire that Susanna had always lit within her, the passage of time dissolving in an instant.

"You have Thomas to take care of and besides, we are not as we were." Susanna took no pleasure in saying the truth.

"We have servants for the household chores and though we share a bed, he is ...." Elizabeth didn't finish, too embarrassed to say more having been unable to stop the thought attempting to escape. Susanna tried, and failed, to suppress the smirk that infected her lips. Her posture was still tense but that too began to relax.

For the first time in decades, they looked at each other. Deeply, truly looked, not just a snatched glance or expressionless stare but one that made their hearts flutter and breath deeper.

Feelings do not fade; they could be ignored, suppressed or twisted into something ugly and unrecognisable but they are always there, gnawing away at, or uplifting, the soul.

The awkwardness soon gave way to a rekindled partnership and the women embarked on clandestine meetings in the woodland that stood tall and proud on the hilly landscape.

8

Hannah Thomas was a young woman, born and bred in the town, but fiercely independent and reliant on no one. She was frugal with the money she had inherited and the small cottage in which she had been raised, was shared with chickens and an unruly rooster. She had been tending the feathered stock since she was a girl, by five she was plucking the hens her mother had just throttled. Hannah's determination and proficiency was witnessed over the years by the landlord, who reluctantly agreed to the tenancy of a single woman, on the untimely passing of her father.

Hannah sold eggs to the many bakeries that lined Mill Street and the avenues that spurned from the main road on the western bank, any excess flogged at the market alongside pies and ornamental pieces to adorn the mantlepiece or to extenuate a ladies finer features.

She would sit late into the evening, working by the light of a candle, to create beautiful decorations from the plumes. She had a reputation amongst the locals for producing bespoke fans. Using the flexible twigs of the willow tree, or occasionally bone, she painted intricate patterns on the ribs and added the fluffiest feathers.

She had learnt the skill of coppicing from her grandfather, which served her well in keeping a useful supply of wood for her crafts.

Stopping off outside the custom house, Hannah leant against the wall to catch her breath. The steep cobbled street was the quickest route to the market but pulling the cart was not easy work and her muscles burned from the exertion.

Temperance was also out early that morning. She was watching the archers take practice shots across the water towards Amberley. Many fell short, the arrows piercing the water with a plop. Boys with as much mud on their faces as boots scurried around retrieving what arrows they could find and returning them to the butts that filled the generous public garden beside the ever-busy building visited by traders daily to settle accounts and pay fees.

Hannah was wiping the sweat from her brow and hands on her stained apron as Temperance shuffled towards her. The sack on her back was weighing her down, making her progress slow and she was happy to stop. Fishing around she pulled out a juicy apple.

"Here my dear, take this." Hannah took the fruit and the two women exchanged pleasantries. She placed it in her cart, offering Temperance a speckled brown egg in exchange.

"I couldn't take that, my dear." Temperance took a step backwards. Hannah did not disguise the offense she felt. Having noted this, Temperance was quick to justify her behaviour. "I meant I have no money to pay for it."

"You gave me food. It is a simple trade good lady."

Temperance held out her hand to receive the offered egg, which she wrapped in cloth and placed in the secret fold of her olive-green frock. They spoke further about the weather, the state of the pathways and their shared appreciation of mother nature.

Hannah, having recovered sufficiently, took her leave and continued to the market. Elizabeth and Grace would be very pleased with her unintentional kindness. She had not expected to meet Temperance but did not squander the opportunity to forge an association.

Grace was to be the one to tempt the dark priestess and steal the devilish book of shadows, but Hannah was a player that the three crones would not see coming. Once the hell bound grimoire was in their possession they could vanquish the demons hold and rescue their corrupted brethren.

The widow Lloyd was as enamoured by the chance encounter. She spent the remainder of the morning contemplating the validity of Hannah's words and seriously considering the possibility that Hannah could be persuaded to join them. It was obvious she had a deeper understanding of the properties of the surrounding woodlands.

Food and friendly words of advice were given, by both women, on every occasion that they saw one another over the coming months. Neither suspected that they were being groomed for their supernatural secrets.

Yet.

Temperance spent little time indoors. Although her bones were old, she was spritely for her advancing years and walked for miles each day, foraging, gathering, begging, stealing.

Mary spent much of her time indoors. Her joints were beginning to twist with the signs of arthritis and her mind was prone to fits of depression, made worse by her consumption of fermented wine, brewed in her own front room. Susanna picked the berries and enjoyed the spoils of Mary's handiwork, as did Temperance.

The women dined most evenings together, talking about enchantments or gossiping, usually about past acquaintances. Sometimes lost in their own dealings, happy to be in the likeminded presence of another, even though no words were spoken.

The town was fortunate to have had some generous benefactors whose wealth left a lasting legacy. Every Christmas, a one-man meal was provided to the poor with thanks to the departed merchant, William Pawley, others were helped due to silk weaver, Thomas Smiths need to be remembered.

Being in line to receive aid was humiliating to Temperance but she was not too proud to take what was offered. She was not alone in the queue of aged widows and the infirm, that snaked for half a mile from the doors of the guild hall. Susanna was often to be found in the same line.

The maintenance of this official building was courtesy of the endowment left by the famous Admiral of the Fleet, Sir Grenville, as was the upkeep of the town's prison. Usually, cash was handed out to purchase essential substance but today each pauper received a small quantity of produce, in varying forms of stale to mouldy.

Temperance had developed a chefs skill to add pungent ingredients to her broth to improve the bland taste. This was not the first time, nor would it be the last, that Temperance and Susanna had to rely on the parish for relief.

Temperance recalled fondly the day that England's dignitaries graced the little white town with their presence. On a tour of the birthplace of the son of the seas, knighted sailor Richard, they visited his family home, an arm's reach from the town hall.

Men in puffed trousers or with skinny legs stuffed inside hoses and finished with a codpiece walked along the swept quay. The shining buttons of their doublets reflected the glittering sun and brimmed hats sat upon nodding heads as they listened to premonitions for the town's industrious future.

The gentlemen were accompanied by two women, finer than any Temperance had ever witnessed. The skirts on their patterned dresses were as wide as a horse's rear end and they both clutched a fan. Dutifully following the men, neither uttered a single word but offered a dainty smile when addressed. Ringlets of ash blonde hair bounced as they strutted long the cobbles, cleaned of manure and vagabonds.

Flags hung from windows and the bridge's parapets flapping in the breeze, a contestant against the beating of the gulls wings.

Children were scrubbed, their clothes washed, and their hair tamed. Residents lined the streets, waving and cheering, as the horse drawn carriage arrived in style. Some ten year prior the town awarded the baronial title to Lord John Granville, for his duties in restoring the throne to King Charles the second, and the whole town celebrated, eating like kings that day too.

The distant memories floated through Temperance's mind as she stood in line, her head down and gaze fixed on an ant scurrying between the cobbles.

Anne Fellow was in town too. The daughter of a gent, she was born with a proverbial silver spoon in her mouth, she wanted for nothing and possessed everything but a decent bone in her body. Anne was mean, distempered and spiteful. She had been set up with many eligible suitors but preferred the lifestyle she was accustomed too.

The apple of her father's eye, to become a wife she would have to forfeit her lavish desire to do as she pleased, and she loved to do as her heart directed her. It was through her blatant disregard for the feelings of others that she found herself mistress to the surviving William Herbert, an agreement that was mutually beneficial, to everyone except Mrs Herbert, who was ignorant to her husband's extramarital relationships.

Temperance was not and had caught them in a compromising position, on more than one occasion.

She had threatened to expose them but William was not intimidated and had threatened back, with his fist.

Anne recognised Temperance from behind and couldn't resist a jibe. She looked down her nose at Temperance, at anyone less fortunate, but Temperance took the insult personally. As Anne drew level she sniggered. Grabbing hold of her pleated plum coloured skirt, Anne deliberately swished it away, as if it could become contaminated just being in the vicinity of the unfortunates in society. The disgraceful display of arrogance did not go unnoticed.

'I'll get you.' Thought Temperance.

She had found a new target.

She couldn't care less about the affair, but Anne had gone too far this time. Temperance would not stand for being treated this way and vowed that Anne would pay for her actions.

9

"Come along Mary." Susanna took the arm of Ms. Trembles and guided her along the well-trodden path of Stambridge Lane. The gated dirt track connected the town to the surrounding hamlets and branched off into various footpaths that weaved through the fields and woodlands that overlooked the slate rooftops and bustling harbour.

Susanna often felt the dark influence of her religious icon when she walked along the lane. Closing her eyes, she'd call the name of the Lightbringer and would feel his presence all around her, imagine his hot breath on her neck and his experienced hands on her body.

The women were deep in hushed conversation as they turned from the path and, hitching up their skirts, climbed over a stile into a field used to graze sheep and bordered with wild flower. They startled a moon gazing hare who sprung from sight.

They weren't the only ones in the woods that Spring Equinox dawn.

With bare feet, cold from the dew-covered ground, the three ladies stood, holding hands, facing East as the sky exploded in a burst of colour from a fiery orange glow into a subtle azure blue. Once the sun was over the crest of the horizon, their lips moved as they mouthed the words of an ancient invocation to bring their endeavours to fruition.

They prayed to the Goddess Ostara whilst tracing with their fore fingers a deosil circle and then a cross, to represent a wheel; a solar circle of the sun and the four seasons. An egg nestled safely in the other hand.

When they had finished their chanting, Temperance, Mary and Susanna drew circles in the air in a widdershin direction and placed the eggs carefully on the ground, an offering to the pagan Gods and Goddess.

They set about gathering the herbs and other plants with magical properties to decorate altars dedicated to the fertility of the sabbath.

"I know where there is an abundant supply of marjoram." Susanna had ulteria motives for offering to fetch the sweet pine scented perennial.

"I'll fetch the oak leaves and lemon balm." Without waiting for a reply, Mary slowly plodded away. "I'll see you at the cottage." She called over her shoulder. Temperance shook her head in disapproval but made no moves to stop her.

Thyme and lavender grew from hedgerows and would be picked as they passed. Temperance's fingers were covered in pollen by the time she had enough Honeysuckle. The delicate white flowers of jasmine poked out from under the cloth that was draped over her basket.

Elizabeth Eastchurch lead the blessing.

"Lords and ladies of the four watchtowers,
Bless this morn and bring the light.
May all things flow.
May all things grow.
May all be well."

Grace and Dorcas joined in. "Blessed be." They said in unison. The women collectively bowed to the East, South, West and North. Fortunately, Amberley's secret weapon, Hannah, was detained by her flock of poultry and was not at the early morning ceremony. In her place was a young apprentice by the name of Agatha Summers.

Aggie was a ten-year-old orphan who had been taken under the wing of Hannah. She happily loaned the girl to the coven, in her place, and Aggie was delighted to learn the craft. She had a natural aptitude and caring nature that leant itself to the primitive art of witchcraft.

Daffodils were the remaining plant, neither group having yet collected their quota, and both had headed to the same sunny spot.

Temperance was stooped over, pulling the bulb from the ground when she heard the unmistakable laugh of Grace. It always pained

Temperance that others brought joy to the woman she once looked upon as an equal.

"Look. Over here." A small, light pair of footsteps beat along the path. "I've found them." The young voice sang with the delight of completing a task.

"Well done Aggie." The nurturing tone of Elizabeth floated through the air. Overjoyed at her find, the youngster was bouncing around like a March hare. "How many should I gather? Should I pick the head, or the whole.." Her voice tailed off when she locked eyes with Temperance and she scurried back to the safety of her clan.

The women greeted each other curtly.

"Run along Aggie. Quickly now." The girl needed no further urging and fled down the track, passing Susanna, who was on her way to her supernatural accomplice.

A war of words ensued between the warriors of good and the weavers of evil.

Temperance's thoughts were consumed with plots and schemes. They had co-existed relatively peacefully, until now.

Mary was in no mood for Temperance's theatrics. Her father had been taken gravely ill and passed away. Susanna stood beside her, holding her hand as tears flowed and her body shook with grief, as he was laid to rest.

Susanna was conflicted. She didn't want to jeopardise her relationship with Elizabeth, nor did she wish to betray Temperance, or the Dark Lord, whose pull was too strong to deny. She left the planning to Temperance whilst she comforted Mary and ensured that her faith did not lapse.

As harvest approached, the town went into overdrive. Farmers slaved late into the nights, with their families and community's winter store at stake, everyone pitched in. Women and children were given the unenvious task of winnowing, separating the chaff and any pests, from the grain. The men wielded scythes and horses pulled carts laden with produce.

The hard work accumulated in a celebration that lasted for days. This year the mead was particularly potent which resulted in a drunken brawl. A handful of men started the fight, which drew patrons from both the legitimate and the back-room bars, to watch or participate. With approximately one drinking establishment to every twenty residents the small scuffle turned into a large array involving many of the town's tradesmen and several women.

Owing to the fact that the quay was little wider than a cart, punches were thrown from precarious positions, resulting in several falling into the river and needing to be rescued by their more sober peers. One was taken by the current and washed up on the silty banks of the estuary, some five miles from where he had entered the water. Another unfortunate chap was trampled by a nine-hundred-pound thoroughbred, stirred by an intoxicated rider.

The constables and well-intentioned peace keepers were no match for rowdy townsfolk. Children could be seen swaying in the street, caught up in the merriment and mayhem of the occasion.

The old pagan sabbath, Mabon, had been claimed by Christianity so could be celebrated openly, though under the guise of another faith. The same can be said for Ostara and Yule.

Leaving the noise and revelry behind them, the three old ladies slowly walked up the town's step paths, to gather in the woods for their own Autumn Equinox ritual. Each took a different route, to avoid suspicion and to make sure they had not been followed.

They had been undisturbed during the intervening three sabbaths, yet Temperance did not trust that the Amberley witches were not meddling in their affairs.

The trio took their places, hidden in the darkness of the night and protected by the wall of trees that surrounded them.

Temperance cast the circle. Her intentions coloured by distrust and vengeance.

Together they chanted:

Beat the water, Trembles' daughter,
Till the tempest gather o'er us:
Till the thunder strike with wonder,
And the lightnings flash before us !
Beat the water, Tremble's daughter,
Ruin seize our foes and slaughter!

As they started to make their way home a fork of lightning lit up in the distance. Mary let out in involuntary squeal, which made Susanna giggle.

Temperance took it as a sign.

10

Temperance worked the strip of leather between her bony fingers. Visualising her intent, the wicked witch pictured Ms Fellow, lying with her eyes closed, the life drained from her body. Taking the awl, Temperance pushed the sharpened tip through the cured hide. A smile erupted from her wrinkled mouth and a cackle escaped her lips.

As the daylight gave way to the encroaching winter, Temperance's thoughts turned to survival. How to end the annoyance that was Anne Fellow was still forefront in Temperance's mind, but she understood she needed to be practical. Afterall, she could do nothing from the grave, which is where she would end up if the food and firewood did not last.

The winter was not as cruel as previous years and the town escaped with a splattering of snow and early morning frosts that dissipated by noon. A chilly mist hung over the estuary giving it an eerie appearance and cattle were clustered in barns, making the fields look deserted.

Yule came and went.

As Imbolc approached the ground had thawed sufficiently for snowdrops and daffodils to poke new shoots above the ground. The countryside, painted in shades of brown, was slowly having a palette of green added to its branches. Birdsong filled the air and livestock populated the fields.

Temperance was excited to try out the incantations that she had been working on as she sheltered from the artic temperatures. Her store of dry firewood was almost depleted, and her food reserve was dangerously low. She was forced to replenish her supplies before she could concentrate on her current deathly dilemma.

It was whilst she was sneaking around the streets, in the light of dawn before the majority of the town had risen, that she happened upon two figures, huddled together in a hushed conversation. The old woman was surprisingly quiet on her feet, owing to the soft soles of her hand stitched boots. From behind the trunk of a large yew tree that dominated the grounds behind the bridge buildings, Temperance could make out very few of the words that were spoken but she recognised those speaking.

Hannah Thomas and Grace Thomas.

No relation that either were aware of, though their ancestry may have merged at some point.

“In honour of Brigid I have a loaf cooling on the sill.”

“Dorcas will bring the milk and Lizzy has a beautiful silver trinket that Thomas gifted her, in the form of a hare. I baked the cake last night; the house smells awfully of fig now you know." Grace exclaimed, her voice, louder then she had intended, carried on the breeze.

Hannah liked the perfumy scent of the versatile fruit but gave a sympathetic nod to her elder.

As the ladies made a date for the evenings celebrations, a realisation dawned on Temperance. Hannah, the woman who she had mistaken for a friend, was in cahoots with the enemy.

Hurt and angered that she had even considered Hannah as an ally, Temperance vowed to use all her power to bring the Amberley coven to their knees, no matter the cost.

Susanna was busy baking, having noticed that Temperance was preoccupied and had not prepared for the sabbath celebrations. Her hearth had burned with the sacred fire for the past twelve days and served well to cook the celebratory food. She hoped that it would not extinguish in her absence.

Temperance dismissed Susanna's concerns, blamed it on being unwell. This was not entirely a lie for she was feeling her age. Her body ached. Instead of wallowing in self-pity, she used the pain that niggled at her joints and sometimes kept her up at night, as inspiration for her campaign to rid herself of the troublesome white witches.

The dark priestess was still in a world of her own as they each made their way, separately, to the meeting point in the woodland bordering the Daddon estate. Each carried a small wicker basket, covered with a dark cloth to conceal the contents.

Susanna's woven carrier contained warm bread, a fig pie, a clay pot filled with butter for which she had ashamedly grovelled profusely, and a corked bottle of nettle wine that she had fermented herself specifically for the occasion.

Marys held a colourful collection of wild flowers and greenery.

Temperance's load was a worn piece of flint, a ships nail borrowed indefinitely from the dockyard and a farthing wrapped in a cloth, to leave as an offering to the divine. In her pocket she had hidden stones collected from the river.

Mary laid the flowers in a circle, their stems interlocking.

Susanna traced the ancient solar symbol of a triskele in the dirt at the heart of the circle. The triple spiral design represented the cycle of life, death and rebirth as the world gives way to winter and welcomes spring.

Temperance distractedly stacked hawthorn branches into a pyramid shape. Taking the flint, she struck it with the iron spike many times before enough sparks ignited the pile of sticks.

Standing holding hands, within the floral ring, they began the ritual. A gust of wind blew through the trees and dislodged a long twig from the burning bundle which fell onto ground, precariously close to the frayed fabric of Temperance's frock.

"Mighty Brigid, keeper of the flame, blazing in the darkness...."

"Temperance! You are on fire!" Screamed Mary. Susanna lurched forward and stamped on the flames before they could engulf her mentor. The air smelt of burnt rags and Temperance's skirt had a large unsightly hole with singed edges. After gulping down a substantial portion of the wine, the tenacious widow completed the rite.

The women danced around the circle, chanting a blessing. As they moved rhythmically, in harmony with the increasing wind, Temperance discretely deposited a stone at the four navigational points. As she did so, she added a silent plea to Dana, the Celtic Goddess of War, to aid her in her endeavours.

A lone crow squawked.

They came to a graceful end and Temperance placed the coin in the centre of the triskele.

That night Temperance's dreams were filled with possibilities.

The following day she requested Susanna meet her in the overgrown lane that ran behind one of the fields used by Mr Tanton to graze his sheep. Several of the flock were lingering by the hedgerow.

Temperance twisted the wiry strands of sheep's wool that she had found clinging to the gatepost between her thumbs and fore fingers as she told Susanna of the spell she had been concocting.

"Let me demonstrate."

11

Temperance continued to twist the wool, this time between the thumbs and fore fingers on each hand. She rotated her wrists back and forth as she pulled strands from the woolly braid she was forming.

With every small clump she removed she held it close to her face and whispered, "From the source I do pull the essence that make them strong and true."

She followed this with a sharp exhalation of breath that sent the discarded fleece into the air. The women watched as it gracefully floated to the ground. As the final white fibres touched the muddy path a startled bleat pierced the silence of the morning.

Leaning over the gate, Susanna inspected the source of the noise. A ram, with horns that curled like cinnamon rolls, was limping away from its unfortunate position behind the hedge.

Temperance was disappointed that the spell had failed to fell the walking mutton dinner but was pleased that the previously healthy animal had been adversely affected by her actions.

The partial success of the charm had impressed her sister witch but Temperance needed to perfect the intention and strength, for a much larger target.

She would creep around in the early hours, whilst most of the residents were in a state of slumber, to test the potency of her invocations. In the course of her experiments, she lamed many more sheep and cattle, much to the bemusement of the farmers.

Susanna and Mary were quick to learn the incantation, keen to cause their own mischief and misery. Individually they were a nuisance but together their diabolical charms wreaked havoc.

Mr Hann was a farmer who moonlighted as a minister, preaching the word of the Lord Almighty and condemning those of differing faiths. Anyone deemed Godless was a target for his beliefs and the three friends had fallen foul of him, owing to having never seen them at a service or on holy ground.

The women, all of one mind, were equally determined to bring him to his knees. He seemed under the protection of the Heaven bound deity for any attempt to harm him was unsuccessful. They turned their attention to his cattle. Conjuring a unique charm, they caused the herd to produce blood in place of milk, much to the great astonishment of the milkers.

Livestock were not the only victims to fall prey to Temperance's ruthless trials. Over the coming years, innocent bystanders mysteriously lost the use of limbs, rendering them infirm, the physicians unable to provide a remedy other than walking aids, ranging from thick sticks to beautifully crafted canes. The basic ingredients the same, Temperance altered her words and intention to inflict suffering upon not only humans and animals but also on the elements and inanimate objects made from substances that once lived.

Standing on the quay, Temperance would gaze out to sea. The salty waters stretching into the horizon. Superstitious seamen viewed the aged widower with prejudice eyes, only interested in trading their goods and satisfying their needs before returning to the open seas.

She found easy targets with those that bobbed on the Atlantic, casting several away, to the loss of many men's lives.

She would later be blamed for these, in addition to nautical mishaps that were the fault of poor crewmen and unscrupulous captains. In the end, she would own every death she had caused but she never harmed a child. She wasn't a monster.

Months slipped by as Temperance worked on her potions. The green shoots of spring grew into bountiful crops. Summer passed into autumn. The golden leaves fell from the trees and the wintery frost spread its icy fingers across the town.

Conflicted, the desire to deal with Anne nagged incessantly like an irritating child, but the need to address the brazen betrayal of the young

Miss Thomas outweighed Temperance's longing to teach Anne a lesson from which she would not recover.

As the seasons passed, Temperance kept meeting with Hannah, each feeding the other lies. The chance encounters appeared to be coincidental but were carefully orchestrated by each coven. Though Temperance was the face of the operation, she had the full support of Susanna and Mary who, behind the scenes, mixed the cauldron and gathered the herbs that Temperance shared with her fellow wiccan.

Unbeknown to their fellow practitioners, Susanna had been meeting secretly with Elizabeth. They had indulged in the company of one another on a monthly basis over the past twelve months, with every intention of continuing over the coming years. Their time was mostly spent in deep conversation, watching bees buzzing from plant to plant, or the delicate birds as they foraged in the undergrowth or bathed in puddles. Susanna was fond of the elusive Nuthatch with its unique upside-down feeding style, sky blue wings, golden chest and a head striped like a badger.

Squatting down, Elizabeth's skirts puffed out and her heels dug into the soft ground. She beckoned Susanna to join her. Rolling the folds of her dress to prevent it getting dirty, Susanna positioned herself beside Mrs Eastchurch.

"Here, give me your hand." Elizabeth grasped the hand that was tentatively offered and held it an inch above the soil. For a brief moment their faces were inches apart and their gaze was lost in the warmth of the other's eyes.

Elizabeth broke the moment first, returning her gaze to the dusty dry earth. Since the passing of her husband, Susanna felt the loneliness that only a content heart could cure. Intimacy had been for the practical purpose of breeding but she did miss having someone to share her thoughts with. She liked that she had someone in her life that could bring a smile to her face and with whom she felt comfortable to be herself, although she kept the darker side of her personality hidden. Elizabeth too kept a portion of herself from the rekindled friendship and enjoyed a contented sex life with her devoted spouse.

Susanna's hand began to get warm. The top was insulated from being held by Elizabeth's, but the heat radiated in her palm. It became uncomfortably hot, and she tried to pull it away, but Elizabeth kept her hand steady with strength that opposed her stature and a look that warned Susanna not to move.

Susanna couldn't make out the incantation that Elizabeth whispered. A deliberate action on behalf of the white witch.

"Crescere planta fortis et sanus. Crescere planta fortis et sanus. Crescere planta fortis et sanus." Repeating the phases that translated as an invocation to grow strong and healthy, Elizabeth's focus was firmly on the floor.

Susanna wiggled her fingers and giggled as her palm was tickled. She looked at Elizabeth, disbelief written across her face. Elizabeth released the pressure she had used to keep Susanna's hand in place but Susanna didn't move, her hand suspended over the ground.

"Go ahead. Have a look." Susanna looked back at her. The craft had only taught her death and destruction.

She gasped in surprise at the succulent green sapling that was not there moments before. The coven operating on the opposite side of the river was dedicated to growth, rebirth and sustaining the environment whereas Temperance and her cronies sought to squander life.

The intentions behind the white witches were pure, their spells designed to bring harmony and peace. They took what little they needed but gave back ten-fold, their practice based in sustainability and working in conjunction with the seasons and the lunar calendar.

A smile that showed her gums spread across the wrinkly face of Elizabeth. Susanna looked from the plant to Elizabeth and back again, attempting to fathom the impossible.

The spell had been adapted from one that had been entrusted to Grace by her former mentor, Madame Ellyott and had taken years to perfect. Recognising the streak of darkness that ran through Temperance's core she had not been privy to the exchange.

The exertion of the enchantment left Elizabeth dizzy and breathless and she sank to the floor. Concerned, Susanna closed the meter gap and held Elizabeth in a tight embrace, stroking her hair. Elizabeth's muscles relaxed and she melted into

Susanna's arms. For several minutes they sat together in the woodland, Elizabeth attempting to compose herself and Susanna in a state of wonder.

Elizabeth, sufficiently recovered to hold her own weight, sat up. She turned to thank Susanna for her assistance and found her face in close proximity to the penetrating stare of Susanna. It was the excitement and a surge of emotion that urged Susanna to throw caution to the wind.

12

The women brushed the dirt from their clothes as best they could and made plans to meet the following evening.

Susanna's mind was in turmoil. The memory of Elizabeth's soft lips on hers teased at a future she knew to be unrealistic.

As agreed, Susanna waited for the sunset before heading out to Amberley. Using a piece of cloth in the frame to deaden the noise, she pulled her front door shut. She crawled under the window sill of Mary's adjoining cottage. It was imperative that she was not discovered.

The tide was high and the waves lapped at the stone arches. The noise created an eerie backdrop as Susanna hurried across the bridge. The wharf was still trading in late night deliveries and the taverns were full of drunken seafaring men and hopeful wenches.

She took one of the lesser used, overgrown paths to the woods where she had agreed to meet

Elizabeth. The walk was the better part of three miles and her legs ached as she slowly made her way up the hill. She lost her footing several times on loose stones, unable to see far in the darkness of the unlit countryside.

It would have made for a smoother journey if she trekked the route via the fort, but she wished to avoid the attention of the infantry men. The soldiers made good customers for the town, their wages paid by the state, and the threat of war eliminated after the dramatic loss some years previous, but they were known to cause trouble, and she did not wish to explain her late-night excursion.

Erected in 1642 by parliamentarian general James Chudleigh, the weaponised building stood at the highest peak of the town, a defender for any land or sea attack.

On more than one occasion she nearly abandoned the journey, suspicious that she was being tricked or lured into an ambush. Only her desperation to believe in Elizabeth and the possibility of uncovering a magic stronger than her own, drove her on. As she rounded a corner, the flickering flame of a candle, caged in a lantern with glass singed with soot, highlighted the bearer.

Elizabeth smiled warmly at Susanna and beckoned her to follow. They walked in silence along a winding path that snaked between trees and hedgerows.

The windows of Amberley's vast farm house could be seen illuminated through the evergreen foliage and contrasting amber leaves of those affected by the changing of the seasons, lit up like fireflies hovering in the distance.

The women were concealed from any keen-eyed residents by a thick line of trees that framed the edge of the sprawling estate, that gave the East of the water its name.

Before they reached the sacred space Elizabeth tied a scarf tightly over Susanna's eyes, reducing her visibility from poor to zero.

"It's just a precaution, to protect my .... to protect myself. You understand." Elizabeth wouldn't have won an Oscar for her performance but she was trying her best. She wasn't accustomed to lying.

Susanna left the blindfold in place and fought against every fibre of her being that was screaming at her that she was entering a trap.

She would not willingly betray either of the feminine forces in her life and this way she was absolved from the lies and betrayal, for she could not disclose what she did not know. She silently called on Hecate to stand by her side and to shroud her in a protective bubble.

Grace hurried from the clearing; the scene was set.

A small fire raged beneath a blackened cauldron, a thin stream of perfumed smoke from the simmering herbs rose into the air, dissolving into the canopy of the glittering night sky.

Elizabeth held the lantern high above her head, casting a shallow glow over the floor of fallen leaves, moss and fertile soil, compacted by the feet of the coven as they danced beneath the sabbath moon. Using a long stick, Elizabeth stirred the contents of the pot, causing a concentrated waft of the intoxicating aroma to fill the external place of worship and fill Susanna's nostrils with the sweet scent of marjoram and mint.

"What are you summoning?" Enquired widow Edwards.

"Ha..." She stopped herself before she broke the confidence of her fellow practitioner. "It's an offering to the Goddess Brigid. I've been working on the potency for some time." Lied Elizabeth.

Her words a fabrication of the truth. The contents of the pot was destined to be a healing balm, intended for human use and would be very beneficial, once they had figured out the balance of ingredients and it had stopped causing an unsightly rash.

Elizabeth had a fiery temperament, rarely shown but a remnant of her difficult childhood. It was a quality that had attracted Thomas, a streak of wild in an otherwise passive personality. She hadn't been an eager participant in the plan to dupe Susanna but understood the importance of converting or extinguishing the evil ones.

The Amberley coven was dubious of Susanna's motives and hoped to plant a seed of doubt that they would watch grow. Susanna's aims were not innocent. Part of her yearned to be in good company, she had spent time imagining what life would be like if she followed a new path now she had let Elizabeth back into her life, and heart. But the other part, the stronger and dominant influence on her affairs, sought to pervert the course of nature. The draw of the excitement she felt when she embraced the darkness was too strong.

Elizabeth talked about where she had foraged for the herbs and the properties of the plants around them. “The environment will provide. You just need to understand what it has to offer.” An owl’s hoot echoed around the trees as it majestically took flight.

Susanna was not ignorant of the goodness that could be derived from the world around them, but she and her colleagues chose to corrupt rather than nurture the light, their philosophy being to take without giving.

Following Elizabeth’s instructions Susanna, stirred the bubbling cauldron seven times clockwise then seven times deosil, until the mixture began to thicken. The witching hour had long passed by the time the two women said goodbye. Susanna eyes were again covered to prevent her finding her way. Guiding her old friend by the hand, both women felt the tender touch of the other and a warmth that was lacking on the cool night air.

The following day Temperance knocked on Susanna’s locked door. Still slumbering, Susanna hadn’t returned home until the small hours and was kept awake with her mind whirling with the destination of her future.

Her eyes fluttered closed as the first rays of light clawed over the horizon. She was astonished by the discipline practiced at Amberley and the dedication to create a brighter path, for anyone willing to walk it. Her own worship had been self-serving and at the detriment of others. Her brief time with the flip side of Paganism had forced her to ponder her current friendships, but searching her feelings brought her he realisation that her soul had been fractured by her despicable choices.

The draw to the dark side was rooted through her core. The overriding emotion she was feeling was guilt and shame that she had considered turning her back on her hooved God, who had rewarded her insolence with a nightmare filled with hellfire and blood.

Temperance's angered pounding on the door stirred her from sleep, but it would be an hour before she was conscious enough to dress. Her eyes bloodshot and her stomach rumbling.

"Where were you?"

"Sorry Temperance. I had an unsettled night, sorry, I slept in."

"Well, get to it." The annoyed dark priestess pointed to crudely nailed together crate, overflowing with unwashed nettles.

As she soaked the stinging weed in a rusty pail of cold water, her mind weighed the experiences she had had with Elizabeth against those with Mary and Temperance. Susanna jumped as a hairy leaf brushed against her wrist sending an irritating itchy pain up her arm. White blisters formed almost instantly. Cursing her carelessness she went in search of a dock plant, to eliminate the soreness.

She located a supply of the thick medicinal foliage at the top of Pitt Lane. The rough track had high hedges on either side and cattle grazing in the fields adjacent. Susanna sighed in relief as she rubbed the leaf over her affected skin.

Walking back, a stock of the healing plant stuffed in her pockets, Susanna heard the approaching voice of Mrs Eastchurch, who was in the company of two of the wives of the town's illustrious merchants.

Susanna could not contain the smile that spread across her face, last night fresh in her memory. She raised her hand in greeting but quickly put it behind her back as she saw the look on Elizabeth's face. It was one of disgust and contempt.

She walked past Susanna with her nose towards the sky, as if the mere presence of Susanna was polluting the air they breathed. Her underlings looked to their guru, who made a disparaging remark, causing them to laugh and Susanna's cheeks to redden in embarrassment. Elizabeth could do nothing to salvage the situation without compromising her cover.

Susanna rushed home, tears streaming down her face. Thoughts of a partnership turned to plans for revenge. Any remaining consideration of her changing her allegiance crushed by the humiliation of public rejection.

13

Tendrils of black smoke rose from the many kilns dotted around the town. The clay was transported from the Meeth or Fremington or specialist white clay from Peters Marland that was used to produce tobacco pipes, to compliment the trade with the American colonies. The town's potters worked industriously producing domestic and trade ware for local use, however the majority was shipped to Ireland or Virginia making a pretty penny for the craftsmen.

Elizabeth Caley's father was a respected tradesman, creating designs drawn by his wife and daughters. He used a technique, developed in the town and known as sgraffito style, where he would scratch the design into the slip to reveal the clay beneath. Once fired the pots, jugs and bowls had a distinctive pattern that was popular across the shores.

The children made trinkets and charms that were sold at market and given as gifts. Despite her families prosperity, Elizabeth, known to all as Betty, was not seen as a candidate for marriage, not from want of trying.

She suffered from hypothyroidism causing severe weight gain and was prone to bouts of melancholy, making her moody and unapproachable. She had a lazy left eye that children mocked, and adults did their hardest to ignore, a feat many failed to manage.

The first time Temperance encountered Betty; she was sat on the banks of the estuary moulding a small chunk of clay into the effigy of a horse. Her shoulders shook as she sobbed, reflecting on the sorry direction her life was heading.

Master manipulator, Temperance, saw a potential ally in the lonely young woman. She sat down beside her and offered kindly words of advice and comfort that Betty's exasperated mother had long since stopped offering.

Though she was old enough to be her grandmother, Betty felt comfortable in Temperance's company and quickly confided in her.

The two women met regularly after that, Temperance grooming her with compliments and long walks through the countryside, pointing out plants and their properties.

Sat in the front room of Temperance's cottage drinking a brew of nettle tea, Betty was introduced to Mary and Susanna. They had been briefed. Susanna distrustful, her experience with Elizabeth marring any new alliance. Mary was more trusting and could find no fault in the plump woman who would be transformed to their cause.

Preferable to digging clay from the banks of the river to create a poppet, Temperance covertly coerced Betty into procuring a lump from her father's stock. She wouldn't win any prizes for her sculptor techniques, but it was a recognisable human form, in the fact that it had a torso, two arms, two legs and a head. Her hands were caked in clay, benefitting from a manicure that did nothing to smooth out the deep creases and bulging veins.

Temperance made sure that she hung around the market, knowing that she would see Hannah deliver stock to the stall holders. Rows of wicker baskets filled with fresh produce and baked goods filled the spacious building. As their husbands toiled on the farms, tending to crops and livestock, their spouses, or offspring, flogged what they had cooked or grown. Carrying a bundle of willow sticks, Temperance made herself look busy, as if she should be there. Knitting the bendable stalks, they criss-crossed forming a durable weave.

Following the failure to bring Susanna into the fold, Hannah was on the back foot. She held her composure around Temperance, smiling sweetly, keeping her tone polite. Temperance was equally cordial. Though she knew nothing of Susanna's visit to Amberley, she had set her heart on completing her mission and would have to be more forceful with her tactics.

The following day, with a plan formulated, she again waited for Hannah.

"Ah, my dear Hannah. I was hoping to see you." Temperance was beaming a smile that was as wide as the Cheshire cats but did not reach her eyes.

They made small talk. Curious eyes watched from under frilly bonnets.

"Here." Temperance thrust a neatly wrapped package into Hannah's hand. "I made this for you."

Hannah held the parcel. "You have no need to give me a gift." She tried to pass the offering back to Temperance, who loudly refused it. "Thank you Temperance, that was very kind of you. I have nothing to give in return."

"I do not require anything. This is a gift for your friendship." Knowing that they had an audience, Temperance outstretched her arms. Hannah, standing taller than Temperance by almost six inches, felt compelled to reciprocate the gesture.

The embrace was lengthy, Temperance squeezing Hannah's arms tightly, under the pretence of love. As she did, she silently spoke a deadly spell in her mind, sending her intention to the darkness that had a hold on her soul. "In this act I do set the connection to flesh and clay. What will pass to one will to the other."

Hannah pulled back as soon as she could without forcefully pushing the other woman away, but it was enough for Temperance to take what she wanted. Several strands of Hannah's curly, mouse coloured hair. Hannah's mouth was not bleeding but she had a metallic taste that was pungent on her taste buds

"Ouch." Hannah put her hand to the spot from which Temperance had roughly extracted her fine locks.

"I am sorry." A lie.

With her prize held tightly against her palm, Temperance took her leave and scurried home. As she came over the hill and into Old Town she saw a single magpie, perched high in a birch tree. Negating the bad omen, she spat on the floor three times and said out loud, "Good morning Mr Magpie, how is your wife today?"

The black and white scavenger had a negative reputation throughout England, if a solo bird is spotted by a fishermen, it is fated that they will catch no fish that day.

Hannah went about her business, distracted by the earlier events, assuming that the old crone had not pulled her hair by accident.

The pie was not poisoned, as Hannah suspected, and the hog who found the discarded pastry thoroughly enjoyed it.

By the light of the full moon, Temperance took the poppet in her left hand. With her right, she twisted the strands of hair around the crude figure.

As she did so, she chanted. "Endings come, and life be lost. As Time comes to pass, these days will be her last. By my blood and all hellfire, do as I command."

Every day, for the next twenty-nine days, until the moon was full again, Temperance repeated the chant, pricked her finger and smudged blood into her creation.

The bulbous ball illuminated the ground below. Stars shone around it like a million tiny fireflies hovering in the night sky. The lunar light cast an eerie glow over the figure clad in a black cloak, a clay doll, stained crimson, held carefully in her left hand.

"My intention is true; it is time to fulfil." As she spoke the final word, Temperance quickly and violently closed her fingers around the figurine, crushing it in her fist, causing clay to seep between her clenched knuckles.

A mile away, alone in her cottage, a shooting pain shot up Hannah's arm and she fell to the ground blood gushing from her mouth.

And that was the end of Hannah Thomas.

Now she could focus her attention on Anne Fellow.

14

The bells of St Mary's church could be heard ringing on the hour, a reminder to Temperance that the town worshipped one God, whose earthly bound offspring's effigy hung proudly above the altar. The small town was a haven for religious sects and had been governed by the Anglican clergy, who lost their living when the preaching protestants took control of the town's spiritual guidance.

The former religious body was forced to seek shelter with compassionate parishioners and to pray in secret from backrooms. The tunnels used by smugglers to deliver contraband booze were now used by escaping ministry, bound for more sympathetic clientele.

For those whose faith was supernaturally bound, each faction was as dangerous as the other and great care had to be taken to avoid raising any eyebrows. The past dictated that the church wouldn't hesitate to vie for the death sentence, yet unwittingly provided substance to those they would see starve.

Normally Temperance would avoid town on a Sunday morning, but the ruckus could be heard in the old part of town and caught her interest. She could not help but investigate. A large crowd was gathered in the grounds of the church. Men, women and children in all their finery, with polished shoes and feathered hats, stood in groups, observing or forming a barrier between the warring men.

She would later learn that the fight was started by the rector, who chased the town clerk, Mr Hill, from the holy building, spewing unchristian language and wielding his staff, which he used to threaten and then assault the officer. John Hill had challenged the rector and called his conduct into question.

"You have broken the ancient custom of this parish." That's what Mr Hill has accused him of, Temperance overheard someone say.

"What did he do?"

"That Mr Hill," The informant pointed at a small man, huddling behind his wall of men. "says that Ogilby has been demanding, extorting and receiving unreasonable, immoderate and unjust fees or sums of money for marrying, baptising or burying us!"

"My aunt did pay unto him an amount so that she may marry quickly. I took advantage of her shameful behaviour." Said the niece of plague hero, surgeon Henry Ravening.

"He is a great drinker, the rector. I have seen him in many a drunken rage! He is a lover of wine and strong drink." It seemed everyone had experienced Michael Ogilby's drunken ways.

"I do believe him to be in permanent state of ebriety." Chipped in another.

Mr Ogilby took his leave for the better part of a year but soon returned spurting profanities and swearing dreadfully against his fellow parishioners. It was a wonder that anyone attended his services, but he had a loyal following of gossip mongering parishioners and was set to cause more trouble for certain inhabitants.

15

Edward Fellow was a distinguished gentleman of the town. He descended from a long line of wealthy ancestors who made their fortune through ruthless acquisitions and careful friendships. Edward was unlike his forebearers, he was trusting and generous by nature, not a trait his daughter possessed.

Anne had lost her mother at an early age. Despite the desperate advances of eligible widows and big bosomed hopefuls, Edwards heart was buried with his wife.

With a beaver hide top hat perched upon his head and a tailored suit over a ruffled white shirt Edward Fellow was an attractive prospect. Accompanying him on his daily stroll through town was his wayward daughter, Anne. He knew he should curb her behaviour but the love for his children ran so deep, he had not the heart to interfere.

His other offspring had successful relationships and employment; however, Anne had gladly chosen to mother her father, idling away her time in the arms of a married suitor or spending her inheritance on trinkets and silk garments. Smiling serenely at her dad's acquaintances and making small talk with their bored wives, Anne understood how to perform in polite society.

Temperance was also in town, on a mission to beg some bread. So far she had been unsuccessful.

"Good morning to you Master Fellow." Temperance curtsied. She cast an eye and an unseen wicked smile at Anne.

"Ah. Madame Lloyd. How are you on this fine morning?"

"My old bones are aching but otherwise I am well." They exchanged further pleasantries

Feeling sorry for the woman old enough to be his own mother, Edward pressed a shilling into her aged palm.

"Thank you. Thank you kind sir." She shook Edwards hand and embraced Anne before she could stop her.

"Ow." Anne rubbed at the back of her head, where Temperance had extracted a few hairs. Missioned accomplished, Temperance shuffled away, feigning a slow pace befitting her advanced years.

"Father, why would you give money to that wretched woman?"

"Anne! You have been brought up to respect your elders and show compassion for those less fortunate." Anne scoffed at her father's dressing down. Edward was not ignorant to his daughters unfavourable view of those whose social standing fell below her own.

Back in her cottage, Temperance moved the stool and lifted the loose floorboard. She recovered the wax figurine. Using the pointed tip of her awl, she pushed the few strands of Anne's hair into the head of the poppet. She placed the effigy back in its hiding place until the next full moon when she would use Lunar magic to set her intention and start the demise of the woman who had crossed her.

With the threat from the white witches looming over them, Temperance had been considering increasing their number. The dark priestess had been taught by Grace Ellyott that three was the perfect number. It represented the past, present and future, the beginning, middle and the end, birth, life and death. Before she abandoned her students, Grace had been teaching them harmony, wisdom and understanding relating to the craft, but her lessons were left incomplete.

By doubling their number, Temperance hoped to double their power.

She had short listed three possible contenders.

Elizabeth Cadley.

Abigail Handford.

Mary Beare.

Temperance had already sown the seed with Mary, the unpopular granddaughter of the towns well-known doctor. Unlike her educated, yet gullible, grandfather, Mary slaved away as a seamstress, her mind wandering to the unnatural as her hands hemmed sleeves and darned holes.

She welcomed the impromptu visits from the mature woman, telling impossible tales and filling her head with magical fantasies that allowed her to escape her mundane existence.

The first unofficial lesson she was taught, as was Betty, was to keep her mouth shut and not utter a word that exchanged between them to another living soul. Not that Mary had anybody to tell.

The night sky was cloudless, allowing the bulbous moon to shine bright, illuminating the world below in a magical glow. Known as the Pink Moon it is closest to the earth's orbit than any other lunar cycle.

In Amberley, four women and one child danced in the moonlight, chanting a rhythmic tune about rebirth and the optimism for the fertility of the land and its people. It's fifth member lay cold in the ground, covered with stones and a sapling taken from the garden she loved, whose roots would wind around her bones. Hundreds of years later, with her body long consumed, the evergreen would stand tall and proud, its purpose long forgotten.

In the woodland that bordered the Daddon estate, five women moved in unison, hand in hand, a small bundle of wax placed in the centre of their sacred circle. For two it was their first practical foray into the world of witchcraft. Temperance drew on the naive energy to strengthen her aim to fill the bound figurine with malicious intent.

Over the course of the next week, Temperance periodically poked her awl into the representation of Anne Fellow, who did die shortly afterwards.

Temperance had claimed another life.

16

Despite having a loving wife, William Herbert was cut deeply by the loss of his lover. He suspected foul play and wasted no time anonymously tipping off the authorities. Even though his position had been elevated since the death of his father, revenge was always lurking at the back of his mind.

The Fellow household was a busy place to be over the coming days. The walls not having seen so many people since the departure from this world of Edwards beloved wife, Anne's mother.

Within hours of his daughter's death, the arrangements for her funeral were underway. Two trained midwives were first on his doorstep. Alongside bringing new life into the world, they were known as layers out of the dead, whereby they would gently wash the body of the deceased before wrapping them in a shroud and, with the assistance of several men, placing them in the coffin, ready for viewing, if the condition of the body permitted it, and for mourners to pay their respect.

Balancing on makeshift legs, Anne rested upon a bed of linen that surrounded her cold body, in the front room of the family home. There she would stay for two days before being interned, with her late mother, in the family plot in the grounds of St Mary's church.

As had happened countless times before, the gravedigger would remove the flagstone, ready for the new deposit before replacing it, once the grieving had left. Her eyes were covered by silver coins and flowers had been arranged around her head and torso.

A steady stream of noir clad neighbours, friends and relatives attended the house from dawn to dusk. Some stayed long enough to appease their own conscience, others were helped from the Fellow abode, their legs wobbly from Edward's hospitality.

Edward's sister, a stern-faced woman who sense prevailed above all other qualities, moved herself in and took over the preparations. Unaffected by the death of her niece, she prevented several charlatans and earnest business men from taking advantage of Edward. One young gentleman claimed to be a professional sin-eater and gladly offered his services, for a fee. Dressed in a suit two sizes too big, he explained that he would pass beer and bread over Anne's body and then subsequently eat and drink them, thusly taking the deceased's sin on himself. Appalled at the allegations that his daughters conduct was anything less than virtuous, Edward himself escorted the greedy entrepreneur from his home.

The trade of being an undertaker was a new concept, taking the organisation of a funeral away from the family and many of the community were reluctant to embrace the change in tradition. Edward was one of those people, rejecting the two gentleman who tried their best to induce Edward to take their services. They too were asked to leave, in a politer manner than the sin-eater.

A man of great faith, he implored the clergy to pray for Anne's soul, just in case she was in purgatory, the additional worship would see her ascend to heaven. Last rites had not been administered as Edward thought Anne would overcome the sickness, but the rector, Michael Ogilby, came in the aftermath to perform a blessing and gratefully took the coins pushed into his hand to make Anne the centre of his thoughts, at least until her body went into the ground and she became a distant memory.

"We thank You Lord for the passing of our sister. We exalt your name for the good life she lived. We pray, oh Lord, that everlasting life be given unto her. And as she abides in your garden, let your angels touch what she cannot touch again. Father, be with her soul and may she rest in perfect eternal peace."

Together, all those in attendance said, "Amen."

Edward was quite exhausted on the morning of the funeral. Having had constant visitors, Edward had not had the time to properly process the fact that he would never talk to or laugh with his daughter again.

He walked sombrely in front of the coffin, that was carried by six pallbearers, made up of family and two of the towns justices. His surviving offspring, elderly mother-in-law and domineering sister walked alongside Edward, at the head of the procession that paraded through the streets on the way to her final resting place.

Locals lined the streets, caps in hands and tears streaming down women's faces, who joined in behind the other mourners on the slow walk to the house of God.

The church bells could be heard before anyone saw the weathervane topped spire, summoning the town's inhabitants to the service. The bells would ring again as Anne's body, safe inside the elongated wooden box, was lowered into the ground.

All around was a sea of blackness. The men wore suits with slivers of white fighting for light behind the black cravats and shaped collars of their tailored jackets with matching trousers, from which the tips of shiny shoes poked out. Top hats sat upon groomed hair, and many carried a cane.

The women wore dresses with neck to toe ruffles of black lace, even the undergarments they wore were devoid of colour. Black ribbons were woven into braided hair and fingers were covered in black gloves. Veils hid their sorrowful expressions and sprigs of rosemary protruded from the bands of beaver fur hats decorated with black flowers and feathers. They maximised the outfits with accessories, all in midnight shades, from brooches to jewellery consisting of skulls and crosses.

Michael Ogilby preached to the gathered audience, collective in their grief and captive to his sermon on heaven and hell and the importance of living a fruitful and Godfearing life, not that he practiced his own advice.

At the graveside, Mr Ogilby read from the Bible as the gravediggers carefully lowered the ropes into the pre-dug hole. Edward could contain his emotions no more and his shoulders heaved as he cried. His youngest daughter threw a scarlet rose into the open grave, others carefully tossed in herbs or handfuls of earth as they said their final goodbyes.

Edward's servants, wearing the black garments they had been bought when Mrs Fellow passed on, had been busy cooking up a buffet and decorating the home for the wake. Laid out on the dining table was the expected feast of cake, in addition to pies and stewed fruit. Flagons of ale provided a backdrop to the silver platters of food.

Half the town traipsed through Edward's downstairs rooms, eating the freshly baked produce and drinking glasses of intoxicating amber liqueur. Their bellies full of delicious pastry and their thirst quenched, Temperance, Susanna and Mary queued up to receive a portion of the money they knew would be distributed amongst the poor.

Temperance felt no guilt, yet the food sat poorly in Susanna's stomach but need made her take the funds offered.

Mary followed the example set to her, placing the coin in the purse camouflaged to the fabric of her shirt.

17

The pounding on the door made Temperance jump and she dropped the cloth she was repairing. Thankfully she was doing nothing damning. The thread she was using to darn the hole was flotsam found washed up on the banks of the river and the bubbling pot contained nothing more than rain water and nettles, seasoned with rosemary.

Answering the authoritative tone of the knocking, Temperance was disheartened, yet not surprised, to find two constables on her doorstep.

"Are you Temperance Lloyd?" The larger of the two specimens asked, in an accent that was not from these parts.

Temperance considered lying but her dishonesty would soon be discovered and would not do her any favours in the eyes of the law. "Yes, good Sir. How may I be of assistance on this fine afternoon?"

The two men exchanged a glance, clearly expecting a struggle.

"You are to be arrested for the crime of practicing witchcraft." Bracing themselves for a fight, or to fend off a supernatural attack, the constables were shocked by the suspected sorceress's reaction.

"Allow me to extinguish the fire in my hearth and I shall duly come with you." Temperance threw a generous helping of dry earth onto the burning logs, using her boot to stamp out the remaining flames. She animatedly threw out her arms, ready to be cuffed.

"If you will be no problem, you may walk beside us as we escort you to the gaol." Temperance obliged the generous offer.

The jailer was not as kindly. The red cheeked, overweigh,t gloried guard reprimanded them for not securing the prisoner and roughly marched Temperance to a dank and dirty cell, without so much as a word in her direction, until the door was slammed shut and locked. "You will wait here until the major is ready for you."

"And how long will that be, good sir?" Temperance received no answer to her question.

Temperance sat on the floor, the crude wooden bench already occupied by two prisoners, both due shortly before the major and his associates.

Temperance was alone when she received her first visitors. They had not come to offer tea and sympathy, but to carry out a search, on behalf of the mayor and in accordance with the procedures of handling a suspected practitioner of the dark arts.

Cicely Galsworthy and three women to whom Temperance recognised from the town but knew not their names entered the cell with all the airs and graces of nobility.

Without any pleasantries Temperance was ordered to strip so that she may be searched for any marks indicative of worshipping the Devil. To refuse would raise suspicion and result in having her clothes ripped from her person so she begrudgingly complied to the degrading demand.

Not a single word was uttered as Cicely and the others carried out their employment. The women were thorough in their search and left not a centimetre of skin free from scrutiny.

Temperance felt humiliated and embarrassed by the intimate inspection. Her body was goose pimpled from the exposure and her mind torn. A part of her was blasé about the experience, after all she had got away with it once, but she couldn't help but feel scared.

What if she couldn't convince the jury to spare her life?

Would her execution be painful?

Would it be public?

Question upon question swam through her mind but she convinced herself to remain calm and put her faith into the belief that she would charm them as she herself had been seduced.

The women found nothing. Not a mark or a blemish that could be blamed on an acquaintance with any demon and used as evidence to convict the widower of the charges that would be brought upon her.

18

Word spread through the town of Temperance's arrest like wildfire. Kids came to jeer and throw stones and a handful of brave adults came to ogle the witch.

"For all of you stand as accusers, not one of you will speak for the years we spent together, when I wished you only good fortune. Would you see me swing for a crime for which you cannot prove me guilty?" Temperance knew the answer.

Even if they did consider her innocent, none would approach the powerful elite who officiated over the town to speak on her behalf, some from fear of being accused themselves, the others out of a wary respect. "Away with you!" Shouted Temperance.

Any remaining spectator scurried home and Temperance was left in peace. Her drunken cellmate was snoring in the corner, their troubles temporarily forgotten. The floor was covered in straw and an unpleasant odour of unwashed bodies and rotting food filled the humid late spring air.

As sleep finally came to claim Temperance she heard the dulled shuffling of feet that were trying to move undetected. "Pssst." A hooded figure lingered at the bars of the inhabited cell. "Temperance, are you awake?"

Groggily Temperance approached the barred glassless window. As she neared, Mary Beare's delicate hand waved a crust of bread through the gap.

"May the Lord bless you for your good deed." To anyone listening, the exchange would have been seen as a kindly Christian act, on both parts, but each woman knew that it was not Jesus Christ nor this heavenly father to which they referred.

The bread was laced with chopped basil soaked in burdock leaves, to bring protection in her time of need. A delivery from her pals, too anxious to make the journey themselves for fear of accusation by association.

Susanna ensured she picked the herbs herself. Owing to an unfortunate mishap early in her witchcraft journey, when she confused the burdock leaves with those of the deadly nightshade, a mistake that Temperance noticed before its devasting consequences wiped them out.

Susanna watched from the window of the bedroom as Temperance was escorted by two compassionate officers. She craned her neck to follow their progress as they walked past the high wall concealing the drum field and towards the top of Medden street, where they would take a sharp left and head down the hill to the town's crammed and compact prison. Susanna lost sight of them ten yards from Temperance's front door, not wanting to be caught hanging out of the window.

She initiated the protocol that had been put in place, in the event of their discovery, by hiding their supernatural paraphernalia.

The icy grip of dread twisted Susanna's insides and she felt nauseous. Aside from her own self-preservation instinct kicking in, which over-rode the feelings of panic and desperation that were coursing through her bones, she struggled with the emotion of relief. She'd be a liar if she didn't admit, to herself, that Temperance's execution would release her from the bond that they had and she would be free to pursue her friendship, and faith, with Elizabeth.

She was confident she could convince Mary to transfer her allegiance but she lacked the courage of her convictions and would remain faithful to the promises she had made.

As she mixed the herbs and chanted a spell of protection she chastised herself for even considering, let alone entertaining, the idea of poisoning her comrade. It gave her a moments peace to briefly fantasise about the fatal deed, which was nothing more than a daydream. The conflict in her mind left her with a temporary dose of insomnia, her eyelid fluttering closed as the sun began to rise.

It was a night of broken sleep and worry, not only for Temperance but for her two friends, who were expecting a knock on the door, which would not come for several more years.

From the moment of Temperance's arrest, Mary paced the floorboards, jumping at any little noise. The spinster was not a born leader, she was happy to follow and felt aghast facing the possibility that one of their number may be lost and that she may have to make decisions in the future. She had a fitful sleep haunted by nooses and chains.

Unlike her mentor, Temperance had prepared Susanna and Mary in the event of her demise. They knew of her hiding places and had secret ones of their own. Susanna would take the mantle of leading the coven, with Mary as her faithful number two. They had instructions to strengthen the flock and carry on the dark legacy to a new generation.

The date is Monday the 15th of May, in the year of our Lord 1679.

Temperance stood in the wood panelled room in front a John Suzan, the mayor, and his posse of justices.

The last time she had been here, against her will, she had been transported to the assizes at the county's capital where her life hung in the balance on the word of a scorned son.

She had successfully won a reprieve and prayed silently to her dark God to work his unholy magic and save her again from a public execution.

Mr Suzan addressed the room, read the official statements in accordance with lawful procedure and adjusted the heavy gold chains that adorned his thick set shoulders.

"Temperance Lloyd. You are accused of practicing witchcraft upon the body of one Anne Fellow, the daughter of Edward Fellow, a gent of this parish. You are charged that you did do some bodily hurt to the said Anne Fellow, and that thereupon the said Anne Fellow did shortly die and depart this life."

Temperance stared ahead making as little eye contact as possible, but enough to be respectful and not defiant.

"How do you plead?"

Temperance denied all the accusations. She had learnt to act the picture of innocence and to draw attention to her withered frame in the hopes that pity would prevail over public persuasion.

A brief statement was made by the victim's father on the general state of his daughter's health prior to her untimely death.

The major turned his attention to the women who carried out the search upon Temperance's person to discover marks deemed to have been left by contact with evil. All four stood earnestly to the left of the examinant, their heads covered by bonnets and their gaze to the ground.

"Mrs Galsworthy, did any of you find any devil marks or witches teats on this woman?" Mr Suzan pointed to Temperance, whose hands were bound tightly behind her back.

"No sir. Myself, nor the others, found not a mark upon her body." Heads could be seen shaking but no one contradicted the lack of findings of many of the women.

"Mr Fellow." Edward stood and bowed at the assembled peers. "There is no proof against Temperance Lloyd that is clear and conspicuous. I cannot find her guilty of the charges brought upon her. What say you on the matter, as the father of the deceased."

"I thank you for your assistance Mr Suzan. I do not wish to further prosecute against Mrs Lloyd." He was a man of great pity and, though he had lost his daughter, he could not pursue a verdict of guilty, without the evidence, and look at himself in the mirror.

With only an anonymous report and no physical or circumstantial evidence, and without the cooperation of the victim's father, the major had no option but to release Temperance without charge. What had been poised to make sensational headlines was over within the hour. Most of the trial was taken up with the formalities of the occasion.

"I find nothing to the contrary to convict you on any charge relating to witchcraft. Under the guidance of the law, you are free to go." In all conscience the major could not conjure evidence or condemn the old lady to death, nor would his integrity allow him to sentence her to spend the remainder of her life behind bars.

Thomas Gist, an aspiring official, vowed that he would exact the justice he felt his superior was lacking. He made up his mind to run for office and vowed that no other woman would demean the court with her wicked lies.

The door slammed loudly as William stormed out of the chamber. He was furious that the woman he held responsible for the death of his father had escaped prosecution, for a second time.

19

It was a subdued celebration in Temperance's tiny cottage. The three women sat on hard wooden stools, in a semi-circle, spooning the contents of nettle soup into their mouths, tankards of mead on the swept floor at their feet. Branches crackled as flames burnt the thin logs in the blackened fireplace.

Temperance recounted the trial and her subsequent acquittal at the honourable hands of Major Suzan. Mary and Susanna listened intently to Temperance's escape from the clutches of the law. She felt invincible. She had stood where others had died for lesser crimes and survived the allegations and harsh conditions of imprisonment.

Mary was glad that they could put the traumatic event behind them and move on.

Susanna was nervous that it was the beginning of the end, that Temperance's cards were marked, and it was only a matter of time.

The tapping on the door was as light as a sparrow tiptoeing across the rooftops. Above the sound of Temperance's voice, the older women could not hear their guest, but the shadow at the window gave her away. It was Susanna who opened the door to find a loaf of bread wrapped in a linen cloth and the retreating figure of Abigail Handford.

Temperance had unwittingly come to the aid of Mrs Handford some months past. Nursing a black eye, courtesy of a drunken blow from her abusive, unfaithful husband, Temperance had made her a soothing balm. She crushed a fistful of river algae and a chunk of apple, that she had bitten off herself, under a stone, into a wet paste.

She advised Abigail to apply the concoction to her swollen eye and cover it with a cabbage leaf. Whilst Mr Handford was topping up the alcohol levels in his system, in his pals backroom bar, Abigail followed the instructions, which reduced the pain considerably.

From that point on, Abigail always had a kind word for Temperance. She had little to offer in the way of material goods, but gave what she could spare, without being caught to those even less fortunate than herself. She had to be creative to make the household funds stretch to cover rent and food, any spare farthing being drunk by her selfish spouse.

The kind smile and friendly word from Temperance was sometimes all that she would receive in a day.

Temperance would use this new friendship to her own advantage. To expand their power and sell another soul into the hellfire of satanism.

Whilst she spent time incarcerated for a crime that she did commit but would lie wholeheartedly that she had not, Temperance devised a ritual to bind herself, Susanna and Mary to each other and to the sacred tools of their craft.

She had finalised the wording in her own mind and spent the afternoon convincing the other two thirds of the coven of the benefits.

Having missed her chance to escape the clutches of the Devil and his minions, Susanna, resigned to her fate, agreed to the blood rite. Mary went with the flow, as she had done most of her life, being washed along, landing wherever destiny stopped.

A small knife, whose handle had been stained black with pitch from the docks, that served as a tool to slice food as well as to cut though plant stems and rope sat in a bubbling pot of water, sterilising the blade to be used on skin. In addition to being utilised in the kitchen and for other domestic chores, it was an athame, a traditional implement used in ceremonial magic.

Temperance's hand was steady as she made an incision in her left palm. Blood instantly trickled from the wound. Passing the athame to Susanna, Temperance supported her self-inflicted injury in her right hand, trying to stem the flow of blood until Susanna and Mary had performed the same action.

Susanna was shaking, her heart beating against her rib cage as she ran the sharp metal knife along her own skin. She winced but bit back a yell.

Mary followed suit but let out a cry of pain as she quickly slashed the soft pink flesh of her own palm.

Following Temperance's direction, the three women linked hands in an awkward three-way conversion of palms, that stung as the open wounds touched. They placed their bloodied palms on top of the grimoire and smeared the pillar-box-coloured bodily fluid into the leather binding of the sacred text.

"We call upon you, Hecate. As three, we call upon you. Hear our words, feel our desire. Join us as one. We give what sustains life, so that this spell has life to fuse our souls, in service of our Goddess and the dark Lord. So mote it be."

The simple action, combined with the words that spilled from their lips, bound a part of them to the book, as well as to each other, eternally.

Blood sisters.

In the following days, feeling closer than ever before, the trio had many conversations about how they should deal with the troublesome supernatural element that were attempting to cloud their beliefs with goodness and light.

Each had their individual tasks.

Together they would train and initiate the downtrodden Abigail Handford.

The mission to end the Amberley coven had begun.

20

A small yet significant posy of wildflowers, by way of a thank you for the bread after Temperance's release, was thrust upon Abigail at their next meeting. On top of a thick stem, the delicate flowers of the wild marjoram plant clustered together in groups of twelve, the tiny petals with a gradation of dark to light pink. The pretty plant was included for protection, mostly against unwanted attention, they could ill afford to bring anymore upon themselves.

The veiny lavender petals of the cuckoo flower were a representation of love and the five-pointed head of the St John's wort brought healing. The striking yellow colouring was as warm as the sun and resembled the five-pointed star of witchcraft.

A few sprigs of stitchwort were also added for decoration, their properties usually used to repel the nuisance woodland pests known locally as Piskies. Annoying miniature creatures, their blood was potent and would guarantee the success of a spell, but they were spritely and cunning so capture was incredibly rare, and mostly by children who were easily influenced and would release them, unaware of their worth.

Mary had been teaching Abigail the ancient art of palmistry. In the younger woman's hand it was easier to point out the relevant destiny lines as they hadn't been withered with age and wrinkles. She had a natural gift for divination and excelled in her lessons.

Meeting weekly at the stream in Westcombe Lane, a popular place for the housewives to clean their family's clothes. Women and children frequented the offshoot of the estuary during daylight hours, dunking filthy linen in the cool water before dragging it home to be dried. Too many garments had been stolen when left to dry on the branches of the trees that lined the eastern bank.

As they were carrying the heavy bundles of wet laundry back up Pitt Lane, Mary heard a noise. At first she dismissed it but as she heaved the soaking fabric onto her back, her ears detected the high-pitched pathetic squeal. She followed the sound to a heap of discarded refuse of cracked slates, rotting wood and broken pottery. Carefully moving the dumped waste, the noise got louder, and the source was revealed to be a small grey kitten.

Around four weeks old, the feline had been abandoned, it's tiny head unproportionally large to its malnourished body. Triangular ears and a striped tail jutted out it's flea-bitten coat.

Mary fell in love with the manky creature and gently lifted it from its junkpile home. She bathed its patchy fur and fed it cream and scraps of meat her sweet nature had extracted from the local tradesmen.

The two developed an inseparable bond. The cat slept on the straw filled pillow on Mary's single bed and followed her on her daily chores yet, always returned home if Mary instructed him too. She named him Bartholomew.

For in the middle of August, it was cold and an eerie mist hung over the river. The year was 1680. Susanna had been busying herself around the town but had nothing more than a few soft carrots and four shiny red apples to show for a morning walking the damp cobbled streets.

On the way home she stopped off at the Barnes residence. After much knocking, Dorcas did not answer the door. A well-to-do family, they were often targeted by the poor, for they had a reputation for providing alms when it suited them to be seen as just and giving. It was dependant on personal preference too, and Dorcas had no intention of lining the stomach of an enemy.

Needing to secure a personal item of Mrs Coleman's, Susanna, in a moment of madness, tried the door handle. It was unlocked. Taking a precautionary glance to her left and right, Susanna eased it open and slipped inside. A creak betrayed her entrance and a floorboard upstairs flexed under the weight of the bed and it's inhabitant. Holding her breath, Susanna stood still, ready to make her escape. All was quiet.

Taking off her shoes, Susanna hitched up her skirt and slowly made her way upstairs, careful to tread wisely. The door to the marital bedroom was open and Dorcas lay fully clothed, yet asleep, on top of the covers. She often had a nap during the day whilst her husband John was working, or drinking, or flirting with the bar staff, or all three.

Using her finger, Susanna traced an inverted pentagram over the slumbering form. Silently she mouthed the enchantment. Her mind screaming the incantation whilst her lips remained closed. “In this room you will be, tormented by the image of me. Come and go, to and fro, I shall pass unseen, unless I deem it so.”

Using a small but sharp knife, Susanna cut a piece of fabric from the back of the quilted petticoat that stuck out from under the folds of expensive fabric.

The blade had been confiscated from her son after he lost a game of mumblety-peg. Punishment for partaking in the dangerous game of skill that had left the tossed knife imbedded in many a body part of the children playing, instead of the ground which was the intended target for the knife. Her son had not only lost the handy tool and the temporary respect of his peers but also a tooth, for the losers must pull up a peg driven into the ground by their teeth.

She had a lock of hair held between her fingers when Dorcas stirred. Her heart beating fast, and sweat dripping down her back, Susanna panicked. She fled from the room, viciously pulling the hair from its roots, waking Dorcas.

Susanna thundered down the stairs and was out of the door in seconds.

Dorcas had been in the midst of a nightmare where she was being boiled alive in an oversized cauldron so was thankful that she had been woken. Her groggy brain took a moment to settle itself after the rude awakening and she mistook the noise of Susanna fleeing for her noisy neighbours.

Susanna crouched behind a hedge. Her back and knees ached as she rose after several minutes, sure that she had escaped detection.

She hobbled home.

Not as brazen or confident as their leader, Susanna had opted to perfect astral projection. She'd demonstrated moderate success, giving Mary a fright appearing at her bedside and she had briefly materialised in Temperance's front room.

It was draining and she could only sustain the projection for short periods. She was left with a headache that bored into her temple, and a strange craving for licking lead.

To travel outside her body, Susanna unanchored her soul from its mortal flesh and blood.

She used this new talent to torment Dorcas, appearing at all hours, a ghostly form invading another's sanity.

She also created a poppet, using the hair plucked from Dorcas' head and the scrap of cloth cut from her clothing. Unlike Temperance, Susanna crafted the doll out of twigs and moss.

Using thorns from a red rose bush that had spurted from the ground opposite her cottage, Susanna pushed one into the stomach area, others into the stick arms and the last she sunk into the mossy chest, where the heart would be in a human.

From that moment, Dorcas Coleman was in constant pain, that no remedy could cure.

Over the next few years Dr Beare would be called out on many occasions in an attempt to ease Dorcas' suffering, but nothing he gave would alleviate it.

The only respite she had was when the coven performed a healing ritual over her shuddering body. Grace Thomas would loan a horse, which would carry the afflicted Dorcas to Amberley where she would bath in the white magic and be soothed by the calming voices of her spiritual sisters.

Despite seeing the apparition of Susanna haunting her waking moments Dorcas refused to accept it was witchcraft and that a fellow practitioner would turn the craft against her, regardless of Elizabeth's insistence.

Owing to the feud, Susanna and Elizabeth Eastchurch's relationship was in tatters. It pained both the women to lose the friendship, again, but it was unsustainable as the battle against good and bad began.

Apart from her blood sisters, Mary had no other friends, apart from the fledglings they were training. She knew people, but no more than to utter a few pleasantries as they passed in the street.

Considering the notoriety she was to accomplish; Mary was an unremarkable woman in every way and her meek manner allowed her to disappear seamlessly into the background.

Temperance was so consumed by her goal that she cared little now for lost friendships, or the feelings of others. Her days were spent strengthening her intentions and her nights were spent praying to Hecate and Lucifer in equal measure.

A hypnotic blend of herbs burning in the fire place aided her communication with the dark forces that drove her actions.

On occasion she felt his presence with her when she lay alone in bed. In the gap between wake and sleep she would experience the carnal pleasure she hadn't felt since her husband had died.

She would relay her visions to Susanna and Mary, urging them to continue on the destructive path with promises they should live and do well if they obeyed his orders. Power was within their grasp should they surrender to his will. Temperance couldn't help but feel a little invincible.

The sweet enticement of the tempting bribe, that they too may get to encounter the demonic glory himself, was enough to extinguish any last flame of hope in Susanna's soul.

It wasn't long before Susanna got her wish.

21

Susanna was beginning to doubt that she would ever get the encounter she had been promised, and she had done her part. She had plagued Dorcas with disturbing visions, infiltrating her bedchamber with haunting apparitions.

Susanna was lonely.

Her pockets were as empty as her belly.

She was starting to lose the faith and regret her decision.

Her morning in town had been a waste of time. There were no charitable patrons on the streets who would even look her way, let alone part with funds or food.

Susanna's legs were weak and her stomach ached. She had to stop at the top of High Street to catch her breath and let her tired limbs rest. After ten minutes she had regained the strength to walk further, however instead of travelling the short distance back to she cottage her decided to head to the woods, to take some time out in nature in an attempt to realign her allegiances and rejuvenate her spent energy.

She opened the gate at Parsonage Close, careful to close it again to prevent the cattle from escaping and started to make her way across the field. She'd only gone a few paces when she felt the presence of someone watching her.

She turned around to see a gentleman, dressed from top to toe in black. His clothes were as dark as his face.

Full of hope, Susanna smiled and, despite the burn in her legs, curtsied to the exotic looking stranger. She looked expectantly into his chocolate brown eyes.

"Do you have no funds to sustain you?" Asked the handsome, dangerous foreigner.

"Yes, good sir. I am poor."

"You will not want for meat, drink or clothes if you grant me this one request."

Excited, Susanna spoke without considering her answer. "In the name of God what shall I have?" Susanna had chosen the wrong deity. Upon hearing her reply, the mysterious gentleman vanished from her sight.

"But...... where did ...... come back ... I meant ..." Susanna stammered a few more unfinished phrases but, apart from the beady eyes of a cow upon her, she was alone again. She was both intrigued and worried as to the identity of her would-be benefactor.

She sat silently in the clearing. Her bare feet connected with the damp ground, and she pushed her fingers into the soil. She tried the spell Elizabeth had taught her, but her mind was too clouded to concentrate.

That night, as she lay in her bed, her eyes closed and her mind began to slip from consciousness and into the realm of dreams. It was then that she felt the thin linen sheet lift and she had the sexual experience she had desired and missed. The memory lingered on waking, as did the faint masculine scent, her breast tender to the touch.

Bartholomew the cat woke Susanna the following morning. A furry paw in her distended mouth made for a rude awakening. He'd had made itself quite at home with the three women and Susanna had fallen for his feline charms. He followed Mary like a lost sheep. Temperance was not as keen. In recent months, Bartholomew had taken to leaving slaughtered wildlife at Temperance's door. His first gift, to align himself in her affections, he had left bedside her bed. She discovered it, in the dark, with bare feet. Her toes squished the cold internal organs of a field mouse into the floorboards with a squelch, it's tiny bones cracking under her weight. After he'd been chased from the room with a high-pitched shriek and the contents of a half full tumbler of water, the wise cat learnt to leave his gifts on the doormat.

Nothing was left to rot. What they couldn't salvage to eat Bartholomew got for his evening meal. The bones were sharpened to make awls, pins, anything that was useful to the kitchen or the craft.

For spells that needed an organic element, Bartholomew's presence had been a blessing.

The beautiful smoky tom was as loyal as any canine and as wily as a fox.

Mary was the last of the three to receive a visitation. She had heard of the experiences of the others, and had no desire for anyone, no matter the reward, to have carnal knowledge of her. As with her co-conspirators, Mary was in the lucid period of falling asleep when the Devil came to her. Her body was paralysed with fear and her mind's eye conjured the image of a lion attacking her. She cried into the silent night, in physical and emotional pain.

Mary's heart beat a frantic rhythm and her breath escaped in deep gasps. Horrific memories of the forced conception of her only child swamped her whole being. She was distracted for days as she fought against herself and her past.

She'd be lying to herself if the thought of running away with Bartholomew hadn't crossed her thoughts, but it was fleeting and she knew, deep down, she would never escape the town, or her pitiful existence.

She sat silently as Temperance dished out orders. Enough was enough swore Temperance, it is time to bring them down. The campaign of terror was to increase its intensity in the new year. They would celebrate Yule then execute their strategic attack.

22

No matter how hard she tried to orchestrate a chance encounter, Temperance had not seen Grace Thomas for some months.

She had not admitted her failings to the others, pretending that Grace's absence was a direct result of her meddling.

Graces' disappearance was indeed the result of witchcraft. However the culprit was neither of the three that resided in the adjoining cottages in Old Town, but herself. Grace had taken on the responsibility of blending the coven's ingredients and she had misjudged the volume of mistletoe. As a result she had come down with a gastrointestinal upset that left her bedridden. Thanks to the quick thinking of Dorcas and a disgusting concoction of ground charcoal and spices, her life had been spared. The natural talent of Hannah with herbology was sorely missed.

It would take months for Grace to build up the strength to venture far from home. Elizabeth took to sending a cart for Grace, her presence essential to the covens numbers. Elizabeth had an inkling that dark forces were at play and a slither of doubt that she could stop them.

In the meantime Susanna had been keeping up her end of the bargain with systematic projections into the bed chamber of Dorcas Coleman, spying on her nocturnal activities, which mostly consisted of snoring and scratching.

Mary disliked the directness, for fear of getting caught, preferring to perform her part remotely. She could not perfect the talent of astral travelling, but she had a knack for creating potent hex bags. The heart of a blackbird, the stomach of a dormouse or the skin of a frog were wrapped inside a parcel of rowan leaves and hazel twigs. Mary cursed each body part she added. As the contents decomposed, Grace would experience tormenting pain, and Mary was never in the vicinity.

Under the cover of darkness, Mary would place the carefully constructed packages around the boundary of the house that Grace Barnes lived in with her husband.

One day in March, heady from an intoxicating brew of mead, Mary, full of bravado tried the front door. The wooden door opened a crack. Having recently passed the Barnes heading into town, Mary knew the house would be empty. Without giving herself time to consider her actions she slipped inside and bolted upstairs. The speed and agility was filled with adrenaline, for which she would spend several days suffering in agony with inflamed muscles and aching limbs. She threw one of her carefully constructed hex bags on top of the free standing and scarpered.

That night Grace woke clutching at her chest, excruciating pain shooting through her chest bones. In earnest Mr Barnes called on Doctor Beare, who could find no cause. By morning the initial onslaught had abated but the attack would leave lasting damage, for which Elizabeth would avenge.

The importance of initiation became a hot topic of conversation between the three elderly ladies. Susanna and Temperance were far from ignorant of their precarious standing and understood the need to increase their power by tapping into the innocent energy.

The upcoming May Day festivities would be the ideal distraction.

The town was decorated with bunting and stalls were pitched in doorways and along the narrow quay. A twelve-foot pole had been staked into the ground adjacent to the bandstand, where musicians entertained the crowds from dawn till dusk. Coloured ribbons fluttered in the breeze, waiting for the pinnacle of the day, when they would be bound together in a choreographed dance. Another sacred pagan ritual the God-fearing collective had claimed. The noise level and everyone's spirts were high. Children rode finely crafted or cobbled together stick hobby horses, enjoying the freedom and generosity of the day. The smell of hog roast almost covered the salty scent of the sea and the aromas of the squalid conditions of the overpopulated port.

Temperance, Susanna and Mary huddled together and watched the revelry from a distance. Shouts of joy and the banging of drums announced the arrival of the colourful and energetic parade. At the head of the procession, the May Queen and the dancing figure of the Jack-in-the-Green lead a very merry following of townsfolk and performers through the streets.

The joyous tones faded as the three amigos took their leave to prepare for their own Beltane celebrations. Each gathered armfuls of dry kindling, which they stacked into a pyramid. A considerably larger version burned brightly on the water's edge, casting mesmerising yet distorted shadows of the Maypole dancers upon the ground. A faint orange glow in the steeped countryside betrayed the location of the Amberley witches. To their advantage, the dark lords servants had departed before the darkness of the sky highlighted their hideout.

The flames licked gently at the wood whilst they waited for the fledglings to arrive. Sprigs of sage, Sandalwood and Jasmine burnt on the pyre, their aromatic flavour leaving a seductively relaxing hint in the women's nostrils. A tree stump served as an altar, upon which they placed a gleaming athame, a stoneware cauldron filled with rain water and a pentagram weaved from willow, its point facing downwards.

They waited.

23

Abigail had slipped unnoticed from the throngs of men, women and children that filled the streets. Mr Handford was on his tenth pitcher of booze and wouldn't remember his wife until he crawled into their marital bed. She pulled her shawl tight over her head and shoulders, hiding her face for fear of being recognised, and the fresh bruise from questions. Her new friends had no need to quiz its origin for they knew it would be a reward from her husband for her steadfast devotion and loyalty, which was rapidly dwindling.

Mary had outright lied to her family, her parents too drunk to care. Besides, she was a grown woman and they hoped she found herself a fella and would finally be out from under their feet. As it happened it would be a tenancy on a small cottage in Old Town that would eventually part her from her childhood bedroom.

Last to arrive was Betty. Breathing short and hard through her mouth, she leant against a tree for support. Her ribs pushed painfully against the confines of her fine dress as her lungs battled for air. Once she got her breathing under control she joined the others who were stood in a circle around the fire.

They were gifted with robes made from moth eaten linen, torn and frayed at the edges. As part of the ceremony they would be cast into the flames as a symbolic gesture, so there was little point in wasting good fabric. The rite was performed skyclad. Five bundles of clothes were already placed neatly on the grass. Betty was all too happy to add to the pile, embarrassed and self-conscious but glad to be rid of the constricting frock. Nobody had seen her naked, bar her parents and it had been many years since she was a child. She was quick to throw the manky cloak over her exposed body.

Temperance, the younger Mary, Susanna, Abigail, Mary. Betty slotted herself into the space between Mary and Temperance, completing the sacred ring.

Temperance invited the four elements, earth, air, wind and fire, along with spirit to enter the circle. Giving praise to Hecate and the Dark Lord she placed offerings at each navigational point.

"To the Lords and Ladies and guardians of the watch towers of the North. O power of earth. Guard our circle and our rites, be with us now. Ground our deeds, make them fertile. By tree, by soil, by stone, by bone. Be here now, ye powers of earth. Blessed Be."

She turned clockwise and said, "To the Lords and Ladies and guardians of the watch towers of the East. O power of air. Guard our circle and our rites, be with us now. Clear our vision, give wings to our thoughts. By wind, by cloud, by blue horizons and morning light. Be here now, ye powers of air. Blessed Be."

To the South with its fiery power. "... Fill us with energy, inspire us. By bonfire, embers and wild lightning strike. Be here now, ye powers of fire...."

To the South and the power of water she asked for healing and wisdom by lake, river and ocean tide, before returning to her space.

The women linked hands.

They walked slowly in a circle until Abigail reached the direction of North. As instructed by Temperance she curled up on the ground, her knees hugged into her chest in the foetal position. The heat of the fire kept her warm as she lay in the dirt. Clearing her mind she breathed deeply, trying hard to filter out the distractions and doubt that gnawed at her and concentrate on focusing on nothing. Her spouse would ring her neck if he caught her dabbling in the dark arts, daring to form opinions of her own, in fact he was that lazy she imagined that he'd report her himself and have the magistrates do it for him.

Pushing her clouded thoughts away she uncurled herself. Removing the robe and carefully placing it in the fire she stood, nude and vulnerable in the clearing. She looked uncertainly at Temperance.

"Now child, raise your arms and offer yourself to the element of Earth. Remember the words we have taught you."

"I call upon the powers of earth, native spirits, Devas." Abigail's voice was shaky. She felt the ground beneath her feet shudder, but Temperance urged her to continue. "I give myself to you as a child of nature. May you bestow in me your protection, grounding and health." She bowed gracefully before turning to the East.

"I call upon the powers of air, ariel spirits, Sylphs. I pledge myself to you as a campaigner for true intentions. May you grant me clear thought, freedom and inspiration." A gentle breeze chilled her bare flesh.

She was getting into the swing of it now, although her arms were beginning to ache.

Rotating to her right, she called upon the power of fire and salamanders. "I will strive to keep the inner fires of spirit burning brightly. May you enhance my creativity, passion and energy." The flames of the small bonfire danced, as if doused by an invisible accelerant.

West brought the spirts of the lake, sea and stream and a dedication to give herself as a servant to the elements in exchange for love, wisdom and compassion.

She turned to face East, lower her arms to waist height. They burnt with the effort of holding them outstretched.

"My Goddesses and Gods, Lords and Ladies, I, Abigail, kneel before you and ask that you accept me as witch and priestess. In complete, free and full understanding of the choice I have made, I set my feet on your path of wisdom and enlightenment. I give myself to you, your ancient names Hecate, Cybele, Medea and Circe. I will abide by the laws of the craft and obey your commands. Guide and teach me in your ways great Horned One, Cernunnos, Herne, Apollo and Lugh. I enter the craft and your protecting embrace with perfect love and perfect trust."

She exhaled loudly. Lowering her arms her fingers began to tingle as the blood rushed back into them.

Temperance broke from her position and advanced on Abigail with a small point in her hand. It contained oil made from crushing the herbs that now burnt on the fire and made the air smell sweet. Before anointing Mary with the greasy substance, Temperance dedicated it by passing it over the fire and the altar.

"May my mind be free. " At the same time Abigail spoke the words, five voices joined in. "May your mind be free." Using her thumb, Temperance rubbed oil between Abigail's eyes.

"May my heart be free." Mrs Lloyds thumb rubbed over Mrs Handford's chest, echoing her words.

"May my body be free." Oil was rubbed over her genitals. Temperance returned to the spot she had recently vacated whilst Abigail faced North.

"Old ones, Goddess and God, powers of the cosmos, I stand before you as witch and priestess. So mote it be."

"Your new life in service to the Goddess and God begins now." Temperance handed Abigail a new robe, who gratefully wrapped the warm cloak around her. Standing between Susanna and Mary the senior, she watched the old crones namesake take her place on the marker for North.

Mary also had trouble quietening her mind, which was more to do with her intake of alcohol than her ability to concentrate. She embraced the initiation, standing proudly and pronouncing her words eloquently.

Betty's legs wobbled from nervousness and cold. She tentatively raised her arms to the skies. Feeling liberated to have the cool night air touch her body, she couldn't help being concerned what the others were thinking of her folds of fat and cellulite pitted skin. Looking at her own reflection repulsed her, she imagined they must feel the same as she moved around the circle, unable to hide her feminine curves under the orange glow of the fire. They did not. Bettys size was of no consequence to them, the three older women cared not for the vessel, only the worth and corruptibility of its inhabitant and the two newly initiated witches thoughts were consumed by the deeds, and mischief, they could accomplish.

Sitting around the fire, Susanna tore chunks from the loaf cake she had prepared especially for that nights feast and handed them to each woman in turn. Clay pots filled with wine helped to wash down the dense, dry mixture. From ingredients picked, blended and preserved the previous Beltane, Mary had stewed and strained the fermenting juice ready for the evening celebrations.

Eating and drinking was a part of the closing ritual, an offering to themself and the deity to which the intention or request was focused.

Abigail was raising her handcrafted pottery glass to her lips to drain the remainder when a large black hound bounded into the circle. Its eyes blazed red in the firelight. She screamed and involuntarily dropped the handle-less mug on the floor, chipping the lip.

Its large paws dug into the dirt. The dog sniffed the air and glared at each woman in turn, its left lip curled upwards in a snarl, exposing sharp white fangs.

With a howl the beast leapt over the dying flames and ran off into the distance.

"He came." Yelled Temperance in excitement. Under her breath but within earshot she muttered, "See Susie." Who couldn't doubt that it seemed the Prince of Darkness had indeed sent a messenger from Hell to attend the service.

Several minutes passed before the younger ladies were calm enough to close the circle. They grounded themselves and said in unison, "Thank you for attending, I bid you hail and farewell. Blessed be."

The coven dressed to the sound of the crunching of dead foliage, ruffling of fabric and a few escaped gasps here and there. An owl hooted in a nearby tree, a small mammal ran through the undergrowth, a gust of wind nipped at skin not yet covered.

Temperance, Susanna and Mary watched the three retreating silhouettes. Temperance was confident in the succession of the coven. She was aware that the vendetta she had started could be the death of her and that she may end up taking Susanna and Mary to the grave. The seduction of the dark side was strong enough to keep her musings to herself.

Susanna had been shaken by the encounter with the hound, not that she would admit it openly. She hid the altar decorations, ready for use at the next sabbath. It was safer than keeping them at home.

Mary was lethargic and ready for bed.

Temperance's parting words were, "We have work to do."

24

"Bloody cat." Swore Temperance, her foot swiping for but missing the agile feline. Fully grown, Bartholomew had silky smooth smoky fur and amber eyes that were ever watchful and vigilant.

Temperance knew that retaliation from Elizabeth and her mystical crew was a very real possibility and that their plans were most likely underway. She was preparing for a physical assault or a magical onslaught, but the attack would come on a different front. But only after the white witches peaceful attempts were spent.

Temperance had noticed that when she woke, her joints were stiff, and she had a crick in her neck that would often take till noon to ease. She'd tried balms and herbs but nothing alleviated the symptoms of old age. Temperance feared that, despite the Devil's assurances, her days were numbered but she was determined to selfishly persist with her mission, and would bring down anyone who stood alongside, or against her. Her heart wasn't faring much better than her bones, and her ninety-year-old kidneys were struggling.

Regardless of her audacity, there was a nagging suspicion that the third time would be the charm, she just needed to avoid being arrested again. For this reason she had negated her role and Grace Thomas was recovering from her bout of sickness, one that Temperance claimed she had inflicted.

The summer equinox had been celebrated and the blistering heat of August had given way to cooler evenings. Preparations were underway for harvest, farmers pitched in on neighbouring enterprises as they all laboured towards the common goal of harvesting enough produce to see the town through the approaching winter months. Crops already ripened had been picked and stored and the land had been ploughed and turned over, ready for new seeds and a new year.

Mary placed a bundle of dried corn between her namesake and Betty. "Today, I will be teaching you how to create a Mabon offering."

Betty raised her hand, as if she were in school. "Mary, I have made these since I was a girl."

"Very well Elizabeth. Then you need not my assistance. Why do we construct them?"

"To ensure a good harvest." Betty was confident in her response.

"And who is it that sees that there is food for all?" An uncomfortable pause fell. Mary opened her mouth but thought better of her answer and quickly looked at the floor. "The farmers." Neither of the apprentices had experienced poverty and both lacked life lessons needed to venture alone into the unforgiving world. Mary knew the reality to be that the officials were the ones with the true power over life and death and could decide who would starve. She was determined that her charges would learn what they needed to in life.

"Yes. They cultivate the land and tend the crops, but it is the Corn Spirit who lives within the handcrafted corn decorations, its essence reborn into the weaved maize. We keep it until the following spring when it will be tilled into the earth and infuse with the new year's crop for a good fertile harvest."

Mary had a captive audience, keen to discover the pagan traditions behind the modern practices. "The equinoxes are a balance of day and night, and we are heralding in a time of rest, but we have much work to do ladies."

Betty picked up three stalks and proceeded to plait them together, her fingers twisting and bending. "One year I used the dried husks of an ear of corn. Father hung it above the hearth."

Mary junior watched the senior Mary, copying her actions. Splinters stuck from the edges and the braid was not tight, but it was a worthy effort.

Bartholomew deposited a monarch butterfly on the threadbare rug beside his mistress. Its orange wings, punctured by the cats pointed canines, jerked with the final movements of life. Picking up the remains of the innocent invertebrate between her wrinkled fingers, Mary encased its lifeless form within the heart of her corn dolly, explaining that it represented the transformation and growth for the following year. She went on to explain that an owl's feather will bring the recipient wisdom and will aid in attracting dark forces and the leg of a frog will bring luck and healing properties. She covered many animals and the magical implications of their dissection and the benefit of insects with exoskeletons who do not smell when they decompose.

Women and young girls worked into the small hours, plating the straw from the last sheaf of corn cut, fashioning them into dollies or farm inspired ornaments.

It had become a competition, the finest looking piece would be rewarded with the place of honour, the centre of the banquet table. The wholesome feasts are held at the large Herbert residence on the Daddon estate. The Amberley tenants held a rival gathering in the farm house in the deer park.

Temperance spotted Grace before Mrs Thomas saw her nemesis. Grace was carefully picking her way down the steep cobbled high street, using buildings for support when Temperance rounded the corner connecting Market Street to the rest of the town's traders. This was Grace's first sole outing since she had fallen ill. Determined to recover a semblance of independence, Grace had waited for her husband and Dorcas, who was visiting daily, to leave before venturing out herself.

'Why is it, that when you want to see someone, they are nowhere to be found, yet when you do not want them in your presence, they are around every corner, their name whispered on every lip?' Thought Temperance to herself, unprepared and daydreaming of a life she could have lived, had not her personality and fate intervened.

Temperance frantically thought of a ploy to get her close to Grace. She acted, at first, as if she had not seen her. Stooped over and looking at her boots, Temperance moved at a snail's pace, until she drew level to Grace.

With movements that were lightening quick, Temperance fell to her knees. A Hollywood worthy actress, tears sprung from her eyes as she pretended to weep with joy.

She threw her arms outwards and reached up towards Grace, who was startled at the performance. She backed away, finding herself pressed against a building. With eyes bulging from their sockets, Grace daintily swatted at Temperance as she clawed at Grace's dress.

"My dear Grace." Temperance forced her voice to break, as if she were about to sob. "You look so strong again." Temperance tried flattery to get closer to her victim. From her position kneeling on the floor, Temperance could not reach Grace's hair and she had raised her suspicions sufficiently that any attempts to cut material from her garments would be fraughted.

"Why dost thou weep for me?" Grace prayed that someone would come to her aid, but the streets were eerily deserted for a Wednesday afternoon.

"I weep for joy to see you well again." If anyone was witnessing the performance, she hoped they would recall her perceived kindness, and report it as such.

Grace edged her way past, having the advantage of standing. She muttered that Temperance need not cry for her and that she had business she must attend to and could not dally. Once she was clear of Temperance's reach she increased her pace, leaving a wicked plan forming in Temperance's mind. Out of misguided memories, Grace did not relay the encounter for some months, knowing that it would be ammunition against her childhood companion.

Knowing that the Thomas household would be empty, Temperance crept down the lane adjacent to the house and snuck in via the unlocked back door. In the front parlour she found a wooden comb on the mantlepiece, in front of a large mirror in a guilt frame. The locks twisted around the bases of the thin prongs were too long to belong to Mr Thomas. The find saved her a painful trip up the narrow staircase. She placed the stolen hair in the secret pocket sewn within the folds of her pinafore.

As she passed back through the kitchen, her goal accomplished, she stopped at the pantry. On a rustic chopping board sat a crusty loaf of bread, the end already sliced, presumably eaten for breakfast. Temperance indulged her whim and sliced a doorstop chuck for herself, along with a wedge of cheese. She ripped off a small chunk that she ate as she walked home, chewing on the soft, cooked dough. With two drops of rose oil, Temperance added the hair to Grace's poppet whilst repeating her intention for Grace's demise.

That night Grace was very sick, and her body was racked with stabbing pains, from her head to her feet. She described the pain to Elizabeth as being stung by a thousand bees but would not reveal her suspicions on the assailant immediately. She hoped that it was a coincidence and that the feud would fizzle out before it turned deadly. She was not one hundred percent convinced that Hannah's death had not been an unfortunate accident, despite her high priestesses assurances that it was foul play, and the hands of Mrs Lloyd and her cronies.

25

This year, to coincide with the lunar phase at its fullest, the harvest feast was to be held on Saturday. The community came together several times in the year, to pull in the crops and share equipment.

The unmistakeable squeal of a pig echoed through the town, followed by the thundering footsteps of several people. The terrified hog had a four second lead on the pursuing teenagers and a knife sticking out of its hide. One teen had mud smeared up his trousers, tunic and left cheek from a failed tackle. The best part of an hour had passed, with the young men showing more fatigue than the pig who had charged out of every cornered avenue and lead his hunters on a merry dance around the narrow, cobbled streets.

The muddy lad made another attempt to capture the petrified swine. He made contact with the animal's hind leg, grabbing the strong thin limb. The pig tried desperately to turn and bite its assailant, but the bulk of its torso prevented it, so the walking pork chop tried to flee. Unwilling to relinquish his prize, the tall adolescent hung on, his body bumping over the smoothed pebbles that formed the pathways, but it slowed the pig enough for another to place a coarse rope lead around its thick neck. It took the weight of three teenagers to move the stubborn beast, who attempted to take a chunk from any that would get close enough. One of the amateur butchers released his grip on the rope and took the hunting knife strapped to his trousers firmly in his right hand. His movement was quick but his aim was not accurate or strong. The serrated blade entered the left side of the pigs throat but he failed to slice through the tough hide. Sensing an opportunity, and the slackened rope, the injured boar bolted, leaving a trail of blood in its wake. It was a mercy that an archer took pity on the tormented creature and shot it with an arrow, for a quick, painless execution.

The shocked teens took some moments to recover from the near-death experience of an arrow whizzing past their faces at ninety meters in a second. In a blink of an eye their prey was dead. Using one lads father's cart, they loaded the carcass and took it to be bled and hung, ready for roasting. Nobody rested in the leadup to the festival, hands, minds and feet were busy from dawn to dusk, but the days that followed were lazy days of hungover heads and overindulged stomachs.

The three witches were no exception. Though they didn't celebrate with their neighbours, they benefited from the vast quantity of food and generous mood.

By Tuesday the cupboard was again bare, forcing Temperance to satisfy her grumbling tummy. Bartholomew perched on the windowsill of Mary's house, a keen eye watching a bird teasing him from a spindling branch of a silver birch. He was flexing his sleepy muscles, ready to jump onto the wall surrounding the drum field when the familiar footsteps drew his attention away from his avian tormentor. Curious, he followed Temperance, at a safe distance. Hiding behind rubbish strewn in the street or keeping her in his sight from under a cart.

The generosity of harvest had dried up and nobody was offering even scraps for a pittance. She was forced to buy bread but the freshest had the highest price, leaving her with a stale loaf that she placed under her arm for the climb back up the near vertical Gunstone street.

The elderly sorceress was out of breath and needed to stop before she reached the top.

"Temperanceeeee." She recognised the slippery tone and the bournville coloured skin.

She had not excepted a visitation. The mid-afternoon sun cast a shadow that fell upon the devilish man and kept the heat from Temperance's sweaty brow.

"You shall go now to Grace. It is time."

"I will not." There was no conviction in Temperance's voice. She knew that she would do his bidding but first wanted to see what he would offer in way of persuasion. His handsome face was temptation enough but if she could get anything above an increased heart rate, she'd take it. She was promised food, drink and a quality of life that exceeded her own and that her deed would go unseen.

"I will put a glamour on you." He said with a menacing grin that showed all his teeth. Raising his hand he blew a powder into Temperance's face. He pushed her in the direction of Thomas Eastchurch's property. His broad eyes urging her on when she looked at him from over her shoulder. Temperance blinked repeatedly in an attempt to remove the gritty substance from her eyes and felt a tingling sensation over her whole body, which was not unpleasant but was unnerving.

With a firm hand on her back, Temperance turned the door handle, desperately hoping the door to be locked. It wasn't. With dark brooding eyes on her every move the widower took a stair at a time until she had reached the landing, her breathing still laboured from her walk up the steep hill.

Grace, lodging in the spacious back bedchamber above the shop owned by her sister and high priestess, was laid on top of the patchwork quilt. Local busybody Anne Wakely was massaging one of Grace's arms to help with the circulation. Temperance's guide had followed her inside and was encouraging her to commit an act of ABH upon the practitioner of white magic. Waving her arms in front of her, she imitated pinching Grace with her thumb and forefinger. She made the action all over Grace's body, unwitnessed by either woman, but to the pleasure of the abusive demon that coerced her into tormenting her former friend.

Bartholomew was waiting outside, posed like an Egyptian statue. Temperance instructed him to hide and spy upon Grace and the Eastchurch's. He meowed in acknowledgement of his task. The cat slunk into the shop, its hips swaying, and tail erect.

The following afternoon, Temperance went again to Grace, with Bartholomew knowingly at her side.

Susanna was beginning to enjoy herself. She used astral projection to visit the far-off lands the merchants talked about. She saw the barren Spanish landscape and the forested shores of America. Once a week she would honour her deal and materialise in Dorcas's bedchamber. Depending on the timing, Dorcas would be alone, her husband drinking away their children's vast inheritance. The following morning, Susanna would see a crow within minutes of waking. The beady eyed black bird would squawk at her before taking flight. She would feel the influence of the dark lord and take the feathered omen as a sign.

The women felt his presence in many forms, a toad that leapt into their path and hopped away, a snake that slithered into the undergrowth or in the many rats that burrowed into sacks of flour and nibbled on the town's refuse.

Stambridge Lane was a favoured place for Susanna. The pretty properties were covered in ivy and thatch with vases of wild flowers visible through the leaded windows. There were no taverns in this part of town, so it was quiet, the only trouble coming from drunken residents returning after a night out. It was outside one of the cute cottages that Susanna was attacked. It was dark, the lamps from the houses not penetrating the darkness outside when Susanna was grabbed from behind, she protested but when her assailant kissed her on the neck, her grumbling descended into gasps of joy. She used a handkerchief to clean the blood, for his teeth were sharp on the sensitive skin of her breast.

Mary was on her way to Dorcas' when she became distracted. The hex bag secreted in her pocket forgotten as she followed her nose, which lead her to the bakehouse halfway up Gunstone street and the rows of game pies that were cooling. Parting with a few coffers and a pleasant smile, Mary secured one of the misshapen pies, too ugly to sell but just as tasty. The dithering on her allocated task earned her a scare. From nowhere, a large black hound charged at her, its teeth bared, a guttural growl coming from its throat. As it ran past on powerful hairy legs it snapped at the frightened servant then promptly bound off over a low wall.

Mary didn't hesitate to deposit the cursed package within the boundary of the Coleman household. As she pushed the stuffed leaf into a crack in the plaster rendering around the doorway, she uttered an incantation to strengthen the spell.

Dorcas woke in the early hours to a stabbing pain, her intestines spasming as if twisted by an invisible hand. Sweat gathered on her top lip and in the creases of her skin, her shoulder length hair stuck to her forehead. Finger nails dug into the straw filled mattress and she panted through the waves of pain.

26

Puffs of icy breath escaped into the air like a pack of smokers as the women huddled in a group, stamping their feet to keep warm and rubbing their arms with mitten clad hands.

The winter solstice, known as Yule, was the last sabbath on the yearly calendar. Creeping out as the witchy hour approached, they took the track adjacent to Parsonage Close and headed to the clearing in the woodland at the top of town. They weren't the only ones in the wood that night.

A bubbling crock released sweet odours into the air. Taking turns to stir the pot, they moved around the circle, in a clockwise direction, humming, chanting and giving praise to the Gods and Goddesses with particular emphasis on the Oak King, who battles with the Holly King for supremacy throughout the year.

John Coleman witnessed them on many times, from the window of his mistresses house, enter the woods. Sometimes he would venture down the track and discretely observe the women, hoping to catch a skyclad ceremony and bouncing bosoms made to look exotic by the light of the fire or glimpse one of the wild orgies that he had satisfied himself too. His lover spent and already asleep, John dressed and followed the ladies into the night. The ground was damp from the winter weather and the trees barren from leaves, but he hid within a nook, carved out by the passage of animals. From his vantage point he was shielded from the harsh wind but was privy to the magical celebrations.

On this occasion, John witnessed another attended the clearing. A tall figure dressed in a black hooded cloak, that matched the witches grey versions, that trailed along the ground, that John assumed to be male. From a satchel carried over their shoulder and body like a sash, the dark stranger retrieved a small item that he placed into Temperance's outstretched palms. She immediately dropped the item into the crock, where it fizzed before sinking into the purple liquid. A burst of laughter got the estranged Mrs Edwards reprimanded. "Susanna, shush." Temperance narrowed her eyes, her lips resembling Bartholomew's bottom, followed by an apologetic bow to the mysterious person.

John could not make out any words, they were spoken too softly, but could detect actions from the glow of the fire. From his bag, the devilish imp produced an object that glowed in the dark, which he handed to each of the mature herbalists. John was getting tired, the alcohol and exercise settling on his ample frame. He rubbed his eyes, trying to stay awake. When he opened them the women were alone, their benefactor having seemingly disappeared. John listened to them as they sung harrowing songs of spider legs, toil and trouble, before he too took his leave, crawling into bed beside his sick wife.

1682 started like any other for the poor. Cold nights and empty bellies.

The riches Temperance, Susanna and Mary had been promised had not materialised, but they weren't starving and had enough fuel for heating. They were discreetly training the next generation, revealing secrets and teaching them spells and enchantments. The students were coming along well, had made novice advancements, were growing in confidence and maintaining a balance within their everyday lives.

Mary had Abigail working on her hex bags. The powerful curses, natural and biodegradable, could be used to weaken defences or to cause to harm. Using the knowledge she had gained, Abigail undertook a personal mission, to rid herself of her controlling husband. She made a small incision in the fabric that housed the straw and linen that constituted the mattress on their martial bed and inserted cut up a twigs from a rowan tree and lavender to calm his temper. She noted a minuscule reduction in his abusive behaviour and vowed to up her game.

Meanwhile, the campaign against Elizabeth's minions continued. When John was at sea, Susanna would turn up unannounced at the home of Dorcas with any excuse she could fathom, mainly to make her presence known to make a point. She was beginning to wonder what the point was, that they were strong and malevolent? She was getting tired, tired of the feud, tired of the constant struggle to survive, she would turn seventy this coming Yule time. Sometimes she felt the loneliness so acutely it cut her like a knife. Temperance was happy alone, and Mary was too scared to trust the opposite sex, but her friends didn't understand her need to belong, to feel needed. She often felt as disposable as the apprentices.

Temperance would sit by the light of the moon or the dying flames of her hearth fire and stick the awl into the wax figurine with Grace's hair. Across town Grace would scream in pain or be woken in agony.

Days faded into weeks and soon the Ostara sabbath was upon them. The ancient festival that Christians commandeered and called Easter is, through the wheel of the year, the ideal balance of light and dark, feminine and masculine, when night and day are in perfect equilibrium at an equal length.

It was a time for planting and sowing, of ideas and intentions as well as horticulture seeds. It is also a time to honour what is manifested since the last equinox and to revel in the sweetness of their blooming destruction.

It was Mary's turn to go into town and beg. Her knee was disfigured from crimping arthritis, some days she could hobble on it but mostly she needed the assistance of a cane. She had been gone some time and Susana was getting fretful. Worried that Mary had fallen, she wrapped a shawl round her head and shoulders and headed out to make sure Mary was okay.

Mary had her back against the wall of the town hall, catching her breath and resting her throbbing limbs. Her belly was grumbling, and she felt a pang of desperation. As Susanna approached Mary let out a heaving sob. She soon calmed down, under the kindness of Susanna who wrapped the tearful Mary in a reassuring embrace.

"Come on. We'll call in at the Barnes, perhaps we'll get lucky." Mary looped her arm through Susanna's as they braced the hill to Grace and John's residence. Once in town they had no choice but to choose one of the roads back home, all of which rose at varying gradients, and all ached tired old bones.

They knocked timidly, at first, on the door. Just as they were about to give up hope they heard movement from inside.

"What do you want?" Grace answered the door, her question directed at Susanna. Mary stood meekly at her side, staring at the ground.

"Please, Grace." Susanna put on her most pathetic voice. "I was hoping for some bread for my dear friend Mary." It was Mary's turn to test her acting skills. "She is so hungry, and we have nothing to spare."

Susanna looked at the servant who was hovering behind her employer. Her eyes widened in horror that Susanna was trying to engage with her. She firmly but discreetly shook her head to signal 'no' and took several paces backwards.

Taking another tact, in her sweetest voice, Susanna said. "We will take meat." Grace also refused this request. Susanna enquired about the man of the house and was told unduly that he was not home, and the door was promptly closed.

Susanna and Mary reluctantly took their leave, but a plan was forming in Susanna's mind. They stopped once they had reached the brow of the hill. Susanna instructed Mary to return to buy a farthings worth of tobacco. It was common knowledge that they dealt in a side-line of smuggled baccy.

"You had not the money for food, how now do you come by funds for tobacco?"

"I. Um." Susanna had not prepared her for such a response. She had expected to be sold the hand rolling nicotine. Grace would hear none of Mary's pleas, again shutting the door in her face.

Susanna was angry and vowed to Mary that Grace would regret her decision.

That night, around one in the morning, John was snoring when Grace woke to the sensation of pricking pains across her upper body. She swatted at her arms as if stung by an army of invisible wasps.

When Elizabeth Eastchurch called in, Grace declared that they would all die if they did not stop their enemies. Grace was deeply worried that Hannah would not be the last of their number to lose their life to the age-old fight between good and evil, light and dark.

Elizabeth assured her that plans were afoot for the demise of their foe.

27

Dorcas had been suffering for several days with pains that pricked at her upper body. No remedy gave her any relief and she slept in fitful bursts when exhaustion gave her no choice.

As Mary was directly responsible, Susanna made the foolish decision to check on her colleagues handiwork. John's uncle had permitted Susanna to visit Dorcas, unaware of the woman's reputation and charmed by her fake smile and kind words.

Dorcas, aware of the accusations by Grace, always sought the best in people and refused to believe that she had fallen victim to the craft and that a fellow townsperson was advocating her murder. Susanna had been alone with Dorcas for a few moments when the front door opened and closed. John had returned home and was furious that Susanna had been granted an audience with his ailing wife. Hearing her husband's angered tone and his boots on the stairs, Dorcas attempted to get up from the chair in which she was sat. The actions of the Coleman's frightened Susanna who hastily said under her breath, "I render you useless, there you will be until you no longer see me."

Dorcas had intended to place herself between her well-meaning relatives and Susanna, but instead slipped to the floor. The feeling in her extremities were numbed by the spell, which left her immobile and speechless. With her heart beating so fast she thought it would break out of her chest, Susanna backed out of the chamber and ran. Dorcas mustered all her remaining strength in an attempt to stop Susanna from escaping, so the episode could be explained rationally, but John and Thomas were struggling to lift her back into the seat

Bartholomew mewed at the window and watched as Susanna fled from the house, followed moments later by Thomas Bremincom. The elderly gentleman watched her retreating form but made no effort to follow her. He also noted the slender grey cat that slunk along in her wake, as she hurried away.

Susanna thought she was going to die. The rapid beating felt out of control and too fast to sustain for any period of time. She placed one hand over her bosom and the other against a wall to steady herself. She'd placed her palm on a jaggered stone but even the pain as the hard rock pushed into her soft flesh didn't compare to the impending doom she was experiencing.

Bartholomew twisted between her legs. The soothing purr of the intuitive moggy had a calming effect on her. Soon her heart was back to its normal rhythm. She gave Barty, as she liked to call him, a well-deserved fussing. Together they walked home,

Susanna looking as frail as her years, a little shaky from her near-death experience. Having seen Susanna to her door, Bartholomew jumped onto Mary's windowsill to take up watch for any stray wildlife that might like to play chase with him.

"Tonight, it is time to end Grace. Enough of these foolish follies."

"But my Lord." Temperance ignored the look of loathing for daring to defy an order and pressed ahead. "They are growing suspicious of us. May I suggest we step back a little." It was self-preservation making Temperance talk. She knew that Elizabeth was on the warpath and hoped to see another winter but wasn't convinced her body would hold out long enough.

"You wish to renegade on our deal?" The tone was threatening, his eyes blazed red like shining rubies.

"No. No. We have done all you have commanded." No response. Seconds passed in silence, though it felt much longer. "Will you glamour us again?" Temperance's voice was small, like a school girl asking the stern teacher to explain a maths equation.

"No. You will go now." The foreign manipulator forcefully kissed Temperance, his hard features pressing against the wrinkled face. Full facial hair and bushy side burns bleed into a mane of hair. He pointed with a long, elegant finger and snarled, "Now." Without further ado, his submissive minion hurried in the direction she was being forced to go.

Her body was ailing, her eyes were experiencing the onset of macular degeneration, but her hearing was as keen as a youngsters. It was this honed sense that had her hiding behind an overgrown rosemary bush in a neighbour's front garden. It was more of a courtyard that surrounded the first foot of the pavement in front of the terraced house. Mr and Mrs Eastchurch came out, Elizabeth with her hand balanced on her husband's arm. The bonnet that she wore had a large peacock feather sticking from the wide ribbon around the brim. The turquoise hue matched the delicate flowers stitched to the dresses bodice.

Grace was not alone in the bedroom that she lodged in, rent free. Anne Wakely was topping up her brownie points by being a good Samaritan and massaging Anne's body. Josephine Mills was sat on the rickety chair at the end of the bed, one uneven leg propped up with a wedge of wood. She had nothing to contribute to the situation other than company. Anna Blackmore was mopping Grace's brow with a wet cloth whilst talking about nothing of any consequence, idle gossip and observations to pass the time and distract themselves from Grace's frequent groans.

Temperance crept to the Eastchurch's door. She peered into the window to the left, her hand shielding her eyes to get a better look. On the kitchen side sat a plate, the contents covered with a checked cloth. Temperance could hear women talking, the sound drifting down from the open window. She learnt that a pie had been put aside to replenish

Grace's strength and a wicked idea formed in her mind. Within the hem of her skirt, she had sewn a tiny vial that contained belladonna. If she was captured, she could simply stand on the delicate bottle, smashing the blown glass so the liquid would seep into the fabric and there would be no evidence against her.

She eased the door open and slipped inside. She caught her skirt in the kitchen door as she closed it so had to release it without making a sound, trapping her in the kitchen. She teased the harmful substance through a hole and allowed three drops to fall into the centre of the pie soaking immediately through the glazed pastry.

Looking up and down the street through the window, Temperance could see the coast was clear and took her opportunity. The door made a dull thud as it closed but the chatter drowned it out. If anyone saw, they said nothing.

That night, with Grace's poppet on her lap, she pricked it with an awl. For hours she stabbed the wax effigy, with each twist of the wooden handle she visualised Grace taking her final breath. She wanted her deal with the Devil to end as much as she wanted Grace's life to end. If she did this, perhaps she could rest at last. In her dreams, she lay with her tormentor, enjoying the spoils of evil and the tantalising treats that she thought she wanted to walk away from. Where she dreamt she had been touched, it was tender to the feel the next morning.

Grace hadn't eaten all the pie, but enough of the poison had entered her system to cause agonising pains in her belly and excess gas that bloated her, so she looked six months pregnant. She had taken to passing out when the pain became too much, her body first convulsing in shock, then fainting, so that she looked dead. A leg hung over the bedframe, like a cadavers on a hospital trolley. This was how Elizabeth found her the following morning. Her scream had Thomas running into the chamber in his bed clothes, the ruckus snapping Grace awake. A daisy prick of dots could be seen on Grace's pale exposed knee.

"Right. That's it." Elizabeth put on her boots and marched out of the door.

28

Elizabeth hammered on Temperance's door. It shook with the force of her blows. Temperance was at the foot of the stairs deliberating what to do. If she didn't let Elizabeth inside the whole street would be privy to her issues with Temperance. Perhaps she could placate her.

She opened the door and Elizabeth marched inside, without waiting for an invitation.

"Mrs Eastchurch, how nice to see you. What may I do for you?"

"You can knock off the pleasantries for a start. I have seen the mark you left upon Grace."

"Grace? Do you mean your sister? I have heard she has been unwell." Temperance made herself look as small and innocent as possible and her eyes as wide as a pleading puppy's.

"Do you think I do not know the mark of the Devil, Temperance? I have known you to be cruel and selfish but you have gone too far this time."

"I know not of what you speak." Temperance shrugged her shoulders.

"What did you use? A poppet? Where is it?" A barrage of questions came at Temperance.

"I have no poppet." Temperance could lie as well as a politician.

"What did you use old woman?" Elizabeth had closed the gap and was stood over Temperance. The dark priestess thought the vessel of light might actually strangle her.

Temperance backed away, her hands raised in front of her in a sign of surrender. Careful to avoid the loose floorboard, Temperance produced a piece of leather from a pot on the mantlepiece.

Elizabeth snatched the rag and left, leaving the door wide open. Temperance sank into the chair by the unlit fire. Her mind raced, full of conundrums - what should she do? What will Elizabeth do? Bartholomew sauntered through the open doorway and made himself comfy on Temperance's lap. She stroked his velvety fur, a plan forming to dispose of the troublesome figure and the person to whom it was modelled on.

"Listen to me very carefully." A pair of large amber coloured eyes stared up at Temperance as she spoke in a controlled manner. "You must take this and place it under the bed in which Grace sleeps." Temperance placed the wax doll on the floor. A wet nose sniffed the object.

"Be swift, be unseen. May the Lord's darkness cloak you as you do his bidding." The cat did as it was instructed. Walking under the counter of Thomas' shop, as if he owned the place,

Bartholomew headed for the living quarters. The shop assistant had his back turned, restocking the shelves and the Eastchurch's could be heard in one of the rooms at the back of the house. Silent paws and quick reflexes meant he had deposited the magical effigy and was back out on the streets in under a minute.

His reward was a smelly, disgusting and hideous fish head from a whiting that accidently slipped its way into Temperance's hand as she passed the crates on the quay that morning.

Elizabeth hunted at the back of the kitchen dresser and pulled out a cast iron pan that she reserved for ceremonial use. From a pitcher of rain water she filled the pan until it was half full.

A row of latticed windows looked out onto a walled garden. Rose bushes and clematises snaked up the stone boundary. Beds of brightly coloured flowers were interspaced between shrubs shaped in spheres or twisted in spirals and baby pink peony's, known to bring protection from negative energies.

Elizabeth positioned herself at the long wooden table, the heart of the workspace, so that she could look out at the yard she had been tending since she moved in with Thomas as newly-weds. Bird feeders were hung from the branches of a mature sycamore tree that partially blocked the sun.

Lighting a candle, Elizabeth invited the elements to join her. she stirred the water, creating a gentle whirlpool. She passed the leather through the flame and placed it in the pan. She continued to stir the water, adding a daisy to bring clarity to her aim, to reveal the intention behind the cursed leather. Was the purpose to maim or kill Grace? The little flower swam around the bowl with the momentum of the water. The two peony petals floated on the surface like two boats caught in a storm.

The hazelnut hit the bottom of the pan with a ding. “Bestow on me the wisdom to follow in your light. Guide me, Goddess, on this journey fraught with darkness.”

“Reveal the truth, let it be shown. If the waters turn black, then death is known.” She dropped the spiked mugwort leaf into the mixture, droplets formed on the spiderweb hairs of the underside as it hit the water.

“With love and light, may the truth shine bright.” Elizabeth repeated the mantra over and over as she stirred the pan.

After several minutes the water was as clear as when she had added it.

Nothing had happened.

Her abilities with enchantments was not under question. The spell had worked.

A lone magpie landed on top of the wall, scaring away a chaffinch pecking at the crumbs scattered on one of the feeders. Upstairs, Grace murmured in her sleep as Anne paced the floorboards. ‘One for sorrow’ she thought, looking from the black and white bird of superstition that perched authoritatively on the wall to the slumbering form of the bewitched woman she looked upon as a kind aunt. For over a month she had tended to her daily, helping her to dress and bath, being her crutch when they took air, keeping her amused or holding her hand when the pain became too great.

Anne was not ignorant of Elizabeth's practices. She had no desire to join them, and even less to report them. The unstoppable witch mania was short lived in this part of England and none she knew had become the targets of the witch finders who went from city to city hunting down suspected practitioners of the forbidden arts. She had overheard conversation between the sisters and knew of the strife between the two covens. With fingers in lots of pies, she knew who to owe a favour for and who to owe one to.

Maybe she could straighten out this whole sorry mess.

Knocking gently on the closed kitchen door but not entering, Anne called out that she had an errand she must complete but would be back in due course.

Anne took her bonnet from the hat stand by the door and strapped it over her head. It was too warm outside but it protected her eyes from the sunshine.

Stepping out into the dazzling daylight, compared to the dim bedroom, Anne didn't see the figure that hovered a short distance away. Turning in the direction of Old Town, she spotted Temperance.

"A word if I may, Mrs Lloyd?" Temperance had nowhere to go, no excuse for lingering in the street.

"How may I help you? It's Anne, isn't it my dear?"

"Why have you sent that bird? Is it to spy on us?"

"I'm afraid I have no clue what you mean."

Anne tried to keep her cool but she found herself inching closer.

"Tell me. Why do you wish such sorrow upon Grace?"

"Has poor Grace been taken ill again?"

Anne was struggling to keep her voice at a level that wouldn't attract unwanted attention. She challenged Temperance further. The exchange lasted for several minutes, neither relenting on their position.

"Maybe it is the devil in disguise, come to take Grace home to hell." Temperance laughed mockingly. She had tired of the accusation and extracted herself from the conversation.

Anne was too stunned to stop her. The bird that had caused all the commotion flew overhead and sent a shiver down Annes spine. She could easily have caught her but instead went for a walk, to clear her head and decide if she should tell Elizabeth.

When she got back, she did.

Meanwhile, in an adjacent street, Susanna was lightly knocking on the door of Dorcas Coleman. She had no reason to be there, other than to satisfy her own morbid fantasies. It wasn't the first time but it would be the last. Dorcas was not the target that Susanna had been tasked with eliminating. She had planned to ask for a spoon, on account that she had burnt hers to a crisp, a frivolous excuse for being there, but nobody answered.

Whilst Anne had been out, it had occurred to Elizabeth that Temperance had tricked her. She had not had a spell fail since she was a fledgling in training, and even then she had a knack of mixing ingredients, on par with Morgan Le Fay. She would have made a great chef, but was born in the wrong body, in the wrong century.

Elizabeth was scratching underneath the units in the kitchen, a stick reaching where her arms were too short, or the gap too low. Nothing other than dust.

She moved into the front parlour and then the back, both searches were unsuccessful. She found a gift wrapped in a green silk scarf that she assumed was for her birthday, so hid it back where she found it. Thomas liked to surprise his wife with trinkets, flowers or exotic fabrics, he worshipped the ground that she walked upon.

Her bedroom turned up nothing she didn't expect to find. Anne returned to find Elizabeth wedged under the bed frame, as if she had been eaten by the patchwork quilt. "Elizabeth, do you need assistance?" Anne rushed forward and squat beside Mrs Eastchurch. Grace was repacking a box of linen, sure that nothing untoward rested between the folds of material.

Elizabeth slithered out, looking dirty but triumphant. In her hand was a small lump of wax, crudely carved into the shape of a person and covered with holes from where a sharp implement had been pushed into the surface. She sneezed. Anne used her hand to brush away the clumps of dusty hair that had gathered on Elizabeth's apron.

"I knew it."

With the offending artifact found, Elizabeth headed to the kitchen. The pan had been emptied into the flower bed but there was enough water in the pitcher to perform the incantation again. She repeated every word and every action precisely, as she had done an hour or two ago.

This time the water turned black.

"I knew it."

Elizabeth had tried being nice, she had tried ignoring the abuse of her fellow witches and she had tried threatening them. Nothing had worked.

Elizabeth felt strongly that there was only one course of action left. It was time to call in the big guns. She did not want blood on her hand but if Temperance persisted that is exactly what would happen, and Elizabeth would swing for her.

Elizabeth waited for Thomas Gist as he left the magistrates court. He pulled the arched door closed; the large iron key, the length of his manly hand, rattled in the lock as he jostled to secure the building.

She nodded her head in greeting. "May I have a moment of your time?"

"Mrs Eastchurch." The slimy, married man took Elizabeth's hand and planted a wet kiss on her sagging skin. "It would be my pleasure."

"It is of a rather delicate manner." Mr Gist's mind raced with elicit musings as to the nature of this beautiful woman's woes. He suggested they retire to his private quarters, but she was happy to conduct their business in the quiet churchyard, huddled together like lovers colluding to elope.

The date was Thursday the 2nd of July 1682.

Temperance was lifting a spoon of nettle soup to her mouth, when she was startled by the noise at her door. The watery content fell back into the bowl with a splash.

BANG.

BANG.

BANG.

The Trial

29

Grace adjusted the bow on her hat so that the loops matched. She'd been pottering around, trying to distract herself from the impending court case, for which she was a star witness. The fate of another's life weighed heavy on her shoulders. She had scrubbed her face until it was red, pressed her dress and squeezed her feet into the uncomfortable Spanish boots that accentuated the feminine pattern of her puffed skirt.

Grace had been an unwilling participant of the witch hunt and the aged witness stood awkwardly before the mayor. She wasn't convinced that the ploy would work and feared that her similar religious practices would be discovered and more lives, including her own, would be lost.

"Please state your name."

"My name is Grace Thomas."

"For what reason have you come to inform us of today?"

"I suffered from great pains."

"Can you describe these pains, Grace?" John Davie asked.

"In my head and all my limbs." Grace went on to elaborate that she had suffered symptoms for six months. "The pains did abate, and I was able to walk abroad to take air."

"Can you tell us more about your suffering Grace?"

"I thought I was cured but in the night season I was in much pain and was not able to take rest." Pressed for more information, Grace did further saith. "I was going up the high street when I did met with that Temperance Lloyd. In the street she did fall down on her knees!" Grace dramatically swung her arms towards the ground, to emphasis her storytelling. "Temperance did say to me 'I am glad to see you so strong again'.

Grace paused for breath. "I did ask her 'Why dost thou weep for me?' and she did reply 'I weep for joy to see you well again.' But she was only pretending." Grace's brow furrowed as she thought back to her encounter with her fellow spinster.

"Why do you think this Grace?"

"That very night I was taken very ill with sticking and pricking pains. It was as if pins and awls were being thrust into my person." Grace pointed to several places on her body. "It was from the crown of my head to the soles of my feet." Grace looked down at her black shoes with pointed tips and a slight raise in the heels. "It was as though I had been placed upon a rack."

"When did this incident happen?" Asked Thomas Gist.

"It was on the 10th day of September now last past."

"Has this happened to you before?"

"Yes. Yes it has." Grace was happy to regale her tale. "On Thursday, the first day of June last past in the night, I did suffer. I felt I was bound and seemingly chained up. I had sticking pains, gathered together in my belly. All of a sudden my belly was swollen, as big as two bellies and it did cause me to cry out. 'I shall die, I shall die' I cried out. I was in such a sad condition that I lay as if I had been dead for a long space, of about two hours."

Grace hadn't finished yet. "On Friday night last, being the thirtieth day of June, I was again pinched and pricked in my heart. I experienced such cruel thrusting pains in my head, shoulders, arms, hands, thighs and legs. It was as though the flesh had been immediately torn from my bones, with a man's fingers and thumbs."

"If you were 'as if you were dead', how do you know you were not sleeping?"

"I had informants in my chamber who told me so. They said I was plucked out over my bed and I lay on the floor, in this condition, for some three hours to come."

"Do you know the cause of your illness?"

"There is not a natural cause. I was bewitched."

"Grace, you say you were bewitched?" Thomas raised his eyebrows, challenging his subject to further commit to her testimony.

"I was. By Temperance. Upon the first day of this instant July, you did arrest that Temperance and did put her in prison. As soon as she was apprehended I immediately did feel my pricking and sticking pains cease and abate."

"Have the pains returned since Ms Lloyd's incarceration?"

"They have not continued so, ever since. But, I still have great weakness of my body. I know it was Temperance Lloyd that hath been an instrument of doing much hurt and harm unto my body. She did prick and torment me." Grace was thanked for her testimony and released from her position as an informant.

Dorcas Coleman was waiting outside the magistrates court for her good acquaintance. She took Grace by her arm and supported her frail friend as the two women trudged slowly through the uneven cobbled streets.

This time it was Anne Wakely who took the stand. She had been brought forward as she was one of the women who entered the jail cell and searched Temperance's body for any evidence that she was colluding with dark forces. Honor Hooper was another. She stood solemnly beside Anne, but it was Anne who answered the questions.

"Who instructed you to search the body of Temperance Lloyd."

Anne pointed at Thomas Gist. "It was Mr. Mayor."

"Were you alone when you searched Temperance?"

"No, I was not. I conducted the search in the presence of Honor Hooper, and several other women, of this town."

"What did you find?"

"Upon searching Temperance's body, we did find, in her secret parts, two teats hanging nigh together like unto a piece of flesh that a child had sucked. Each of the teats was about an Inch in length." Anne Wakely did not wavier under the scrutiny of the men. "I did demand of her, Temperance, whether she had been sucked at that place by the black man." Anne was a woman who liked to please. She was a faithful and obedient wife and served her town in any capacity she could. However, if she was conflicted, her moral compass could be swayed with a pleasant compliment and a persuasive chat. If it was permitted for women to run for office she would have.

"Who do you mean when you say, 'the black man'?" The gentle jangle of chains echoed around the room as Thomas shifted his weight on the unforgiving wooden chair, styled to look like a throne.

"I mean the Devil, Sir." Honor timidly nodded her head in agreement. "Temperance did acknowledge that she had been sucked there often times by the black man and the last time that she was sucked by the said black man was on the Friday before she was searched."

"That was the thirtieth day of June last past." It was a statement rather than a question.

"Yes Sir. I witnessed her witchcraft for myself. Thursday, now last past, I did see something in the shape of a magpie to come at the chamber window where Grace Thomas did lodge. It was in the morning." Anne carried on without hesitation. "I did demand of Temperance Lloyd whether she did know of any bird to come and flutter at the window. And she did then say that it was the black man in the shape of a bird. I pressed her further and she doth say that she was at the time down by Mr. Eastchurch's door."

"Did you see Temperance at the time you saw the bird?"

"I did not see her, but I believe she was at the door."

"And this happened on the twenty-ninth of June last past?"

"Yes Sir." Honor corroborated every word that Anne had said.

"Thank you ladies. You are dismissed."

Both women gave a polite bow and left the room. Both women headed in the direction of Mr Eastchurch's house. The dwelling would be full by the time the owners returned.

30

As with Grace, Elizabeth was in all her finery. She was an upstanding citizen and would present herself to the court as such. She used the juice of a beetroot to add colour to her lips and styled her hair with pins. She'd eaten a hearty breakfast and was ready to teach Temperance a lesson she would never forget.

Elizabeth Eastchurch was eager to take her place in front of the adjudicating men. Elizabeth politely answered the formal questions before launching into her version of events.

"Grace had been staying with us, the kindness of my husband permitted Grace to lodge within his house. On the second day of July, in this year of our Lord I did hear Grace suffer. She was complaining of great pricking pains in one of her knees." Elizabeth pointed to her own knee, as if the men needed an education in the physiology of a human being. "I made Grace show me her knee and I did observe for myself that she did have nine places in her knee which had been pricked. It looked as though it had been pricked with a thorn!" Elizabeth emphasized the last word. "I knew Temperance to be responsible and went immediately unto her. I demanded to know whether she had any wax or clay in the form of a picture whereby she had pricked and tormented Grace."

"How did Temperance respond to your accusations?" Enquired the Alderman.

"She did deny that she had made a poppet."

"And this was not satisfactory to you?"

"No, it was not. I pressed her further and she did admit that she had no wax or clay. But she did confess that she had only a piece of leather which she had pricked nine times." Mrs Eastchurch was thanked for her contribution and dismissed.

Outside, in the shade cast by the northern corner of the church, Elizabeth spoke briefly to her husband.

She did not wait to support him during his recounting of the evidence, as other dutiful wives may have done. Elizabeth hurried along the narrow quay, dodging carts and horse manure, to catch up with Grace and Dorcas. Their reports had been damning and conclusive.

The mist hung low over the river and the sky was a pitiful grey. Thomas Eastchurch, owing to his status as a gent, had not the need to work in order to gain an additional income and could therefore afford to pass his time with leisurely activities and concern himself with the business of others. He had plenty of staff to operate his businesses. Thomas was a charitable man also, but persistent begging grated on his good nature, and he was weary of those, of a far lower standing, who attempted to befriend his wife or relations.

Thomas watched the ship's crew as they scurried around loading or unloading the magnificent vessels, whilst he waited to be called in front of his brethren. From tobacco and wool to fishing, the sea was the life blood of the town.

The shipping industry brought a lot of work to the people of the town. There was constant trading on the river edge, both legal and illicit, with goods being loaded or unloaded by townsfolk and men from across the continent. At the northern tip of the quay sat the shipwright yard where one-man fishing boats to impressive frigates were built. The vessels that meet an untimely end at the bottom of the sea were reclaimed and the timbers used as beams to construct the town's houses as the population increased.

The ships didn't only bring bounty, once they brought death. In 1646, one ship carried the plague which killed over two hundred, twenty percent, of the town's residents as well as many livestock. Flea infested wool saw the black death ravage the maritime metropolis. Physicians moved from house-to-house, bloodletting and boil-lancing, but the treatments were ineffective against the deadly infection. The Ravening boys, who played upon the plague infected merino wool, were the first to succumb to the deadly disease. Their surgeon father would die too, but only after he worked diligently in the houses of horror in a desperate attempt to stop the spread. John Strange, of Ford house, set up blockades to prevent travel to and from the town and to contain the virus, whilst the mayor and other dignitaries fled. Temperance was among those too fearful to step foot outside.

For weeks, her, Mary, Susanna, and countless others hid behind the safety of their walls, gradually starving. The smell of burning aromatic herbs wafted from the homes of the infected and disease free alike. Anyone with a symptom was treated like a leper and confined to their own residence, to die alone. Not one street was untouched by a red cross and the costumed plague doctors stalked the streets, that were soon overgrown with grass and weeds. People returned tentatively to the market, fearing a second wave of the pandemic but too hungry or poor to keep away from society any longer. Mass graves were dug around the outskirts of the town, with the dead stacked upon each other. The land on which they were interred would remain barren for generations, until they were forgotten, and the earth reclaimed their bodies.

"We thank you, Mr Eastchurch, for taking the time to explain the issues you have experienced at the hands of one Temperance Lloyd, of Biddiford." Thomas Gist envied the wealthy gentleman stood before him and fought hard to keep his mind on the proceedings.

"It is with pleasure that I stand before you."

"Please present your evidence Mr. Eastchurch."

"Upon yesterday I saw Temperance was returning to her home, from the bakehouse with a loaf of bread under her arm and I did hear Temperance Lloyd say and confess that she, Temperance, did meet with something in the likeness of a black man ....."

"That was the thirtieth day of September last past to which you are referring?" Interrupted John Davie.

"Yes, it was." Thomas straightened his already vertical back and roughly readjusted his already perfect waistcoat. "As I was saying, I did hear her confess of her knowledge of this black man and that it was the black man who did tempt and persuade her to go to my house to torment Grace."

"What relationship to you is Grace Thomas?" Enquired the mayor.

"Grace is my sister-in-law."

"Where did Temperance meet with this 'black man?"

"In a street called Higher Gunstone Lane, within this town. "

"Did Temperance meet willingly with this said black man?"

"Temperance did first refuse the temptation, saying that Grace had done her no harm, but afterwards, by the further persuasion and temptation of the said black Man, she did go to my house."

"And what happened when Temperance arrived at your house?" Mr Gist had managed to focus his mind on the task at hand.

"She went up the stairs after the black man and confessed that both of them went into the chamber where Grace was."

"Was Grace alone?"

"No. There they found one Anne Wakely."

"The wife of William Wakely of Biddiford?"

"Yes."

"What was Anne doing in the chamber with Grace?"

"She was rubbing one of the arms and one of the legs of Grace."

"Is that all you have to present?"

"No. Temperance further confessed that the black man did persuade her to pinch the said Grace in the knees, arms and shoulders. She imitated with her Fingers how she did it." Thomas re-enacted Temperance's re-enactment of her actions. Thomas anticipated the interruption and continued. "And when she came down the stairs again into the street, after tormenting Grace, she saw a braget cat go into my shop. Temperance did believe it to be the Devil."

"Has Temperance confessed, or have you overheard her to say, on any other occasion that she caused deliberate and malicious harm to Grace?"

"I did hear the said Temperance to say and confess that, on Friday night last..."

Thomas Gist got in first. "This was the twelfth day of September last past to which you are referring?"

"No. It was the thirtieth day of June to which Temperance was now speaking of. She did say the black man did meet with her near her own door, about ten of the clock of that same night, and there did again tempt her to go to my house, and to make an end of the said Grace Thomas! And she did go unto my house and into the chamber were Grace lay." Grace had moved out of her own cottage when it had flooded, and never left. The banks of the stream couldn't contain the onslaught of water, following a particularly wet May, resulting in the homes being drowned under a monsoon of cloudy water.

Pausing just long enough to steady his voice, Thomas continued his sister-in-law's tale of woe. "Temperance did further confess, that she did pinch and prick Grace again in several parts of her body, declaring with both her hands how she did do it." Thomas mimicked the actions as he spoke the words.

"Thereupon, Grace did cry out terribly! Temperance said the black man told her that she should make an end of Grace and he did promise her, Temperance, that no one should discover her or see her. Temperance also confessed, that about twelve of the clock of the same night, the black man did suck her in the street in her secret parts. She was kneeling down to him and afterwards he did vanish away out of her sight."

"Did Temperance describe this devilish black man?" "She did say that he had blackish clothes and was about the length of her arm. He had broad eyes, like a saucer, and a mouth like a toad."

"To your awareness, was this the sole occasion Temperance attempted to 'end' Grace Thomas?"

"No, it was not. It happened previous. I heard Temperance to confess, that about the first day of June last past, the said black man was with her again and told her, that on that night she, being Temperance Lloyd, should make an end of Grace Thomas. Temperance did admit that she had that night gripped Grace in her stomach and breast and clipped her heart and that Grace did cry out pitifully. Grace said that Temperance was about the space of two hours tormenting her. Temperance was gleeful that the black man stood by her in the same room also and that Anne Wakely., who was present in the chamber with Grace, could not see her, the said Temperance."

"Do you have anything further to say regarding Grace Thomas's sickness?"

"I suppose that Grace, in her sickness, had been afflicted through a distemper arising from a natural cause. We did repair unto several physicians, but Grace could never receive any benefits prescribed by them."

"Thank you for your time and contribution Mr Eastchurch." The actual whereabouts of Thomas whilst his ill-fated inherited relative was harassed by the elderly woman was not addressed. The fact that he would have been being entertained in one of the more reputable drinking establishments was ignored.

"Gentleman." Thomas gave a short tight nod and left the town hall.

31

The knocking at the shabby door shook the frame and the thin glass of the adjacent window was nearly dislodged. One of the constables tried peering through the grimy window panes as the other continued to pound on the door.

The warning gave Temperance little time to conceal the tools of her trade under the loose floor board and just as she was pulling the rug into place with her foot, two burly law enforcement officers barged through the door and into the small living space. A small, charred pot of nettle soup hung over a pathetic fire in the hearth.

"Are you Temperance Lloyd?"

"Yes."

"You're coming with us." As the constable who had been knocking on the door moved to grab her arm, Temperance took a step backward.

"I'm not going anywhere." Said Temperance defiantly.

"You are to be brought in front of the mayor." There was no further discussion on the matter and all pleas by Temperance were ignored. She was forcefully dragged from her home and marched in the direction of the town hall. The ruckus caused Temperance's neighbours to pile out into the street, speculating about the old woman's crimes.

The crone was surprisingly strong for her age and the tight grip the constables were forced to use left deep purple bruises on her arms.

Temperance's thoughts ran wildly around her head. She couldn't focus on a single one. Her eyes darted back and forth, scanning the crowds that had started to gather as she was escorted down the hill. People she knew, people she liked, people she didn't, looked at her in disgust not sympathy. She could do it she told herself, she'd got away with it before. But she was tired, she was old and questioned if she could face it all over again.

Dread filled her heart as she trudged up the stairs, sandwiched between the arresting constables.

The large room, dominated by wood and testosterone, was unchanged from her previous two involuntary visits. She had not faced this assembly of men before and prayed to Satan that she could charm them as she had the others. Other than those appointed to rule on behalf of the town, Mr Eastchurch had been permitted referential viewing, purely as a spectator and in gratitude for his orchestrated speech earlier that day.

Resigned to her current predicament, Temperance stood dutifully in the spot on which the constables had left her. She knew there was no physical means of escape for they were now guarding the entrance; to keep her in as much as to keep prying noses out.

"Temperance Lloyd. You stand before us upon the complaint of one Thomas Eastchurch." Temperance did not react, choosing to stand rigidly and stare blankly ahead. "You are charged upon the suspicion of having used some magical arts, sorcery or witchcraft upon the body of Grace Thomas, spinster of Biddiford." Temperance's only acknowledgement of the fatal charge laid against her was to exhale loudly, seemingly bored with the proceedings. This only served to anger the mayor who added. "You are also charged with having had discourse or familiarity with the Devil in the shape of a black man. What have you saith for yourself?"

Temperance could see that her silence was having the desired effect and continued to bite her tongue, for she knew her fate was sealed, and this was simply a formality to appease the judicial system. If she was going to win her case, it would not be here with prejudiced and self-righteous locals. The mayor was on a personal quest for vengeance to see that Temperance would not get away with her religion for a third time. He thought his predecessor lacked the convicted needed to prosecute a witch, with the previous trial ending in an acquittal of the charges. Mr Gist was not prepared to lose, and neither was Temperance.

"Temperance Lloyd." Mr Gist somehow controlled the volume but could not hide the distain in his voice. "I demand you inform us how long since you had discourse or familiarity with the Devil in the likeness or shape of a black man."

Temperance enjoyed seeing the mayor uncomfortable in her company but knew that she couldn't evade answering the questions and the more she irked him the greater her suffering would be. "On about the thirtieth day of September, in the year last past, I did meet with the Devil, as you described him." Irritated foot tapping promoted the accused to continue, without delay "I met him about the middle of that afternoon in Higher Gunstone Lane when he did tempt and solicit me to go with him to the house of Thomas Eastchurch to torment Grace Thomas.."

"And you went willingly with him?" The disgust oozing from his tone.

"At first I did refuse."

"But you did go?" The men had heard the story from several sources already.

"Afterwards, by the temptation and persuasion of the Devil, I did go to the house of Mr Eastchurch." Temperance pointed a bony wrinkled finger at Thomas, who, watching cowardly from the corner managed to shrink back further, frightened that the impoverished widow would cast a spell upon him.

"I went up the stairs, after the black man and we did both go into the chamber where Grace was, but Grace was not alone. She was in the attendance of one Anne Wakely.

"Is Anne the wife of William?"

"I do not know but she was rubbing, chafing and stroking one of Graces arms and several parts of her body, at the same time." Temperance's futile attempt to pass the blame was not believed and she was pressed further into confessing. "Then and there I did pinch Grace, with the nails on my fingers, in the shoulders, arms, thighs and legs." Her attempt to implicate Anne had failed, so her next ploy was to involve an innocent animal and she recanted how she watched a grey cat enter Thomas's shop. Anne Wakely, also present during Temperance's examination, affirmed that she had not seen Temperance, or the Devil, in Grace's bedroom, despite the insistane of Temperance that she was there too.

"We demand you inform us if you went anymore unto Mr Eastchurch's house."

"I did go again, the following day, invisible to his house." Again, Temperance pointed directly at Mr Eastchurch who was filled with fear and would have run had the door not been blocked. Proudly she gloated, "I was not seen by any person, but I did see and met that grey cat, who did leap and retire unto the shop that he...." The skeletal finger again sought out the cowering Mr Eastchurch. "...owns."

"And this was the last time you visited the premises of Mr Eastchurch?"

"No. That would be upon Friday the thirtieth day of June, of this year."

"And did you go alone?"

"No. The Devil was with me." If they wanted answers, she would make them work for them.

"Temperance Lloyd. You will saith and confess all that you did do to Grace Thomas."

With a sigh that resonated around the room, Temperance's will dissolved, and she told them what they wanted to hear. "In the chamber we found Grace lying in a very sad condition. Notwithstanding this, I did torment her again and had almost drawn her out of her bed. I did it on purpose so that I could put Grace out of her life. I did do it because the Devil did promise me that no one should discover me. Mr and Mrs Eastchurch were absent. We did torment Grace for the space of two or three hours." Temperance went on to confess that she had shared her secret parts with the seductive gentleman, both privately and in public, and in celebration for inflicting pain on others.

"Did you mean to cause bodily harm to Grace Thomas?"

"Yes. We tormented her by pinching and pricking her with the intent to have killed her."

"How does this Devil appear to you?" The mayor and alderman were a formidable team and were satisfied with their questioning, although Temperance knew first hand that they had only touched the surface and were no match for the skilled inquisitors of the country's capital.

"He was about the length of my arm and his eyes were very big. He hopped and leapt about before me. He doth vanish clear away out of my sight after he hast laid with me in my bed."

Instead of being returned to her dwelling, Temperance was rudely escorted to the town's clink. The magistrates had decided to defer the trial so the chain of evidence could be thoroughly investigated. The following day, the town was buzzing as the circumstances of the accusations were related. Preachers urged anyone in earshot to heed the word of the bible and the terror-stricken town's folk gasped in terror at the news. There was talk of nothing else and wouldn't be for weeks.

The investigation to discover witches marks was the same as last time, her dignity and clothes stripped. Hands searched around her body, fingers caressing her skin. This would be the last time she would be touched by the hands of another, and she took what pleasure she could from the humiliating moment. Mary was consumed by shame whilst Susanna stood tall and proud, not flinching at the cold fingertips or recoiling at the intimate examination.

There were quadruple the amount of rats as there were prisoners and the smell reached them before the depressing moans of the incarcerated. As she sat contemplating her future, she remembered her dinner, which she envisioned bubbling away above a tiny inferno and prayed that it would not engulf her home.

That evening, under the cover of darkness, and at the risk of being named a collaborator,

Susanna made the daring trip to visit Temperance. She was soothed to know that Temperance had not betrayed their coven and revealed its secrets.

Susanna was tasked with retrieving the grimoire and their sacred tools, held by Temperance as she was the senior priestess. Living in the adjoining cottage, it was a feat she managed with ease. Fortunately, the inadequate quality of the kindling meant that the fire had extinguished itself and the pot of watery soup was cold, but would not be wasted as Susanna took it, as well as the hidden paranormal artefacts.

Whilst Susanna was scurrying around desperately trying to save the life of her dear friend, and escape the threat of the noose herself, there was a hushed meeting around the table at the Eastchurch residence. Much grumbling regarding the perceived facts of the case took place prior to them formulating a plan of their own, which they would execute the very next day. Thomas had questions he wanted answered, and if Gist wasn't man enough to get them, he would be.

Susanna was an intelligent woman and understood the nature of humans, and their need to control and rule. She was aware that she stood at risk of being accused of practicing witchcraft due to her friendship with her incarcerated pal. She knew that Temperance would not betray her but her clandestine relationship with Elizabeth Eastchurch might. Removing the stone, she exposed a hidey-hole that she had created within the breast of the chimney. It was a tight squeeze for the book and tools but she managed to conceal them so that they wouldn't be found, unless you knew where to look. To protect their dreadful legacy, Susanna had tasked another with the responsibility of keeping their secrets and educating the next generation of dark necromancers.

The forefathers, the kings of old, have reigned over the mysterious and the unknown for eons, slaughtering their magical brothers in fear of what they refused to understand. The murder of a non-believer would weigh lighter on their souls than following a path that led away from the garden of Eden.

32

The imprisoned were not idle, they were forced to toil the day away, in return for a measly helping of gruel and pest infected damp straw to sleep upon. The punishment largely unbefitting to the nature of the offence. The men would be forced to carry out manual labour while the dexterity of the woman's nimble fingers were used to repair fishing nets or work as unpaid seamstresses.

Well-meaning busybodies would sneak in stale crusts of bread or cloudy shots of mead, to appease their own conscience as much as easing the suffering of the deemed criminal element of their society.

Temperance had a dreadful night. Alone and at the mercy of the howling wind that whistled through the barred windows, her dreams were plagued with visions of death in what little sleep she had managed. Her waking moments were consumed with self-pity and teased with unfeasible ways to free herself from her lethal predicament.

Dawn had scarcely broken when the jailers rattled the sturdy bars to raise the occupants for a day of hardship and toil.

After stopping off at the town hall to obtain permission from the mayor to implement their scheme, Thomas and his posse of faithful woman marched directly to the jail.

Temperance was huddled in the corner of her cell, surrounded by fishing nets in need of repair. The bulging knuckles on her arthritic hands meant she was unable to participate in the fine needle work required to sew holes in clothing. The smell of salty seaweed and rotting fish entrails lingered in the air. Once the nets were mended she had a pile of willow branches, ready to be woven into weir baskets. The crown wasn't going to pass on the opportunity for free labour.

The rector, Mr Michael Ogilby, was pottering around the church garden. The early morning sun cast shadows from the spire which topped the seventy-foot square tower and danced around the sacred ground. The plain tower was constructed from the same common stone as the bridge and housed six harmonious bells that rang out across the tide. The religious man's head was pounding from the previous nights over indulgence. Pigs had broken through the churches defences and had wreaked havoc amongst the flowers and shrubs. Beautiful petals lay slain in the dirt and broken branches hung limply from green hedgerows. Sweat dripped from Mr Ogilby as he cleaned up the vandalised yard under the heat of an early summer morning and under the watchful eyes of a gaping and excited crowd who had gathered long before the appointed hour to get a view of the arch-witch before she was exorcised. Seeking sanctuary inside the cool walls of the house of worship, Michael straightened a candle and dusted the life size idol of his God's earthly son. He hadn't yet sampled the confessional wine, a daily routine, when he heard determined shouts of "she's coming".

After seven ceremonial laps of the church, they staggered through the open church doors, half dragging, half carrying a thin, confused and tottering Temperance. The two constables wrestled the bound woman to the chancel of the church whilst Thomas, Honor Hooper and Anne Wakely acted as bouncers. A choir of angelic voices sang Te Deum. A reluctant congregation huddled at the west end, their shuffling feet the only betrayal of their presence. Elizabeth Eastchurch was several paces behind the others after struggling to carefully close the heavy arched doors. The town's mayor and clerk remained outside.

Rector Michael Ogilby stood wide eyed in disgust and open mouthed as the heathen spectacle was paraded down the nave. He wished he'd had that drink. More candles than normal burned brightly on the altar, from behind which the rector was protected from the witch.

Before the God veering Ogilby could formulate any words, Thomas Eastchurch recanted the events of yesterday. He listened with a mixture of fascination and horror whilst pondering the reasoning for bringing a worshipper of Lucifer into a house of God.

"Why have you brought this wretched beast here today?"

"Because we were dissatisfied in some particulars concerning a piece of leather she had confessed of unto my wife Elizabeth. She did say that she had no wax nor clay, but she did confess that she had only a piece of leather which she had pricked nine times. Grace, who hast been staying with us, did cry out from great pricking pains in one of her knees. I did observe that she did have nine places in her knee which had been pricked, as if by a thorn." Thomas was a man on a mission and used plenty of body language to accentuate his claim. The ladies nodded obediently when required. "We are conceived that there might be some enchantment used in or about this said piece of Leather."

"Under whose authority do you come here today?"

"I have the leave and approbation of Mr. Gist to bring Temperance into this church and present her to you."

"What has this wicked creature been accused of?" Michael knew the answer but wanted to hear it spoken.

"For using and practising of Witchcraft upon the Body of Grace Thomas."

The rector formerly addressed the obedient flock and rather impressively, under the unusual circumstances, delivered communion to the sound of

Miserere Mei Deus vibrating gracefully through the sacred space.

Until now, Temperance had not been addressed. As Michael unwillingly adjusted his gaze, he was startled to see that Temperance's eyes darted feverously around the room.

Temperance did not ignite into a fiery inferno, as superstition would have her believe, but she did feel uncomfortable under the scrutinising gaze of the Christian icon. Aware that Exodus 22:18 advises thou shalt not suffer a witch to live, she prayed to Hecate that the rector would not follow the guidance in his bible.

Undeterred Mr Ogilby demanded, "Tell me how long since the Devil did tempt you to do evil?" Temperance did not answer immediately and the tension in the hollowed air was palpable. "About twelve years ago I was tempted by the Devil to be instrumental to the death of William Herbert and the Devil did promise me that I should live well and do well." Arrogance seeped from her mouth and her eyes, now cold and focused, fixated upon the clergyman.

"Were you an instrument in the death of William Herbert?"

"Yes."

"And what have you to say of your involvement with Grace Thomas?"

"On the Sevenight I did come into Thomas Eastchurch's shop in the form and shape of a cat and fetched out of the same shop a poppet. I did carry it up into the chamber where Grace Thomas did lodge and left it about the bed whereon Grace did lie." She would take the blame for what she had made Bartholomew do, his would not be a life that she would take with her. She'd had word that the devoted familiar had found refuge with Betty and knew that Mary would be pleased her beloved pet would be well cared for.

Pressed further by both Michael and Thomas, Temperance refused to confess that she had pricked any pins in the poppet. So far the men had kept their tactics verbal, using their gender and size to intimidate the decrepit femme fatale.

Michael loomed over Temperance; his foul breath almost as intolerable as the stench of the cell that she longed to be back in. The rusty shackles that restricted her movement cut into her skin as Michael sadistically twisted the clanking metal. He was particularly demanding that she should provide him with a sufficient answer.

To stop the infernal chatter about the effigy that resembled a child's doll, Temperance rashly and with instant regret, admitted to the slaying of Anne Fellow, three years previous. Her confession momentarily stunned her accusers. Elizabeth had taken a seat in one of the pews for fear that she would faint under the pressure of the informal examination. Anne dutifully hovered beside her whilst Honor stood with the men, keeping a manner of dignity to the proceedings.

The erection of the chapel had been completed by Temperance's forefathers under duress and on the penalty of death, for another man's God. Temperance looked to the rafters in the hopes that she would find a hidden effigy to her own faith. Amongst the carved human faces grotesques peaked out on the congregation, offering absolution to the pagan's transgressions. So many had died at the hands of another's devotion over the centuries. She knew in her heart that she was done for too. She had no defence that would combat the ferocity with which her accusers had come at her.

'To Hell with it.' She thought to herself. She was tired, hungry and truth be told, not long for this world anyway. She had been preparing Susanna to take over her role and was confident that If she gave a worthy enough performance, their secrets would not be discovered. Their names would not pass her lips.

A war of words would lead to the discovery of all the enchantresses and condemn each one to a public execution, but the supernatural battle of curses and charms they fought had spilled into the public arena. As with every aspect of life, there is a balance of good and bad, black and white. In witchcraft the divide was as vicious as opposing sides of an army and each side had given it their best shot to eradicate their counterparts, for the perceived betrayal of the craft.

If she was going to be ripped from this world she would damn well leave her mark on it.

As the rector tried to stammer out a response to the frank revelation, Temperance calmly stated, "I was the cause of death of one Jane Dallyn, the late wife of Symon Dallyn who is a Mariner. I did do it by pricking of her in one of her eyes. I did so secretly perform this, that I was never discovered or punished for it." The corner of her mouth hinted at a snarl of a smile. Pride could be heard in the voice that croaked with age. She wasn't finished yet. Before the stunned trio could utter a word, she continued.

"I declare that I did bewitch unto death one Lydia Burman." Upon hearing that she was in the company of a serial killer, the gasp combined with a yelp of distress that escaped from Mrs Eastchurch echoed around the virtually empty church, startling Temperance mid confession and causing her to glance in the direction of the source. Elizabeth was in real danger of fainting.

Thomas was delighted that his actions had produced such results. Undiscovered crimes resolved, thanks to him and the condemnation of a witch, although his internal rejoicing was tinged with concern for his beloved. He liked to believe that people looked up to him and for the most part they did. He was an incredibly successful and wealthy, yet generous man. For all his faults and qualities, his greatest flaw was the spell that his wife had over him. He would move Heaven and Earth if she bid him to.

Recovering a little, Ogilby managed to interject, "Why would you do such a wicked thing?"

"Because she had been a witness against me at the trial of my life and death at the Assizes when I was arraigned for the death of William Herbert. And deposed that I had appeared unto her in the shape of a red pig. But she was drunk because at the time she was brewing in the house of one Humphry Ackland."

Fearful that the curse may remain long after her soul had been dragged to the underworld and he would be forced to endure the pitiful suffering of his related house guest, Thomas urged the rector to further demand repeatedly in what part of the house or Grace's bed had she left the poppet.

Temperance refused to tell them and would only say, "I will not nor must not discover for if I do the Devil will tear me in pieces." Temperance had handed them their golden goose on a platter. A double-edged gift of a confession before a representative of their almighty God and a seed of doubt over her willing involvement.

Realising that there was no further information to be gleaned from the interrogation Mr Ogilby desired Temperance to say the Lord's Prayer, which she imperfectly performed, on purpose. The rector gave her a good many appeals, but it was more fun for Temperance to torment the devoted man of the cloth with her feigned attempts.

Exasperated from the witch's refusal to correctly recite the infamous Christian invocation, Michael Ogilby politely excused himself and departed his own sanctuary. But not before he delivered a solemn exhortation to fear the darkest superstitions and seek the light of the Lord.

The return journey to her holding cell was a solemn affair, each lost in their own thoughts. Once Temperance was safely in the hands of the burly guards the gang thusly reported back to the mayor, who was eagerly awaiting their return. Thomas Gist was determined not to fail the town as the previous holder of office had and would not be taken in by the charms of a witch.

33

Another inhabitant of the town that was out for blood was William Herbert. News of Temperance's arrest soon reached William's ears. Upon hearing that his sworn enemy had been incarcerated he downed tools and headed straight for the clink. Cutting over fields he made a beeline for the filthy building that was the town's jail.

Slipping the guard a shilling for his troubles and discretion, Temperance was escorted to a private room for a little chat with the man she had since desired to call her stepson. William puffed out his chest to make himself as menacing as possible. Temperance shrank into her frame to appear as fragile and innocent as she could. Neither bought the others pretence.

They went back and forth for a while with accusations and denials, with wagging fingers and raised hands.

Temperance was tired. The first night locked up had brought nightmares when she slept and equally disturbing daydreams as she lay awake listening to the congested breathing of her cell mates or the squeak of a rat as it passed, looking for any scrap of food.

"I demand of you, what did thy do to my father?" The same question, again.

"Maybe he was bewitched by my beauty!!" Temperance batted her eyelids. A wicked smile teased at her lips.

William was not above hitting a woman but he somehow retained his composure as Temperance goaded him. The old crone could see in his eyes how riled up he was, his fists were clenched in frustration, and it took effort to keep his voice from rising.

"Yes William. I surely did kill your father. Is that what you wish to hear, that I confess to the downfall of the late, great Mr Herbert?"

It was what he had wanted to hear. He cared little for what truth there was in the statement, only that he had been proven right. By the time his visit was over, William had also gleaned a confession for being the cause of the death to Anne Fellow, as well as a GBH charge against Jane Dallyn and Lydia Burman.

William would be worth his weight in flesh to the prosecutors and would be expertly used to demonstrate premeditation and that the supposed witchcraft was not simply a case of whimsical fancy on behalf of the witnesses.

To visit Temperance would be inviting the Spanish Inquisition into their lives. Susanna and Mary had no choice but to forge ahead without their illustrious leader. They knew what was expected of them, their fate tied to Temperance's through the actions they felt compelled to take at the behest of a dark, handsome stranger.

Mary had devised a cunning way to keep in communication with their doomed chief. Either she would draw a pictogram of her message, she had never been taught, nor mastered the art of writing legibly or Susanna would scribble a note to keep Temperance informed of their progress. She would attach the parchment to a makeshift collar and Bartholomew would deliver it. Nimble and quick he would squeeze between the bars, under the cover of darkness and past sleeping or drunk guards. Once she had read the letter, she ate it. It tasted horrible but she would not risk being caught and endanger any hope she may have of surviving her current predicament, though she knew, in her heart, that she would not walk away from this. Third time would be the charm but not for Temperance.

Bartholomew always settled with Temperance until she fell asleep, keeping her company and connected to the friends that she missed more than she cared to admit. Despite not being overly fond of him, Temperance felt at peace stroking his soft fur and was grateful for his companionship.

The other inmates wanted nothing to do with her. Too scared to make eye contact in case she put a spell on them or get close enough that she may touch them and turn them to stone. Temperance was indifferent to their treatment, carrying out the daily tasks set with her eyes cast to the floor and her mind thinking of her glory days and the mischief she had got up to, to distract herself from the pangs she felt from lacking any real nourishment and the niggling pains in her joints from the unsavoury working conditions.

In a last-ditch effort, Susanna and Mary threw everything at the assault on the weaker members of the Amberley coven. Susanna lacked the heart to take the fight directly to Elizabeth, choosing to systematically eliminate the sisterhood around her. With Temperance incapacitated, the white witches had become complacent and relaxed their guard, leaving them susceptible to magical attacks. Elizabeth, with her own failing, failed to maintain the protection she had put in place to repel the physic and physical harm their foes had demonstrated themselves capable of.

Susanna had noted a change in a people's attitudes, as if a silence had descended on the town. The calm before the storm. She saw a wariness in the eyes of her neighbours that hadn't been there before. She had never been one to feel intimidated, had always stood with her shoulders raised, even when she was a quivering wreck inside. She had braved the humiliation of begging and stepped into old age with relative grace but her exterior was cracking, to match her fractured soul.

Mary, a dab hand at divination, had foreseen her destiny. She was alone in this world and had tired of her existence. She pitied the future of her prodigies; the world was not accepting of their blend of the craft. Life had brought her nothing but hardship and her exit would be a blessing to her. She shared none of these feelings with Susanna.

With the support of each other, the pair carried out every task as a duo from laundering their clothes to cooking their evening meals.

They had been out since dawn, picking fruit and hovering around the shop doorways, looking suitably pathetic in the hope that pity would be bestowed on them. It wasn't.

Grace was walking back from town with a bundle under her arm. Susanna had seen her come out of the butchers and stepped into her path as she walked through a side street. She tried flattery to entice Grace to part with a little of her purchase but Grace ignored the pleas. A threatening stance and menacing eyes helped to sway the decision to tear off a small strip of meat, which she handed to Susanna, who gave the tiniest of nods and walked away without a word. The Goddess had taught Grace to be harmonious, to be kind to all the creatures on earth and to walk in perfect love and perfect trust. She knew their dark counterparts were to blame for the illnesses that had befallen the members of Amberley but she also knew that she only need withstand the pain a little longer.

Susanna persuaded Mary to follow Mrs Barnes. Grace had sensed Mary's aura but carried on, keen to know what Mary may do. Mary edged her way along, occasionally stopping to 'pick something up' or gaze in a window before continuing her stealthy pursuit.

Mary watched as Grace opened the front door and disappeared inside. She gave Agnes the package and told her she was tired and would retire for an hour or two. From her bedroom window she could see Mary standing five houses down, looking at the door she had just come through. After a couple of minutes, Susanna joined her. She handed Mary a white pot and pointed at Grace's home. Mary nodded and nervously walked in Graces footsteps.

Grace started whimpering and calling out, putting on a stellar performance. She threw herself on the floor and writhed around in 'agony'. The commotion brought those in the house crashing into the room, where they attempted to hold her down.

"Do I hear someone at the door?" Agnes asked the assembled party. As they listened they heard shuffling on the cobblestones outside. Agnes was sent to investigate whilst the men stayed with Grace, in case she suffered another fit.

"What do you want?" Agnes was not a fan of the most in need of society.

Before Mary could answer, the remarkably strong voice of Grace Barnes shouted from upstairs, "Who is that at my door?" Upon hearing that it was Mary, Grace cried out in a fit of pain.

"Shut the door. Come inside Agnes. Arrgghhh. Quickly." Agnes did as she was bid and ran up the stairs, two at a time.

"Grace, you are in pain again"

"I fear it is witchcraft. I am so afraid that they have performed a magical act on me, and I may die!" Part of Grace's camouflage was to publicly portray an external image of fear of the supernatural. That should prevent suspicion that she would practice it, when in fact she was a skilled spellcaster. "Ouch." Grace rubbed her arm, "I feel I am being pricked, ouch, with pins."

That night Grace was plagued with nightmares. She huddled into her husband's sleeping body but still felt unseen eyes were watching her.

The following day, William Edwards was enjoying a steaming cup of tea in the front room of the Barnes home. Bookcases or paintings covered the walls so the hand-drawn design on the background behind was barely visible. Heavy drapes hung over the window frames and a large rug filled the centre of the room. On top of the woven carpet was a low table surrounded by a semi-circle of wooden high-backed armchairs, upon which sat John Barnes and his skilled blacksmith friend.

"So it is agreed, William. You will tell the mayor that you overheard them confess that they did make themselves invisible and did come into my house to pinch and prick my wife."

"Aye. I shall swear an oath that is what I heard." William had made several advances, in the past, towards Susanna and had been rebuffed on each occasion. He had waited a long time to get revenge for his dented pride.

34

John Barnes was one of the town's Yeomans. He managed his freeholding through renting out the land to small tenant farmers looking to hold a small plot within the confines of the town, to store or grow produce.

With the formalities stated and recorded, it was time for John to alleviate his wife's condition with his damning words.

"Upon Easter Tuesday, which was the eighteenth day of May last past, my wife was taken with very great pains."

"can you describe her affliction, Mr Barnes?"

"Yes, Grace described them unto me. She has great pains of sticking and pricking in her arms, stomach and breast. It is as though she had been stabbed with awls. She described it to me in such a manner that I thought that she would have died immediately."

"Did Grace recover?"

"No sirs, she has not. My Grace is in such sad condition she hath continued unto this present day, in tormenting and grievous pains."

"Are these the same pains experienced by Grace Thomas?

"I do not know of the other Grace's predicament." Whether this was true, it was not investigated further and Mr Barnes continued unchallenged.

"Upon Sunday last, which was the sixteenth day of July instant Grace was again taken ill. It was about ten of the clock in the forenoon when my wife was taken worse than before. In so much as four men and women could hardly hold her."

"And these men and women can validate your claims?"

"At the same time one Agnes Whitefield was present."

Thomas Gist interrupted, even though he knew there to be no other Agnes. "And is the Agnes to which you speak of the wife of John Whitefield, cordwainer of Biddiford?"

"Yes, this is the Agnes of which I speak. The said Agnes, was in my house and on hearing somebody at the door, she did open the door and found one Mary Trembles."

Thomas was quick to interject again. "It is Mary Trembles of Biddiford, single woman, who came to your door?"

"That is what I was informed sir."

"Why had Mary Trembles come to your door?"

"I do not know. She was standing with a white pot in her hands, as though she had been going to the common bakehouse. Thereupon my wife did ask of the said Agnes, who was it that was at the door?" John paused, expecting to be prompted but he wasn't. "Agnes did unto answer that it was Mary Trembles. My wife did reply and said that she, the said Mary Trembles, was one of them that did torment her, torment my wife, and that she, Mary, had come now to put her out of her life." It was established that Grace was still alive, and John had no further information or conjecture to add.

William Edward's forearms were as thick as tree stumps, his shoulders broad and his legs powerful. A blacksmith by trade William sported a heavy leather apron and a black smudge that graced his cheekbone. His deep voice reverberated around the room.

He was also privy to the conversation, on the seventeenth of July, in which Susanna admitted that the Devil had carnal knowledge of her body and had sucked from her breast and secret parts.

During this overheard confession, William added, "Susanna did say that she and one Mary Trembles did appear hand in hand invisible in John Barnes house, where his wife Grace did lie in a very sad condition." True to character, it was confirmed that the data involved the same Mr and Mrs Barnes, which the previous informants had claimed were the victims of a vicious supernatural attack.

Completing his performance, William added, "I did then also hear Susanna to say that she and Mary Trembles were at the same time come to make an end of her. Of Grace." A strike to his anvil would have been less condemning than the words he had just spoken.

Before word spread of the further indictments, this time against Mary and Susanna, the two women were arrested to thwart further outbreaks of witchcraft and prevent them from absconding.

The fame of convicting one notorious witch would be nothing to the notoriety Mr Gist would receive for taking down a coven of evil doers. He would have acted on a lesser declaration; he would have taken action on a rumour.

35

It was two weeks after her husband stood in this spot, that Grace Barnes told her sorrowful tale of self-pity and suffering. She had not volunteered her statement but been dragged to the town hall under duress, at the request of the town's mayor. Grace had no prior intention of condemning a former acquaintance, even though the two women had fallen out of favour with the other.

The tormented Grace was manhandled by a constable, Anthony Jones and several others, her thrashing body making it hard for the men to keep a controlled and steady grip on her. Supported and lead through the filthy streets, Grace had no option but to go with them.

Inhabitants watched with morbid curiosity or fascinated horror as Mrs Barnes was escorted to the dingy and cramped official building.

Susanna Edwards watched with suspicion; her vantage point through the small, latticed window, not as concealed as she had assumed.

Susanna's fingertips were cold, she had been restrained and the blood flow compromised. Subconsciously she wiggled her fingers to improve the poor circulation and warm them up. The weasely form and nasal voice of Mr Jones irrationally aggravated Susanna. His appearance made her skin crawl, since she had spurned his advances when she was publicly mourning the loss of her husband and income, he would take any opportunity to mock her. "Transfer the pain, in this moment of gain. Twist my pleasure, blow him down like a feather." With the eagle eye of a farmer who could notice a diseased ear of corn at fifty paces, Mr Jones spotted the source of Grace's aliment. Subsequently, the healthy Mr Jones succumbed to a moment of gripping pain that left him behaving like a rabid dog. Foam oozed from his mouth, and he leapt around as if he had fire in his muddy boots.

"Wife, I am now bewitched by this Devil." Screamed Mr Jones, capering as if a tune played only in his own mind. As quickly as his body was seized with pain it was tendered helpless and Mr Jones lay in a state of unconsciousness for some thirty minutes. The remaining men ushered their wards into the deserted hall as Mrs Jones attended to her husband and the justices attended to the disorderly rabble and restore peace, which took a considerable amount of time.

Owing to her ailing condition and the dramatic convulsions that gripped Mr Jones, Grace was permitted the use of a chair from which she answered the questions put to her.

Upon her oath, Grace said that she hath been very much pained and tormented in her body these many years. She confirmed that she had sought near and far for a remedy to cure her.

"I never had any suspicion that I had had any magical art or witchcraft used upon my body, until about a year and a half ago."

"If you did not suspect witchcraft, why do you now?"

"I was informed by some physicians that it was so. I also had some suspicion of one Susanna Edwards, of Biddiford."

"The widow Susanna Edwards?"

"Yes Sirs."

"Why do you suspect Susanna Edwards?"

"Because Susanna would oftentimes repair unto my husband's house upon frivolous or no occasions at all."

"Do you have anything further to add Mrs Barnes?"

"About the middle of May last past, I was taken with very great pains of sticking and pricking in my arms, stomach, breast and heart. It was as though divers awls had been pricked or stuck in my body. I was in great tormenting pain for many days and nights together, with very little intermission."

Unlike her male counterparts, Grace waited for the invitation to expand further. "Upon Sunday the 16th day of July, I was taken in a very grievous and tormenting manner. At which instant of time I did hear a knock at the door. Agnes did look out...."

True to character, the mayor interrupted the proceedings, to clarify the details. "Is this Agnes Whitefield, the wife of John, of whom you speak."

"Yes Mr Gist. Agnes did open the door and looking out, found one Mary Trembles standing before the door. I did ask Agnes who it was and it was Agnes who answered that it was the said Mary Trembles." Grace looked to the mayor, anticipating clarification, which she provided. "I was fully assured that Mary Trembles, together with Susanna Edwards, were the very persons that had tormented me, by using some magical act or witchcraft upon my body."

Grace's words were recorded, and she was assisted from the town hall. Supported on one side by her husband and on the other by Agnes. The trio moved slowly through the streets and Grace retired to bed as soon as they had manoeuvred her up the creaking staircase.

36

The sun shone through the wispy clouds casting glittering rays of light across the murky river. The smell from the clink was an unpleasant aroma that infiltrated the nostrils of the unfortunate visitors and passers-by. The incarcerated soon became accustomed to the overpowering smell of rotting food and human excrement. The use of mint leaves gave Joane Jones an advantage when visiting those left to suffer behind the thick bars of the town's prison. She rubbed the aromatic leaves between her fingers and then inside her nostrils, repeating every few minutes.

Joane was in attendance, sweeping the stained and damp straw, when John Danning from the neighbouring town of Great Torrington, paid a visit. John had forged an alliance with many of the town's residents when they fought a bloody and unsuccessful battle against the King's royalists. It was through these allegiances that John came to learn of the town's witch problem.

The townsfolk had taken an active stance against the sovereign and erected forts at strategic points on the coastal entrance to the town. General Fairfax's soldiers has been marched through the area as a warning against an uprising, which served more to antagonise the population. In preparing for battle the town found itself cut off from trade routes on land and was forced to rely on supplies shipped from the neighbouring town of Barum.

The battle was long forgotten in most people's minds. Moss had grown over the graves of the dead, and no one talked any more of the crushing defeat at the hands of Captain Digby's horse mounted cavalry, joined by a battalion from Cornwall.

Master manipulator, Hopton, had stirred the locals into a frenzy and by the time summer ended tempers were fraught and the men of the town were riled up to fight. A plan was formed.

Thinking the threat more hearsay than dangerous, the captain had sent the majority of his men on the long march home, just a fraction of his force remaining in Torrington to deal with any dissenters. The rival men could be heard a mile away, singing with God in their hearts and swords in their hands. Fired up from the lengthy sermon, they were late to their rendezvous with their allies, costing them victory. Reinforced boots and horses hooves thundered towards Digby's vastly outnumbered army, who were fuelled and fed up of the wait. They attacked with such fury that many of the men at the rear fled without seeing a drop of blood spilled.

In the light of a new day, some two hundred men and boys lay lifeless on the ground, blood puddled from whatever injury had claimed their lives. An equal amount were captured and imprisoned as conspirators to the crown. Those that returned told tales of garrisons of trained killers, of ambushes along the riverside and of supernatural horrors that befell them. Others boasted that they had slain a formidable warrior or defeated ten men with one blow, while others proclaimed themselves to be cavaliers and their egos grew as big as their bellies. The truth would filter through, and Temperance would realise that the men she had admired, had thought strong and invincible, had run away, their tails between their legs.

For reasons known only to him, he took it upon himself to visit the town and carry out his own talk with Susanna yet failed to record or report his findings to the appropriate authority. His loss at the infamous battle did nothing to curb his enthusiasm for poking his nose into another's business, thinking himself superior in all manners.

John rode his faithful steed across the twenty-four arched stone bridge which connected the east and west sides of the town. The exhausted mare, having just trekked seven and a half miles, plodded at a snail's pace up the steep hill. Realising he wasn't helping the situation; John dismounted and led the grateful horse the remainder of the way. He left the chestnut thoroughbred to graze on a nearby grass bank whilst he visited Susanna in her prison cell.

Joane avoided eye contact with Susanna, who stood silently in the corner of the room. Chains weighed on her old bones but she stood defiantly as she was forced to listen to the accusations against her, grateful to be away from the poor conditions of the stinking cell.

"Are you Joane Jones, the wife of Anthony Jones, husbandman of this town?" The woman to follow John Barnes and William Edwards confirmed her identity.

"Twas Friday the seventeenth of July and I was present, with Susanna Edwards, when one John Danning, not of this town, came in to see her. He did demand of her how and by what means she became a witch."

"And how did Susanna answer?"

"Susanna did answer unto the question that she did never confess afore now but now she would."

"And did Susanna confess to being a witch?"

"I heard Susanna confess unto the said Mr Danning that she was on a time gathering wood when she did see a gentleman draw nigh unto her and she was in good hopes that he would give her a piece of money."

"Does Susanna want for money?" It was an obvious question that Mr Gist knew the obvious answer too.

"For she is a widow Sir, I am sure she is in need." Mr Jones was permitted to continue. "Mr Danning further demanded of Susanna where she did meet with the said gentleman and Susanna did answer that it was in Parsonage Close."

"Was this the only confession that Susanna did make?" Thinking that the day may come to an early end and he would be holding up the bar before the clock struck three, Mr Gist shifted his robed body on the stiff chair.

"No Sir, when Mr Danning was gone I did hear Susanna confess that two days prior, she with Mary Trembles , and by the help of the Devil, did prick and torment Grace, the wife of John Barnes."

"And this was the extent to which they did perform witchcraft upon Mrs Barnes?" It was becoming more likely that Mr Gist would not make it to the tavern in the time scale of his choosing.

"No Sir. I did hear both Susanna Edwards and Mary Tremble to say and confess that they did this present day, being the eighteenth of July, torment and prick the said Grace Barnes again."

There appeared to be a disagreement between the two aged close friends that Joane reported in detail. The alderman was fully engaged in the testimony whereas the mayor's mind and gut were thinking of mead.

"Mary did give Susanna a mild poke in the arm and declared 'O thou Rogue, will now confess all; for tis thou that hast made me to be a witch and thou art one thy self and my conscience must swear it."

"And how did Susanna react?" Mr Gist's interest peaked at the possibility that the two women would come to blows.

"Susanna did reply that she did not think that Mary wouldest have been such a rogue to discover it, and further confessed to me, with provocation, that the Devil did oftentimes carry about her spirit."

"Did Susanna or Mary confess to harming any other?"

"Yes. Susanna did further confess that she did prick and torment one Dorcas Coleman, the wife of the mariner John Coleman."

"Did Susanna confess to any other contact with the said Devil?"

"Yes Sir, I did hear Susanna say that she was sucked in her breast several times by the Devil who, in the shape of a boy, lay in her bed and that it was very cold unto her. She also did say that after she was sucked by him, the said boy or Devil, that he had carnal knowledge of her body."

"Were you the only person to witness this confession?" That drink was becoming less of a possibility.

"No Sir, my husband Anthony Jones did observe Susanna also. He saw her gripe and twinkle her hands upon her own body. He did say to her 'Thou Devil, thou art now tormenting some person or other'."

Joane mimicked the motion with her hands. Joane's face changed, and a darkness came over her features as she recounted what happened next. "Susanna was displeased with my husband and said 'Well enough. I will fit thee'. At that time, she did no harm to Anthony but at that present time, Grace Barnes was in great pain with pricking's and stabbings unto her heart."

Joane went on to describe how her spouse was part of the group of men that were accordingly dispatched under order of the mayor to bring Grace Barnes before them, which was done immediately and with much ado. As Grace was hauled to the town hall, Joane's tale recommenced. "Susanna Edwards turned about and looked upon my husband and forthwith my husband was taken in a very bad condition as he was leading and supporting Grace Barnes up the stairs of this town hall. In front of you and the justices my husband did cry out to me that he was now bewitched by the Devil and forthwith he leapt about and capered like a madman. He then fell, shaking, quivering and foaming and lay for the space of half an hour like a dying or dead man. As you know, at length, coming to his senses again, my husband did declare unto me that the said Susanna had bewitched him."

"Have you known your husband, Mr Anthony Jones, to be ill of character?"

"I have never known my husband, Anthony, to be taken in any fits or convulsions. He is a person of sound and healthy body and has been since we have been married."

"Thank you Mrs Jones for your in-depth account." Mr Gist practically ran to the inn, pushing past waiting patrons to quench his insatiable appetite.

The fit farmer took a day to recover from his sudden bout of being hexed. He stood in front of the men, senior to him in status and position and confirmed everything his wife had stated the previous day, though the retelling of the events was less dramatic than his spouse's. All except for his use of the word 'Devil', that he spat out viciously, and always in the direction of Susanna, who simply returned his venomous gaze with one of her own, equally poisonous but accompanied with a knowing smile.

37

Mary had never been as terrified as she was now. She'd had a hard life and faced many a hardship but now she was facing her own mortality. She could twist no tale, nor strengthen any lie enough to make her captors believe her innocence.

It was Mary's turn to stand alone and face the consequences of being a poor spinster with a damning choice of friendship.

As he had done previously and for the final time this trial, Thomas Gist addressed those gathered with an official statement, as much to bolster his inflated ego as to inform Mary, in no uncertain terms, that she had broken the law and would be punished.

"Concerning all manner of murthen felonies, poisonings, enchantments, witchcrafts, forgeries, trespasses, forestallers, regraters and extortioners whatsoever, and concerning all and singular other evil deeds and offences, of which justices of the peace of us, our heirs and successors may or ought lawfully to enquire by whomsoever or howsoever, of this parish, heretofore done or committed, or which shall hereafter be attempted, done or committed, shall stand before us and God and satisfy to us the sanctity of their actions. Thomas gist inhaled deeply; his oxygen spent on the lengthy disclaimer.

"Mary Trembles. You have been brought before us, on this day, the eighteenth day of July, Anno Domini 1682, and accused of practicing of witchcraft upon Grace Barnes, wife of John Barnes of Biddiford yeoman. We demand you to tell us how long you have practiced witchcraft?"

For a moment Mary stood staring blankly at the men. Any answer she had formulated danced on her tongue, not yet ready to be spoken.

"What do you have to say for yourself woman?" Thomas Gist was in no mood for the antics of the female of the species, who he saw and treated as a lesser version of their male counterparts.

Mary found the words that she hoped would save her life. With a voice that shook with nerves, she spoke them. "About three years last past, one Susanna Edwards did inform me that if I would do as she said, that I would do very well. I did yield and did do as Susanna did." Mary's confession was swift and direct and to the narrative the women had created in the vain hope of survival.

"And how would you do very well Ms. Trembles?" John Davie, though determined to get to the truth of the matter, spoke to the elderly woman with a modicum of respect.

"Susanna did promise that I should neither want for money, meat, drink or clothes." Mary went on to confess that after she had made the bargain with Susanna, she was visited by a stranger, who lay with her in her bed, and as a result had sensual knowledge of her body. “The Devil came to me in the shape of a lion.” If they didn’t believe her, maybe she could appear insane.

Thomas Gist revelled in this part of the tale and pressed Mary to elaborate on the nature of her relationship with the supposed evil incarnate.

“He did suck me in my secret parts.” Mary looked at the floor, ashamed. “His sucking was so hard that it did cause me to cry out in pain.” The men had no sympathy for the woman’s plight and demanded in an uncaring tone that she should continue, digging her own grave with the words that came tumbling from her lips. “On Tuesday in Easter week of the eighteenth of May, I did go into town to beg some bread and I did meet with Susanna on my walk.”

Mary went on to say that she had been unsuccessful in securing any nourishment and together with Susanna had happened upon the notion to beg at the door of Mr Barnes, in the hopes that he would be generous. John was not home when the women came calling and instead were met at the door by his wife Grace and their servant. The two enchantresses failed to perform their magic and were refused any meat and were sent away, with proverbial fleas in their ears. “Afterwards, on the same day, Susanna did bid me to go unto John’s house and request a farthings worth of tobacco. I did go but could not get any and returned with nothing for Susanna. She was displeased with me and with the Barnes."2

"And why do you assume Susanna was displeased with the Barnes?"

"Because Susanna did say to me that it should be better for her, meaning Grace, if she had let me have some tobacco." Many of the men had made their mint as pioneers trading tobacco with Maryland and Virginia, silk with other American colonies and goods with France and Holland. The Spanish had forgotten their defeat and had many rich through the importing and exporting of wool. The important little English port, made famous as the birth place of Sir Richard Grenville, led directly to the Atlantic Ocean making it a powerful force for its size. A testament to this were the merchants impressive three storey houses, built side-by-side up the length of Bridgeland Street.

"Did you hurt Grace with your witchcraft?"

"On the sixteenth day of July, I, with Susanna, did go to John Barnes house and went at the fore-door invisibly into the room. We saw John Barnes in bed with his wife Grace, who was on the inner side of the bed, and we did pinch and prick Grace almost unto death."

"We demand to know; how many times did the Devil have carnal knowledge of your body?"

Mary took a moment to consider her answer before replying. "Besides the time mentioned, the Devil had knowledge three other times. The last being upon the sixteenth day of July, when I was going towards the common bakehouse."

"On the same day that you did torment Grace?" Thomas did like to interrupt proceedings to clarify a point. The day was getting late. The last rays of the setting July sun cast an amber glow through the lead lined window.

"Yes. I did beg of her again for food for at that time, with the help of the Devil, I would have killed Grace, if she had not spilt some of the meat she was then carrying unto the bakehouse."

During the proceedings Temperance and Susanna had been collected from the cells and stood silently at the back of the room, each between two strong guards. The officers expected to be seized with pains and maledictions performed by the witches at any moment.

The three pagans were to be told their fate, which the mayor had already decided before a word of proof was uttered.

The women were weary and despondent.

They could do nothing for their friend.

Before the mayor had the opportunity to ask Mary anything further a raven flew at the glass, repeatedly striking against the window. The sound made everyone jump in fright. The bird was declared as an evil omen, a visitation from a demon. The occurrence brought a smile to the tired faces of the condemned and their demeanours brightened greatly as the room was thrown into a credulous panic.

The men had had quite enough of hearing of the dire acts and amongst the chaos adorned the verdict. The accursed were returned to their respective cells. Her march up the hill meant that Mary fell several times and arrived with grazed shins and cut palms. Mary cried until no tears were left.

Both men were aghast at the identical suffering, perpetrated at the hands of other women. Although Mr Gist had been desperate for the woman to implement each other, he couldn't help but commended their loyalty to Temperance. He knew that his position offered him the servitude of others he desired, but Temperance had no such standing to exact her influence. He was satisfied that the woman had signed their own death warrants with their confessions and that he could rest easy that he had helped to rid the world of evil. His only concern was that the assizes would fail in their responsibilities, as they had before, although he was confident that his examination had been thorough.

38

Susanna walked carefully up the staircase; her legs had been unshackled but her hands were still bound behind her back. On a few occasions she almost lost her balance and her shoulder slammed into the wooden panels that lined that walls.

The proceedings commenced quickly, and the mayor was talking before Susanna had a chance to gather her thoughts. The number of people known to her that lined the streets to hurl insults had unsettled her and the unkind words were circulating around her mind like a whirlpool. She numbly confirmed her name and the charges that were being brought against her.

"We demand you inform us how long since you had discourse or familiarity with the Devil."

"About two years ago I did meet with a gentleman in a field at Parsonage Close. Here in this town." Susanna, whose arms were still held behind her, nodded her head in the direction of the top of the town. Susanna went on the say that the gentleman's apparel was black and that she did hope that he would give her some money.

Susanna was quite the flirt and enjoyed the company of men. She readily confessed to curtsying for her devilish acquaintance, as she would do for any gentleman, in the hopes of falling in his good grace.

"What and who is the gentleman you speak of?"

"The Devil." Susanna went on to describe her dire financial situation and that she was targeted due to being a poor woman. "Thereupon he did say to me that if I grant him one request I should neither want for meat, drink nor clothes.

"What was his request?"

"I do not know, for I said, 'In the name of God, what is it that I shall have?' Upon which the gentleman vanished away from me." The tone of Susanna's voice betrayed the disappointment that her knight in black armour had disappeared. As with Mary's confession that was to come, Susanna also admitted to laying with the man reported to be the devil who performed the intimate act of sucking at her breast.

"Were these the only times that you did meet with this 'man'?"

"No Sirs. Afterwards I did meet him in a place called Stambridge-Lane, where he did suck blood from my breast."

"Have you harmed anyone at the behest of this man?"

"On Sunday the sixteenth of July, together with Mary Trembles, we did go unto the house of

John Barnes and nobody did see us." Susanna's voice again betrayed her true feelings, this time there was a hint of pride. "Mr Barnes is a yeoman!" Susanna's attempt to justify her actions against the wealthy couple fell on deaf ears.

"We are aware of John's position in the community."

"We were in the same room where John's wife, Grace was. There we did prick and pinch Grace with our fingers." As Susanna talked, the fingers that were grasped behind her back replicated a pinching action and her arms strained against the rope that held them. "We put her in great pain and torment, in-so-much that Grace was almost dead!" A wry smile teased at Susanna's lips.

The mayor had noticed the movement and requested that Susanna's arms be freed, allowing her the freedom to condemn herself.

"Was this the only time you have inflicted pain upon Grace Barnes?"

"Today I did prick and torment Grace Barnes again." Playing straight into Mr Gist's trap, Susanna intimated with her fingers how she did it. Realising her mistake, Susanna was quick to lay the blame. "The Devil did entice me to make an end of her, of Grace. He told me that he would come again to me once more before I should go out of town." The pride was back in her voice. "I can go unto any place invisible and yet my body shall be lying in my bed."

"Can you describe this devil?"

"He wore black and appeared unto me in the shape of a lion."

The Alderman raised his eyebrows in disbelief at Susanna's claim. "I demand to know if you have done any bodily hurt unto any other persons, besides Grace Barnes."

The realisation that the men had been privy to witnesses testimony promoted Susanna to confess more, in the misguided hope that her declaration would save her life. "I did prick and torment one Dorcas Coleman. And I gave myself to the Devil when I did meet him in Stambridge-Lane" Susanna lived in a small two roomed cottage that was a stone's throw from the gated entrance to the next parish and the lane in question ran behind the row of cottages and provided access to the wells. The new confession concerning Dorcas would add more fuel to the fire of the public hatred building against the accused.

"What is your relationship to Mary Trembles, Single woman, of this town and borough."

"Mary Trembles was a servant unto me, in like manner as I was a servant unto the appellation of a gentleman."

Susanna was thrown into the cell beside Temperance. Falling to her knees she grabbed handfuls of golden straw and roared at the wall, the primal scream echoing into the dusk.

39

Dorcas Coleman stood in the centre of the wood panelled room. She fiddled with the layers of her skirt and smoothed down her bodice as she stood before the scrutinizing gaze of her contemporaries. Sat on a high backed ornately carved chair was Thomas Gist, the town's mayor. Mr Gist took too much pleasure from donning his official chains and conducting his investigations against the common citizens of the town in which he presided. He felt important with the fate of the innocent and the guilty in his hands and relished the power he had to chastise and punish delinquents against the ordinances and statures of the borough. The ruffles protruding from his collar pushed is greying beard outwards. To his left sat John Davie, Alderman for the town. Mr Davie also revelled in the respect he was owed for his role in the community. Mr. John Hill, the town clerk, sat at a desk, paper and quill ready. One of the Justices of peace sat in the chair adjacent to Mr Gist, the other stood to his colleague's right. Originally intended to advocate for the poor and the aged, the justices mostly served as jurors in local matters to support the town's officials.

"State your name."

Dorcas looked at the assembled men. "Dorcas. Dorcas Coleman."

"Are you the wife of John Coleman, mariner?"

"Yes I am." Dorcas glanced around the room. She wished that her husband was by her side. Dorcas had many reasons to accuse Susanna of a crime that could result in her execution. One of those reasons was Dorcas's belief that her beloved husband's heart had been stolen away.

"I did suffer from tormenting pains."

"Can you describe these pains Mrs Coleman?"

"I was pricked in my arms, stomach and heart." Dorcas touched the parts of her body where she'd experienced discomfort.

"When did this happen to you?" Dorcas felt that she was on trial, with four sets of eyes penetrating her resolve.

"About the end of the month of August."

"What year was this Mrs Coleman?"

"In the year of our Lord God 1680."

"This was twenty-three months ago Mrs Coleman. Why have you taken so long to come forward with your accusations?"

As Dorcas considered her response she pushed a stray hair back into the safety of her bonnet. "I have no explanation sirs." Dorcas knew that petty accusations and hearsay would not guarantee a conviction against the woman whose friendship she mistook for malice in a fit of jealousy.

"Have you experienced these pains before?"

"I have never before then been taken with such torment." Dorcas replied, her head bowed. She continued without prompting, "I was bewitched!"

"Why do you claim this, Mrs Coleman?"

"It was Doctor Beare, he said I was." Dorcas spoke with conviction, as if the Doctors words were gospel.

The assembled panel questioned Dorcas as to why the town's physician would blame witchcraft for Dorcas' aliments. She could offer no reason other than his failure to cure her. However, she had her own condemning evidence that she was to share with the town's appointed official.

Any previous nerves that Dorcas felt standing in front of the town's elite evaporated as she seized the opportunity to seal Susanna's fate. "I saw her."

"Saw who, Mrs Coleman?"

"Susanna Edwards." Dorcas went on to state that Susanna would enter her bedchamber and had been doing so for the most part of two years. "I saw her."

"How did she get into your bedchamber, Mrs Coleman?"

"She used witchcraft. She bewitched me." The acting detectives probed Dorcas on the validity of her allegations. "She told me. I went to the clink and she said she did do this to me. She did cause bodily harm against me."

"Was anyone with you at the time?"

"No, we were alone and she did ask me to pray." The jurors urged Dorcas to continue with her statement. "But I would not. Not with a witch."

Dorcas was proud of her testimony. John walked her home before returning to give his own testimony.

The next witness to be hauled in front of the egotistical leaders of the town was Thomas Bremincom who stood on the same spot as Dorcas had. Holding his tatty wide brimmed hat with both hands, Thomas waited confidently for his inquisition to begin.

"It was some two years past that Dorcas became very sick."

"What is your relationship to the Colemans?"

"I am John's uncle."

"And how come is it that you were dispatched to Doctor Beare, and not the good lady's husband?"

"John was at sea. He had been for some weeks prior. Dorcas did beg me to go unto the Doctor and seek out a remedy to ease her pains."

Although Thomas showed no anxiety in his statement, his hands betrayed him under the accusing gaze of his peers. He discreetly wiped his sweaty palms on his olive-green breeches.

Thomas corroborated Dorcas' testimony, that Doctor Beare attended his patient and that it was beyond his skill to cure her. "She was bewitched!" Thomas almost shouted the doctor's verdict.

The mayor continued to question Thomas, who revealed that he too had witnessed Susanna in the bedroom of Dorcas Coleman and the strained nature of the relationship of the ladies.

"Dorcas tried attacking Susanna?" John Davie was secretly amused at the rivalry between the two women.

"Dorcas did try but she was unable to raise from her seat." Thomas looked around the room, dominated by various shades of brown. The attire of the justices matched the depressing décor. "She saw Susanna, in her very chamber and tried with all her might to strike her. It was the pains that stopped her. The pains that Susanna did inflict upon her." Thomas was urged to continue with his confession. "I tried to help her up, as did John." The gentleman clarified who was in attendance and had witnessed Susanna enter the bedroom.

"Yes, John was there also but Susanna did back away and escape."

"Why did you or John not approach Susanna and stop her?"

"Because Dorcas did slide from her chair in her attempt to go after Susanna, however her legs would not comply with her demands."

"Could John not attend solely to his wife whilst you apprehended the suspect?"

"No. We, together, could not. Dorcas was in such a sad condition but we could not lift her from the ground."

"Two men could not lift one infirm woman to her feet?"

"It was Susanna." Thomas gestured wildly with his hands, his hat flapping with the force of his movements. "She spelled her to be lame, until the witch was gone over the stairs." Thomas was so desperate to back his friend that he expanded his oath to include his conjecture on practitioners of the craft. "Dorcas could neither see nor speak, by reason that her pains were so violent upon her. That is the hold that Susanna had on Dorcas but she did surely know which way Susanna fled."

"If Dorcas could not see or speak how do you know this."

"She, Dorcas, pointed with her hand and I did follow."

"And what did you do when you chased Susanna out the fore door?"

"I watched her, then returned to John and Dorcas." The men enquired as what happened further. "Dorcas was improved with Susanna gone. John had sat her in her chair."

Having given his testimony, Thomas was expelled from the company of the gathered justices and took up the company of the local rouges, drowning the memory in malty ale whilst he waited for his nephew.

A short recess was called for refreshments. All this sitting around listening was tiring work.

John Coleman strode proudly into the room. He held his head high and faced his old childhood friends.

Stating his name and occupation John prepared to give his evidence against the woman he secretly harboured feelings for.

"My wife has been suffering a long time from a sickness."

"Can you describe this sickness?"

"She is affected in a very strange and unusual manner." The men's facial expressions gave John cause to continue with his explanation. "She did say she is tormented by pains." John confirmed that he had not witnessed much of his wife's sickness and relied on the support and testimony of Thomas to care for his wife.

"What have you done to ease your wife's suffering?"

"I have sought far and near for remedy."

"And you have found none?" Asked John Davie.

"No sirs. I have found none. Not in my travels and not in Doctor Beare. I have been prescribed no directions to heal her. " Thomas shook his head in recognition of his failure to find a cure for his wife. He answered faithfully the questions put forward to him. Johns profession meant that he could be at sea for days or months at a time, escaping from his wife's manic episodes. John was a sought-after mariner and navigated many trips to foreign lands as well as frequently sailing the English coast, importing and exporting local goods.

"It is my uncle Thomas who resides with us. It is he who informed me that the good doctor said my wife is bewitched."

"Do you agree with the doctor's verdict?"

"Why it is past his skills, so must be the work of the witch Susanna." John corroborated the evidence of his wife and uncle. "Some three months last past Susanna did come to visit my wife."

"And what happened between the two women?"

"Susanna did curse my wife to be speechless." John's voice was starting to raise, yet he was prompted to continue. "Dorcas was sitting in a chair, in our bed chamber, when that hag Susanna did enter." John took a stained cloth from the pocket of his sand-coloured trousers and wiped his perspiring forehead. Composing himself, John affirmed that his wife did indeed fall from the chair, blaming the presence of Susanna for his wifes deteriorating condition and subsequent recovery, once the alleged sorceress had vacated the property.

"Is it correct that your wife did try to attack the aforesaid Susanna?" Mr Coleman was quick to defend his wife's actions. Mr Gist could see the genuine fear in his eyes as he recalled his wife's fragile frame crumbling to the floor, from where he was unable to help her to her feet.

"Is there anything further you would like to add Mr Coleman?"

"Only that my wife has had this sickness ever since unto this day, with some intermissions. And I did witness them on many occasions, at midnight, mixing something in a crock. The Devil did give them something from his hand that they did immediately put into the babbling crock. He then put his hand into a bag and did pull out something bright. He carried the bag at his side."

"What did he do with this bright object?"

"He handed it to each of the crones and did then disappear into the trees by the rectory at Parsonage Close. I know it to be them, I recognised the cracked voice of Susanna." John went on to tell the mayor that the women, dressed in grey hooded cloaks, burst into wild laughter as they sang songs. "I was riveted to the spot at the sight of the wild orgie."

This had the justices wishing they had been present, and they conjured erotic thoughts of half-naked women cavorting in the woodland.

"I did see one of them take a bucket of water, seize her broom and perform a spell, but I could not hear the words she used but she saith that thrice the brinded cat hath mewed." Mr Coleman genuinely believed the cat to be a familiar of the witches and as devilish a creature as its masters. The mariner took little prompting to continue. "Upon the chanting, a ferocious wind suddenly arose and lightnings flashed angrily through the sky as I rushed away home, and when I got to my door a black cat did dash through it! I was trembling with fear and perspiring with affright when I did hear my wife Dorcas cry out in pain. I concluded at once my wife was bewitched."

John gave a short respectful bow before exiting the local court room and joining Thomas in the tavern.

They had their pick of drinking establishments. Despite the councils promise to force the residents of Biddiford to reign in their drinking, they had failed to curb the enthusiasm for alcohol. They issued fines and imprisoned offenders but it had little to no effect on the inhabitants of the small harbour town. If they stopped the supply routes by land, the booze would arrive by boat, by legitimate or unlawful means. For every monitored legal drinking den, there was a back room keeping the residents inebriated.

The uncle and nephew made it home without incident. Susanna did not get any cell mates that evening.

40

Every day was a little worse than the last. With every passing day they lost hope, they lost weight and they lost their determination.

The jailers treated them according to their own conscious. Jacob, who had been brought up by his maternal grandmother, treated them like nannas in a care home, slipping them an extra crust or lightening their work load. Most were indifferent, ensuring the inmates did not escape or kill each other until their shift was over and they could forget the smell and harshness until their next time on duty. Martin was one of the cruel ones, who got too much satisfaction from their role. Setting impossible goals so they could beat the enslaved workers when they weren't met or mixing dust into the gruel that was fed to the convicts.

Temperance was defiant in the face of adversity. She had won twice before and projected the confidence that she would be victorious again. It was not a confidence that she felt when the hush of night settled over the distraught inhabitants. Mary had sunk into a deep depression, her spirit for life extinguished. She missed Bartholomew.

There was a room inside the jail, not much larger than a broom cupboard that was reserved for punishment, a kind of solitary confinement. When their wasn't a poor soul being held in darkness, devoid of food and interaction, it could be used to interview a suspect, when an official record wasn't required.

Susanna waited in the cell; the door was open but there was no possibility of escape. The chains around her wrist were secured to a massive iron ring bolted to the wall. Susanna racked her brain for the reason and could only fathom that it was Mr Gist, come to offer her a deal to testify against Temperance or Mary. It was Dorcas Coleman who had come for a word with the captive. It was evident in Susanna's demeaner when she realised that the meeting would be of no benefit to her.

"If you tell me what you have done I will put in a good word for you." No amount of reasoning or pleading had brought the answer from Susanna's lips that Dorcas was hoping for, so she changed her tactics. "I know what you are and what you have done. I swear to the Great Goddess Diana that I will not stop until you burn. The truth, Susanna. Tell me" This brought the confession that Grace had been bewitched. Susanna was hungry and her leg ached from being stood. She could see in people's eyes and their body language that they were scared of her and fear bred self-preservation which lead to witch hunts, which cost lives. Susanna was not a fool; she knew it would take a miracle to save her life.

The town was concentrated on the emerging trial. Trails of people walked past the cells daily, hoping to catch a glimpse of the of the eminent witches. Some were expecting elaborate displays of magic but, much to their disappointment, what they saw were bodies ravaged with age, lack of sleep and physical chores that drained what strength remained. Not that it would stop idiotic townsfolk from embellishing the facts to fanciful proportions.

Betty, Abigail and Mary were scared witless. Abigail had bravely broken into each cottage in turn and ransacked it of magical paraphernalia, the same night that her mentors were detained by the authorities. Betty would have happily taken the job but her size was not conducive to breaking and entering, she had the stealth of an elephant, not a cat. All they could do was wait and keep everything crossed that their tutors did not betray them. They worried their new associations would lead to their arrests but the women had been discrete in their training and the only three that had knowledge of their involvement would take the secret to the grave.

The property's would not stay empty for long, there was a long list of the needy who would be housed in the adjacent homes, but, until the sentence was passed the witches were the unpaying tenants and their possessions were their own.

A candle could be seen through the window of Temperance's front room. The naked flame moved around as if the holder was searching for something. "Damn you old woman. Where in the Goddesses' name is that book?" The would-be thief left drawers upturned and furniture overturned, neither careful nor respectful in their search. Susanna and Mary's house would also be informally raided and neither would provide the answers that were sought.

With the power of light and dark on her side, Elizabeth would be unstoppable.

This was William Herbert's second chance to avenge the death of his father. His statement came rather late in the proceedings but he was granted an audience and it would be valuable evidence in the substantial case they had built.

He was on the doorstep of the town hall before the astute men arrived, though he would have to wait patiently for his turn to talk. Cleaned poorly by the light of a candle, his boots gave testament to his farming legacy. As far as he was concerned, they could have his mud as well as his pent-up anger over the death of his father.

William sped through the formalities and introductions so he could have his say. He tried his hardest, unsuccessfully, for his distain of Temperance not to seep into his voice.

"Near, or upon the second day of February, in the year of our Lord God 1670, I did hear my father to declare on his deathbed, that Temperance Lloyd, of Biddiford, had bewitched him unto death."

"Can you state for the records the name of your father?"

"My father was named William Herbert also."

"Do you have any further information to give."

"Yes sirs. My father did declare that I, with the rest of my father's relations, should view his body after he is deceased and that by his body we should see what prints and marks Temperance had made upon his body." William took a moment to steady himself for the death of his father still hurt him deeply.

"My father did lay his blood to charge Temperance and desired to see her apprehended for the same, for his death."

"I believe that Temperance was indeed arrested on your accusation."

"Yes, this was accordingly done. She was accused for the same but she was acquitted at the assizes."

"But you believe that she was guilty, Mr Herbert?"

"Yes. Upon the fourth day of July, now last past, I went to the prison, in Biddiford, where Temperance was, concerning Grace Thomas. I did demand of her whether she had done bodily harm or hurt unto my late father. Temperance answered and said, 'surely William, I did kill thy father. I did demand of her further whether she had done any hurt or harm to one Lydia Burman."

"Who is Lydia Burman?"

"A spinster of Biddiford." William had been conducting his own trial and was there to present the evidence he had gathered. "I did get Temperance to answer and she said that she was the cause of death." The two woman had come into the others orbit as they vied for the attention of William's father. Neither of the ladies had any chance of winning. Mr Herbert's kind nature had misguided their hearts.

"Temperance was charged with no crime against a Lydia Burman."

"No sirs. I demanded of her why she had not confessed so much when she was in prison the last time and she did answer that her time was not yet expired."

"And how did Temperance know this?"

"For the Devil had given her greater power and a longer time." William wasn't content to stop at the two deaths, he had more information he wished to convey. "In addition, I did hear her, Temperance Lloyd, to confess that she was the cause of the death of Anne Fellow, and she said she was the cause of the bewitching out of one of the eyes of Jane Dallyn." William had finished with the unfounded allegations.

"Do you refer to Anne Fellow, daughter of Edward Fellow, a gent, of Biddiford?"

"Yes, that is correct." Like his father, William junior was a handsome specimen but his heart was twisted and mean, unlike his fathers. William expected a return on any investment he made, whether that be in money or affection. In return for the haberdashery repairs Anne made, she would be rewarded with a tryst in the barn. It was an arrangement that William's wife remained ignorant of but one that affected him adversely in the groin, for Anne was his favourite lover.

"And the Jane to which you make a remark, is that the wife of Simon Dallyn of Biddiford, a mariner?"

"Yes Sirs, that is also correct." William's evidence was recorded, and he returned, contented, to the family estate.

41

People lined the streets to watch the three eminent characters leave their home town for what would turn out to be the last time. The atmosphere was wild with excitement. Fearful mothers covered the eyes of their babes as the trio of accused women passed, lest their precious offspring become bewitched, and their ears as fellow Biddifordians shouted jibes and execrations or hissed. Chained together by the wrist and ankle the progress from the jail to the town hall was laborious down the steep cobbled hill. Dirty rags acted as gags, to prevent them from spelling any other person. Intrigued teens watched from windows and rooftops. Nosey crew keen on gossip to take back with the wool they were exporting leaned against the wall, pipes billowing with thick chocking smoke. A brave soul risked the wrath of a witch by hurling a rotten pear in their direction. The aim fell short and the decaying fruit exploded in pulverised mess at the justice's feet.

Mary lingered for a moment on the doorstep of the town hall, under the arched doorway, her heart breaking at the hatred and fear that surround her. A tall woman, far braver than the fruit thrower, rushed forward from the heaving crowd. She grabbed hold of the old, withered arm and tore the flesh down the full length of Mary's bony limb, with a bodkin. Onlookers yelled in delight as a crimson trickle of blood dripped methodically into a stream and Mary cried out in pain. Her injury was crudely bandaged.

After being presented at the town hall, the women were loaded into a waiting cart, to be transported to prove their innocence, or be punished for their guilt, at the assizes. On the rear of the cart, a cage had been constructed to hold the prisoners, owing to many having been lost over the years. Several fell to their premature deaths over the side, for the journey to Exeter was long and fraught with many dangers on the winding, bumpy road. One had escaped during the driver's extended stay in one of the hundreds of taverns that littered the wayside and another had been freed in a daring, yet successful, prison break by friends unwilling to lose their partner in crime. The outlaws and highway men were a constant threat to the officers but rarely attacked a consignment of stinking, unfortunate convicts.

A thick chain and heavy ornate lock secured the door. An arm could be thrust through the lattice of squares that formed each wall, not that it did those captive inside any good. Unless the day was mild they would arrive sodden or dehydrated for the construction exposed them to the elements and allowed common folk to torment the jailbirds by prodding them with sticks, ogling or jeering at the unfortunate spectacles.

Temperance, Susanna and Mary had been deliberately kept separate during their stay at His Majesty's pleasure. None of the women had been permitted even a minute in the others company since each of their arrests, for fear that they would collude on a spell so powerful they couldn't be stopped.

Temperance was the first to be roughly forced to mount the rickety steps and needed to steady herself on the bars. She looked around for a last reprieve but none were forthcoming as Susanna was unceremoniously escorted to the cart. Temperance shuffled pathetically towards the driver to make room for her doomed companions. Mary's head hung low, too ashamed to make eye contact with the folk she had known all her life. Ms Trembles sunk to her knees in the stale filth that lined the bed of the wagon.

The beautiful scenery of rolling fields dotted with cotton candy sheep and magnificent forestry teeming with wild animals was ignored by the women as the uncomfortable holding cell wound its way towards Rougemont castle and they were lost in their own troubled thoughts. Temperance stood proudly and disobediently, swaying with the motion of the cart. Susanna initially stood rebelliously alongside her before her arthritic joints forced her to sit beside Mary, where she attempted to comfort the sobbing apprentice.

A fanfare of curious onlookers heralded their arrival at the former roman legionary fortress. Without stopping, the driver negotiated the open archway, passing quickly under the fortified iron gate, a spiked guillotine if the mechanism failed. The horse's hooves resonated off the cobblestones as the cart screeched to a halt. From their raised vantage point, they could see the scaffold of the Maudlin drop which featured a single gallows whose noose swung stiffly, as well as a blackened stake, onto which the bodies were tied as searing flames engulfed their hair and clothing, the crackling of skin and the smell of burnt flesh wafting towards the river Exe.

A semi-decomposed body stood lopsidedly to attention in a gibbet, a stark warning against committing an offence, could be seen clearly from the entrance. Ravens clung to the bars with their talons and pulled off chunks of dead flesh, squawking at rivals eager to pluck away a squishy eyeball or peck at a lifeless digit. It was reminiscent of the two near skeletal remains that hung from cages suspended from the top of St Thomas' church that they passed as the horses thundered into the city.

The expansive grounds of the castle were lined with trees, whose leaves now in full bloom would soon fall and litter the manicured landscape. It was a beautiful yet taunting place to spend the final days of your life. For those that commit their crimes within the confines of the city's ancient walls, their lives would be terminated in this picturesque setting. To whom the sentence of death was imposed for an offence orchestrated beyond the city's boundaries, their condemned souls would be taken to Gallows Cross in the neighbouring village of Heavitree.

It would be a month before Temperance would confess to anything. It was reported that she made a free confession of her discovered crimes and many more exploits, including the wanton destruction of sailing vessels.

42

The date was Tuesday the 18th of August 1682.

The three women stood at the bar whilst the indictment against them was read out. None had impudence enough to deny what they there were accused of. Temperance's attitude was deemed as unreasonable and she owned the accusations, stating that she had been in league with the Devil twenty years and upwards and that in the term of those years she had been guilty of many cruelties and by hellish power afflicted both man and beast. The persistent unearthly presence that had been consistent in their lives had abandoned them to their fate, going no further with them than the prison door. They no longer felt the guiding pull of Hell to direct and justify their actions.

Susanna and Mary, who were instructed in the damnable skill of witchcraft by the old influencer, acknowledged that they had served five years to her to learn her accursed art and during this time they saw and were acquainted with many wonderful and unlawful tricks.

They confirmed that they had not been idle in their hellish practices but had served their master faithfully and been gratefully rewarded for their diabolical indulgence.

"We have been the servants to the old one for five years, to learn the arts and misery of hellish, damnable, accursed and most to be lamented witchcraft." Susanna spoke on behalf of herself and Mary, who was suffering badly with depression. She had assumed they would survive the trial as Temperance previously had and had all but forgotten the plan they had devised on their way to the assizes.

"What did you do in these five years?"

"We grew to be as dexterious as our devilish tutor, trying our experiments upon man and beast, to the Injury of both."

"You committed these acts willingly?"

Susanna and Mary appeared pensive, as they had planned. "She was the introducer of our misery and we served both the Devil and her for five years of slavery." The women had concocted that their best defence would be for them to appear meek and gullible beside the temptress Temperance.

"Do you think they will get away with it?" The middle-aged woman sandwiched between Mr Deacon and her husband said, her gentle voice full of concern.

"No" Replied Mr Deacon. "Heaven's vengeance never fails to follow such offenders who do wickedly, presumptuously and profanely, make use of the Devil to satisfy their impious wills. These hellish agents find themselves outcasts from everlasting happiness and have grown insolent in the cursed conceits. It is clear they are making use of the art, which they will dearly pay for, and you shall see that will be the case. "

The judges, jury and all the other men and women in the room, listened to how Temperance was first tempted with a devilish encounter. This destitute woman was accosted in the early afternoon, whilst on her way home and labouring under an almost insupportable burden of brome, with a civil offer of friendly assistance. But on viewing him, she discerned his feet to resemble those of an Ox! Her reply to him used the name of our Lord God and the tempter immediately transformed himself into a flame and so disappeared. Upon arriving at her own poor habitation, she saw a black dog going along the entry. She thought it grew still bigger and bigger but that in vanishing, she presently saw the same black gentleman, who but a little before met her in the brome field.

Now, being grown a little wiser than he was before, proceeded with those subtle insinuations that he prevailed with her to consent to his contract. She signed it with her own blood, which the ingenious Devil drew from her with little or no pain. No sooner was the instrument signed, he immediately issued out his commands. The First of which, was for her to go to one Madam Thomas and hurt her. Which she could not have done without the assistance of her patron, who conveyed her invisible into the room where the gentleman and his lady were asleep in bed. There she did bruise the said Madam Thomas in a most cruel manner. They left unseen. They lay together. She was not yet devil enough for his more pernicious enterprise to kill Grace and refused to comply to his command. As punishment the Devil struck her across the face, leaving the mark of his fist.

The Devil's feud with the ageing Ms Thomas, a white witch who worshipped the Goddess Diana and could not be corrupted or influenced by his dark charms, had lasted for several years. Her devotion to the Huntress was pure and good. He tormented this poor gentlewoman regularly with some supernatural affliction or other, for which she received no remedy from any physician that was sufficient. Sometimes she would be seized with fits of raving, sometimes of laughing but always of pain.

Much of what had been established in Biddiford was rehashed, rephased and the answers repurposed to fit the new judge and jury. They admitted to the physical torture and their improper relationships. This time they impeached one another.

"It is alleged that the door was closed." The Lord Chief Justice Sir Frances North relished his coveted role as judge. If he had his way he would be the jury and executioner too.

"That is false, for the door was open!" was shouted out in an attempt to provide their own defence. However, the response was seen by the judge and jury as a tacitly implied act and consequently helped to convince the panel of their guilt and that of the other two.

"It is put to you that you have been the cause of the destruction of many ships. By what means do you cause this devastation?"

"I have often placed eggshells in the sea." Temperance was questioned repeatedly regarding her nautical behaviour, when she made a startling announcement that brought a momentary silence to the hearing. "I am most repentant for throwing a youth overboard." Her voiced oozed with commendation as she spoke of the youngster's shape and beauty.

Sir Thomas Raymond, who served as co-judge was a passive, mild mannered man who lacked the dexterity or spirit of his colleague and would not oppose the popular opinion. Regardless of his own conviction, he was merely the puppet of the experienced and ruthless Sir Frances North and would do little personally to impeach or exonerate a case. Overseeing the case was the Lord Chief Justice, the Lord Keeper Guilford. Mr Guildford had happily let Sir Raymond represent the crown on his behalf at such cases as those that involve women stricken with melancholy madness. However, he was in attendance for fear that Sir Raymond's inert morals would result in the hangman's employ.

Additional justices had been drafted in to manage the proceedings. Word of mouth had spread like wildflowers and interested, or nosy parties had come from across Devon to witness the trial of the grand witch who had escaped the wrath of God and hatred of King Charles the second. Twice. The volume of evidence and number of witnesses meant that the trial would last two days. That night the inns were full and the taverns drunk dry.

Amongst the revellers was the Lord Justice, who for the most part enjoyed his job. Mr Guilford however did not believe in the existence of witches or the use of witchcraft and creatures such as Lucifer and dreaded the trying of a witch, which luckily was seldom in his career. For this he had himself been accused of having no religion, which is why he would side with the verdict of the judges to appease the assembled audience and carry out whatever sentence was deemed proportionate to the crime, regardless of his opinion of guilt.

"When a poor wretch is brought to trial upon the account of witchcraft, there is, at the heels of her, a popular rage that does little less than demand her to be put to death." Mr Guilford was seated with educated gentleman, some of the same persuasion, who nodded at the sentiment and some whose faith was strong, opposed Mr Guilford's views.

Mr Justice Rainsford told of a case he had presided over the previous year in which Sir James Long had complained heavily about a woman he claimed to be a witch and petitioned the Lord keeper, that if she were to be found not guilty, to keep her under lock and key for fear that his estate should be worth nothing if she were to be freed. Against his better judgement and for the bribe of a crown, or two, or three, Mr Rainsford complied. At the stately cost of 2s 6d a week, the innocent victim remained in prison in Salisbury. The following week she was sent to be cared for at her local nick for the much cheaper sum of 1s 6d weekly.

Guilford recalled a case at Taunton-Dean, in which a wizard was tried for bewitching a young girl. The adolescent spat straight pins from her mouth and onto the floor as evidence of the sorcery against her. Mr Guilford was inclined to think she had the pins concealed within her mouth, for curved pins would have been a more magical allure but was forced to find him guilty under the wave of popular consensus and the physical effects of a supposed enchantment.

"I can only hope that a judge is so clear and open as to declare against that impious vulgar opinion, that the devil himself has the power to torment and kill innocent children, or that he is pleased to divert himself with the good people's cheese, butter, pigs, and geese but I fear that they too will be influenced by the scriptures of God." He knew they would have likely been raised on the same Christian values as the ignorant and foolish rabble who so desired the terminal punishment but he would not act on his own virtues or principles.

"To mistake requires a very prudent and moderate carriage in a judge, whereby to convince, rather by detecting of the fraud, than by denying authoritatively such power to be given to old women. But power they do give to them by naming them as witches and name their preternatural exploits." Several of his peers found his atheist approach unsettling but his demure nature retained their respect.

43

Deacon had a pocket full of sharpened pencils and a wad of paper where upon he could scribble notes and important details, which he would later embellish for the amusement of his audience. Where he couldn't attend a newsworthy event in person he would use second hand evidence to vilify his claims. He had written several publications and basked in the moderate success of having his name in print. He liked to start with a brief introduction to the reader and would often forgo a prologue, keen to deliver the facts as he believed them to be.

He'd heard talk in the tavern of the impending witchcraft accusations and was determined to make his fortune with the demise of the accused.

"Ah yes." He marvelled at his own genius "Man's enemy, soul destroyers. All three, authors of wickedness, stricken in years, which might have taught them more grace." He was on a roll and his fingers worked as quick as his brain. "These poor souls made an unfortunate interchange, accepting a Hell for a Heaven and in doing so, they lost the love of the Great Creator, whose smiles are more precious than refined gold, and were damned to everlasting destruction for pleasing the Devil." Mr Deacon was a man that had never missed a Sunday service. A righteous man, he could not fathom why any person should take delight in nothing more than conversing with Devils, who he had been taught, seek nothing but destruction , Gods dishonour and to overthrow man by emptying Heaven and filling Hell.

"They have aimed at nothing but ruin, embraced folly instead of wisdom and presented pleasure for eternal pain in taking flames for crowns. They have misery for happiness, have changed God for a Devil, and a soul for Hell." The gathered patrons agreed wholeheartedly with the medieval journalist's sentiments and assisted him with names to which they called the Devil.

"He is the inventor of mischief, an author of lies." Said one woman. "He is the betrayer of souls." Said another. One to his right said. "Lucifer is an unsatisfied deceiver and an enemy to God." The same woman, dressed in a plain frock and with matching bonnet, described the witches as inhumane and was horrified at their preposterous actions.

Temperance stood resolutely and feared not what should become of her immortal soul.

"I have caused several ships at sea to be cast away, to the loss of many men's lives and the prejudice of many others."

"And you alone, or together, are responsible for the death of the boy?"

The women had, so far, confessed to all the accusations. "No. We did no harm to the boy or sink his ship. He fell from the topmast of another ship and did break his neck or drown. For that we did not do."

"What will you confess too?"

"I was instrumental in the death of Hannah Thomas." She audaciously declared.

"How did you end Hannah's life?"

"By the pretence of love. I squeezed her in her arms so long, until the blood gushed out of her mouth." Several of the female members of the crowd swooned at the thought and had to be supported by men folk. Temperance was impudent that she had done many wicked exploits by the power of her hellish discipline.

"Have you harmed others?"

"Why yes, we have been the death of two more, besides several others that we have lamed by our hellish art." They all confessed to the destruction of many castle, both great and small, as well as many petty and tedious crimes, that paled in comparison to murder.

"We have a report that you, all being of one mind, exercised your devilish arts upon one Mr. Hann who is a minister in those parts. What have you to say for yourselves." Mr Hann was described as a person of good repute and honest conversation.

Mary and Susanna nodded at Temperance, who said "We did intend mischief and misery to Mr Hann, but an overruling power prevented us."

"And did you seek revenge for failing to exercise your diabolism upon his body, for he sought his souls eternal happiness whilst you designed your everlasting ruin."

"Yes. We laid our charms upon his cattle, so that those cows that used to give milk, when they came to be milked would gave blood." The judge consulted the statement from the astonished milkers.

Michael Ogilby was called to the stand to give his testimony. New evidence was introduced in which Michael graciously described the inflicted suffering from abnormal fits of giggling. He took the credit for apprehending the slippery sorceress. Strangely, Temperance seemed extraordinarily joyful at the sight of her old adversary.

"I know something more than the country physicians of the effects of sorcery. I instructed that the bottoms of her feet must be held and covered with hands, to good success for it always stayed her laughter. It provoked consequently more effectual than the magical charm by which she was enchanted." The Amberley witches had tried various herbal cures and acupuncture techniques to ease the side-effects of the warring covens.

Before Michael was swallowed up in the seething onlookers, Temperance begged to touch his hand. Surprisingly, he complied with her request. Her bony fingers dug into the flesh on his hand as she grasped it tight and said, "I know not but that your advice and prayers might do me good."

The grip on his hand was intense and as he went to pull away, Temperance told him, "The time you were riding between Banton and Taunton and your horse become stuck in the midst of the water; I was there." Doubt flicked across the rector's eyes; he had seen no-one. "It would neither go forward nor backward until you whispered, 'well Satan, thou hast not long time to continue to torment to human nature before thou shalt be chained up'." Fear was now reflected in his bloodstained eyes as he recalled the unnerving event. Temperance continued, "At your words the Devil fled away in the shape of a bull, roaring most terribly." With a wink she said, "I was there though invisible." She released her hold on him.

Dumbfounded, Michael stood gawking at the crone. He puzzled how she had she known.

Another witness was sworn onto the stand, then another, and another. This continued as the judges and jury, all men, heeded similar tales of torment and witchcraft. Protagonists Susanna and Mary were portrayed as lesser villains, their parts not as monstrous. It was a last-ditch effort; Temperance played her part well; in the hopes the others would receive a lesser sentence.

Sitting in the court, Lord Keeper Guilford read the information taken by the justices, which were laid out upon the table. Much of the evidence he found trifling and the transfiguration into animal form he found absurd.

With the evidence and defence having been presented, it was down to the jury to decide the fate of the three eminent magicians. Whilst they deliberated the gaoler was ordered to secure the prisoners and Mr. Guildford took one last chance to influence the sentence.

"These women are scarce alive." He uttered discreetly to the judges. "They are overwhelmed with a sadness and waking dreams,and so stupid as no one could suppose they knew either the construction or consequence of what they said. Do you not think, in light of their opinions of themselves being false, that their confession ought not to be taken against themselves, without a plain evidence that it was rational and sensible? They are acting no more than that of a lunatic, or distracted person." The judges, equally resolute in their holy merits, would not be swayed against the full and fanciful accounts of the dark arts in all its preternatural glory. Though the Lord Keeper didn't want innocent people to die, he feared more the re-emergence of the witch hunting craze that had been prevalent for a century and taken countless lives on the flimsiest of testimony.

The minister was brought forth to offer the witches the chance to purge their souls before God and denounce their dedication to his fallen son. They received a lecture full of wholesome, yet entirely useless, advice. Susanna and Mary remained silent. Temperance, with a lopsided smile that showed missing teeth, puffed her chest and launched into the common prayer, with a few alterations of her own.

"Our father, who art in Heaven, hallowed be thy name: thy kingdom come; thy will be done on earth as it is in Heaven. Give us this day our daily bread; and forgive us our trespasses as we forgive those that trespass against us and lead us into temptation, deliver us to evil. For thine is the kingdom, the power and the glory, for ever and ever." She ended with neither faiths version of 'so be it', protesting that she could say no more.

In his closing statement Sir North reminded the jury that Temperance was a seventy-year-old who had been the Devil's slave for thirty of those years. An exaggeration from an earlier statement. Justice Raymond took a moment to address the jury himself. He had the title and authority, which afforded him the opportunity to gently speak his mind, though he wielded no real influence because he simply was not callous enough.

After a long day of testimony and hearsay, Sir Raymond turned to the jury and expressed his personal opinion of the three innocent women who he saw as simply being weary of their lives, yet greatly skilled to convict themselves with detailed descriptions delivered in such a natural fashion that he feared the jurors could not disbelieve them. He implored the jury to come to the verdict they know to be true and right. "Consider that it is proper for them to be carried to the parish from whence they came and that the said parish should be charged with their maintenance."

Just the suggestion that the women would be brought back without punishment had the neighbours, who had travelled the distance and suffered greatly due to their diabolical practices, up in arms. They needed to ensure that the hard work they had put into place in their home town came to fruition here.

"If these witches are sent home in peace, none of us can be promised a minutes security on our persons or estates." The disembodied voice, which belonged to Anne Wakely, rose over the congregation.

He had sought out the position under the impression that he would carry out the law, prosecute the guilty and be a saviour to the innocent. He soon learned that doing right thing and being righteous, were not the same and his outlook would often differ to his colleagues. He had earned his position in society and had not forgotten his roots. In his opinion, it was the oppressing poverty in which they lived that had constrained them to their current predicament and may have aided their apparent death wish.

"Can you believe the wicked life and miserable death of these three gross offenders, chiefly the cunning old serpent Temperance? I shall call them witches and not women." Mr Deacon turned to the woman to his right.

"Surely, I would not have believed it had I not heard how they slighted God's commandments and despised a Christ in favour of laying with the Devil, the original source of all knavery and vice."

"Nine nights together Agnes. Nine!" The lady to the right of her had joined in the discussion.

"And with paps an inch long the Devil did suck her cold body to provoke her lechery!!!" The youngest of Deacon's literacy harem piped up, jiggling her own breasts in the restrictive corset. "But she was a poor woman and earnt her living by the sweat of her brow."

"Surely he did take hold of her poverty in laying his bait and it is the Devil's politics to fish in troubled waters and erect his trophies upon the destruction of such miserable creatures."

Martha, a sensible Christian woman on his left muttered, "And they lost Heaven to purchase Hell, at the dear rate of their immortal souls."

"They said the Devil would come to them at night in several shapes, sometimes like a hound. A hound Agnes! And I thought your William was an animal in bed." The flirtatious youth received an elbow in her ribs for her remark.

"And he hunted before them. I wonder what he caught."

"Souls my dear. No doubt he was on the hunt for souls." Martha chose to ignore the incorrigible young adult and try her own divine interpretation. "The poor wretch did struck hands with the insulting master and have become his bond-slave and instruments of hell and mischief."

The jury returned a verdict.
Guilty.
The judge delivered the sentences.

Death.
Death.
Death.

44

The date was Friday the 25th of August 1682.

The trek to the hanging tree was a mile and half from Rougemont. It started with much commotion on behalf of Mary who was extremely obstinate and would not go freely. She lay on the ground and refused to get up. The guards were forced to drag her from the cell and transport her on horseback. She was thrown over the stallions back and tied down to prevent an unlikely escape or the risk of a fall that would render the hangman's job obsolete. Temperance's only worry seemed to be consuming as much food as she could and she went all the way eating, seemingly unconcerned.

The procession had grown in number, hangers on pursuing like pack mules, shouting words of pity or condemnation. Mr. J. Deacon was one such individual who had been avidly following the case to its conclusion and was quick to comment, to all that would listen, how Mary was very loath to receive her deserved doom and how the old witches had recited the Lord's Prayer backwards. However, for someone with such an opinionated persona, he had incorrectly stated both Temperance and Mary to have the surname Floyd, proving Mr. Deacon was not as scholarly as he proclaimed himself to be.

They arrived to find a scene of confusion, the noise deafening. It took the sheriff several minutes to calm the crowd and bring a sense of order to the proceedings. It didn't last long.

As was usual on such occasions as a public hanging, Heavitree was packed with spectators who come to watch as the life drained from the eyes of the dying. Hordes of curious men, women and children from across Devon assembled in the late morning sunshine.

Michael Ogilby stood on the brow of a small mound. He could see well enough and had no need to hear their last words, he had heard enough. He hoped his distance was a safe one from any curse that may fall from their dying lips. That didn't stop the knot of dread that twisted at his insides, neither did the sip of whiskey from his hip flask.

The morbid entertainment would be talked about at the market for days and some executions had been known to inspire a sonnet or two. This one would spawn a ballad that was sung for centuries, as a warning. Amongst the crowd was a young woman by the name of Alice Molland. Three nooses hung from a branch as thick as a man's torso, beneath each rope a simple trestle was positioned.

Itchy robes had replaced the threadbare clothing they had arrived at the gaol in, and their feet were bare and bleeding from the walk to the place of their execution. Stones lacerated the soles of their wrinkled feet and they shoulders ached from having their hands tied tightly behind their backs. Long silver hair that was normally tamed into a bun or plait was now wild and free.

'This is crazy.' John Carwythen thought to himself. He feared the women may be lynched If he didn't commence with formalities quickly. Hearing the substance of the last words and confessions of Temperance, Susanna and Mary was a challenging feat for the sheriff, owing to the volume of noise and mayhem caused by the crowd baying for blood. Amongst them were some familiar faces including that of Mr Gist, who had travelled, comfortably, to the counties hub to ensure that his version of justice was carried out.

"Mary Trembles." The minister, Mr Hann addressed the youngest of the accused. "What have you to say as to the crime you are now to die for?" As the minister integrated the woman for the final time, the executioner hooked the nooses around their necks, in preparation for their imminent deaths.

"I have spoke as much as I can speak already; and can speak no more." Mary's frail voice was barely audible above the racket the mocking crowd was making.

"In what shape did the Devil come to you?"

"The Devil came to me once, I think, like a lion."

"Did he offer any violence to you?"

"No, not at all but he did frighten me," Mary tried her hardest to look like a sweet old granny. "and did nothing to me." She quickly added. "And I cried to God and asked what he would have and he vanished."

"Did he give thee any gift, or didst thou make him any promises?"

"No."

"Had he any of thy blood?"

"No."

"Did he come to make use of thy body in a carnal manner?"

"Never on my life."

"Have you a Teat in your privy-parts?"

"None." Mary could see the children in the front row sniggering.

"Mary Trembles, was not the Devil there with Susan when I was once in the prison with you and under her coats? The other told me that he was there but is now fled; and that the Devil was in the way when I was going to Taunton with my Son who is a minister. Thou speaketh now as a dying woman and as the Psalmist says, I will confess my iniquities and acknowledge all my sin. We find that Mary Magdalene fed seven Devils, and she came to Christ and obtained mercy." The kids who were giggling were now showing visible signs of boredom and drawing circles in the dirt with their equally muddy footwear. "And if thou break thy league with the Devil and make a covenant with God, thou mayst also obtain mercy. If thou hast anything to speak, speak thy mind."

"I have spoken the very truth and can speak no more: Mr Hann, I would desire they may come by me and confess as I have done." Mary inhaled deeply and fixed the sheriff with a deathly stare. Mr Carwythen returned the gaze, unmoved. He gave a slight nod and a noose was placed around Mary's neck. The coarse rope rubbed against her sagging skin. The world slowly closed in on Mary, she hardly registered the words that were spoken beside her and the roar of the crowd became hushed whispers to her ears. Images of her late father swam in and out of her thoughts, the cold still body of her only child and the memories of casting spells played out in her mind.

Agnes, Martha and their cronies were in the crowd, in addition to a few of their acquaintances who had not been present at the trial.

"It was that one there." Agnes pointed at Temperance. "The eldest and worst who was the introducer and cause of the other two's overthrow."

"She's an old hag." Disdain was written all over Martha's pinched features.

"But those other two are somewhat younger than the Old Shape of prince Lucifer." Observed one of the newcomers.

"Aye but they too are carnally charitable with the Devil." A gasp of shock escaped the lips of those who were hearing of their wicked, accursed and damnable actions for the first time.

Mr Hann turned to Temperance. The sheriff stood at his side.

"Temperance Lloyd." The minister projected his voice so that he could be heard over the rabble. "Have you made any contract with the Devil?"

"No." Temperance knew this was not the answer he wanted to hear, but this was her final chance to play the part of an innocent.

"Did he ever take any of thy blood?

"No."

"How did he appear to thee first, or where in the street? In what shape?"

"In a woeful shape."

"Had he ever any carnal knowledge of thee?"

"No. Never." Temperance's acting was Oscar worthy, and she would have brushed her brow in a mock swoon, had her hands not been tied.

"What did he do when came to thee?"

"He caused me to go and do harm."

"And did you go?"

"I did hurt a woman fore against my conscience. He carried me up to her door, which was open. The woman's name was Mrs. Grace Thomas.

"What caused you to do her harm? What malice had you against her? Did she do you any harm?"

"No. She never did me any harm: but the Devil beat me about the head grievously because I would not kill her: but I did bruise her after this fashion." Temperance managed to manipulate the bindings and lay her two hands to her side, as she had shown the jury here and at home.

"Did you bruise her until the blood came out of her mouth and nose?"

"No."

"How many did you destroy and hurt?"

"None but she."

"Did you know any mariners that you or your associates destroyed by overturning of ships and boats?"

"No. I never hurt any ships, bark or boat in my life."

"Was it you or Susan that did bewitch the children?" Temperance stole a glance at Susanna. They would not be judged on her authority.

"I sold apples, and the child took an apple from me, the mother took the apple from the child, for which I was very angry. But her child died of the small pox." Any woman in the crowd that had any ounce of sympathy remaining was appalled at the notion and moved firmly to team execution.

"Do you know one Mr. Lutteril about these parts, or any of your confederates? Did you or them bewitch his child?"

"No." The minister was getting frustrated.

"How did you come in to hurt Mrs. Grace Thomas? Did you pass through the keyhole of the door, or was the door open?"

"The Devil did lead me upstairs and the door was open. And this is all the hurt I did."

"How do you know it was the Devil?"

"I knew it by his eyes."

"Had you no discourse or treaty with him?"

"No. He said I should go along with him, to destroy a woman and I told him I would not: he said he would make me and then the Devil beat me about the head."

"Why had you not called upon God?"

"He would not let me do it." Temperance could keep the act going no longer. She was tired and broken.

"You say you never hurt ships, nor boats; did you never ride over an arm of the sea on a cow?"

"No. No Master, 'twas she, meaning Susan. She was the cause of my bringing to die, for she said when she was first brought to goal, that if she was hanged, she would have me hanged too; she reported I should ride on a cow before her, which I never did." In their final moments, the lifelong friends became enemies. The hemp rope that had been used to snap the necks or asphyxiate their prey was pulled over Temperance's skull. Strands of her long hair snagged in the knots as it was tightened around her throat.

45

The minister now turned to Susanna.

"Susan. Did you see the shape of a bullock? At the first time of your examination, you said it was like a short black man, about the length of your arm."

"He was black, Sir."

"Susan, had you any knowledge of the bewitching on Mr. Lutteril's child, or did you know a place called Tranton-Burroughs?"

"No." Susan wanted desperately to interrupt the minister and inform him that the correct pronunciation of her name was Susanna. It wasn't as if her situation could become any more dire but she had been brought up to be respectful and to use the manners which she had been taught.

"Are you willing to have prayers?" The noose was placed over Susanna's head.

Many of the crowd fell to their knees and prayed alongside the sheriff, who could have doubled as a pastor. The convicted witches would not partake and pray to the Christian God but they did sing a part of the fortieth psalm, at the desire of Susanna. If she was leaving this world, she'd enjoy her last few minutes in it. Despite her desire to leave with joy in her heart, she mouthed the last of the hymn.

Temperance told the spectators to take warning of her and begged they shall pray for them.

"The Lord Jesus speed me though my sins be red as scarlet, the Lord Jesus can make them as white as snow. The Lord help my soul."

Susanna Edwards was then executed.

The sheriff turned his attention to the spinster who was trembling from witnessing her best mate die.

She was permitted her final words, and they were. "Lord Jesus receive my soul. Lord Jesus speed me."

Mary Trembles was then executed.

Temperance remained unfazed by the swinging corpses of her friends.

Without waiting to be invited to speak, Temperance said, "Jesus Christ, speed me well. Lord forgive all my sins; Lord Jesus Christ, be merciful on my poor soul." She waited; her eyes narrowed in anticipation of the violent jerking motion that would hang her from the old oak tree. Instead of hearing the rush of death in her ears, she heard the monotonous tone of the sheriff, who was not yet satisfied with his interrogation.

"You are looked on as the woman that has debauched the other two. Did you ever lie with Devils?"

"No."

"Did not you know of their coming to gaol?"

"No."

"Have you anything to say to satisfy the world?"

"I forgive them, as I desire the Lord Jesus Christ will forgive me. The greatest thing I did was to Mrs. Grace Thomas. And I desire I may be forgiven for it and that the Lord Jesus Christ may forgive me. The Devil met me in the street and bid me kill her and because I would not he beat me about the head and back."

"In what shape or colour was he?"

"In black like a bullock."

"How do you know you did it? How went you in, through the keyhole, or the door?"

"At the door." Temperance was consistent in her recollection of events.

"Had you no discourse with the Devil?"

"Never but this day six weeks."

"You were charged about twelve years since and did you never see the Devil but this time?"

"Yes, once before. I was going for brooms and he came to me and said, 'This poor woman has a great burden and would help ease me of my burthen. And I said, 'The Lord had enabled me to carry it so far and I hope I shall be able to carry it further'."

"Did the Devil never promise you anything?"

"No. Never."

"Then you have served a very bad master, who gave you nothing. Well, consider you are just departing this world. Do you believe there is a God?"

"Yes."

"Do you believe in Jesus Christ?"

"Yes. And I pray Jesus Christ to pardon all my sins."

Knowing that her breaths were to be her final ones Temperance used them to make an enduring impression on would-be Satanists and God-faring believers. "Lord God almighty, who desirest not the death of a sinner but that he should turn from his wickedness and lives; grant, I beseech thee that this my late repentance, may be true and not too late.

I do protest sincerely, as far as I know my own heart, that were I to live my days over again, I would lead such a life, as should leave no room for doubt. But, feeling my minutes are but few, I can do no more than can be done in such a time and my confidence is, that though the merits of my saviour, all my former iniquities, shall be blotted out, which I beg for his sake alone, in whom I hope to find mercy."

Temperance Lloyd was then executed.

As a choruses of 'Amen' and 'Hallelujah' rang out, a salty tear raced down Alice Molland's cheek who bravely mouthed the words, "Blessed Be." Alice would soon experience for herself the force of a witch hunt.

Alice would be tried before Chief Baron Montague on the twentieth of March 1684 for witchcraft on the bodies of Jane Snow, Willmott Snow, and Agnes Furze. She was found guilty and sentenced to death. She would succumb to the brutality of the jail system before she made it to the gallows.

46

Mr Deacon had found another group of willing participants who would bolster his ego and word count.

"How does this sound?" Mr Deacon helped up a sheet of paper, put on his most authoritative voice and read out loud. "Let this then be a caution for all sinners to forsake sin and Satan, whose end and design is to ruin souls, to enslave mortals, and without doubt were it possible, to pull God's Almighty majesty out of his Everlasting throne."

"Tis a great pity that some have so little esteem of their jewels, which Jesus Christ the son of the Almighty, purchased at so dear a rate." Mr Deacon took this as confirmation that his closing address was well written.

"Do they not know how they crush Christ, how they wound his already wounded side for sinners?" He was stirring up an angry mob of zealots.

"Yet vile sinners, never call to mind, or at least very seldom, what Labyrinths of misery they involve themselves in." Everyone, it seemed, had an opinion and Mr Deacon would print the biased views as his own. "These women sought the Devil's aid, knowing the price that must be paid."

"But now to conclude. Take a poor sinner's advice, walk uprightly and justly and let not the fruition of present enjoyments of which, is beyond expression and the loss thereof of eternal misery, destruction and ruin." Mr Deacon carefully folded his manuscript, happy that it would be viewed by generations and placed it within the internal lining of his coat. He considered it his duty and for the benefit of the public, especially in Scotland where witchcraft was prevalent, to produce the guide to which educate on the use of witchcraft in the form of using an effigy, by tickling and how insoluble countercharms may be successfully and laudably applied. He would be on the doorstep of the printers the following day.

The bodies of the three women swung where they were slain. Those that were not claimed by family, or the academics, were interned in a mass grave. The surviving kin of the dead old ladies did not have the funds, or the inclination, to have the remains transported home. With short sharp blades children approached the hanging figures to cut off mementos of rope and hair before the executioner returned. In a practice that had become customary at high profile hangings, the man responsible for the rope that ended the life of the convicted would get money for the old, used rope by slicing it into small lengths and selling it to the public that had witnessed the government killings, as a keepsake.

They were left hanging for several hours before their bodies were cut down and they were laid to rest upon the decomposing remains of other Devonians, a thin scattering of soil separating each burial.

The tale of three eminent witches from a small harbour town on the coast of North Devon would be retold for generations. From taverns to farms up and down the county and beyond, three names, and their wicked deeds were the subject of anecdotes, plays, warnings and a lengthy melody. Minstrels made a living off the back of the execution. Playing violins or flutes, they retained the practiced and popular tune of Fortune My Foe, changing the words to fit the supernatural deeds. Children sang the words as they played, mothers hummed it as they slaved away at household chores.

Now listen to my Song, good People all,
And I shall tell what lately did befall
At Exeter a place in Devonshire,
The like whereof of late you nere did hear.

At the last Assizes at Exeter,
Three aged Women that Imprisoned were
For Witches, and that many had destroy'd;
Were thither brought in order to be tryd

For Witchcraft, that Old Wicked Sin,
Which they for long time had continued in;
And joyn'd with Satan, to destroy the good
Sweet Innocents, and shed their harmless blood.

So these Malicious Women at the last,
Having done mischiefs, were by Justice cast;
For it appear'd they Children had destroy'd,
Lamed Cattel, and the Aged much annoy'd,

Having Familiars always at their Beck,
Their Wicked Rage on Mortals for to wreck:
It being proved they used Wicked Charms,
To Murther Men, and bring about sad harms.

But now it most apparent does appear,
That they will now for such their deeds pay dear:
For Satan, having lull'd their Souls asleep,
Refuses Company with them to keep.

A known deceiver he long time has been,
To help poor Mortals into dangerous Sin;
Thereby to cut them off, that so they may
Be plung'd in Hell, and there be made his Prey.

And that they had about their Bodys strange
And Proper Tokens of their Wicked Change:
As Pledges that, to have their cruel will,
Their Souls they gave unto the Prince of Hell.

Wands Up Witches

The Country round where they did live came in,
And all at once their sad complaints begin;
One lost a Child, the other lost a Kine,
This his brave Horses, that his hopeful Swine.

One had his Wife bewitch'd, the other his Friend,
Because in some things they the Witch offend:
For which they labour under cruel pain,
In vain seek remedy, but none can gain.

But Roar in cruel sort, and loudly cry
'Destroy the Witch and end our misery'
Some used Charms by Mountabanks set down,
Those cheating Quacks, that swarm in every Town.

But all's in vain, no rest at all they find,
For why? all Witches are to cruelty enclin'd;
And do delight to hear sad dying groans,
And such laments as wou'd pierce Marble Stones.

But now the Hand of Heaven has found them out,
And they to Justice must pay Lives, past doubt;
One of these Wicked Wretches did confess,
She Four Score Years of Age was, and no less.

And that she had deserved long before,
To be sent packing to the Stigian shore
For the great mischiefs she so oft had done,
And wondered that her life so long had run.

She said the Devil came with her along,
Through Crouds of People, & bid her be strong

And she no harm should have, but like a Lyer,
At the Prison Door he fled, and nere came nigh her.

The rest aloud, crav'd Mercy for their Sins,
Or else the great deceiver her Soul gains;
For they had been lewd Livers many a day,
And therefore did desire that all would Pray

To God, to Pardon them, while thus they lie
Condemned for their Wicked Deeds to Die:
Which may each Christian do, that they may find
Rest for their Souls, though Wicked once inclin'd.

Nothing much changed in the small maritime town. News of the executions reached home. The three apprentices held a vigil to honour the teachers whose bodies lay cold in the ground.

Upon Susanna's arrest, Abigail Handford had risked life and limb to retrieve the grimoire that Susanna had hidden within the chimney breast, safe from prying eyes, but not other witches. Betty Cadley had been the one responsible for keeping the book safe, and she did exactly that. The pages would not see the light of day, or the light of the moon, for many, many generations.

They had the basic knowledge. Each could cast a circle and call upon the elements and had perfected grounding themselves, intending to teach the next phase of witches and warlocks the supernatural order of the universe. Using the pages of the book of shadows, that had been entrusted to their possession, they performed ritualistic magic; however they lacked the expertise to create powerful new spells.

Before they had the opportunity to groom any new students Mary Beare was arrested on a charge of witchcraft. One, luckily, that was unsubstantiated and thrown out by the major John Darracott. Betty and Abigail would also be brought in front of the magistrates and suffer the accusation of being sorceresses and both would walk away with their lives and reputations intact.

They also walked away from the craft.

Three hundred and forty years after their deaths, the names Temperance Lloyd, Susanna Edwards and Mary Trembles were still falling from the lips of the people of the town, known to men, women and children across the globe.

Their legacy had not been lost in the passing of time; their lives not forgotten.

The sigma of witch attacks on passing trade forced the town to change its name to Ducksberry.

Now

47

The date was Friday 17th June 2022.

The world was in a mess.

Mother nature was attempting to fight back. For over twenty years the words global warming and climate change had been whispered on the lips of the empathetic, with Greenpeace and animal right activists using the media to spread the word. It fell on deaf ears. The profit of commercialism outweighed the need for renewable energy and sustainable resources, which were now the keywords being used to drive the change needed to save the planet.

She had tried to drown her sorrows in tsunamis and cull the population with pandemics but the human race survived like cockroaches, coming back stronger and more determined.

Those in power seemed incapable of learning from the past, making the same mistakes but on a grander scale. The more man advanced the more nature fell by the wayside, ignored or abused, it's delicate beauty replaced by machines. The western world had become a throwaway society, with generations of entitled brats failing to grasp the need to reuse and recycle. The big corporations had no accountability for their conduct, nor cared about their impact on the environment.

Not everyone could see the need for mankind to slow down, that the automated processes that had been programmed in recent years had the potential to develop a conscious to rival their creators and start a new age of steel and destruction. Those that did were starting to shout louder, were beginning to be heard.

Starr Anderson, a self-proclaimed eco-warrior, was one of Earth's moon children who felt it's destruction as a personal slight. Her hair was splattered with blues and purples, braids and knots from lack of brushing yet it was neither dry nor greasy.

Waving the lime green banner high above her head, Starr held tightly onto one wooden pole as the four-foot message was buffeted by the wind. A colourful crowd surrounded her waving their own flags demanding the truth. The demonstration had started small but had gathered momentum as passers-by joined in and social media rallied the troupes. Bored police looked on, ready to jump into action to prevent any unruly behaviour and squash any loud protests. Traffic was flowing, any holdups taken in good nature, sympathetic to the cause and appreciative of the effort.

In London the low-level disturbance made for major delays and loss of profits but here the drivers are used to tractors and stray sheep holding up the highways. There was nowhere else to shop so the customers would either wait, take one of the many alternative routes into the large neighbouring town or simply return another day. It was at least entertaining to watch the hippies that had come out of the woods for the day to take over the town. Also unlike London, there were no choreographed performances or extreme costumes, just like-minded individuals in ethically sourced clothing and no deodorant. Starr understood the need for collective change but was not sold on all the tactics used by those concerned about the extinction of the human race but did have a few ideas of people she would like to be extinct. One of those people was the ex-boyfriend who broke her heart.

Starr had strived to live an alternative lifestyle since her teens. When she felt troubled she turned to art to express her frustration. Thick layers of oil paint covered boards salvaged from bins or bought cheap in charity shops. Pieces she liked she hung on her bedroom wall, the rest she stored in the garage. Her conservative parents struggled to understand their wayward daughter and why she couldn't or wouldn't conform to their perfect idea.

More concerned with her carbon footprint than her grades, Starr was a constant source of disappointment to her mother and father. Christened Jane, the unhappy youth went by the name Starr for her formative years at secondary school. Her older brother, Johnathan, was the families golden child. An A-star student he was studying astrophysics at the university of Bath and had a promising career to look forward too. Starr had scrapped pass grades at GCSE level and dropped out of college. Starr rarely felt good enough. Seventeen years of growing up in her brothers shadow had been a challenge, to which she was about to forfeit the possibility of overcoming.

Starr had mastered the art of sneaking out of the house when she was dating an undesirable older lad who only cared about what swung around in his trousers. Her parents headed to bed around nine, had no idea what their daughter got up to as they slept. The blueish light of a screen shone from under Johnathan's door and, if you listened hard enough, the tapping of the keys on the keyboard confirmed, along with his grades, that he was studying and not on any x-rated websites.

Starr was not adverse to learning but she found the forced school subjects tedious and the teachers boring. Using the library she'd built up an extensive knowledge of the supernatural. She was fascinated by the occult and drawn to gothic imagery. She considered her soul as dark as her eyes.

Starr worked. She had a Saturday job in a café, collecting plates and washing dishes but it gave her a little independence and allowed her to indulge in her mystical hobbies such as tarot reading. She had a handful of shifts after school but made the most during the school holidays where she covered waitressing duties and got a bigger share of the tips.

One of the common meeting places for the underage drinking element of the town was St Marys church. Quiet and dark, teenagers would sit against the cold stone wall, drinking or kissing. Starr's alcohol of choice was vodka, which she would swig from the bottle. The clear liquor burnt and she would screw her face in disgust after each dram, but she liked the euphoric feeling the spirit gave her.

Cigarettes had been upgraded to vape pens but someone always had rolling tobacco and some marijuana to make a joint that was passed around the group of adolescents. A party trick that took no time to master, Starr clicked her jaw to produce smoke rings, much to the delight of her peers who would contort their faces in the most peculiar ways trying to imitate the skill.

Only once had Starr tried a class A drug, a tab of acid that dissolved on her tongue. The LSD was concealed in an innocent smiley face that tasted of nothing. She experienced heart palpitations and didn't like the lack of control she had over her limbs or thoughts. She had a spliff sandwiched between her fingers when three police officers responded to a complaint from a local resident of unruly behaviour in the graveyard. They were not being loud or aggressive but they were underage drinking and smoking narcotics.

Regardless of ages, the troupe was rounded up and taken to the neighbouring town to have their details recording for further prosecution.

Unfortunately one of the arresting officers, sergeant Daniel Smith, played snooker with Starr's father and insisted on bringing her home in person. The town's drug problem would be put on a temporary hiatus owing to the disappearance of local drug dealer, Logan Keene. His cronies were still trading but the supply was low, outpricing teens from the market.

The humiliation of neighbours seeing one of their offspring being brought home in the early hours of the morning, in a squad car, was too much for Starr's dad.

"How am I supposed to show my face at the club now? After what you have done?" Was all that came out of his mouth for several days, once he had regained the ability to speak to her. Starr had no response, nor did she care to give one. Her mother would just sigh as she passed, displeasure etched into every line on her face.

Starr had borrowed a holdall from a friend and filled it with as many clothes and personal possessions as she could cram into the canvas sack. As soon as she heard the key turn in the lock she headed to her parents room and riffled through the drawers until she found her passport. Tucking it in between a neatly folded t-shirt and pair of jeans, Starr made herself a sandwich and took a selection of snacks from the cupboard, which she managed to squeeze into the large sports bag.

Then she left, with no note and no intention to return.

48

The gallery was quiet. All commissions had been completed or were drying. Two were parcelled and ready for dispatch. Bubble wrap and wooden crates held the one-off sculptures, wire framed hares dancing under the moonlight for installation in the customers country retreat.

Julie Slater sat at the reception desk of the glass fronted building, her legs swinging from the high stool. Yesterday had been the final day of an exhibition she hosted for an ex-student who had moved to London and embarked on a promising marketing career in digital art. It had brought a varied footfall into the contemporary workspace, with exposed brick walls and art deco lighting. Julie giggled as a fat cat misjudged it's arial abilities and plummeted to the floor having missed, by some way, it's intended target.

It was rare that Julie wasn't busy but her to-do list was empty and the gallery was experiencing a lull after the popular exhibition and pop-up shop of merchandise, that made the show viable to all parties, had travelled to the next location of the national tour.

YouTube was a quick, convenient place for funny cat videos that whiled away the time until the courier arrived. Julie had learnt from experience that if she was expecting someone, they would only turn up when she had given up waiting and decided to start a messy job that involved time and protective clothing. Today she chose to sit and wait patiently, losing herself in the misfortunes of other peoples beloved and rather stupid, pets.

Julie had studied art in Rome, painted breath-taking scenery in the footsteps of the masters but a relationship breakdown brought her back to her family home on the cold shores of a small English harbour town. Julie had quickly settled into life. Within several years of returning she had established her own studio and gallery and hosted workshops for promising future artists and hobbyists who wanted to expand their portfolio.

She loved animal but cats were her passion. And the supernatural. She had created a range of products based on a cat called Socks, owing to his white feet. Socks was a street cat that spread his time over many residences, one being the small, terraced house she had shared with Lizzie Summers. Lizzie had recently moved in with her fiancé, leaving Julie in need of a roommate.

She wasn't having much luck finding a replacement.

The online advert was saved to her laptop but not uploaded and the hand written note was sat on her desk. She was hoping that someone would pop up at the right time, that fate would intervene and she wouldn't be forced to interview a bunch of hopeless individuals that she had no desire to live with.

She wanted someone like-minded, who didn't mind the messiness of an artist and who believed in the supernatural. When she meet Lizzie, she had little knowledge of otherworldly entities but an overnight vigil at Amberley House convinced Lizzie that ghosts may exist. Family research showed that Lizzie was a descendant of Aggie Summers, a reputed witch who lived over three hundred years ago.

She could sustain the rent for a few months on her own and delighted in the freedom of living alone but reality was a stark reminder that, whilst her paintings were selling, she was a long way from the fame of Banksy and would soon deplete her savings with rent on two properties to pay.

Government initiative and grants, alongside shaming on social media had forced many business to go green. A lot had established recycling programmes within their stores or offices and there were plenty of companies you could pay to dispose of the packaging that most premises used, through choice or because their suppliers encased the products in meters of bubble wrap or polystyrene.

To find sustainable ways to handle their waste whilst turning a profit was another challenge the managers faced. Big conglomerates had stepped in at a national level to enforce further targets to meet customer expectation and maximise on the value of employment.

Julie was conscious of the materials she used. Since she was young she had been aware of the damage happening to the planet and begged her parents to buy her anti-animal testing body shop toiletries and she shopped for clothes in charity shops. Furniture was upcycled and trinkets came from eBay or corporations she knew to be ethical in their practices. Mr and Mrs Slater had always been proud of their caring daughter who put the needs of others before her own.

As a proprietor she sought eco-friendly supplies and encouraged but did not force, her customers, family and friends to think about the environment too. The paint she used was created as it was centuries ago, using mineral pigments, the brushes made from bamboo and her canvas were made of raw cotton. It was as vibrant in colour as anything chemically produced, after all, it was good enough for the artists whose masterpieces are still looked upon with admiration hundreds of years after the creators themselves turned to dust.

Fair trade was associated with expense, as was the word organic and regrettably that is still the case, out pricing some from living the natural lifestyle they wished too. A new breed of artisans were resurrecting the trades of the past, from butchers to craftsmen, using traditional tools and methods.

Julie was not a political person but could see the need for an effective group to push for change. So far she was yet to find one whose ethos matched her own and whose message she could fully get behind without finding fault with some element. She was a member of Greenpeace, had adopted multiple animals from the World Wildlife fund and supported local nature organisations. Solar panels were mounted on the top of houses and in fields to capture the energy of the sun's rays, with an engineer booked in for next week to add two reflective panels to the roof of Julies rented terrace property and she was in talks with the landlord of the gallery to do the same.

She was an advocate for an offshore wind farm but every consultation was meet with local opposition that it would impact on their view of the flat horizon of the Atlantic ocean or hydroelectric energy for its supposed impact on marine biology. Stuck in their ways, they were too reliant on fossil fuels to seek out an alternative, until they will be presented with no choice but to change suppliers.

A movement that the locals were behind was the drive to be rid of plastic, on land and in the sea. The popular grassroots charity, Surfers Against Sewage, had been campaigning for generations for pollution free water ways, dedicating their time and efforts to safe beaches and healthy oceans. Stickers appeared in shop windows and on website banners stating a plastic free status with television ads and celebrities endorsing the abolition of single use plastic and collecting discarded pieces to be turned into clothing, building materials and even components for gas guzzling cars. The uses for reformed plastic were growing with every new conscientious inventor, as were the companies who dealt with the deadly substance. People-powered plastic free demonstrations and petitions were starting to filter through to the government, with independent companies and big conglomerates jumping on board to claim their status as plastic-free or moving from single-use manufacturing to a sustainable way to source their products. Further understanding was emerging on the importance of wetlands and ways to stop pollution from controlling agricultural waste and sewage in addition to preventing further urbanisation. Common folk were taking a stand, having their say and acting on behalf of the environment to highlight and educate those who did not share their united vision to reconnect with and promote nature and the natural products whose production did not impact on the global need for change.

Julie had been working on a tender to secure some commissions to create a globally recognised symbol to represent the dedication to saving the planet of those partaking in the scheme. She had been approached by a forward-thinking government backed biosphere company who had branches dotted around the UK. Through a combination of graphic design and hand drawn images, Julie created a range of colourful logos that she submitted with a wordy application.

The mornings post brought bills, junk mail and a white A5 envelope with a circular bird and fish motif in the top left corner. She anxiously turned the sealed decision over and over in her hands, putting it down only to pick it up again minutes later, unable to concentrate on anything. She made herself a mug of herbal tea and opened a packet of biscuits, supermarket own brand bourbons. She was feeling nauseous. The tea didn't help settle her nerves.

'Do it.' She commanded herself. She picked up the envelope and started to ease it open. An inch in, she shook her head, said 'I can't do it' to herself and put the unopened letter back down.

She put a sign on the door and went for a walk by the river. As she watched the sun twinkle off the gently rolling waves she thought about her life.

She was happy. She was single, currently lived alone, except for Socks, the stray cat that would wander in when he felt like it. Her business was going well, her art was selling, she was building a nest egg and she was very content with her social life. It wouldn't matter financially if she didn't get the contract, she had plenty of work in the pipeline but she felt like she was missing something. It wasn't a hope to be in a relationship. Like most girls, she didn't consider herself overly pretty, just sort of average but she got plenty of attention when she was out and had no trouble pulling when she felt inclined. She couldn't put her finger on it.

When she returned to the gallery, the envelope was sitting where she had left it. She had hoped that it would have magically disappeared so she wouldn't have to open it.

'It doesn't matter what the outcome is. There would have been tons of competition.' The pep talk wasn't working. The envelope remained firmly on the desk.

'Get a grip. Come on. Come on. Just do it!' Julie picked up the envelope. She felt sick again.

She closed her eyes and carefully carried on from where she had abandoned her first attempt. She pulled out a folded letter.

Julie took a deep breath and opened her eyes. She had to squint to focus on the small writing, owing to her hands shaking .

She won the commission.

Julie slumped into her chair. Elated, shocked,

After her hearing had recovered from her mother's screams of joy as she told her the news, she phoned Lizzie.

Lizzie rallied the troops and they headed to the Ivy that evening to celebrate.

For the next month she would be working all the hours she could, so the search for a flat mate was put on hold.

49

Steve Smith was head barman at La Iveson, aka the Ivy, the town's leading restaurant. Hip and modern with traditional values and ale, the establishment was popular across the age ranges of the town.

As bar manager, it was Steve's responsibility to carry out the interviews for new bar staff as he would be working with and training them up, ensuring they were a good fit with the existing squad. He wasn't looking for any mavericks, just team players with a strong work ethic. There were late nights and rowdy customers, it wasn't a job for the faint hearted.

Jobs rarely came up; it was a fun place to work and everybody was valued for their skill set. Steve had a knack for producing tasty and intoxicating cocktails. Poppy's was her aura, she oozed positivity and the customers loved her. Her appearance was in direct conflict with her personality. Black eyeliner and facial piercing matched her punk rock clothes and tattooed limbs. A raven skull necklace hung from her neck and silver rings decorated every finger, glistening with onyx's or

Celtic symbols. The rare vacancies arose from maternity leave, a resignation due to the unsocial hours and the employee having a day job they refused to leave and the approaching holiday season, where extras were drafted in to cover the peak times. Usually these positions went to uni students looking to earn cash through a summer job, happy to part time work to pay for their summer drinking. Half the town seemed to have applied for the positions at the popular eatery.

The online application form weeded out some of the candidates and a phone call had crossed a few more from the long list but Steve still had a diary crammed with back-to-back interviews, a checklist of questions and a scoring system marked one to five.

By the time he took a break for lunch, the calibre of prospective colleagues was not as strong as he had hoped and he prayed the afternoon would deliver a more enthused and experienced crowd. It was clear a couple had been forced by the jobcentre to attend and one had the competency level of a slug. Three was the highest mark he had written against a name so far.

It didn't.

With the exception of Jade Johnson.

She had no experience but came with a charming attitude that was teased out from behind nervous smile and fidgeting hands.

Promised a phone call, either way with a decision, Jade picked her way around the tables towards the exit. Steve put a tick next to her name, the second of the day. By the end of the day, the total number of ticks had risen to three.

Jade Johnson was over the moon to get the call from Steve. She answered her mobile as if the caller was going to deliver a life-or-death verdict.

Her life had been a catalogue of disasters since her earliest memories.

Brought up in care, her mother had died when she was two years old. Her father was as elusive as his name on the birth certificate.

She had no idea on her family history. She had tried looking, tried asking but nobody could give her any answers. To the best of her knowledge and to that of her foster parents Pauline and Joh Abbot, nobody had come forward to claim her. No aunts or uncles, no nans or grandads, no cousins or siblings. On the discovery of her mums passing, she was handed to social services by the police officer who attended the scene of her mother's demise, following repeated reports of a child crying in distress. The flat they lived in was sparse. There were no family photos, no letters, nothing to identify a relative, no clue to her ancestry, other than the colour of her skin and a crumpled birth certificate. There were no personal touches to the property bar a box of second-hand toys and a wardrobe of stained or threadbare clothes.

The woman from social service took what food was in date and whatever toys were not broken. The only item that travelled from home to home with Jade was a small, jointed teddy bear with one leg that flopped around, dislocated at the seam and an ear that had been stroked to hairlessness.

Jade was an easy child. She didn't express any behavioural or emotional issues associated with early trauma or stress and rarely cried. She never wet the bed or developed idiosyncratic tendencies to displace her feelings. Despite this, she found herself pushed around the foster system, a resident of several homes with children who were angry, wanting others to feel as rejected as they did.

Jade never did.

But she did feel like she never belonged, that no one wanted her. Until she was welcomed into, what she saw as, a mini mansion on the Devon coast.

Jade looked out the window in awe at the boats that bobbed on the estuary and strained to look out to sea as the car she was in sped across the bridge. She had never been to a beach.

The five bedroomed detached farm house was double fronted with a gravel drive. It looked like a stately home to a wild eyed eight-year-old from London who thought sharing a crammed room with other children was how all children were raised. Nicknamed JJ, Jade preferred to go by Jay, which is what her newest family called her.

Jade was introduced, her paperwork was signed and she was left in the care of total strangers, again. She had the choice of her own room, or she could share with a sweet natured seven-year-old with moderate learning difficulties and club foot, that needed corrective footwear.

Jade chose to have a roommate. Discarded by her perfect parents owing to her diverse conditions, Jade's new friend would let her play with her toys and held her hand when Pauline took them to the park.

Pauline Abbot and her husband John started the sanctuary for wayward and unwanted children after the unexpected death of Johns parents and the arrival of a well thought out inheritance. They struggled to have a family. Pauline had conceived on several occasions but all ended in devasting miscarriages, less than nine weeks into each pregnancy. They revaluated their lives and jobs; John was an accountant and Pauline worked as a career, working with elderly residents. The decision to relocate to the destination both had holidayed in as a child was a no-brainer. Theirs sold within weeks of going on the market leaving them renting whilst in search of an idea retreat.

John tinkered as a handy man, taking on jobs that peaked his interest and repairing the old farm house. He had built a tree house that was sturdy enough to take the weight of two adults and had seen countless children use as a secret base, a club house or a hideaway.

Pauline was the primary care giver, an agony aunt, the cook and the cleaner. She drove a people carrier, whose bumper and driver's door was scratched and in serious need of some TLC, to ferry the children to school and for weekend outings to the coastline or den building and camping in woodland.

Jade had spent over half her life living with the Abbots. She was happy there. She felt at home. She had people there she considered family, cared for like they were blood.

As much as Pauline loved the majority of the children who passed through her doors, her hands were tied with legalities and procedures. She was a small cog in a big machine and couldn't enforce the change she knew needed to happen. The rules were, when a child reached adulthood, at the vulnerable age of eighteen, they would be turned out into the world, ready or not.

With no care order in place, Pauline could longer claim for Jade's upkeep and the bed was required for another child in need. The cost of living was high in the backwater marine town so the Abbots could only afford to sustain the children for a short period with their own staying put project.

Jade needed a job and a place to stay, urgently.

50

There was a summer house at the bottom of the large garden. John had built it from reclaimed timber and fitted a miniature kitchen, with working appliances and a space saving bathroom. It was designed as a transition into independent living for the children whose time in care had come to an end. A stop gap whilst they found employment and themselves.

It had been used and abused in the past but every child was given the chance and the opportunity.

Jade's possessions filled two medium sized suitcases packed to the brim with clothes, books and ornaments that Pauline had bought her as birthday or Christmas presents. A child's shoe box of mementos was her life before the Abbots took her under their wing. It was carefully wrapped in a crotched jumper that was now to small; a handmade gift on her first Christmas, made for all the wards by Pauline's mum.

"When can you start?"

"I. Um. As soon as you need me?" Jade's response was said as more of a question than an answer.

It was arranged that her first shift would be Saturday night.

Jade ran straight to the house to tell Pauline, who was on the phone to the council trying to secure accommodation for Jade. Thirty minutes on hold, she was waiting for the housing officer, who offered a room in a hostel style halfway house or helpfully recommended to rent privately. He agreed, after realising Pauline had experience of the rental market, to post out an application for Jade to access the discretionary fund which would cover a deposit on a place of her own. Now all she had to do was convince the landlord to take on Jade as a tenant.

Miss Johnson burst through the backdoor like she was being chased by a pack of wolves, leaving it wide open and calling for her foster parent as she made her way through the ground floor of the house.

The ruckus brought John running from the shed, wondering where the fire was, then promptly chastising Jade for letting the cold air in and the cat out.

Pauline beamed like the Cheshire cat. She had always treated the kids as she would her own, revelling in their glories and wiping their tears through the pain.

Jade's shift went well. She shadowed Poppy, watched her mix drinks and work the till. She delivered orders to customers with a smile and poured her first pint, with a head inches deep. She had expected to start as base level, washing dishes and collecting glasses but

Steve could see the potential and had thrown her in at the deep end, with Poppy as a life line.

Jade accepted any and all shifts offered, she had no social life to miss. A three-day working week soon doubled but so did her pay packet. She didn't have many friends. Her best friend was at university studying to be a doctor and the rest were more acquaintances than confidants, not trusted with secrets or invited back for tea from the playground. This was partly due to her circumstances, the Abbots had to be careful who they invited into their home, the safeguarding of the children was their priority and income.

Jade was a quick learner. She had mastered the till by the end of her first week. Not that it took a rocket scientist, most customers were attached to their phones so ordered and paid with an app and for those that didn't, the till was electronic with a touch screen scroll feature so all she had to do was select the same options the mobile tooting clients did.

Carrying trays of drinks was a harder skill to perfect. She spilt several but none on customers or herself. The uniform was supplied, jet black with a trail of ivy imprinted up the right side. Above the door, a lit sign said La Iveson but locals called it the Ivy.

A group of young women, laughing, walked in. Steve shouted greetings across the room, waving from behind the bar. This was returned with flirtatious smiles and winks from Julie, who had known him since nursery. Poppy sidled up to the party, giving

Julie a hug and congratulating her. "Shift finishes in 40. Save me a seat."

"What about a drink Pops?"

"Line them up Lizzie!"

"Gotta get back to it." Poppy went back to work.

The girls got out their phones to order food and drinks. Julie had pizza with a side of onion rings and a double vodka watered down with cranberry juice to neutralise the burning taste of the spirit. Lizzie had burger, locally sourced in a brioche bun with a rhubarb gin in a pretty glass. Curries, more burgers and a seafood platter arrived for the other guests along with more gin and a bottle of house red.

The drinks were flowing and the food consumed. Julie was sandwiched between Lizzie on her right and Francesca on her left. It took three trips to clear the table of empty plates and spent glasses. The noise level rose in a chorus of "thank you's" as Jade carefully balanced the plates of uneaten salad on a tray, her attention acutely focused on the breakable dishes.

Julie' bladder couldn't hold any more liquid. Reluctantly she headed to the toilet, knowing that once the flood gates were open, it would be endless trips to the loo for the rest of the evening. She was washing her hands whilst checking her reflection when Poppy came in.

She'd slammed down a shot of vodka before coming to get changed. Swapping her work top for a low-cut t-shirt with a studded skull on the front. She produced some goth style accessories from her bag, applied a dramatic flurry of makeup and transformed herself into a Goddess of the night.

"So Jue, what we celebrating?" Julie explained about securing the design work. "Nice one mate. Congrats." Poppy nodded her head in kudos to her friends achievements. "Sounds like things are working out for you."

"Life's good. I just gotta find a lodger." Julie made a face at the prospect. She knew she really should get onto it, living alone was slowly draining her income. "You ready to put your big girl pants on and leave home?" Julie was only half serious about the offer.

"No way! Mother still does me laundry for me. And leaves me food when I'm on lates. I'm never moving out! Well, not until my tattooed knight comes along on his Harley and whisks me away!" Both young ladies giggled. Poppy thought wistfully for a moment of her perfect guy. "Not on the lookout for a fella?"

"Haven't got the time to be honest." Julie knew she had the time for a relationship, just not the willingness to commit right now. She enjoyed her freedom. If she wanted to stay up to four in the morning painting or binge-watching American sitcoms on Netflix, it was her prerogative.

"Or a girl pal?" Poppy winked and blew a kiss towards Julie. The girls descended into fits of laughter.

Whilst they'd been talking Poppy had ordered herself a round of drinks.

"Right, downstairs, I've got some catching up to do." Supporting her tipsy friend, they returned to the celebration.

Poppy downed the drinks that had arrived at the table before she did.

They were the only customers left. Steve turned the lighting down and the music up.

Jade brought over the last legally served drinks, one tray at a time. She placed a pint of Guinness in front of Steve, who had joined the party.

"Hey Jay." Shouted Poppy, a little louder than she had expected, making her colleague jump a little.

The tray containing empty glasses that Jade had balanced on her outstretched palm shook. The room froze for a moment. The glasses clinked in a harrowing melody before settling, damage free. Jade let out a breath she didn't know she was holding.

"Sorry. My bad." Poppy raised her hands in mock surrender. "You still looking for a place?"

Jade nodded timidly.

Gossip went hand in hand with the job, little of the staffs private lives remained that. It was meant without malice; they were more like family than work mates. The worst culprit was Poppy, whose well intentioned mouth was often activated before her brain.

"Jules needs a paying flat mate, don't ya Jue? Problem solved!" Declared Poppy triumphantly.

Julie widened her eyes at her drunk friend. Her words slow from drink and thinking on her feet. "I, well, I do but I really need to concentrate on this.."

Jade's cheeks began to redden, her gaze on the tray she was desperate to deposit in the kitchen. Before Julie could finish Steve stepped in to save the day, a tattooed knight in black cotton but not the one Poppy was looking for.

"Once you've loaded the dishwasher you can head off for the night. I'll clear up the rest."

"Okay. Thank you. See you tomorrow." Jade didn't make eye contact with anyone except a fleeting glance in Julies direction. "Have a good night ladies."

Julie was too inebriated, her mind too woozy to give it consideration but the thought would subconsciously gnaw at her.

51

Starr had been couch surfing since she rashly absconded the family home. She'd spent a few cold and lonely nights sleeping in a disused railway tunnel on the trail running beside the river Taw, before seeking refuge on friends sofas.

Amongst the few possessions she had crammed into the holdall was her art supplies. Tubes of paint, pencils, brushes, chalks etcetera lived communally in an old fishing tackle box salvaged from a dusty shelf in the garage. Her father used to be an amateur angler but the pastime fell by the wayside as the kids got bigger and his work commitments grew. She loved the box and the connection to her dad.

Both parents and her brother Jonathan, had sent multiple texts begging her to come home. She had let them know she was alive but would remain absent from their lives for the foreseeable future. To her mother this meant she was stoned, too high to act responsibly, a demonstration of her immaturity. Her father had led a wild existence before falling in love with his future wife and understood his complicated daughter. He wasn't happy with her antics but had empathy for her fight against society and a secret streak of pride for her defiant attitude. Jonathan's opinion was a mixture of his inherited views but he missed his little sister and worried for her. The texts to her brother were truthful and raw. Despite their differences, they shared a close bond, she brought a little bit of crazy to his organised world and he brought normality and stability to hers.

The small amount of savings in her bank account was dwindling. She'd applied for jobs as a cleaner, a career, a shop assistant but no interviews had come through yet. She had little experience and minimal qualifications and her appearance put off potential employers. Facial piercings and multi-coloured hair was not always a desired look for an establishment but Starr would find her fit.

The council had placed Jade on a waiting list. She had been offered a bedsit, smaller than the summer house, in a halfway house, which Pauline rejected on her behalf. Jade handed over a fifth of her wage packet as rent on the vamped up, insulated garden shed.

With her second pay packet she went shopping. Not for groceries but for fun, frivolous stuff. From the discount store she came back with a bag of knickknacks; signs, candles, fake succulents, nothing of any practical use. She also had a look around the antique shops, to which there were several around town, interspaced between the numerous charity shops, cafes and banks. Jade adored history. She liked looking at old items, imagining a past for them, who used them and why they no longer wanted the item that had found its way onto the packed tables or locked display cabinets.

In the second vintage packed store she visited she was drawn to a wooden handled awl. The pear-shaped base was smooth from centuries of being held, the metal tarnished with age but still sharp. As a hobby, Jade felted. She liked to keep her mind and hands busy. She made brooches and decorations but specialised in animals. Her creations were dotted around the Abbot household, given as gifts to her foster family. The outcome was a more detailed product and it was easier than trying to remember how to knit. She'd sat for hours with Pauline's mum, creating unsymmetrical scarfs and always needed help to cast on and had nobody who could remedy her dropped stitch. Pauline lacked any creative skill and the interest in developing one, which she made up for with a loving nature and was a talented baker. The awl would be handy to fashion large holes and it was old.

Using a bundle of sage that she had picked and dried herself, she cleansed the awl to remove energy left by previous owners but not for several days after the purchase and not before she had pricked her finger. A droplet of blood swelled quickly to the surface. Putting the injured digit in her mouth she sucked it until it stopped bleeding. She had learnt to do this from the #witchtok community, an app of the popular social media craze of TikTok, who were educating a new and old generation on modern witchcraft, spells and harnessing the power of crystals.

Jade loved to read in her downtime but the late-night shifts meant she was too tired to concentrate and the words jumped around the page. She often fell into a deep dreamless sleep, exhausted from her shift and thinking of the future. Tonight she dreamt fanciful tales of magic and spells, of transforming cats and handsome wizards.

Julie likes history too. It was the ruins and historic culture of Rome that she missed, not the inadequate lover that she left there. At the time she returned with a bank account and heart in tatters but was now a successful artist with her own gallery.

Julie had been flat out on her commission. Working late into the night and starting early, her single status allowed her the opportunity to do just that. She had no one to care for but herself and the stray cat, who just went to one of his many other homes for food and cuddles.

Her corporate contract had been fulfilled. The designs were at the printers and the invoice was in the post. She closed the gallery and took a rare day off. Treating herself to a holistic massage, the tension ebbed from her muscles as the practitioner dug into her flesh with her thumbs.

Ambling along the estuary with an award-winning ice cream, Julie stopped to watch the ducks, leaving behind the remnants of her cone as an afternoon treat for the amphibious birds. Two jet skiers shot up the harbour, causing the moored boots to rock in the wake of the thrill seekers.

To finish the day she indulged in a little retail therapy. She left a charity shop twenty quid lighter but with a bag for life stuffed with new to her clothing and a couple of paperbacks. She picked up a bottle of Chardonnay and chocolatey treats from the off licence and finished the day with a wander round her favourite antique shop. Two floors of old castoffs and salvaged goodies.

She was drawn to a cabinet at the back of the shop, almost eclipsed by a grandfather clock and polished officers chair, on which sat an assortment of threadbare teddies. On the second shelf down, alongside snuff boxes and silver ornaments, was a small knife. It's handle had been stained black with pitch.

Julie had no use for it but knew she had to have it.

Four minutes later she was walking out the door, her new purchase wrapped in newspaper and tucked carefully in her handbag.

Socks was on the doorstep. He snaked around her legs as she jiggled the key in the lock, shopping bags hanging from her arms getting heavier with every second it look her to get through the front door.

Julie put the new apparel into the washing machine, a habit she had got into after bringing home a donated item that was funky but festering. The wine she placed in the fridge and the chocolate in a bowl, ready for munching on later. She reached into her bag to take out the knife but it had worked itself free of the wrapping and sliced her palm. She recoiled in shock, instinctively closing her fingers over the wound and covering her fisted hand with the other. Her face scrunched up in pain as she washed the incision under cold running water before dressing it with an oversized piece of gauze and copious amounts of medical tape.

As with Jade, Julie understood that the energies of previous owners could leave an imprint on an item. Objects hundreds of years old would have passed through many hands and the nature of the knife meant that blood had most likely been spilt by the weapon.

The blade would be placed under the rays of the next full moon to cleanse it of negative vibes and charge it with lunar power.

Julie often dreamt vividly, her nightly subconscious fantasies playing out like a movie. Tonight she dreamt of spells and charms.

The inch long cut on her palm was sore when she woke and was an angry red colour. She painfully bathed it before applying a soothing balm and wrapping it back up.

She was back to the grind stone, her day of vacation felt like a distant memory already.

The town council was organising a heritage day in honour of a trio of women, slain three hundred and forty years previous, accused of practicing witchcraft upon fellow townsfolk and for the deaths of several other locals. The town had a rich history and liked to celebrate the anniversary of its famous residents. This and her dream, inspired Julie to create a witch line of products. She painted beautiful pictures, designed useful coasters and mugs as well as a cartoon range of affordable products featuring hares, black cats, owls, bats, moons and brooms.

They were selling like hot cakes, through the gallery and online to national and international fans of the craft.

52

When Julie was a kid, much of the town was still green fields worked by farmers. She fondly recalled getting chased by a heard of cows, having to seek refuge in a tree with her best friend. Scared and laughing at their predicament and the prospect of spending the night in the branches of a strong sycamore, she smiled at the memory.

Much of the land had now been built on. Makeshift football pitches were now housing estates and cattle had been replaced with cars. Amberley was still a haven for wildlife, a landscape of greens and a testament to the beauty of their slice of the world.

The history of the town was not lost. Plaques commemorated the great people and events that shaped the area. Buildings centuries old stood tall and proud, their purpose having changed over the years. Not all the town's secrets had been revealed, many were still buried or hidden behind false walls, waiting to be discovered. Behind a bricked-up fireplace, builders pulled out a witches bottle. The blue glass contained a rusty nail and the dried remains of a plant, the stopper sealed by candle wax. Another company had found a silk pair of child's slippers with a hand written note, the writing to faded to illegible and a piece of dried heather that crumbled as they carefully removed the artifacts. Donated to the town's museum, they helped to show the beliefs of a time long past.

One of Starr's refuges was the overgrown graveyard located in Old Town, a now largely residential area leading from the top of the steep high street. It had been the resting place of the town's inhabitants for a hundred and seventy years. It had once been a recruitment field for the military, coercing drunk young men to join the forces. Comprising of two sections, the hallowed ground was untouched, reclaimed by nature. Headstones lay were they had become party to some unfortunate incident; others bore the signs of childish vandalism though most stood intact but weathered. Ivy climbed all over the stones, obscuring the inscriptions of the dead and their families, long forgotten by most. The unconsummated section had been converted into a playground and child's football pitch, before Starr was even born. The headstones had been dug up and placed along the boundary wall, no consideration paid when a stray ball smashes into the last reminder of a life once lived.

Starr liked to think they would appreciate someone acknowledging that they had existed. She would trace the letters of their names with her fingertip, say them out loud. Working out the ages at which those whose bones lay under her feet died. She imagined the life they may have led and the circumstances that caused their demise. Feeling especially drawn to the grave of a two-year-old boy, John Box, the date of his death the same as her birth, with an age gap of over ninety decades. She would often sit beside his headstone and watch the birds as the sang a cheery lullaby or hoped between the branches hoping to disturb an insect from its hiding place.

Starr enjoyed the aesthetic element to the engravings. Most insignias here were the common IHS, graveyards in the surrounding villages had much better ones. Her favourite monogram was of two skulls, back-to-back, looking left and right. She had assumed the abbreviation IHS stood for 'in his service' until a chat with the caretaker at the newer cemetery ground. He had dutifully informed her that it in fact represented the name Jesus, translated from the Greek as 'ihsous'.

Starr had slept rough that night. The weather had been glorious for weeks, the ground was dry and the wind was warm. Cuddled up in her sleeping bag in the nook of an ancient oak tree she watched the stars as they twinkled before her eyelids fluttered closed.

Starr's phone had no battery, or credit. Being frugal with her shrinking supply of cash she bought a meal deal on her way into town. John's internment was on the edge of the cemetery, six places from the entrance, second row with his mother, father, his older brother, who lived to only half of Johns age. A supporting low stone pillar provided a convenient seat beside the grave of the deceased youngster, on which Starr could be found most days, her back against the cold stone wall, her face to the sky.

She was half way through a pasta pot when her attention was drawn to the arrival of a large truck and three workmen in orange vests. Soon the tranquillity of the dead was disturbed by power drills and shouting.

The storm had come before the calm in the form of gale force tail winds that wreaked havoc on the small harbour port. Trees had been uprooted, blocking the roads or snapping power lines, boats were overturned by the colossal waves and trampolines transported into neighbouring gardens.

Gale Force winds had felled a tree which crushed the old stone wall, exposing a casket. Through the gap in the masonry the earth had fallen away, exposing a coffin that had been surrounded in chains, ensuring the occupants would never raise from the grave.

The remaining burials had decomposed into the soil, the wooden structures and bodies reclaimed by mother nature. Nails and bones were the only testament that they had lived.

Watching from her vantage point over a high wall eight yards from the repair, Starr saw the coffin before they had the responsibility of protecting the scene. Iron struts has prevented the soil from compressing the tomb and its contents into the mud but hundreds of years had forced the wooden panels to bow. A skeletal hand of a long dead inhabitant poked through the soil.

What they had assumed would be a few hours work had turned into a mini renovation project as the coffin had to be removed and the inhabitant relocated to a modern casket and a local archaeologist brought in to oversee the removal and reinternment of the deceased, who took up temporary residence in a funeral directors adjacent to the plot.

A white tent had been erected around the gravesite. Protecting the public from seeing the dead, it caused a media frenzy with reports on social media stating a suspected murder, or major drug haul. One poster suggested a find of sixteenth century treasure, hidden by seafarer and reputed pirate, Richard Grenville.

The workmen had moved on to the next paying job whilst the appropriate team were compiled to assist in the excavation. In the meantime, morbid curiosity got the better of Starr and she snuck into the tent, after the orange clad men had left. It was gloomy. The thick white fabric let in little light but offered enough for Starr to get up close and personal with the deteriorating burial. It would later emerge that rumour had it, the grave contained three bodies. The Chinese whispers were not wrong. The remains were buried pointing in the direction of West, two had their hands tied behind their backs, as the small bones were found under the pelvises, examined and confirmed a belonging to women of advanced years. Each skull was found with the precautionary measure of a stone placed in their mouths. A custom usually reserved for suspected vampires but occasionally used to scared townsfolk to protect themselves from supernatural forces. If the persecuted could not move their mouth they could not perform the spell to resurrect themselves.

On the side that could be seen, Starr noticed symbols carved into the wood. They were hard to decipher but did not look Christian in origin. There were circles and crescent shapes, triangles and spirals. Starr drew them in her sketch book.

She touched the bony finger. It was dry and cold.

Twelve inches or so from the surface Starr noticed an unusual pattern. It wasn't soil, debris or stone. It was material and it seemed something was wrapped inside. Starr pulled at it. The fabric broke into pieces. The pages were not made of paper as they did not tear but they were delicate and forcing them out would destroy them. Using her hands she dug around the item that had been deliberately buried. She was covered in mud past her elbows but succeed in freeing what would turn out to be a book, the pages made from animal hide, the writing faded. The sludge of wet earth had seeped through the material and stained the object which Starr hid inside a jumper from her backpack. She had no idea what she would do with the stolen item but knew she wanted it.

Ding dong. Lizzie stood at the front door that she used to have a key for. Popping round to see her best mate, future maid of honour and former lodger for a cuppa, she had brought her fiancé Ned, to discuss wedding ideas.

They sat around the kitchen table, the loved-up couples arms touching. Lizzie had found her soul mate. Only in her early twenties, barely into adulthood Lizzie had experienced a string of disastrous relationships but her connection to Ned was instant, love at first sight. He felt the same.

In 1712 they had been embarking on a courtship, him the lord of the manors son, her a servants daughter. It was doomed before it began, the two hearts waiting over three hundred years to find each other again. Lizzie believed she was the reincarnation of Elizabeth Summers, the granddaughter of Aggie Summers, a reputed witch of the Amberley coven and skilled herbalist.

Julie's family had a long association with the town. Her ancestors were not of great importance to history but they were studious hard-working folk who preserved their time on the earth through writings and objects. And they were hoarders, seeing the value in items that was lost on others, each generation added to the collections. She assumed her love of history probably came from living with furniture, ornaments, paintings, handed down through the generations.

Julie's parents feed her enthusiasm for the past. When she returned to the UK and settled in her home town, her mother gave her a wooden puzzle box, crafted from a thick branch, that had been entrusted to the first-born girl of the family tree, which could be traced back to the sixteen hundreds. The tale of the mysterious object, covered in supernatural sigils, says there was once a note that read 'Keep it safe. Aggie'. The heirloom was in Julie's care when it inexplicitly combusted into ashes when Lizzie and Ned consummated their union.

The girls had drunk a bottle and a half of rosé and the trio had settled on a colour scheme of lilac and cream. An appointment had been made online with a bridal shop to try on dresses. The cap unscrewed with a pop and Ned topped up the empty wine glasses. Too tipsy to make good decisions, talk turned to work with Julie showing the soon to be Mrs Millburn her adorable new goth range.

"Here." Lizzie handed Julie a small package, wrapped in tissue paper and secured with a pink ribbon. Inside was a jewellery box containing a necklace.

A disc with a convex dome the size of a two pence coin hung from a delicate silver chain. The pattern inside looked like an artistic wave with gradients of blue swirling to a point.

"We have matching ones." In tandem Lizzie and Ned held up almost identical pendants. "They are made from the ashes of your box." With tears in her eyes, Julie thanked and embraced her friend.

Conversation turned to the empty room.
"What about the girl from the Ivy, she seemed sweet." Julie conceded that she did need to get her

arse in gear but she was distracted with a new business venture forming in her mind.

The following day she popped into the funeral homes based in town with a proposition. She hoped to offer a memorial service to their clients providing posthumous photography of deceased loved ones with sensitive, keepsake images and a selection of options for cremation jewellery and other decorative ways to celebrate a life they wished to remember.

53

Julie had used antiepic cream but the cut on her palm was not healing. Salt wash hadn't worked. She was reluctant to book a doctor's appointment over a simple slash but the incision, that ran parallel to her head line, was still red and sore to touch. She preferred a natural approach where possible so turned to the internet for advice. The position made it difficult, as making a fist or typing put pressure on the wound to open again.

The market had a stall dedicated to bee's. From cuddly critters to patterned material, the buxom woman sold pollinator related products, sourced locally. Julie bought a jar of set honey, if it didn't work, she'd eat in on toast.

It did. Her hand was sticky but the inflammation had gone down within twenty-four hours and in thirty-six the wound had closed and showed signs healing nicely. She transferred some of the honey into a small pot that she kept inside her handbag.

“Garçon.” Lizzie clicked her fingers in the air. Both girls burst out laughing. A lunch date to discuss bridesmaids outfits had morphed into a daytime drinking session with more talk about the past than the future. Julie’s single status being the main area of conversation.

Loved up Lizzie wanted her friend to experience the admiration she had for her fiancé.

“Ladies.” Steve put the drinks on the table.

“Oooo, personal service today!” Steve rolled his eyes at Lizzie’s jovial comment. Steve, as head bar man, didn’t often come out from behind the counter but Poppy wasn’t on shift and Jade was not feeling well. Ms Johnson had been feeling rough for a few days, a temperature was causing her to sweat and her injured finger was throbbing. She felt like a real-life version of princess aurora, her finger also pricked on a sewing implement, just like the immortalised fairy tale who was cursed to die. Jade felt she could sleep for a hundred years.

“No Ned today?” Asked Julie.

“Girly dresses aren’t really his thing! He’s tasked with sorting the ushers, so I get free reign on my escorts! Besides, he’s surfing.” Ned, a keen skateboarder, had joined the surfing community. Trading wheels for water, he had embraced the sea and the freedom of riding the waves and not a halfpipe.

Three miles up the coastline was a resort populated with expensive beach huts, seafood restaurants and novelty shops selling flipflops and sticks of rock. In the summer it was crammed with tourists, trapsing sand through caravans and basking in the sun. In the winter it was a ghost town, the business kept afloat by the hardy residents.

Not only had he signed up as a member of the water sports club, he'd also joined the grassroots charity Surfers Against Sewage, a movement protecting the marine environment, fighting against pollution in the sea and arming activists with resources and knowledge for a thriving ocean. His social media was filled with posts about beach cleans and urged his followers to recycle. Individually they'd always done their bit, used the kerbside collection for household waste, separated bottles at work but Ned had become obsessed with saving the planet. He picked up litter on walks through the wood and town. Lizzie was happy to bag crisp packets from tree branches and sweet wrappers from hedges but was embarrassed when he did it walking the streets. She knew she shouldn't be but part of her was jealous. He got complimented for his dedication to bettering the area, which swelled her heart with pride but made her feel inadequate that she wasn't as devoted. Their house resembled a Chinese launderette. Washed plastic hung from the clothes line and hooks he'd put into the conservatory ceiling, ready to be sent away and turned into clothing or other useful household items by specialist companies who shared his passion.

"You know I told you about his need to find any stray bit of litter he can lay his hands on?"

"At least it's not cats! But yes, he's certainly turned into a little eco-warrior"

"Tell me about it. He's only gone and teamed up with one of his new surfing buddies, you know Kev, that fit builder who works for Francesca's uncles firm."

'I wish I did', thought Julie. "I bet you do!" Said Lizzie, correctly interpreting her best friends body language to the name, knowing exactly what she was thinking. "Well, this guy's misses is a primary school teacher and they've teamed up on an environmental awareness project to build huts out of eco-bricks and mud. I've got stacks of bloody two litre bottles stuffed full! Get this," Lizzie was in full flow. It wasn't that she didn't care but her wedding was her priority, "he's got to chop it all up into little pieces so it is heavy enough to use!"

"Teaching kids young to save the planet is a good thing."

"I know but while I'm trying to arrange the seating plan, he's jamming crap into bottles!" Whined Lizzie. Julie couldn't help laughing at her friends selfishness.

The world was slowly waking up to the need to reduce and reuse.

The fourth round of drinks was served by Jade. Having delivered the full glasses safely to the recipients, Jade turned to head back to the kitchen when she felt light headed. The last thing she saw was the table come towards her as she fainted.

She was only out for a matter of seconds but was woozy and took a minute to get her bearings, which was the floor of the Ivy. From her vantage point she saw the underneath of several tables, one of which was akin to a school desk with chewing gum carelessly stuck by an ignorant patron.

Steve helped her into an adjacent chair whilst Lizzie disappeared into the kitchen and came back with a glass of iced water.

Julie noticed Jade's red fingertip. She quizzed her on the nature and treatment of her injury. Turning over her hand to show her recently healed palm, Julie took the tub of honey from her bag and applied some to the tip of Jades finger. The relief was evident of Jades face as the natural product took effect. Julie was warming to the girl; she could see her potential and that they were kindred spirits but was not yet ready to open her house to her.

"Here, take this." Lizzie handed Jade a small tube. It contained aloe vera oil. "This will help sooth it."

"I use turmeric paste." Interjected Steve. Lizzie made a face. "don't you knock it Summers. It smells and stings a bit but it works. It's no different from your witchy remedy." It was true, the spice was renowned for its anti-properties.

"Achoo." Starr blew her nose. She'd come down with a cold. The sky was bright and the day warm but Starr shivered and her body convulsed as she tried to stifle a cough, which burst out of her in a spray of saliva.

With the sodden book in a carrier bag, a bulging backpack and holdall over one arm, Starr was on her way to beg refuge at an acquaintances house. Jade was slowly walking home; the buses were infrequent, and she couldn't justify the cost of a taxi. Steve had let her finish her shift early and she was hoping that the fresh air would be of benefit. Her finger was no longer a source of pain but her leg hurt. She suspected that a deep purple bruise was forming from her abrupt descent to the patterned carpet of her employment.

Jade stopped half way along the old bridge, looking out at the river. The sun glinted off the water, small boats bobbed on the waves and a family of ducks emerged through the archway, the ducklings merrily quacking as they dutifully followed their mother. A portion of the quay had been roped off for safety as an immense ship was loaded with stone from the quarry. Jade watched the crane as it manoeuvred its load into the cargo hold.

Starr was also gazing out at the tide. Her friend was away at a training course so the hopeful wish of a night under cover was not an option. She was stubborn enough to refuse to go home and insecure enough to worry they wouldn't have her back. Afterall, she was an adult. Most of her friends hadn't gone to university or got jobs, found partners but she had followed a different path. Always a lone wolf, Starr struggled to fit into conventional society. Her appearance could be considered by some as unapproachable, maybe a little scary but she had a heart of gold and a passion for saving the planet.

Starr hadn't realised she was crying until she heard the gentle approach of footsteps and a soft voice that said, "Hey. Are you okay?"

Starr looked up with tears in her eyes at a young lady with skin the succulent shade of a Galaxy bar. A tangle of curls was pulled into balled bunches and caring eyes looked through black rimmed spectacles.

"Not really. Achoo."

The stranger offered Starr an opened packet of pocket tissues. Jade felt somehow drawn to the punk rock themed traveller, there was something about her aura that called to the intuitive barmaid.

"snuufff. Thank you." She blew her dripping nose and dried her face, with a fresh one.

The two struck up a conversation that concluded in Jade offering Starr a roof for the night. Owing to safeguarding issues with the children in the main house, visitors needed to be authorised so she would need to sneak Starr through the woods and into the garden. They made a mad unseen dash across the lawn to the safety of the summer house, Jade's temporary lodgings whilst she found a place to rent.

Jade heated a microwave meal while Starr took a shower. The hot water felt nourishing on her dirty skin. She indulged in Jades cruelty free Body Shop cleansing wash, closing her eyes as she inhaled the scent of berries.

With a towel wrapped round her head like a turban, she had changed into a pair of jogging bottoms and woolly jumper. Tesco's own brand lasagne sat steaming on a plate with a condensating glass of coke and side of garlic bread. Starr was overwhelmed by Jade's kindness and burst out crying. A hug from her saviour calmed her down and they ate in silence, apart from the sound of sneezing. Starr's belly grumbled in equal measure of protest and pleasure at the warm meal.

"Use this." Jade offered Starr the tube of aloe vera she was gifted by Lizzie that morning. Mixing a tablespoon of honey into boiling water, Jade used Julie's natural remedy in the hope it would help cure Starr, like it had soothed the pain in her finger.

That night Julie, Starr and Jade had vivid dreams of walking a familiar yet new trek through woodland where weird and wonderful mythical creatures frolicked and fanciful spirits left trails of colour in their wake, weaving through the trees and over shrubs.

Starr woke the next morning feeling fresh and revived. Her nose was not blocked or running and her chest felt clear. She'd made a new friend and life was looking up.

54

The car parks were full and vehicles were abandoned on the side of the road as visitors and locals turned up for the highly publicised heritage day. Stall holders framed the edges of the large park whilst the town band and it's assortment of instruments and enthusiastic musicians played from the bandstand. The sun had also come out for the day, a rare occurrence when the town had an event planned.

Julie was one of the stall holders. Placed between a couple selling homemade cakes and a farmer with savouries made from his livestock, Julie stood the risk of eating her profits. She'd already consumed a mouth-watering rich brownie with her thermos of hot chocolate and the customers hadn't even arrived yet. She'd paid for a delicious smelling pasty and was adding the finishing touches to her table when she heard the booming voice of the town crier announcing the mayoral party and dignitaries.

Behind the black cloaked assistants and flag bearer was a grey-haired potbellied man, weighed down with gold chains and a heavy fur trimmed red robe and lacy cravat, accompanied by his wife in a suit befitting princess Diana. They were followed by a judge and representatives from the armed and emergency forces. Next in the procession were men, women and children decked out in medieval dress, those imitating tradesmen in tunics and puffed out breeches walked in front of dirty faced females in long dresses and simple bonnets.

In addition to the usual annual heritage displays was the commemoration of the three hundred and fortieth anniversary of the execution of Temperance Lloyd, Susanna Edwards and Mary Trembles. Much of the day was dedicated to witchcraft with stalls offering scented candles and homemade spells, dried herbs and crystals. Alongside her cat range, Julie was selling her supernatural creations. Pocket money gifts to highly priced originals, strands of fake ivy and pentagrams decorated the table, with a cauldron full of sweets to entice potential customers.

A sea of witches walked slowly behind the official congregation, dancing and waving their arms rhythmically to a pipe playing wizard. There were sexy witches, haggard crones, wizard of Oz and Harry Potter cosplayers, people dressed in multihued frocks with feathers in their hair and children in pointy hats, carrying wands.

Jade and Starr sat on the harbour wall and watched as the colourful crowd went past. Conversation turned to religious beliefs, each trying discretely to determine what faith the other followed. Starr had been christened as a child, attended Sunday school and learnt about Jesus and his disciples but as she grew she challenged the fundamental theories behind the worshipping of one all-encompassing God. The church took offense to her questioning the doctrine they taught and she was expelled from the congregation.

Starr was delighted to share details of her wild child ways. “I only asked things like, what did Jesus do from aged eighteen to thirty and surely he was getting it on with Mary Magdalene.”

“I’m well behind that Dan Brown and the holy grail being Jesus’ bloodline.”

“I know, are we expected to believe he was a virgin like his mother?!”

“Who was clearly shagging around.”

“Hey, the lord will smit us you know!” Both girls burst out laughing but cast a precautionary glance towards the heavens. They talked some more with the chat turning towards the craft, learning that each believed, or at least wanted too, that magic had existed once and maybe still did.

“Did you see Britain’s Got Talent the other night, with the girl on the bike?”

“No Jay, I didn’t.” Starr made a ‘doh’ gesture, her new friend aware of her homeless status.

“Sorry. Let me see if I can find it on YouTube.” Jade’s lightning-fast digits whipped over the keyboard and seconds later she held the phone up so they could watch the uploaded clip.

“I wish I had magic. I’d have so much fun.” Starr clicked her thumb and middle finger on her right hand, “Money.” And again with the word “Love”. Her next hand gesture was to point at a passing car that took the bend in excess of the speed limit, narrowly avoiding an elderly woman who was slowly crossing the road with her shopping trolley. She flicked her index finger, visualising the power she wished she had, removing the dangerous driver and their rusty lethal weapon from the road in a dramatic roll that involved a lamp post. A nice person at her core, Starr had a savage streak of wicked cruelty towards her fellow humans but always with an underlying humour, that ensured she'd never become a serial killer, despite her outward projection.

"If only, but it's probs a good thing you don't, considering your choice of actions. Magic isn't supposed to be for personal gain." Starr made a disappointed face. "Let's have a look around." Jade steered Starr in the direction of the noise, hidden behind mature trees and the long line of hyperactive children at the ice cream van.

Julie's insides were doing somersaults as the mayor said a few words on the history of the town and the public were released to take part in the activities and hopefully part with some cash. Smiling at anyone who came within a foot of her stall it concealed the nerves. When someone came into the gallery, it was usually with a view to make a purchase but here customers would prod and examine the artwork, put it back and wander aimlessly to the next stall, repeating the action but keeping their wallet firmly in their handbag. By lunchtime Julie had sold baskets full of the cheap product and was hungry. The pasty tasted as good as it smelt and for dessert she was back at the cake stall for topping heavy cupcakes and another brownie.

There was a lull in custom. A larping display with shining armour and clashing swords had the crowds enthralled, leaving the traders twiddling their thumbs. Julie seized the opportunity to have a browse herself as she made a beeline for the axe throwing, whilst checking out the hot guys in chainmail but none took her fancy. She'd tried archery before but found her aim off using the bow. Holding the sharpened tool in both hands she followed the instructors directions. From over her head she swung the axe forward, letting go as her arms became parallel to her jawline and missing the target. Her second attempt hit the wooden board but the axe bounced off it. She got three of the fifteen tries to lodge into the painted bullseye and had a thoroughly good time doing it. She stopped to say hello to the women weaving baskets and operating old fashioned looms, as one was a valued customer who owned a wall of original Slater art.

Julie never judged anyone on appearance but she suspected that the two approaching punters would not have deep enough pockets and was conscious for sticky fingers. As they got closer she realised one was Jay from the Ivy, the other she thought had a vague familiarity about her.

"Wow, look at that bat, it's so sweet." Starr loved bats. Where most people saw disease and sharp teeth, Starr thought their turned-up noses and oversized ears were cute.

"That's Bartholomew the Bat. He's been a sell-out in coasters and keychains." The three talked some more about the artwork, each pulling out details they liked and how it accentuated the picture.

"I bet. I wish I could draw." Jade looked wishfully at an image of Socks the cat in front of the interior of a witches kitchen with herbs hanging from the ceiling and a full moon shining through the curtainless lead paned window.

"Just keep practicing. Everyone is artist in their own way."

"Not me, Starr is amazing. She's got an imagination I could only dream of." Jade's confidence was for appearances sake but Julie did put her at ease. It was something about Ms Slaters approachable eyes and calming persona that made Jade relax in her company. They pointed out the 'stay wild, moon child' range, stencilled onto mugs, sign and tote bags. It was a term that Jade used to describe Starr, who was an ultimate definition of the new age slogan.

Embarrassed Starr replied that she wasn't that good, to which Jade answered she had seen her sketches and to stop belittling her talent. An enquiry about taking on an apprenticeship was meet with a gentle rejection but also with a suggestion to volunteer. Every businessman loved a bit of free labour and Julie knew several who would happily oblige. She had been in the same position once, putting yourself out there was scary but it had been worth it not to be stuck in a job she hated, just to pay the bills.

As they chatted, Julie felt a positive vibe from the two girls. Jade and Starr experienced the same energy. Julie felt a spiritual vibration emanate from the girls that she wanted to explore but felt the timing wasn't quite right but would be soon.

Half an hour was lost like it was five minutes, the three like-minded young women sharing views on sustainability and accountability. They differed to a degree but the common theme of saving the planet ran through their cores.

Looking around the remaining stalls, Starr was lost in thought about her future and Jade was thinking about her living situation and her unofficial lodger. They found themselves coerced into looking at an array of apparel to keep their head and neck warm, that they had no intention of purchasing by a trader who sounded like she should have been at a London market.

"This one would suit you." Before Jade could stop her, the enthusiastic vendor wrapped a tie-dyed tasselled scarf around her neck, flicking a side over her shoulder.

Jade gasped and pulled the garment from her throat. Apologising she practically threw the soft fabric at the woman and hurried off.

Starr found her sat on the harbour steps, a mallard quaking it's protest at the lack of bread.

"What was that?" Starr had only known Jade for a few weeks and had not seen her behave in such a fashion.

"It was nothing."

"Jay, you freaked right out and ran off, that ain't nothing." Starr wasn't one to push others, preferring to tactfully take a step back but she couldn't understand the reason behind the panic she saw in Jade's eyes.

"I don't like things around my neck. Never have. I panic if anything touches my throat." Jade felt ridiculous telling Starr about the phobia she had since she could remember. She could recall no reason for it. "I can't wear turtle neck tops or sleep with the covers pulled too high. I know, it's lame"

"No it's not. I'm terrified of spiders, even the little ones."

"Everyone's scared of spiders." Jade could see what Starr was trying to do. She often wondered over the years why she felt so worried about pressure on her neck. Pauline had never exposed any physical abuse from her early years and Jade sensed it was more ingrained in her soul than something that had happened to her in this lifetime.

"Maybe you were a witch in another life." Hanging was the fate of most found guilty of witchcraft in England. There was the occasional burning at the stake but that was a practice reserved mostly for Europe. The British favoured stringing up those deemed deserving of the penalty of death.

"Maybe I still am!"

55

Starr meet Jade after her shift at the Ivy. She had good news to share.

Part of the employee perks were free meals, on days you worked. They spilt the cost of Starr's food. They shared a bed so Jade was happy, for now, to share her finances.

"You don't look impressed with the menu."

Starr's a vegan. She sometimes had to sacrifice her integrity and eat vegetarian in order to survive but took the animal product free option at every opportunity, refusing to let meat pass her lips.

Poppy brought the order too the table. Jade sank her teeth into a locally sourced burger dripping with cheese, limp lettuce and a rasher of streaky bacon. Starr chose a vegan lifestyle yet she did miss the juicy taste of a steak but was to stubborn to relent on her decision.

"How can you consume something that innocently walked this earth?"

"Cos it tastes good and it's a great source of protein."

"Eat a pig or chicken instead. You can get plenty of protein from beans and pulses you know."

Jade made a revolted face and looked at Starr's steaming paella. The pungent scent of pepper overpowering her sense of smell. "But it tastes gross. I'm helping climate change, too many cows farting out methane is damaging the ozone!"

"That's due to their digestive system cos they eat food inedible for humans so what does that tell you? And the greenhouse gas comes out their mouth, not their butt! It's no different to what's produced at landfill, hence the need to recycle."

"Hey, I recycle thank you and I don't flush if I don't need to. Besides, if we weren't designed to eat meat, why do we have canines and what about the essential job of plants to the environment, we need them to oxygenate the world, don't we? If you munch all the trees, what's going to clean the air?"

Starr was not a biologist and had no comment on human evolution but she had plenty to say on the treatment of animals in the food chain, regurgitating PETAs aims to overthrow the meat industry. Jade was subjected to a friendly but passionate lecture on factory farming and the cruel conditions animals are kept in before being slaughtered.

"I don't judge your choices!" Jade was behind any campaign for the better treatment of livestock but had not been swayed to a plant-based diet. "Well, you do you but I'm eating this cow. It's dead anyway."

The two new friends agreed to differ, respectful of each other's views.

"I popped into Taser tattoo parlour today. Guess what?"

From the smile Jade could see Starr was trying to suppress, she had a solid idea of the news but didn't want to spoil the excitement of Starr telling her.

"I'm going in Wednesday!" Starr's voice raised in pitch as she told Jade about her visit to the skin artist. She'd been handed a piece of paper and brief and had to design a tattoo befitting the description. Lawrence was the size of a WWE wrestler and tattooed from head to toe. A gentle giant, Lawrence was impressed with the youngster who had walked in and thrown herself at his mercy. With a little tweaking the customer commissioned her design, to be inked on their right bicep.

She'd also signed up for a free workshop in street art. She wasn't a fan of tagging but there were some beautiful pieces of graffiti brightening up the disused buildings around the town. Her portfolio was growing.

Her volunteer work would eventually led to an apprenticeship. Within a year Star would transition from artist to tattooist with aspirations to open her own studio, with an all-female team.

She scored a part time job in a new vegan café. The single fronted shop was a community initiative. Starr washed dishes and took orders but she was on a payroll and had direction in her life.

Starr had started to build up a friendship with Julie. She had popped into the gallery a few times for advice and Julie had kindly offered to give over a display stand for Starr to show her work. Julie knew the importance of collaborative working and it was in her nature to give people a chance. Starr's work was different to her own, rawer, which would bring in an alternative clientele. She made frames from drift wood, 3d pictures from beach glass and small stones and pebbles with topical designs. There was competition over the desirable range of bee accessories, popular with the masses and appearing, in some way, on almost every household linen and kitchen ware as well as clothing and jewellery. The busy insects and their diminishing plight had captured the heart of the nation with people rushing out with sugar water to revive flagging drones and planting flowers filled with pollen to attract them and feel they are doing their part to protect the species. Julie's pollinators were scientific studies with accurate proportions, Starr's were crazy looking and bright. Both versions were selling well to the locals and tourists.

The world is in the grips of a climate crisis. Activists, young and old, are shouting for change but those with the money and power aren't listening. In their ivory towers they can escape to untouched islands while the masses fight to make the planet a better place.

Lone voices try to lead the way but most blindly followed the corrupt whose end goal is their own bank account. The wealthy could portray an eco-friendly existence buying organic and donating vast sums to charity but they seemed to care little for the carbon footprint they left in their wake. They advocate a less consumerist lifestyle then revel in the spoils of the aftersales of their targeted marketing ploys. The poor had little choice but to continue to contribute to the sales of processed food, locking them in an unfair cycle of guilt. The plight of the decreasing resources and impact on ecological systems such as the rainforest was a real threat that people want to support but their budgets only allowed them to purchase the cheap replacements sold alongside the sustainably sourced ones. As much as the average family wanted to put their money towards positive change they often had to sacrifice their ideals to eat or keep a roof over their heads. Purchasing power was all well and good, if you had the spare capital.

Large industries had proactive ways to offer reassurance to consumers that they were ethically sourcing their material but they often came with a hefty price tag. Proudly stamping a universally recognised symbol on their products and packaging show that they have contributed to protecting the environment and have adhered to strictly regulated guidelines. With the reality of busy lives, rushing from one task or job or another, people grabbed what had become habit, not having the time to examine labels and make judgements on the eco-friendly elements, it came down to cost. Good intentions are laid down, a shop is carefully planned and executed with healthy meal choices and fresh produce but it is human nature to revert back to their old ways for ease and comfort.

Social media, with its trends and influencers bred consumerism with generations glued to phones following one sided opinions and buying what society tells them they need.

56

The council had found Jade accommodation. With the previous tenant on permanent vacation to a secure unit, a one roomed bedsit had become available and Jade's name was top of the list. It was in a shared house with folk that looked dodgy and smelt of stale beer, cigarettes and cannabis.

The last thing Jade wanted was to agree to move in but agreed as the summer house was only a temporary arrangement, that wasn't strictly within the guidelines of fostering so she felt she had to take it. Pauline and John had been exceptional carers and she was sure they knew that Starr was on the scene so she accepted out of an empathetic sense of duty.

She had an appointment the following week to sign the paperwork. It would be two o'clock before the property as ready as it needed airing and repairing. Pauline had mixed reactions to the news. She hated to see any charge leave but found satisfaction in their independence. She brought down some boxes and bubble wrap for Jades limited possessions.

"I need to find some ways to save money." The prospect of the new unfurnished property meant that Jade would have to pull in the purse strings or she would be sleeping on the floor and eating pot noodles for the foreseeable future.

"We can make our own cleaning products, it's easy." Starr had been an emerging eco-warrior since she was old enough to form her own opinions and saw through the pesticides used on weeds, to which she poured boiling water on the roots to kill the unwanted plant and the chemical-based cleaners. Her mother would sock the worktops and floors with toxic household sprays making the house smell like a swimming pool. Mrs Anderson had tried a natural shop once but the refill was more expensive than the original product, so she never returned. She considered Starr's homemade concoctions inferior to the cleaning power of bleach but jade's perfected mixture of vinegar, baking soda, lemon and a scented essential oil left the taps sparkling and the side disinfected..

Within the year, Starr would find herself volunteering once a week at the packaging free initiative. Based in a low impact shop housed below a two-storey apartment the shelves were lined with dispensers containing cereal to shampoo. Customers brought in their own receptacles and filled them with as much, or little, as they needed. The ethos was to reduce waste and improve environmental footprints.

"At least we don't have to worry about paying for petrol." Neither girl had a car, or a licence to drive one.

"With the emissions from all these gas guzzlers I wouldn't drive, even if I could!"

"I've seen you push a shopping trolley; I'm not getting in a car with you!"

"Bring back the horse and cart, I say." Starr wasn't into history like Jade and Julie were but she understood the need to return to the old ways and carved out a unique existence that impacted as little on the environment as she could.

"I'd happily ride everywhere." Jade had learnt to control a horse living with the Abbots. For a short while, a wheelchair-bound girl lived with them and would be taken off for horse therapy at a specialist stable. Jade had accompanied her as she was anxious around strangers and it gave the city chick a feel for the countryside.

"By not using cars in the first wave of the pandemic, the ozone layer showed signs that it was repairing." A nasty infectious disease caused by the SARS-CoV2 virus had swept across the world, killing young and old and causing havoc to the economic status of most countries, stretching health care to its limit. "Besides, you miss so much shooting round on transport and there's such beauty here."

"We could get bikes." Jade's suggestion was meet with a disapproving look from Starr.

"And risk my life on the roads! I've never been that steady, or safe, on two wheels, I'd rather walk."

"Probably safer. Not much fun in the rain though. I hate wet trousers sticking to my legs, feels so icky." Jade re-enacted how she responded to having clothing clinging to her skin.

"Nice look!" Both girls descended into fits of laughter.

Gaining her composure Jade said, "Rain is the reason I won't get a dog. Having to walk it and get wet, nah-ah. I'd like a cat."

"Me too. I prefer cats. My own familiar." Starr smiled in a playfully wicked way. "Animals are so in tune with the elements, we need to pay more attention to them."

"All hail the voice of our planet, David Attenborough."

"Trouble is the right people aren't listening." They got into a discussion about endangered species and mankind's impact on nature, trying to imagine unthought of ways to balance the ever-increasing population and decreasing resources.

"It'd be fab to work for one of those wildlife charities, rescuing bears and tigers."

"I've been to a Greenpeace rally." Starr recounted her day trip to Bristol. Having skipped school and caught a bus to the train station she used the money she was supposed to have been spending on her lunches to attend the demonstration. It was the first time she'd experienced so many people jammed into one place. The rush to leave the cinema was nothing compared to this. The tone was calm with an underling feeling of disquiet brewing but it fed Starr's desire to be different, to stand up for a cause, to be heard. The grounding and detentions had been worth it.

"I've never done anything like that. Not even handed in homework late."

"Come along to the XR demo on Saturday." A large demonstration had been organised in the country's capital to protest for an end to the fossil fuel economy and withdraw fossil fuel investments. Jade wasn't sure it was her scene but reluctantly agreed to accompany Starr.

The morning of the appointment to sign her first tenancy agreement was overcast with dark, threatening clouds lingering in the distance.

"I couldn't sleep. I just have a feeling that something good is going to happen today." Starr was tiptoeing excitedly, rubbing her hands together gleefully.

"Really? Are the council going to magically find me a new place to live? Come on, let's get this over with."

Jade trudged down the hill, Starr following light footedly behind. They stopped on the footbridge and looked across at the built-up town, a last reprieve before heading across the bridge and to her fate. The buildings facades barely changed from those in the paintings crafted long before the time of photography.

Jade sighed and pushed herself away from the steel railings.

In her pocket her mobile phone vibrated.

It was an unknown caller.

Jade considered ignoring the call.

She answered on the eighth ring.

57

"Are you serious?"

"Yes. I keep meaning to call. I get good vibes from you. Please accept my apologies, I twisted Steve's arm to get your number."

"No, that's okay, this is perfect. Are you sure?" Jade was jiggling with excitement, looking at Starr who was oblivious to the identity of the caller. The price was within her budget and in a far more respectable part of town.

"When would you like me to come over?"

"How about this afternoon, 2 o'clock? You can have a look at the room."

"You'll never guess who that was." Jade could hardly believe her luck, things rarely seemed to work out to her advantage. She'd found in her life that she had to work her way back from oblivion to see the lightness and leave behind the negative.

"The council with a miracle apartment down on the wharf!"

"Not quite. It was Julie, she's offered me a room." They still had the logistics to talk about but the room was furnished, cheap and Julie was a much better prospect than Joe the Junky. Jade was buzzing with joy.

Starr was subdued at the news, their plans for her to unofficially share the bedsit lay in tatters. Julie's invitation had not been extended to the activist artist.

At two minutes to two Jade knocked on the door of 17 Rectory Drive. As Julie answered a black and white cat sauntered out. He looked up at Jade, rubbed his head on her leg and walked off down the short garden path. His paws criss-crossed like a model performing for the camera, his tale erect pointing to the sky and his head held high.

"That's Socks. Do you mind cats, he comes with the house I'm afraid." Jade assured Julie that Socks would not be problem.

After a tour of the house, they sat outside with a glass of water. The back garden was compact, just like the terraced house it belonged to but it was big enough for a water butt and compost bin. Raised planters ran along the edges and were stocked with herbs and vegetables. Growbags with tomatoes and beans were stacked in front. Hanging baskets of wild flowers attracted bees and butterflies to the sympathetic town garden.

Jade complimented Julie on the attractiveness of the property.

"I can't take credit for the décor, that was Lizzie, she had a flare for interior design. This is my baby though." Julie pointed to the planters. "I used to help Grandad on his allotment, he taught me everything I know." She went on to explain that she had taken over management of her grandfather's allotment which had been broken into several times. His tools had been stolen and produce had been ripped from the ground. They hoped it had been done by a hungry thief and not by mindless vandals so that the trauma cased was not in vain. The damage had knocked her elderly relatives confidence and he wouldn't garden alone. Julie had taken the mantle, hoeing and sowing the ground and drinking cups of tea from a flask as her granddad pottered around the plot.

"I'm not that green fingered." The house plant she had was dead, drowned from over watering.

"I can teach you. I genuinely think we'll face severe food shortages before long. The cost of importing is skyrocketing and all the use of GM is poisoning the wholeness of our crops."

"That the message on the news, that we're in a cost-of-living crisis. What's GM?"

"GM stands for Genetically Modified. Farmers modify the organism in the seeds to improve the yield and they use sprays to keep away insects but the chemicals in the pesticides are damaging the soil,and we're eating food grown in it from a manipulated DNA in the plant that does not occur naturally. Amberley House has a wonderful permaculture garden up there. They are very sensitive to nature and investing in our future."

"Isn't that where all the hippies are?"

Julie giggles at the reference to the nomad community that's in residence in the grounds of the ancient manor house. "I suppose, their lifestyle portrays a traveller existence. They are lovely people, well most of them anyway". Julie's old school friend Hazel was head gardener so she'd had a biased insight into the culture of a true eco-warrior. Dreadlocked hair past her waist and skin tanned from daily exposure, Hazel was the epitome of sustainability. The ethos at the nine-hundred-acre estate needed to be put into practice across the world. Likeminded individuals and family's resided in a commune style arrangement of camper vans and large yurts; part of the rent paid was maintenance on the land and a zero-tolerance policy on waste.

"If you're interested in the room, we can go over some of the house rules."

"I am." Jade's response was instantaneous, ecstatic she had been rescued from the housing from hell. She took a breath before she continued, at a slower and less desperate pace. "Lay them on me!"

"Turn off any electronics if you're not using it. I only leave the microwave and sky box on standby. Same with the water, use as little as you can. Every time I shop I add a well dated can to the stock pile, that's what's in those boxes in the cupboard under the stairs. No room for a boy wizard, cos I'm filling it with supplies!" Jade smiled at the reference and nodded in agreement. "I make wicked casseroles, even if I do say so myself, from left overs. That's normally weekend tea. I also add an item to the food bank trolley. Your choice but it's my way of paying forward. What else? I put any spare change into the demijohn by the front door. When it's full I use the money to buy a tree or I donate the money to an eco-based charity."

"These are such generous idea." Jade was impressed with Julie's commitment to the planet and her fellow humans.

"Thank you. Just a little to help out. The last tree I planted with Lizzie, after she moved out, was down at the communal gardens, that's why the bottle is quite empty. I saw it yesterday; the first apples are starting to form; we did the pear one too." Julie was proud of the benefits of her direct action and the philosophy she was hopefully inspiring in others. "I think that's all. No, I don't like the use of plastics, I have massed quite a collection of tubs to use instead. I make beeswax wraps as well, excellent for wrapping up sandwiches or as covers for tins" There was a lull in the conversation as Jade digested the information and Julie hoped she hadn't come across to bossy, or crazy.

"What do you think?"

"I love the room. I love the house." Jade had a difficult decision to make. She had the upfront funds for a month's rent but not enough to cover the deposit in full. She explained to Julie that she was two hundred pounds short on the deposit so would have to disappointingly pass on the opportunity. She had what she had saved to spend on second hand furnishing but it was not enough.

"How about an extra fifty quid a month until it's paid? The landlord's a good bloke. " Julie understood that starting your life independently could be a struggle. Jade burst out crying at the thoughtful offer. She was desperate to avoid the council lottery and had cancelled her appointment so would not be offered emergency accommodation for a while but her conscious nagged her to reconsider the generous offer.

She snapped up Julie's suggestion, making her the newest house mate and co-career of Socks.

"I'm surprised Starr didn't come with you. You seem joined at the hip!" Jade tactfully talked about Starr's housing situation.

"Leave it with me. I'm not making any promises but I have an idea." Julie was thinking on the go and of the three-way split of the bills and reduction in rent. She was kind but practical. The spare room was small but not that tiny it couldn't easily accommodate a young lady and she suspected that Starr would spend most nights in Jades bed anyway. It was only a storage room for canvases and Julie had more than enough space in the master bedroom to have an easel. It wasn't as if she was using it as a love shack so it didn't need to look like a showgirls boudoir.

There was just the small matter of Starr's lack of funds but she had faith that the youngsters drive would take her places, if they could see past her appearance.

The landlord was flexible and easy going. He had a large portfolio of properties, each with long standing, happy tenants. As long as the rent was paid, the place was looked after with no dramatic interior, or exterior, expressions and local constabulary had no reason to pay a visit they were free to do as they wished.

Three days later, a tearful Pauline pulled up outside the mid-terraced house. Ten minutes later the car had been unloaded and Pauline was waving goodbye.

Jade put the front door key on the keychain that one of her foster siblings had made her. An autistic seven-year-old who could plait embroidery cotton into beautiful friendship bands and tags.

Jade was embarking on the next chapter of her life.

She was nervous. She felt slightly alone and abandoned all over again but this time there was an element of excitement. The feeling that something big was about to happen.

58

Starr texted Jade's mobile at 7.05am to make sure she was up. She was fuelled by coffee and the righteous feeling that her voice may be heard and her protests would make a difference. She had been sofa surfing whilst Jade settled in, a friend on compassionate leave from university had offered her a few nights on the settee. Grieving for her nan, who was more of a mother than her alcoholic parent. Starr's mate was regretful of the company and assistance in dealing with her intoxicated family.

The train was comprised of regularly dressed travellers, business men in suits carrying briefcases and unwashed campaigners holding signs calling for change and retired grans on a mission to get arrested. Starr spoke to a dreadlocked couple with matching tie-dye tops and more silverware in their faces than a jewellery shop had in a cabinet.

Jade wanted to embrace the experience but she felt uncomfortable. She was dressed conservatory and had no intention of falling foul of the law, which she thought could be a very real possibility.

The train picked up more passengers along the route. By the time they arrived in the city, people were stood in the walkways, holding onto the back of seats, swaying with the motion of the carriage, trying not to fall over.

A swarm of people, including Jade and Starr, moved in unison from the platform to the cities high street, meeting in the grounds of the cathedral, dedicated to Saint Peter. There were already hundreds stood around chatting, waving banners and talking to anyone who showed a smidgeon of interest in their cause.

Jade could see that Starr was in her element. Her bright eyes were fliting around the crowd, hunting out other activists she had previously protested with. Jade followed her around like a lost puppy, keeping an eye on the ring of police that stood alert, yet silent, ready to pounce on any trouble.

Julie had been tempted to go along when Jade told her about the extinction rebellion demo but she had mountains of work and deadlines to meet. Jade had been tempted to convince work to call her in and give her an excuse not to go but she didn't.

Starr could tell from her friends wide-eyed expression that she was wary of her current situation and attempted to instil the passion of the parade on her. "Come on Jade, this is our rally cry."

"It's yours." Jade instantly reprimanded her for her uncaring attitude but she had been brought up to respect rules, not flout or challenge them. Starr, who portrayed a confidence she didn't feel inside saw the wariness that Jade viewed the constabulary, remembering her pals worry of incarceration.

"What are rules really?" Before Jade had a chance to answer, Starr continued. "They're just guidelines to make your think, aren't they? I don't adhere to them."

"Usually they are to established to govern our conduct or keep us safe."

"Or are they to control us? They stop stupid people from having to use any common sense! And they are such fun to break." Jade didn't have the opportunity to offer a convincing argument and hear Starr's counter intuitive response as a middle-aged woman with braided hair and a megaphone, called for order.

The officers, all stood like the letter A, visibly tightened their attention on the group, readying themselves for action.

"We are unprepared for the danger our future holds. We face floods, wildfires, extreme weather, crop failure, mass displacement and the breakdown of society. The time for denial is over."

The assembled assortment of men, women and children roared in agreement.

"It is time to act."

A chorus of voices repeated the sentiment.

"Conventional approaches of voting, lobbying, petitions and protest have failed because powerful political and economic interests prevent change. Our strategy is therefore one of non-violent, disruptive civil disobedience."

The speaker was riling up the avid listeners. Starr could feel the adrenaline pumping through her. She felt connected to the hive consciousness, punching the air with her fist. Jade didn't like it. Her heart beat a frantic rhythm as the throng of bodies pressed in from all sides. She'd much rather sign a petition.

The crowd focused on the speaker as she spoke about the impact global warming was having on the planet, she quoted scientific statistics on the climate breakdown and the need to form a citizens assembly. Her words were met with whoops and cheers and cries of, "Be the change".

Jade had thought about a career in politics once, when she was fourteen and had realised she stood out like a sore thumb in the annual school photo. She wasn't bullied, to any greater extent than the usual teenage banter, nor was she popular but she lacked the confidence to pursue her convictions. She was wise enough to know that change needed to come from the top and the only way to make it happen was to infiltrate the system that governed the decision makers. Pauline and John supported her ambitions but she lacked the ruthlessness needed to be a politician. The passion soon faded, replaced with dreams of being a nurse.

Several hours after they had joined the fray people began to disperse, a few at first then small groups began to break away, back to the grind of their daily lives. The young Miss Johnson could see the ideology the organisation was trying to portray but she thought that the way in which they went about things, causing a nuisance and irritating people, which didn't make them sympathetic to the message. Change was needed, there was no doubt but it had to be delivered in a way that encompassed all the positive elements of what each separate group was trying to accomplish, with appropriate funding to achieve their sustainable goals. Jade was aware that they could be the last generation that can do anything to stop destroying the world. Those that went before knew the impact they were causing on the environment but progress was put ahead of green future of their descendants.

Jade seized the opportunity to make an exit, which was a slow progress as Starr hugged goodbyes to fellow warriors.

Thankful to be back to the normality of a crowded shopping experience, Jade popped into The Body Shop, treating herself to a moving in present and a thank you gift for Julie. Before she crossed the threshold the sweet scent of the samples worked like a marketing charm.

Looking for somewhere secluded to have a picnic the girls stumbled upon the ruins of Rougemont Castle. The former Norman construction commissioned by William the Conqueror had been used to defeat armies and later as the counties assizes, sending countless prisoners to their deaths.

The girls took in the formidable site. Something about it held an eerie echo of the past. Jade felt a little giddy as she looked up at the remains of the gatehouse seemingly towering over her. Starr held her left hand against the crumbling stone wall and closed her eyes. Despite the bright day, the chilly temperature of the stone seeped into her veins, shooting icy jolts to her core. A wave of panic wept through her body and she heard whispered reverberations of the screams of souls doomed long ago.

The distress was evident in Starr's face. Jade reached out and shook her shoulder, pulling Starr from under the castles spell.

"Wow. That weirded me out." Starr tried explaining what had just happened but it sounded more like a terrifying daymare.

"Look at this." Jade pointed to an engraved plaque attached to the wall memorialising the execution of three women for the crime of witchcraft. "These are the ones from the heritage day."

"They weren't the last you know."

"This says they were. The town's historians seem pretty proud about its morbid claim to fame." Jade pointed at the bold statement.

"I've got a list somewhere, there's something like fifteen other folk who have been killed. Take Mary Bateman. She was hung for her practices in 1809. Just because the king did not believe in magic, didn't make them any the less a witch. And they were tried under the witchcraft act, well those that made it to trial." Starr was in full rant. "Back home, it's got a dark past you know. It was secured on a pirates legacy and riddled with smugglers. To distance itself from its harrowing history, it became known as

Ducksberry." Starr stopped long enough to take a breath and take in the interested yet amused face of her bestie. "What? I like local history."

The girls walked around the perimeter of the old fortification looking for a nice spot to eat their homemade sandwiches and nibble on strawberries. Neither were hungry and both were feeling a little off. They couldn't pinpoint it; it was like a nervous anticipated dread in the pit of their stomachs but they didn't feel afraid.

The train ride back was subdued. The carriages were half full, leaving a choice of seats. Chatting about irrelevant topics they were soon back at their stop. The bus was late leaving an overcrowded ride back to the small harbour port they called home.

Jade returned to a note on the kitchen table. Julie was at Lizzie's for wedding planning prep and wouldn't be home before the wee hours, with an additional scribble that she'd probably sleep over as there would be wine.

In between talking about bouquets and table favours, Julie told Lizzie about her new flat mate and her plan to extend the invitation to Starr. Julie trusted Lizzie, she had a sixth sense for wheedling out the wronguns in society. Her own life may spiral in crazy directions but it always worked out in her favour. Just a year ago she had no job or partner but was now climbing the career ladder as section leader in one of the areas internationally owned supermarkets and was engaged to her soul mate. She was behind the idea to spread the rent three ways and considered Jade a good judge of character. Julie's mind was made up, she'd tell the girls when she was sober.

Starr stayed the night. It was a wake-up call that she needed to get herself sorted out. Sleeping on the streets was a novelty that had long lost its shine and winter would be coming. Making a mental list of the steps she knew she had to make, contacting the council was at the top, at the bottom, crossed out, was go home. She was relaxed here, felt at home and wished that she could live there too. Not just to be closer to Jade, there was an energy in the place that called to her, she was comfortable inside it's four walls.

59

Humphrey, Julie's sunshine yellow classic Beetle, was parked directly outside the house. It was surprisingly spacious in the back with a seat that ran the width of the vehicle. With the help of Jade, the excess art supplies from the soon-to-be reinstated third bedroom were loaded into Humphrey.

Hidden by canvases was a futon, pushed against the outside wall, with a foldable dayglow green mattress. It wasn't the most comfortable sleep but it was a bed and would be sufficient. Painted splattered overalls and winter coats hung from the freestanding clothes rail and a 1950s bedside table sat below the flaking windowsill. After a trip to the gallery the girls headed to the hardware store for paint and McDonalds drive through for lunch. Choosing the popular battleship grey for the walls and storm cloud grey for the woodwork the housemates got to work. By evening, the compact box room had been revamped and was looking fresh and modern.

Julie couldn't resist adding a few finishing touches. Above the window, she wrote 'Stay Wild, Moon Child' in an elegant Edwardian font with the eight lunar phases cascading down to the right of the cleaned glass. She painted it with the recipient in mind as she too saw Starr as one of the worlds unique and a curious souls who prefers to live in their fantasy, like moon gazing hares on a hazy summer evening.

Knowing that Starr followed a vegan diet, Julie prepared a vegetable curry packed with peppers, spinach, chickpeas and seasoning. The dessert was curtesy of the free-from range at the multinational store that Lizzie was employed by. She took a punt on the wine; it was unfiltered but did not bare the trademark V.

Julie left the gallery early to prepare the meal, that was presented under the guise of a new home dinner for Jade, who was in on the ruse.

Two small gift boxes sat teasingly in the centre of the table. When the food had been eaten and a bottle and half of wine drunk, Jade passed Starr the first box.

"It's Bartholomew! Thank you." Starr swung the bat keyring from her right index finger. Since it's sell-out at the heritage fayre, Julie had prioritised making more.

Julie passed the other box across the table, nearly knocking over the opened bottle of sweet intoxicating grape beverage.

Starr pulled the ribbon which unravelled. Opening the lid she was a little confused by the contents. On a foam bed lay a shining silver yale lock key. Looking between Jade and Julie, who were beaming smiles of teeth and gum, Starr could tell she was missing some inside knowledge behind the gifts.

"They go together." Jade made a poor games master as her clue was lost in translation. As instructed, Starr threaded the key onto the stiff keyring but was still none the wiser.

"Try it." Julie was clueless in the hint department too.

"Try it where?"

"Duh. The door." Jade was still no help.

The conspirative glances and supressed sniggers frustrated Starr but she obscured her annoyance. "Okay." Playing her role, Starr turned the key over in her hand. The only yale lock in the property was the front door but she couldn't fathom why she would have a key for a house she did not live in. Her and Jade weren't an item, not a such, more very good friends with benefits. The glances were urging her to take action.

Starr got up and went into the hallway. Julie and Jade followed close behind, a glass in one hand and a concealed party popper in the other. Starr pulled the door open and placed her key in the barrel.

"Do it properly." Jade shoved Starr the remaining distance onto the front step and closed the door. Julie snorted in amused approval.

Starr turned the key and opened the door to a barrage of explosions and paper confetti.

"If you want it, the room's yours." Starr was overwhelmed. She did want it. The following morning they would have a sober discussion about the logistics and unavoidable payment options.

The remainder of the night was given over to a third bottle of wine whilst the girls celebrated.

Using the large screen indicative of the Chinese Xiaomi mobile the girls drunkenly choreographed moves to a TikTok recording, uploading the least wobbly version. The trends streamed by celebrities and their followers were a viral sensation, with armatures attempts to copy the practiced moves amazing and shared around social media.

"Check this out." Starr typed in the search bar and brought up WitchTok, a supernatural sister to the short-form video app. The girls viewed the short clips with wonderment and naivety. The spells were uploaded for entertainment purposes but were based on real magical theories and practices. It was the intention and thought behind them that made them powerful.

Julie scrolled through the archived posts on the social media platform. She came across a purple haired TikTokker with a pillar candle burning and a large amethyst pendant hanging from her neck. The video bore the hashtag #bindyou.

Fundamentally, sorcery was the same as it was centuries ago. The herbs and words used remained largely unchanged, just modernised to fit with the current era. A gift from the Goddesses, it was how it was used and the will behind it that corrupted the essence of the magic. The internet had spawned numerous outlets for research from wiccan led pages to scanned images of old documents, hand written by wisemen and women.

For thousands of years mankind lived in harmony with nature, giving what they took.

It is time to return to the ways of old.

The girls watched the charm several times before performing it themselves. It was not shared with the world, unlike their twerking and twirling attempt early in the evening.

All three had fitful dreams filled with magic, mayhem and mystery.

60

Julie dreamt that she was walking between the graves in a cemetery when the ground began to shake. The earth cracked and headstones fell as a thunderous roar erupted through the gaps. Billows of emerald-green smoke and flashes of light lit up the tombs and revealed the beauty of the dominating yew trees. Wisps of pink flame twisted through the ground like creatures escaping cruel masters in a choir of disembodied voices said, "Follow our path, hear our cry, trust in the Goddess is the only way."

Jade dreamt of ships sinking in stormy waters and the desperate hands of sailors disappearing into the sea. Women thrashed around in pain holding their stomachs and clutching their chests, a crazed look in their eyes. Cattle lay dying in fields of succulent grass and sheep lay stiff on their backs. Whispered words too faint to recall played in the background like a CD on loop.

Starr dreamt of limbs emerging from the darkness, grasping at strangers as they passed. Havoc was being wreaked upon innocents as they cowered from the figures that haunted the shadows. Cries of vengeance reverberated around Starr's head. Tendrils of mist from hexes licked at the feet of the descendants who played a part in convicting the murderous crones who once walked the same streets.

The following morning none of the girls could remember their dreams. They had vague imprints but failed to recollect any details. Starr blew her nose so loudly it woke Jade who lay slumbering beside her. The visages of sleep fell away and she became aware of throbbing in her finger. The wound inflicted by the awl had flared up overnight, leaving her finger pulsating with pain. A mountain of tissues was piling up beside Starr as her nose dripped like a leaky tap.

In her bedroom Julie's eyes were fluttering open. She instinctively rubbed at the scar that had formed as a result of the slash to her palm, exacted by the antique knife. It itched as if something was trapped under the surface of the newly formed skin. Julie reached for her bag that contained the pot of healing honey which she applied liberally to her inflamed skin.

Coming downstairs, Starr was sporting a comically red nose, sore from being wiped. Instead of coffee she added the boiling water to spoonful's of the nectar remedy which Jade used to smother her aching finger. Paracetamol and a hearty breakfast helped with the collective hangover but their heads would remain fuzzy for the day.

"Do you remember the pact we made last night?" Starr was excited at the prospect.

"Which one?" Asked Jade, snippets of collective drunken ramblings coming back to her.

"To get inked together."

Julie was still keen. She'd always fancied getting tattooed but hadn't had a purpose or design she truly wanted on her body, forever. Now she did.

"Sure." Jade wasn't as convinced as her words suggested. Permanent sketches on her skin wasn't something she had given a lot of consideration too but the interlinking unbroken arches of the triquetra was a pretty triple knot design.

Starr had aced the drawing aspect of her apprenticeship with Lawrence showing she can create exquisite original designs as well as produce perfect copies of traditional images. Learning the practical application was her next step. She'd nailed strips of uncooked crackling, bought off the artisan butchers round the corner from the tattoo parlour, to planks of wood to get used to the texture and movement of skin. A few marks had gone astray but generally the finished article lived up to her expectations and Lawrence was satisfied that she could start bringing some cash into the premises. Her next move was to find consenting human guinea pigs.

Having signed disclaimers, Julie was first in the chair. Once Jade had been inked Starr turned the gun on herself. They had chosen the inside of their left wrists as the mutually agreed location, for the matching ornamental design popular in medieval manuscript illumination and a representation of the past still current in today's future, so Starr, being right-handed could tattoo herself.

In line with his employees believes, Lawrence had invested in a brand of ink derived from plant pigment, imported from America. The Sea Shepherd range raises funds for direct-action campaigns in oceans around the world, making Lawrence feel good that his contribution may save marine life. The hourly rate was more using the natural alternative but it was a service some clients were willingly to pay more for and a fabulous marketing ploy.

Julie loved the inking and despite the unpleasant scratching sensation, she knew she would have more, succumbing to the addictive body modification. Jade barely made it through without fainting. Starr would become a human canvas with arm and leg sleeves of mythical monsters and imagery that was an expression of her creative mind and strengthening beliefs in the supernatural.

Whilst in the chair, Julie's thoughts grappled with a new movement. She'd listened avidly to Starr's passion for activism and Ned's desire to recycle but also to Jade's drawbacks and Lizzies gripes. There was nothing on the market that encompassed the beneficial world saving, eco-friendly elements and embraced the sustainable ethos of all the crisis inspired companies or charities without causing disturbance and upset to some sector of the population. She had decided to make it her mission to create one.

She was still ironing out the kinks but she had the feeling it could be a campaign to change the direction of the planet. Religion would be the only stumbling block she didn't yet know how to navigate around.

Wands up, Witches.

WUW was the brain child of Julie and her merry band of eco-mercenaries.

After weeks of research and compiling data, Julie correlated all the positive benefits, messages and purpose led initiatives each group was touting. Brain storming sessions ran late into the night and ideas were bounced around, some deflating on scrunty, others striking a goal for the future of the species that had destroyed its own habitat. Graphs and spider diagrams were blue tacked to the living room walls of 17 Rectory Drive, the makeshift hub of operations.

Cohorts needed to be targeted in different ways and the inbred thought processes broken, allowing freedom of information to reign supreme. Ned tasked his brother to create a game-based app that rewarded the player with points to redeem on real-life housing schemes or investments in social enterprise to target the digital generation, who would be left with the ruins of society if the movement failed.

Websites were operational, roles were defined, promotional materials were ordered and the logo was designed.

"We can be the change." Said Starr, the driving force that kept Julie's momentum going. They had the power within themselves, everyone did, now they needed the people.

It was a motto batted around the world and in principal it summed up perfectly the direction many were heading but needed drive and intention behind it, not just a hashtagged post to make the individual feel good about themselves. They had a long road ahead with some wrong turns along the way but the final destination was one of harmony and peace.

Since the young ladies had formed a platonic threesome they had undergone an altered state of consciousness, as if something had been awoken in their souls that had laid dormant, waiting for the right time to rise to the surface.

When Jade stepped outside, the world was alive with colour. For the first time she saw the separate hues of green in the landscape or the blue tint to a blackbirds feathers.

Starr could see people waking up and opening their eyes to the destruction around them. She could see the small steps she hoped would turn into big leaps, of faith and wisdom.

Julie often now felt tingling in her fingertips. Like magic was tangible and ready to explode from her at any given moment.

The possibilities were endless ....

WANDS UP, WITCHES
WE HAVE A
WORLD TO SAVE

Map of Bideford
The important streets in the tale of the Witches
Daddon
Stambridge Lane
Witches cottages
Parsonage Close
Old Town
Pitt Lane
Westcombe Lane
Pannier Market & Buttgarden Street
Witch Trail
St. Marys
High Street
Gunstone
Cold Harbour
The Quay
Amberley
Map not to scale

English Witches ~ R.I.P

1324
John of Nottingham - Died in prison – Coventry

1441
Roger Bolingbroke – Hung, Drawn & Quartered – Tyburn – November 18th
Margery Jourdemayne, 'The Witch of Eye' – Burnt – Smithfield – October 27th
Canon James Southwell – Died in prison – London

1534
Elizabeth Barton – Hung – Tyburn

1536
Anne Boleyn – Beheaded – London – May 19th

1538
Mabel Brigge – York

1565
? Waterhouse – Hung – Dorset

1566
Alice Nokes – Hung – Chelmsford

Ellen Smith – Hung – Chelmsford
Agnes Waterhouse – Chelmsford – July 29th

1574
Mrs. Arnold – Hung – Barking

1579
Elizabeth Frances – Chelmsford

1582
Elizabeth Bennet – St. Osyth
? Gabley – King's Lynn
Ursula Kemp – St. Osyth

1585
Margaret Hacket – Tyburn – February 19th

1589
Joan 'Coney' Cunny – Hung – Chelmsford
Joan Prentice – Hung – Chelmsford
Joan Upney - Hung – Chelmsford

1593
John Samuels – Hung – Warboys – April 4th
Alice Samuels – Hung – Warboys – April 4th
Agnes Samuels – Hung – Warboys – April 4th

1595
Helen Calles – Braynford – December 1st
Joane Newell – Barnett – December 1st
John Newell – Barnett – December 1st

1596

Elizabeth Wright
Alice Goodridge – Derby
Isabel Cockie- Burnt at the cost of 105 silver pieces

1597
Edmund Hartlay – Hung – Lancashire – March
Thomas Darting the Baron Boy – Staffordshire

1599
Anne Kerke – Tyburn

1603
Mary Pannel – Yorkshire

1606
Joanna Harrison – Hertford
Daughter Harrison – Hertford

1610
Katherine Lawrett – Chelmsford
Richard Wilkins – Hung – Exeter

1612
Mary Barber – Northampton – July 22nd
Arthur Bill – Northampton – July 22nd
Agnes Browne – Northampton – July 22nd
Joan Browne (nee Vaughan) – Northampton – July 22nd
Helen Jenkenson – Northampton – July 22nd
Jane Bulcock – Hung – Pendle, Lancaster – August 20th
John Bulcock – Hung – Pendle, Lancaster – August 20th

Elizabeth Demdike - Hung – Pendle, Lancaster – August 20th
James Device – Hung – Pendle, Lancaster – August 20th
Elizabeth Device – Hung – Pendle, Lancaster – August 20th
Alison Device, aged 11 – Hung – Pendle, Lancaster – August 20th
Katherine Hewitt – Hung – Pendle, Lancaster – August 20th
Alice Nutter – Hung – Pendle, Lancaster – August 20th
Margaret Pearson – Hung – Pendle, Lancaster – August 20th
Jennet Preston – Hung – Pendle, Lancaster – August 20th
Anne Redfearne – Hung – Pendle, Lancaster – August 20th
Isobel Robey – Hung – Pendle, Lancaster – August 20th
Elizabeth Southern – Died in prison – Pendle, Lancaster – August 20th
Anne Whittle – Hung – Pendle, Lancaster – August 20th

1613

Mother Sutton – Bedford
Mary Sutton – Bedford

1615

Joan Hunt – Hung – Middlesex

1616

Agnes Berrye – Hung – Enfield

Elizabeth Rutler – Hung – Middlesex

Mary Smith – Hung – King's Lynn

John Smith – Hung – Leicester

1619

Anne Barker – Hung – Leicester

Joan Flower – Died in prison – Lincoln

Margaret Flower – Hung – Lincoln

Phillippa Flower – Hung – Lincoln

Ellen Green – Leicester

Joan Willimot – Leicester

1620

William Perry the Bilson Boy

1621

Elizabeth Sawyer – Hung – Tyburn – April 19th

1628

Dr. Lamb – Stoned by mob – St. Pauls Cross, London

1630

Old Wife Green – Burnt – Pocklington

? Utley – Hung – Lancaster

1631

Edmund Bull – Hung – Taunton

1636

Kathryn Garner – trial by water and found innocent – Shropshire

1640

Meggs the Baker – Norwich

1644

2 women named Wanderson – January

1645

Mary Cooke – Died in prison – Lamgham – May 29th
Elizabeth Gibson – Died in prison – Thorpe-Le-Soken, Essex – June 1st
20 people executed in Norfolk on the evidence of Matthew Hopkins – July 26th
20 people condemed in Chelmsford on the evidence of Matthew Hopkins – July 29th
Anne Alderman of Chattisham – Hung – Bury St. Edmunds – August 27th
Mary Bacon of Chattisham – Hung – Bury St. Edmunds – August 27th
Henry Carne of Rattlesden – Died in prison – Bury St. Edmunds – August 27th
Alice Denham of Ipswich – Hung – Bury St. Edmunds – August 27th
Thomas Everard of Halesworth – Hung – Bury St. Edmunds – August 27th
Mary Everard of Halesworth – Hung – Bury St. Edmunds – August 27th
Mary Fuller of Combs – Hung – Bury St. Edmunds – August 27th
Nicholas Hempstead of Creeting – Hung – Bury St. Edmunds – August 27th

Jane Linstead of Halesworth – Hung – Bury St. Edmunds – August 27th

John Loues vicar of Brandeston – Hung – Bury St. Edmunds – August 27th

Rebecca Morris of Chattisham – Hung – Bury St. Edmunds – August 27th

Susan Manners – Hung – Bury St. Edmunds – August 27th

Janet Rivet – Hung – Bury St. Edmunds – August 27th

Mary Skipper of Copdock – Hung – Bury St. Edmunds – August 27th

Mary Smith of Glemham – Hung – Bury St. Edmunds – August 27th

Margery Sparham of Mendham – Hung – Bury St. Edmunds – August 27th

Sarah Spindler of Halesworth – Hung – Bury St. Edmunds – August 27th

Catherine Tooly of Westleton – Hung – Bury St. Edmunds – August 27th

Anne Wright – Hung – Bury St. Edmunds – August 27th

Mary Dowes of Yoxford – Hung – Bury St. Edmunds – August 27th

Anne Leech – Hung – Suffolk – August 27th

Mother Joan Lakeland – Burnt – Ipswich – September 9th

Joan Cardien – Faversham, Kent – September 29th

Elizabeth Harris – Faversham, Kent – September 29th

Joan Williford - Faversham, Kent – September 29th

Jane Holt - Faversham, Kent – September 29th

Hellen Bretton – Hung – Kirkby

Sarah Bright – Hung – Manningtree, Essex

Elizabeth (Bess) Clarke of Bedingfield – Hung – Manningtree, Essex
Ellen Clarke – Hung – Manningtree, Essex
Anne West – Hung – Manningtree, Essex
Rebecca West the daughter – Hung – Manningtree, Essex
Elizabeth Gooding/Goodwyn – Hung – Manningtree, Essex
Anne Cate/Cade – Hung – Maidenhead
Mr. Cherrie of Thrapston – Died in prison – Thrapston
Alice Clipwell/Cisswell – Hung – Great Yarmouth
Mary Cooper – Hung – Great Clacton
Joan Cooper – Died in prison – Great Clacton
Elizabeth Heare – Hung – Great Clacton
Alice Dixon – Hung – Wivenhoe, Essex
Mary Greencliffe – Died in prison – Arlesford
Margery Greure – Hung – Wolton-le-Soken
Sarah Hating – Hung – Ramsey
Elizabeth Harvey – Died in prison – Ramsey
Marian Hocket – Hung – Ramsey
Margaret Moone – Died – Thorpe-Le-Soken, Essex
Susan Cocke – Died in prison – St. Osyth – Found innocent
Rose Hollybread – Died in prison – St. Osyth
Joyce Boones – Hung – St. Osyth
Margaret Landish – Hung – St. Osyth

1646

Susanna Wente – Died of plague – Langham – April
? Louis – Suffolk

1647

Dorothy Waters - Died of Plague – Clacton – February

Mary Coppin – Died of plague – Kirby-le-Soken February

Mary Blackbourne – Hung – Great Yarmouth

Elizabeth Bradwell – Hung – Great Yarmouth

Elizabeth Dudgeon - Hung – Great Yarmouth

Bridget Howard - Hung – Great Yarmouth

Dorothy Lee - Hung – Kings lynn

Moore of Sutton – Hung – Cambridgeshire

Grace Wright – Hung – Kings Lynn

Mary Wiles – Hung – Great Clacton

1648

Bridget Mayers – Dies in prison – Holland, Essex

1649

Elizabeth Anderson – Hung – Newcastle Town Moor – March 26th

Matthew Booner – Hung for wizardry & shape-shifting – Newcastle Town Moor – March 26th

Isabella Brown – Hung – Newcastle Town Moor – March 26th

Margret Brown – Hung – Newcastle Town Moor – March 26th

Matthew Bulmer – Hung – Newcastle Town Moor – March 26th

Elizabeth Dobson – Hung – Newcastle Town Moor – March 26th

Jane Hunter – Hung – Newcastle Town Moor – March 26th

Jane Koupling – Hung – Newcastle Town Moor – March 26th

Margret Maddeson – Hung – Newcastle Town Moor – March 26th

Margret Moffit – Hung – Newcastle Town Moor – March 26th

Kathern Wellsh – Hung for using a witch alias – Newcastle Town Moor – March 26th

Elleanor Rogers – Hung – Newcastle Town Moor – March 26th

Anne Watson – Hung for using magick to have her wicked way with a lord – Newcastle Town Moor – March 26th

1649

Elizabeth Knott – Hung - Worcester – Summer

Jane Martin, millers wife of Chattin – Hung & burnt

John Palmer – Hung – St. Alboins

1650

John Allen – Hung – Old Bailey, London

Mr Billington – Hung & burnt – York

Mrs Isabella Bittington – Hung & burnt – York

1652

Joan Peterson – Hung – Tyburn – April 12th

Anne Ashby – Hung – Middleton – July

Mary Browne – Hung – Maidstone – July

Anne Martyn – Hung – Maidstone – July

Mary Reade – Hung – Maidstone – July

Anne Wilson – Hung – Maidstone – July

Mildred Wright – Hung – Maidstone - July

Catherine Huxley – Hung – Worcester – Summer
Francis Adamson – Durham
? Powle – Durham

1653
Anne Bodenham – Hung – Salisbury
Elizabeth Newman – Whitechapel

1655
Mother Boram – Hung – Bury St. Edmunds
Daughter Boram – Hung – Bury St. Edmunds

1658
Jane Brooks – Hung – March 26th
Mary Oliver – Burned – Norwich
? Orchard – Salisbury

1662
Nathaniel Green – Hung – Hartford – January 20th
Mary Green – Hung – Hartford – January 20th

1663
Mrs Julian Cox – Taunton

1664
Rose Cullender – Bury St. Edmunds – March 17th
Amy Dunny – Bury St. Edmunds – March 17th
Joan Argoll – Faversham
Margaret Agar – Brewham
? Green – Brewham
Henry Walter – Brewham
? Warberton - Brewham
Anne Bishop – Wincanton

Alice Duke – Wincanton
Elisabeth Stile – Died in prison – Wincanton

1674
Anne Foster – Hung – Northampton

1675
Mary Baguely – Hung – Chester

1682
Susanna Edwards – Hung – Heavitree, Exeter – August 25th
Temperance Lloyd – Hung – Heavitree, Exeter – August 25th
Mary Trembles – Hung – Heavitree, Exeter – August 25th

1684
Alice Molland – Suspected died in prison – Exeter

1693
? Chambers – Died in prison

1694
Mother Mannings

1699
Old Widow Coneman – Coggeshall

1700
Amey Townsend – Mob violence – St. Albans – January 8th

1705

Mary Phillips – Northamptonshire – March 17th

Marie Potts – Northamptonshire – March 17th

Elinor Shaw – Hung – Northamptonshire – March 17th

1716

Mary Hicks – Huntingdon

Elizabeth Hicks, aged 9 – Huntingdon

1727

Janet Horne – Burnt – Dornoch, Sutherland

1750

Ruth Osbourne – Mob violence – Tring, Hertfordshire – April 22nd

Joan Osbourne – Mob violence – Tring, Hertfordshire – April 22nd

1808

Alice Russel – Mob violence – Great Daxton – May 20th

1809

Mary Bateman – Hung – Yorkshire – March 20th

1857

Nanny Morgan – Murdered – Westwood Common

1865

Dummy – Mob violence – Sible Hechingham

1875

Ann Turner – Murdered

Covens

1582 – St. Osyth, Essex
Ales Hunt
Ales Manfield
Ales Newman
Annis Glascocke
Annys Heade
Cysley Celles
Elizabeth Bennet
Elizabeth Eustace
Joan Pechey
Joan Robinson
Margaret Grevell
Margery Sanmmon
Ursley Kemp

1612 – Pendle, Lancashire
Jane Bulcock
John Bulcock
Elizabeth Demdike
James Device
Elizabeth Device
Alison Device
Katherine Hewitt
Alice Nutter
Jennet Preston
Anne Redfearne
Isobel Robey
Anne Whittle

Jennet Hargreaves

1649 – St. Albans, Herts
Anne Smith
John Lamen Senior
John Lamen Junior
Mary Lamen Senior
Joan Lamen
Mary Lamen Junior
John Palmer
Widow Palmer
John Salmon
Joesph Salmon
Judeth Salmon
Mary Bychance
Sarah Smith

1664 – Brewham, Somerset
Alice Duke
Anne Bishop
Catherine Green
Christian Green
Mary Green
Alice Green
Dinah Warberton
Dorothy Warberton
Mary Warberton
Elizbeth Stile
Henry Walter
Jone Syms
Mary Penny

Margaret Agar
Margaret Clarke
Rachel King
Richard Dickes
Richard Larmen
Thomas Bolster
Thomas Dunning
? Durnford

1663 – Taunton, Somerset

Christopher Ellen
James Bush
John Combes
John Vining
Julian Cox

1673 – Northumberland

Anne Driden
Anne Foster
Anne Usher
Elizabeth Pickering
John Crawforth
Lucy Thompson
Margaret Aynsley
Michael Aynsley
William Wright
Margarett (whose surname she does not know)
+ 3 other unnamed members

New Forest

C1300s - Horsa Coven

Molly Lee – 1700s
Sybil Leek – 1917-'82

Author's note –

I don't normally feel the need for an author's note but this novel is a little different from my previous ones and deserves some words of explanation!

There were three separate recorded accounts of the trial of Temperance Lloyd, Susanna Edwards and Mary Trembles. One was the account of the trial in Bideford before the mayor, the second was by J. Deacon who recorded what he heard or was told from the trial at assizes in Exeter. The third is a little know publication, that took three years to track down, by an unknown author and was printed in London in 1687. Exeter does not hold a record of the trial. It is possible there is a record at Kew, in London, under references ASSI 23/1, 23/2, 24/37, 24/22 and 24/23 but there are also large gaps in these records, and I have been unable to visit Kew, owing to the COVID 19 pandemic, to look for myself and the cost could spiral into hundreds for staff at Kew to look at the records, for there to be no record.

The accounts differed. For example, In Biddiford there was no mention of the destruction of ships or harm to crewmen, which seemed central to Exeter's trial. An entry in 1874 by R. Chope quotes different information gleaned from A.H. Norway, Mr. Karkeek and Mr. Inderwick who can't agree who presided over the trial. In their analysis of the accounts from a book and in the letter from the Lord chief justice the number of witches and their fate differed, yet they seem to be talking about the three Bideford witches. R. Karkeek says there were two women and at least one was hung, when another contemporary pamphlet at the time states they are all tried together. There is mention of the judges horses refusing to pull the coach to castle lane, yet the same source states Mary was tied to the horse, in which case why was she not placed in the coach? These aren't the only inconsistences - Sir North said Temperance was a seventy-year-old who had been the Devil's slave for thirty of those years (other accounts from Exeter say it was twenty years). And then there is Tedrake's booklet, which seems to contain information of their arrests, not stated in the original documents. The three songs used were sung at the time of the trial and after, as a tribute to the memory of the convicted. Another place where recorded accounts differ from fact is the statement of John Barnes who states an incident took place on Eater Tuesday, which was then listed as 'the 18th day of May 1681'. According to the Genuki website Easter Sunday was on the 3rd of April that year.

I have created part two, the trial, directly from the original resources and have used their own words where, as recorded over three hundred years ago. For example, where the conversations happen during the trials, these are the recorded words of the suspected witches and witnesses, I have added the conversation on the part of the mayor or alderman. I have changed the order of some events recorded to best fit with the other accounts and for the tale to flow. For example, one historian suggested they were all arrested on the same day, yet Temperance is arrested on the 3rd of July, with Susanna on the 10th and Mary on the 18th. Temperance does not mention either of her friends, nor are they brought up at her trial so it's not logical they were arrested on the same day.

Historians and researchers claim Temperance to be the daughter of John Babbacombe, christened on 20th April 1589, making her 93 years old at the time of her execution!!! In one history book about Bideford, it indicates 'that most lived a short and harsh life'; is it reasonable to believe that a poor beggar really lived into her nineties? Personally, I'm not convinced. Nor could I find a discernible record of the marriage to a Lloyd but Temperance Bellem/Bellew did marry Henry Dulin in 1618 and Temperance Harris married Thomas Hopkin in 1652. I could not find a birth record of either of these Temperance's. I could find no evidence of children either. Realistically, how many Temperance's can there be in a small town, though the population was approximately 1,100 people. Back in 1680's Bideford, there is no record of who owned shops or where these shops were, so I find it impossible to believe that anyone can state with any certainty which house in Gunstone belonged to the Eastchurch's and which property was home to the Colemans. It is believed that number 36 Coldharbour (a street off Higher Gunstone Street) was a bakery but it is also not stated in any record what type of wares Thomas Eastchurch traded in.

However, Susanna Edwards the likely illegitimate the daughter of Rachel Winslade was christened on 2nd December 1612, making her seventy years old, the age stated in one account of one of the witches, they do not state to whom they refer. The Ballard states one to be 'four score years of age' making one eighty years of age, a little younger than Temperance Babbacombe by thirteen years and older than Susanna by ten, could this be referring to Mary or where the men writing the publications basing it on appearance rather than fact? There are several possible children for Susanna, four being born to a David Edwards between 1641 and 1653, the mothers names are not recorded in the official document, only the fathers, unless the child was illegitimate, then the mothers name will be stated. A David Edwards married Susanna Winslade on 9th October 1639.

Research is only as good as it is interpreted, which is why I looked through copies of the original christenings, marriages and burial records, parish registers and records, and anything else the records office had that I could look at, that related to the people of Bideford.

Much of the data from the time has been lost or is undecipherable, view copies of them for yourself at the local records office in Barnstaple or on findmypast.co.uk, where copies of registers and censuses have been scanned. Having looked through the christening, burial and death records from 1562 to 1690 I could find no birth record for a Trembles. In the Andrew Dole book of charity received, in 1681 there is an entry for Widow Edwards and below a possible entry for Temperance, however it shows her last name as Floyd. There is nothing known about these women other than the fact that Susanna and Temperance are stated as widows and Mary a spinster. Susanna and Mary appear to have hearth tax relief too. I have fabricated the friendships with others as well as their employment and history prior to 1670.

It is generally accepted that the inflicted at the Salem witch trials in Massachusetts, in 1692, were suffering from ergot poisoning due to eating infected grain. I cannot identify a poison in the UK that would have similar symptoms to those experienced by the Graces' and Dorcas. Nearly all poisoning leads to vomiting or diarrhoea, not symptoms reported in this instance of witchcraft in Biddiford. Strychnine poisoning causes spasms in the head then to every muscle in the body but derives from a plant not native to England. The over indigestion of mercury is a slim possibility with a diet consisting solely of fish, and they are stated to eat meat, although research would indicate that mercury in fish is the result of pollution in waterways due to industrialisation. The most common result for an internet search of their symptoms is some form of nerve damage to the peripheral neuropathy or a pinched nerve due to injury or illness. In my personal opinion (and I have zero medical training) there are a few high contenders - Neuralgia presents as a stabbing, burning, and often severe pain due to an irritated or damaged nerve that is caused by age or a disease such as MS or diabetes, neurological disorder transverse myelitis, radiculopathy - which is a pinched nerve in the spine and can cause sharp, shooting pains, weakness and tingling or paraesthesia which happens because of pressure on a nerve and causes a "pins and needles" feeling.

And the other possible cause – witchcraft. Could they have been real witches with the power to cause harm with hexes?

I wasn't there to comment accurately on a time when all we have is the record views of a small representation of the population, who readily admit to believing in the power of witches. Besides, shamanism is strong in many cultures across the world today, and it is well known that people have practiced herbalism and held ritualistic ceremonies for centuries.

Who am I to say witchcraft and magic isn't real, because maybe, hopefully, it is!

The extract from the census records showing the execution of Temperance, Mary ad Susanna.

Sources –
Bideford trial document – Bideford Library
Exeter witch pamphlet - Bideford library
J. Deacon record
North Devon Record Office
Devon and Cornwall Notes and queries by John S Amery
www.archive.org
www.genuki.org.uk
www.nationalarchives.gov.uk
www.exetermemories.co.uk
www.findmypast.co.uk
Heavitree local History Society
A History of Bideford by John Watkins (1792)
A History of Bideford by Duncan Fielder
Tedrake's guide to Bideford & North Devon – 3rd edition

SURFERS AGAINST SEWAGE
IS THE COAST CLEAR?
Get the free Safer Seas Service app for live sewage alerts.
Safer Seas

THE
BODY
SHOP
MOTHER NATURE'S
SEAL OF APPROVAL

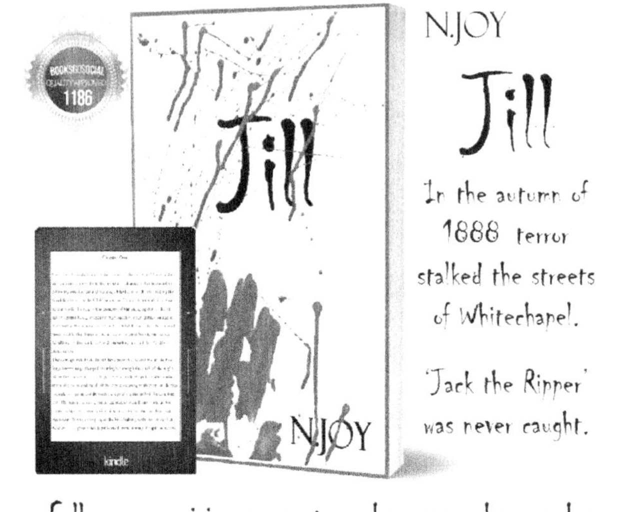
N.JOY
Jill
In the autumn of 1888 terror stalked the streets of Whitechapel.
'Jack the Ripper' was never caught.
Follow a surprising suspect as she weaves her mayhem into a tapestry of blood and lies in a twist on one of Britain's most notorious unsolved murders.
What if Jack was a Jill ?
www.nljdesigns.co.uk
Nickie is a born and bred Bidefordian with a passion for literature. She hopes you will enjoy her debut novel, Jill.
Available to purchase @ amazon

The ghosts of Amberley House

N.JOY

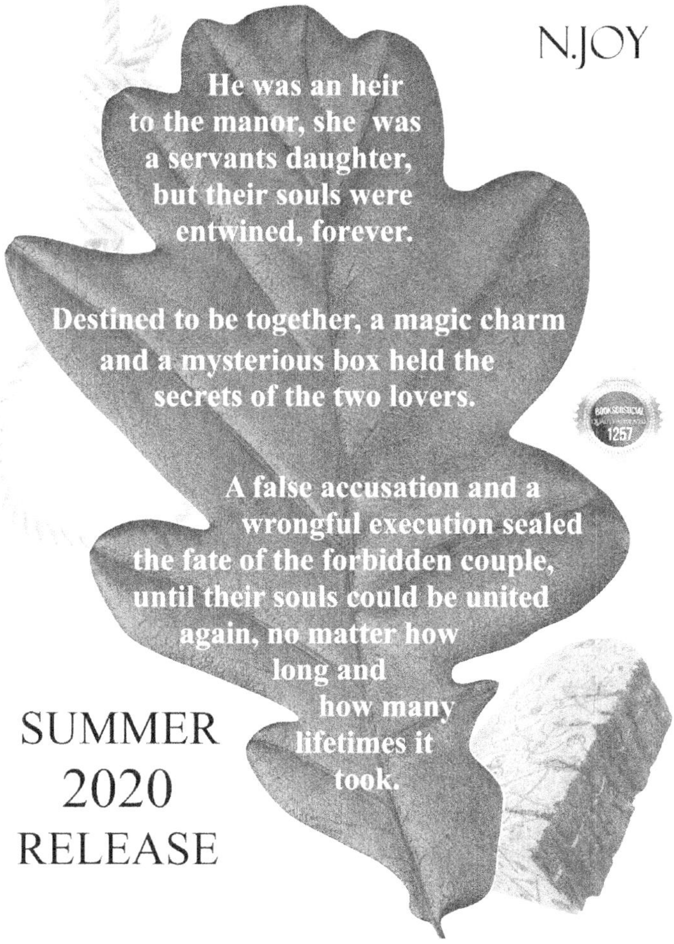

SUMMER
2020
RELEASE

MURDERLICIOUS
N.JOY
POLICE LINE DO NOT CROSS
Available in paperback and eBook
amazon
nlj Designs
Have you ever wished that you could get away with murder?
Have you spent hours dreaming of ways to dispose of that problematic person in your life?
Louise Wilson had. Louise didn't want a divorce, or an affair she didn't really want her husband dead, she just needed a break.
Join Louise as she daydreams about her spouses demise, in this hilarious dark comedy.
1
2
3
4
www.nljdesigns.co.uk

Printed in Great Britain
by Amazon

22884411R00245